Peter Ho Davies

Born in Coventry in 1966 to a Welsh father and Chinese mother, Peter Ho Davies was raised in England and spent his summers in Wales. He gained a degree in Physics at the University of Manchester before going on to study English Literature at Cambridge. Subsequently, he worked in publishing before moving to the US, where he gained an MA in Creative Writing at Boston University.

Peter Ho Davies's first collection of stories, *The Ugliest House in the World*, won the John Llewellyn Rhys and PEN/Macmillan awards while his second collection, *Equal Love*, was shortlisted for the *Los Angeles Times* Book Prize and was a *New York Times* Notable Book. In 2003 Davies was chosen as one of Granta's Best of Young British Novelists. He is currently teaching on the MFA Program in Creative Writing at the University of Michigan.

The Welsh Girl, his first novel, was longlisted for the 2007 MAN Booker Prize.

'Fresh and engaging . . . Davies handles complex and often conflicting themes of identity intelligently and sensitively . . . Some sentences and passages are crafted so beautifully and seemingly effortlessly that it provokes envy.'
David Cornett, *Sunday Express*

'Davies charts his characters' feelings with a mesmeric precision that demands slow reading but creates a sometimes startling level of intimacy between reader and character . . . the novel has a deceptive depth and power'
Sebastian Harcombe, *New Statesman*

'Distinguished, beautifully written . . . quietly stirring'
Richard Eder, *New York Times Book Review*

'Deeply compelling and utterly uncompromising, *The Welsh Girl* beautifully conjures a place and its people, in an extraordinary time . . . This book is a rare gem'
Claire Messud

'The book has a compelling power . . . Davies is an unflashy writer and his vision of the way that the contingencies of wartime brings strangers together has a quiet, moving profundity'
Tina Jackson, *Metro*

'A beautiful, ambitious novel . . . Emotionally resonant and perfectly rendered, I believed in every character, every sheep, every last blade of grass.'
Ann Patchett

'It is the skill with which he investigates [the characters'] inner lives, making thoughts and the ways in which they develop entirely plausible, that confirms *The Welsh Girl* as a fine piece of work'
Stephen Knight, *Times Literary Supplement*

'Utterly riveting . . . His style is his strength, drawing on a subtle vividness to paint a Technicolor image of wartime Britain . . . epic, lucid and compelling'
Big Issue

'He approaches the Second World War with a fresh contemporary style, a gift that he shares with Kazuo Ishiguro'
Russell Celyn Jones, *The Times*

'In this skilled, beautifully empathetic novel, the intersection English troops, German POWs, and Welsh families with the yields surprising insights into what it means to have a ho Peter Ho Davies is a wonderful writer.'

The Welsh Girl

PETER HO DAVIES

SCEPTRE

First published in Great Britain in 2007 by Sceptre
An imprint of Hodder & Stoughton
An Hachette Livre UK company

First published in paperback in 2007

1

A CIP catalogue record for this title is available from the British Library

ISBN 978 0 340 93827 0

Typeset in Sabon by Hewer Text UK Ltd, Edinburgh
Printed and bound by Mackays of Chatham Ltd, Chatham, Kent

Hodder Headline's policy is to use papers that are natural,
renewable and recyclable products and made from wood grown in
sustainable forests. The logging and manufacturing processes are expected
to conform to the environmental regulations of the country of origin.

Hodder & Stoughton Ltd
338 Euston Road
London NW1 3BH

www.hodder.co.uk

For Owen

welsh, *v*. Also **welch** [Of obscure origin]
    1. *trans.* To swindle (a person) out of money laid as a bet.
    2. *intr.* Const. *on*. To fail to carry out one's promise to
(a person); to fail to keep (an obligation).

– *Oxford English Dictionary*, 1928

Prologue: September 1944

O *utside, the technicolor sunset is giving way to the silvery*
sweep of searchlights over distant Cardiff as a hand tugs
the blackout curtain across the sky. There's a scraping of chairs,
then the snap of a switch as the projector starts up. The room
fills with the sharp chemical smell of acetate, the ionised stink of
scorched dust.

'Lights,' Rotheram calls, and the lamps are extinguished. On
the makeshift screen – a bed sheet tacked to the wall, ironed
creases still visible – an image blooms, blurred at first, then
twisted into focus. Clouds. Wispy, cotton-wool clouds slide
across the screen, and then the camera dips beneath them, and
there's the city, spread out like a map. The screen fills with
gothic script, Triumph des Willens, *and beneath it in shaky*
subtitles, Triumph of the Will.

The watching men flicker in the reflected light. They're seated
in a rough semicircle, a handful of dining chairs flanking a
cracked leather armchair. Only the armchair faces the screen
squarely. The men in the dining chairs are half turned from the
film, looking back towards the projector, their eyes narrowed
against its glare, studying the figure at their centre.

On the screen behind them, Adolf Hitler rides through the
streets of Nuremberg in an open car. Crowds throng the side of
the road, arms thrusting into the air, the salute rising and falling

I

like a great wave. In the car the Führer himself holds his arm up, not at the same sharp angle as the rest, but tipped back at the wrist, fingers slightly arched, as if balancing a silver salver.

The screen dissolves to a shot of Hitler on a podium as a battalion of men, glinting spades on their shoulders, march past in powdery sunlight. Beside and a little behind him on the stage is a severely handsome man, slimmer and taller than the Führer. In the next scene, this same figure is at a lectern, a glinting microphone before him, passionately exhorting the crowd. His hand saws the air; a shining lock of hair falls across his brow. He ends his speech crying 'Sieg heil' over and over until the crowd rings with it.

The reel runs out, and as the film is being changed a hand reaches out of the gloom and offers the figure in the armchair a cigarette. He fumbles it out of the pack and bows his head to take a light. There is the flash then flutter of flame, and in it his face is momentarily visible. Older, gaunter and more dishevelled, it is still recognisably the man from the screen: Rudolf Hess, former deputy führer of the Third Reich.

The film had been Rotheram's idea. He'd seen it first in 1936 in Berlin, taking a tram across town to a cinema in a district where he didn't think anyone would know him, not telling his mother where he was going.

She had been pressing for them to leave Germany for months by then, ever since his grandparents had fled to France the previous year. 'But they're Jewish,' he'd told her, as if she might have overlooked the fact. 'It's disgraceful how they've been hounded. But we aren't.' His father, long dead, had been, but his mother was the daughter of German Lutherans, who'd settled in Canada and made a fortune in timber. They'd sent her back to the motherland to study in Göttingen, where she'd met his father in 1912. In the eyes of Jews – the eyes of his father's family, say, who had spurned his marriage and supported his son and widow only from a distance – Rotheram wasn't one of them. Yet in the eyes of the Nazis he was. A *mischling,* at least: a half-Jew.

He'd been dead set against leaving, even after seeing a fellow beaten in the street. It had happened so fast: the slap of running feet, a man rounding the corner, hand on his hat, chased by three others. Rotheram had no idea what was going on even as the boots went in, and then it was over, the thugs charging off, their victim curled on the wet cobbles. It was a busy street and no one moved, just watched the man roll on to one knee, pause for a moment, taking stock of his injuries, then pull himself to his feet and limp hurriedly away, not looking at any of them. *As if ashamed,* Rotheram thought. He'd barely realised what was happening, yet he felt as if he'd failed. Not a test of courage, not that, he told himself, but a test of comprehension. He felt stupid standing there gawking like all the rest. Too slow on the uptake to have time to fear for himself. When he told his mother, she clutched his hand and made him promise not to get involved in such things. He shook her off in disgust, repeated that he hadn't been afraid, but she told him sharply, 'You should have been.'

So he had gone to see the film the next week, to prove something. He arrived early and slipped into a seat towards the rear, hoping it would be a small crowd, but by the time the main feature began the theatre was full. He sat through the first half hour, his shoulders hunched, his arms crossed tightly to avoid any contact with the fellows sitting on either side of him. They were with their girlfriends – it had been a mistake to sit near the back – and when, after about ten minutes, the boy to his left started to kiss his girl, Rotheram didn't know what was making him more uncomfortable, the film or the couple. He was actually grateful when someone behind them harrumphed loudly, 'Show some respect.' When twenty minutes later the boy on his right tried something, Rotheram distinctly heard the girl slap the fellow's hand away.

By then, though, he was caught up in the film, its ecstatic

3

pageantry. The fervent masses on the screen seemed to merge with the crowd around him in the theatre. It might have been the two couples flanking him, but by the time the film was over he felt violently lonely. He wanted to have even a bit part in this great drama, and for a brief while in the darkened cinema, invisible in his seat, he felt as if he did. But then the lights came up and he hurried out, panicked by the sudden piercing thought that, if he could, he would want nothing more than to join the Nazis. In his haste, he trod on the toes of one of the girls, fleeing before he could apologise, fleeing from her little hiss of anger, her pointing finger. Outside, he must have run half a mile, feeling as if the crowd were at his back, ready to kill him for stepping on some girl's toes.

That was the day he realised he and his mother would have to leave.

It was her old Canadian connections that made it possible for them to come to England. Rotheram wondered what his father, killed at Verdun, would have made of that. Conceived in 1915 during his father's last leave, Rotheram had never met the man, although he still kept his frayed campaign ribbons pressed in his wallet, as proud of them as he was ashamed of having run from Germany.

He'd shown them, with a kind of shy defiance, to Colonel Hawkins one night in 1941, shortly after he'd been seconded to the Political Intelligence Division as a document translator.

'Ypres?' The old man had whistled in admiration, pointing to one decoration. 'Lord, we might have traded potshots. Staunch soldiers, those fellows. Took everything we threw at them.'

Rotheram's mother had been killed in the Blitz months earlier, and it was the first time he'd talked about his father to anyone since.

'Neither fish nor fowl, eh?' Hawkins said when he told him his background, and Rotheram nodded. He still wasn't sure what he could call himself – not German, not Jewish – but

4

serving under the CO, he'd felt for the first time as if he weren't running from something, but being led somewhere.

Back in 1941, the war had seemed as good as lost, the papers filled with defeats, yet Hawkins was winning small victories every few days across the interrogation table. The first story Rotheram heard about him was how he once questioned a suspected spy for thirteen hours straight, cracking him in the end only when he told the man he was free to go – told him in German, that is – and saw the fellow's shoulders sag in relief. Hawkins made winning the war seem a matter of wit and will, and Rotheram had been thrilled when the CO personally selected him from the translation pool to sit in on interrogations. Hawkins spoke excellent German himself, of course – he made Rotheram self-conscious of his own accented English – but he didn't always want to let on to the prisoners. 'Helps sometimes to let them think they know more than me.' It was a tactic he'd learned from his days as a journalist between the wars. Springing his German on them when they weren't expecting it was one of his simpler tricks.

Over the months they came up with other stunts. A couple of times, Hawkins had Rotheram translate so sloppily that the infuriated prisoners lost patience and broke into English themselves. Later, he began leaving Rotheram alone with a prisoner, stepping out to the WC while Rotheram offered the man a cigarette, warned him what Hawkins was capable of, advised him to talk: 'It's nothing to be ashamed of; anyone would.' He posed as a British student of German literature, professed an affinity for things German. 'You've a talent for sympathy,' Hawkins told him.

In truth Rotheram despised the prisoners, loved to see Hawkins break them. Once, they'd reversed the roles – boredom, as much as anything, dictating their tactics – and Hawkins had played the sympathetic one, hamming it up so much Rotheram thought he was being mocked. He listened from behind the door as Hawkins offered the prisoner a smoke, warned him that Rotheram was a German Jew, implacable in his desire for revenge. The man had talked even before Rotheram returned to the room. He'd felt a stark thrill, but afterwards, in Hawkins's office, he told him, again, that he wasn't a Jew, and Hawkins eyed him carefully and said, 'I know, old boy, I know. It was just a ruse. No offence intended.'

'None taken,' Rotheram told him. 'Why do you think he believed it though?'

And Hawkins said, 'The reason most men believe anything. He was scared it was true.'

Rotheram had laughed. He couldn't say if loyalty to one man could grow into patriotism, but the harder he worked for Hawkins, the more suspects he questioned, the more British he felt.

Still, by the late summer of 1944, there were fewer and fewer prisoners at the London Cage, and Rotheram was missing the interrogations, missing the war, really. He'd been agitating for a transfer for a month. Quayle and his gang had moved across the Channel in late July; most of the questioning was being done in Cherbourg or by roving teams at the front. According to Hawkins, it was a miserable detail, France or no. So many men surrendering, hundreds a day – it was nothing but paperwork. 'Besides, I need you here, dear boy, to help put the jigsaw together.' They were beginning to identify defendants and witnesses for the prospective war crimes trials. The pieces of the puzzle. Rotheram had nodded and gone back to the dry work of processing the boxloads of interrogation reports coming in from Normandy.

There wasn't even much doing at Dover by then. In June and July, in the wake of D-day, he'd been used to heading down there two or three times a week, to the old racetrack where the POWs were processed, for a 'chat', as they called it, with the more interesting and recalcitrant cases. Once or twice he persuaded the local MPs to give him a captured uniform and put him in with the unprocessed men to eavesdrop. He'd been shocked by the thrill of it – playing with fire, he'd thought – delighted in calling himself 'Steiner'. He'd got results, too, bagged a handful of officers posing as non-coms. By mid-August, the Allies closing in on Paris, he'd begged permission to make another visit to Dover, and tried the stunt again, but he must have seemed overeager. He'd been rumbled, had a rib broken before the guards could get to him.

Hawkins was furious when he heard about it. 'Why would you take such an idiotic risk? Seriously, what do you think you were playing at?'

Rotheram shrugged. 'I was going round the bend, sir. And now with Paris liberated . . .' The news had broken two days earlier. 'Sometimes it feels like I'm the bloody prisoner here.'

Hawkins smiled thinly.

'Then you should be able to fake it better. How did they spot you, by the way?'

'Lice,' Rotheram said, making a face. 'I didn't have any. They saw I wasn't scratching.'

The other shook his head.

'And how's the rib?'

'Sore, but I can work.'

'All right. You want some excitement, then?'

'Sir?'

Hawkins began writing out a chit on his blotter, and Rotheram felt a surge of excitement. Paris!

'I'm giving you a staff car, sending you on a little trip. You're off to Wales, my boy.'

'Wales?' It sounded like a joke. 'With respect, sir, I want to go east, not west.'

'Think of it as a little holiday,' the CO said drolly. 'You're going to see Hess.'

Rotheram paused, watching Hawkins's pen twitch across the page.

'Rudolf Hess?'

'No, Rudolph ruddy Reindeer. Who do you think?'

Rotheram had seen Hess once before, in Germany, in '35. The only one of the party leaders he'd ever glimpsed in person. It was at a football match. Hertha Berlin and Bayer Leverkusen. Hess had arrived with his entourage a little after kick-off. There'd been a popping of flashbulbs, a stirring in the crowd, and then the referee had blown the whistle and stopped the game for the players to give the Heil Hitler. Hess had returned the salute smartly and gone back to signing autographs. He'd been deputy führer then, a post he'd held until 1941 when he'd flown to Britain. It had been a sensation at the time – was he a traitor? was he on a secret mission? – but now Hess was almost an afterthought.

'Even if he has any secrets left they'd be old hat,' Rotheram observed.

'He still has at least one, apparently,' the CO said, placing the travel orders on top of a thick file. 'We don't know if he's sane or not. He's tried to kill himself a couple of times, and he's been claiming selective amnesia for years. Says he has no recollection of anything important. Not of his mission, not of the war. It's all a fog, supposedly.'

'He's acting?'

'If so, he's doing a splendid job. He's been maintaining the same story pretty much since landing in Scotland.'

Rotheram looked at the file on the desk between them, the dog-eared pages bound together with ribbon.

'What makes you think I'll be able to crack him?'

'Not sure you will, my boy. Plenty of others have had a go. Medics, intel bods. The Americans.'

'But you don't trust them.'

The CO sighed. 'Hess is the biggest name we have so far, and if there's a trial when this is all over, he's likely to be a star in it. Only not if he's gaga. Not if he's unbalanced, you follow? It'll make a mockery. Problem is, if we don't put him up, it'll smell fishy to the Soviets. They're convinced he came here to conclude a peace between us and the Nazis to leave them free to concentrate in the East.' Hawkins shook his head. 'The one thing for sure is if he does end up in the dock, we'll be the buggers building the case. I just want someone I know to have a look-see.'

'This isn't exactly what I had in mind when I asked for a transfer.'

'"In which we serve," dear boy,' the CO told him with a shrug. 'You're going up the wall, so I'm giving you something.' He smiled, then craned forward again. 'You want a role in the trials? You want to play a part in that? Well, this is the beginning. Do this right and you might do yourself some good.'

It had been damp and overcast in London – Rotheram needed to let out the choke to get the car started – but by Cheltenham it was warm enough to roll his windows down, and motoring through the Marches into Wales, he found himself lifted by the rippling emerald country, the bright broad skies, so different from the narrow greyness of London.

Still, climbing into the Black Mountains felt like crossing into autumn. Fat drops of rain splattered the windscreen, and by the time he arrived, the metal of the film canisters was cold enough to sting his fingers as he carried them in from the car. He walked up the gravel drive to the manor house, remembering something Hawkins had once told him, that the gentry had put in gravel to announce their visitors. He had a moment to take in the ivy-bearded brick, the leaded windows crosshatched a second time with safety tape, and then he heard the bolt draw back on the heavy oak door.

'Ah,' the pinch-faced lieutenant who met him declared, 'I see you've brought our feature presentation.'

The lieutenant, a doctor in the RAMC who introduced

himself only as Mills, showed him into the parlour, where a projector had been set up. 'You've eaten already?' he asked brusquely, but Rotheram shook his head. There'd been only a meagre lunch at a sullen pub outside Cirencester. The doctor looked disconcerted. 'Well, look, not to be inhospitable, but could you possibly wait? Unless you're ravenous, I mean. Only, he's an early riser, so if you want to show it this evening, best start soon.' He smiled apologetically. 'Can't promise he won't nod off, otherwise.'

'It's fine.' Rotheram began loading the film. His fingers were so chilled they trembled, and it took him long minutes to thread the first reel through the sprockets.

'Nervous?' Mills asked.

'Cold,' Rotheram said, rubbing his fingers. 'Those will have to be turned,' he added, indicating the neat row of chairs and making a circling gesture, 'so we can watch him.'

'Right you are,' the other replied agreeably enough, although Rotheram noticed he didn't offer to light the fire in the grate.

Finally the film was ready, and Rotheram ran it forward for a few seconds, watching the test numbers flicker and count down, and then the opening shots from a plane descending over the city, the image ghostly in the still-bright room.

'Action,' Mills called jauntily.

Rotheram snapped the machine into reverse and the camera lifted back through the wispy clouds, the medieval rooftops dwindling, the soundtrack discordant and garbled. He'd tracked down the print at the censor's office – they'd impounded half a dozen copies at the start of the war – and he'd run it for himself the night before in his office, to make sure it was whole and to refamiliarise himself. He'd waited until everyone had left for the evening, afraid of being caught, as if it were pornography.

'All right,' he said, and Mills opened the door.

Someone must have been waiting for the signal, for less than a minute later there were footsteps in the passage outside.

Rotheram expected a guard to come first, but it was Hess himself, stepping into the drawing room as if it were his home. He was greying and more drawn than Rotheram recalled from his pictures, his nose as sharp as a beak and his cheekbones swept up like wings under his skin, as if his face were about to take flight. Out of uniform, in a navy blue cardigan, darned at one elbow, he seemed stooped, retired, more a shy uncle than the fiery deputy führer. His shirt was pressed and buttoned to the throat, but he wore no tie, and Rotheram recalled he'd made two suicide attempts, according to the file: once opening his veins with a butter knife he had stolen and sharpened on an iron bedstead; a second time hurdling a third-storey banister. He was limping from that fall still, as he approached and held out his hand. Rotheram stared at it, slowly held out his own, but to one side, gesturing to the armchair. Hess ignored the insult, taking his place with only a wry *'Vielen Dank'*, to which Rotheram found himself automatically mumbling, *'Bitte.'*

Two burly MP corporals followed Hess into the room, one taking a seat flanking him, the other carrying a salver with decanter and glasses, which he set on the sideboard. Last through the door was a delicate-featured officer whom Mills ushered over and introduced as Major Redgrave.

'Captain. I gather we have you to thank for the evening's entertainment.'

'I hope it'll be more than that, sir.'

'You've seen it already?'

Rotheram nodded, though he didn't say where.

The corporal appeared at his elbow, proffering glasses.

'Scotch, sirs?'

'And how do you propose to manage this?' Redgrave asked softly when they all had drinks.

'I'll run the film, observe his reactions, debrief him afterwards.'

'You think you'll know if he's lying?'

Rotheram watched the corporal bend down beside Hess and offer him the last glass on the salver.

'I hope so. There are signs to look for.'

Redgrave exchanged a glance with Mills. 'You know we've tried pretty much everything. Over the years.' He said it gently and without impatience, and it occurred to Rotheram that it was meant to comfort him, that they expected him to fail.

'Yes, sir.'

'Very well, then. Can't hurt to try. Whenever you're ready.'

Redgrave took a seat halfway between the screen and Hess, lowering himself stiffly, tugging up his trouser legs by the creases. Hess smiled at him questioningly, but the major just shrugged. Rotheram motioned Mills to draw the blackout curtain against the sunset, then threw the switch and took a seat across from the lieutenant and the major, studying the man in the armchair.

Back in London, the CO had offered Rotheram this job as if it were a plum, but until this moment he had felt like little more than a glorified delivery boy. Now here was Hess, one of the leading men of the party, right in front of him. And it occurred to Rotheram, stealing a glance at the screen, that the last time Hess had been in prison was after the Munich Putsch. He'd been Hitler's cellmate. He'd taken dictation of *Mein Kampf*.

Initially, Hess seemed entertained, watching the stately procession of staff cars, the pageantry. It was a captivating film, Rotheram knew, queasily fascinating in the way it made the ugly beautiful. He could see the two corporals were rapt, one of them moving his mouth to read the subtitles, and Mills and Redgrave kept swivelling their heads back and forth between the screen and Hess as if at a tennis match. But it was no effort for Rotheram to keep his eyes on the prisoner. The whole scene, since Hess had entered the room, seemed unreal. He couldn't quite believe he was in the man's presence, like the night he thought he glimpsed Marlene Dietrich getting into a taxi in Leicester Square but afterwards could never be absolutely sure. If he took his eyes off Hess, he thought the man would disappear.

Hess himself watched with interest, but without comment, sipping his whisky, his foot occasionally keeping time with the music. Only once did Rotheram notice the man's gaze drifting towards him, then flicking away almost coyly. At the first reel change, he seemed inclined to talk, started to lean forward, but Rotheram, wanting to keep the film moving, busied himself with the projector. Hess accepted a cigarette from Mills, and the major asked him if he knew what he was watching, and he said yes, yes, of course. He recognised Herr Hitler; he understood that this was Germany before the war. He said he admired the marching. But when Redgrave asked if he remembered being there, Hess looked puzzled and shook his head.

'Your English is good,' Rotheram called from where he was bent over the projector. He didn't like the others asking too many questions.

'Thank you,' Hess told him. *'Und Ihr Deutsch.'*

Rotheram looked up and a loop of film slipped off the reel he was removing, swinging loose.

'I only meant you do not seem to need the subtitles, Captain.'

Rotheram recoiled the film tightly.

'But perhaps I should be complimenting you on your English instead.'

Mills barked out a little laugh and then looked puzzled. 'I'm not sure I get it.'

'It's not a joke,' Hess said pleasantly. 'I'm asking if Captain Roth-eram' – he drew the name out – 'is a German Jew.'

Rotheram felt the others turning to look at him, the major sitting up straighter. He kept his eyes on Hess but felt himself colouring in the gloom.

'Well,' Mills said. 'I'd never have guessed.'

'You have to know what to look for,' Hess said nonchalantly, as if it were a parlour trick.

'But Jews can't be German, Deputy Reichsführer,' Rotheram told him flatly. 'Or did you forget that also?'

Hess's lips twitched, a small moue.

'Besides, you're wrong.' But even as he said it, Rotheram was conscious of his accent asserting itself, as it did when he was tired or angry.

'My mistake, I'm sure.'

'Captain,' the major called wearily. 'Let's press on, shall we?'

The second reel moved to the evening events of the 1934 Reich Party Day, a grainy sea of flags waving in a torchlit parade, and finally to footage of Hess himself, starkly pale under the floodlights, rallying the crowd, leading the ovation until his voice cracked with the effort. In the drawing room, Rotheram watched Hess closely, saw him flinch slightly, his nostrils flaring as his younger face stared down at him. His eyes, beneath his bushy brows, widened as he watched, and he seemed to clutch himself, his crossed arms drawing tighter, his leg hitched higher on his thigh. The tip of his cigarette glowed in the dark, and the smoke twisted up through the projector's beam like a spirit. At the next break, he called for some light and said he needed to stretch his legs. He rose and walked twice around the room quickly, his limp jagged, his head bent.

Mills tried to join him. 'Are you cold?' But Hess waved him away, and the doctor approached Rotheram instead.

'How much longer?'

'One more reel.'

'Good. I don't want him too agitated.'

Rotheram looked up. 'Isn't that the point?'

'It's *your* point, my friend. My job's to keep him healthy. I don't want him stressed or overtired.'

'I understood—'

'You understood wrong,' Mills hissed. 'And don't be thinking you can go around my back to the old man. He and I have an understanding.'

Rotheram looked up and saw the major watching.

'Do you mind?' he asked Mills steadily. 'I'd like to start this.'

Mills turned and motioned curtly for one of the corporals to light a fire. There was a clatter of coal from the scuttle, and for a few seconds they all watched as the flame caught.

The final reel showed Hitler addressing the crowd, and Hess sank against the seat cushions as if he were trying to smother himself in the chair. Rotheram, glancing round, noticed Redgrave and Mills thoroughly engrossed in the film, intent on the younger Hess, the one formed from shadow and light. Turning back, he found Hess studying him. Their eyes met for a moment – Hess's dark, but shining – before Rotheram had to look away, his heart racing, as if the figure on the screen had met his gaze.

Afterwards, pacing the room once more, Hess repeated that yes, of course he recognised himself in the film, so he must accept that he had been there. Yet he had no memory of the events depicted. He touched the side of his head with his fingertips as if it were tender. 'All that is black to me.'

'No memory?' Rotheram asked. 'None at all? And yet you seem agitated. Disturbed.' The room was very still now without the tick and whirr of the projector.

'I wouldn't say so. Troubled, perhaps.'

'Troubled, very well. Why?'

'Troubled that I can't remember, of course. How would you feel if you were shown and told things you had done that you had no memory of? It is as if my life has been taken from me. That man was me, but also like an actor playing me.'

Hess sniffed. The chimney was drawing poorly. Mills raked through the coals with the poker, making them spit.

'Do you even want to remember?' Rotheram asked.

'*Natürlich*. A man *is* his memories, no? Besides, I'm told the tide has turned. Paris fallen? Germany facing defeat? I should like such memories of happier times.'

'The film made you happy, then? You enjoyed it?'

'Not happy!' Hess cried. He raised his hands in frustration, let them drop with a sigh. 'But you are trying to provoke me.'

There was a moment's silence, and then Mills said, 'You must be tired.'

'Yes,' Redgrave added. 'Perhaps it would be best if we conclude this evening, turn in.'

'Major,' Rotheram began, but when he looked at Redgrave's hangdog face, he stopped. He had been about to say that this was his interrogation, but it occurred to him suddenly that Mills was right. As far as he and the major were concerned, it was no interrogation at all. It wasn't that they thought Rotheram couldn't determine whether Hess was mad or not; they thought it was irrelevant. That unless Hess was raving or foaming at the mouth, he'd be put on trial. They believed the decision had already been taken. That was why they couldn't see any point in this. It was a sham in their eyes and, worse, to continue it a cruelty.

They expect me to find him fit, Rotheram thought, because they believe I'm a Jew.

He became aware that Redgrave and Mills were staring at him, waiting.

'I suppose I am finished,' he muttered.

Only Hess was not. He was standing at the pier glass scrutinising his own reflection. Turning his head from side to side to study his face.

He ran a hand through his lank hair, held it off his brow. 'Another thing I don't remember: growing old.' He smiled bleakly at them in the narrow mirror.

Rotheram spent a restless night in his bare cell of a room – the former servants' quarters, he guessed, up a narrow flight of stairs at the back of the house.

It was all so unreasonable, he thought. He'd been brought up, nominally at least, Lutheran, his mother's faith; knew next to nothing about Judaism. In truth, he'd always resented his grandparents, refusing to write the thank-you letters his mother asked him to send in reply to their begrudging gifts, and he'd been secretly pleased when they'd fled to Paris, as if this proved something. Even when, two months after they'd left, his father's pension had been stopped, Rotheram had been convinced it was simply a mistake. The Nazi bureaucrats were just fools, too dense to understand a subtle distinction like matrilineal descent, something his mother had explained to him in childhood. He was in his second year of law at the university, but when he tried to register for classes the following term, he was told he wasn't eligible to matriculate and realised he was the fool. It made him think of an occasion years before, when, as a boy of thirteen or fourteen, he'd asked his mother yet again why he wasn't Jewish if his father was. Because the Jewish line runs through the mother, she'd told him. *Yes, but why?* he pressed, and she explained, a little exasperated, that she supposed it was because you could only be absolutely sure who your mother was, not your father. He went away and thought about that – deeply and narrowly, as a child will – and finally came back to her and asked if she was sure his father *was* his father. She'd stared at him for a long moment, then slapped him hard across the mouth. 'That sure,' she said.

Just before her death, she told him how she'd been spat on in the streets of Berlin in 1919. 'After Versailles,' she said. 'Because I was Canadian. *That's* what your grandparents could never forgive. I was a reminder of the enemy who'd killed their son. I wasn't *German* enough for them, you see?'

Among her possessions, after her funeral, he'd found a photograph of his father he'd never seen before. It must have been taken on that last leave because he looked gaunt, his tunic loose on his frame, his features sharpened almost to caricature, no longer the smiling, slightly plump figure in a close-fitting uniform that Rotheram had seen in earlier poses. This was his father, he thought, and the figure had seemed to rebuke him.

And yet the following week he'd gone ahead and anglicised his name.

He looked at his watch – not quite one a.m. – and decided to try the CO. Hawkins was an insomniac – his own sleep ruined by so many round-the-clock interrogations – and often spent nights at his desk catching up on paperwork. Sure enough, he picked up on the second ring, sounding more alert than the sleepy operator who put Rotheram's call through.

Barefoot, greatcoat over his pyjamas, Rotheram huddled over the phone in the draughty hall and said he was ready to head back to London.

'You've made up your mind about Hess? That was quick.'

Rotheram hesitated, stared at some movement down the hall, realised it was his own reflection in a mirror.

'Not really.'

'What? Speak up.'

'No, sir,' Rotheram enunciated. He cupped his hand around the mouthpiece, conscious of the stillness of the house around him. 'I'm just not sure I'll be able to, under the circumstances.'

'So spend some more time. Take another run at him.'

'I don't think that'll do any good,' Rotheram offered.

'But why, for heaven's sake?' Hawkins seemed to be shouting in the quiet of the hallway.

And Rotheram was forced to admit that he was reluctant to find Hess sane because the thought of confirming Redgrave and Mills's assumptions rankled.

'Let me get this straight,' the CO said. 'You believe you can judge Hess fairly, but you're concerned that others won't see that judgement as impartial because they think you're Jewish. Those are the horns of your dilemma?'

'Yes, sir.'

'Well, but do you ever think you might not be so impartial after all?'

'I'm sorry, sir,' Rotheram said tightly. 'Even if I were Jewish, I'm not sure why it should make me any less impartial than a Frenchman or a Russian.'

He heard Hawkins take a sip of something, and then another. Finally he asked, 'Tell me, my boy, honestly now, don't you ever think about your family? Your grandparents made for Paris, you say. Don't you wonder where they are, what's become of them?'

Rotheram was momentarily taken aback. He began to say no and stopped, unsure. Hawkins had taught him to recognise the pause before answering as a lie. It came to Rotheram that whatever he said now would seem false. So he was silent, which as Hawkins had taught him might mean a man was holding something back, or simply that he didn't know.

'I'm sorry, sir,' he whispered now. 'You'll have my report Monday morning.'

There was a long sigh at the other end of the line, and Rotheram felt how he'd failed Hawkins. But when the CO spoke again he sounded brusquely hearty.

'No need to hurry back, my boy. There've been some new orders, as a matter of fact. The POW department want someone to visit their camps up in North Wales. Something to do with screening and the re-education programme. Denazification and all that. Thought you'd be just the fellow to liaise. Anyhow, the orders should catch up with you there later today, or tomorrow at the latest.'

'What—?' Rotheram began, and stopped, silenced by the sound of his own cry in the still house as much as by Hawkins's steely jocularity.

Gripping the receiver, Rotheram told him stiffly that he

understood, and he did, although dully, as if his head were still ringing from the blow. The CO had been flattering him with this mission, he realised; more than that, it was a consolation prize. The decision *had* already been made, but not by Rotheram. Hess would be going to the trial, but Rotheram wouldn't. The closest he'd come to Germany, any time soon, was the image on the screen.

'You will be missed,' Hawkins said. He was the one whispering now. 'It's just that there's a sense that Jews ought not to be a big part of the process. To keep everything above board, so to speak. To avoid its looking like revenge. Can't stick a thumb on the scales of justice and all that. And really, that stunt at Dover.' He laughed ruefully. 'That's what you get for playing silly buggers.'

Rotheram was silent and the CO filled the pause by asking, 'By the way, how is Rudi, the old bastard?'

'Probably as sane as you or I,' Rotheram said, and Hawkins laughed again.

'Well, that's not saying much, dear boy. That's not saying very much at all.'

Rotheram held the receiver long after it had gone dead, reassured by the weight in his hand, until he heard a floorboard creak overhead, and finally set it gently back in its cradle. He wondered who else might be awake, whom he might have woken. Hess's room was on the second floor, and suddenly he hoped the Nazi might appear, escaping, any excuse for Rotheram to take him by the throat. On the landing, he peered down the corridor. There was Hess's guard, the corporal who'd served them Scotch, slumped in his chair, giving off a series of soft, flaring snores. Rotheram only meant to wake him, but as he stood before the guard, it seemed as easy to step over his outstretched legs and lay an ear to the door.

Nothing. Rotheram wondered if he was listening to an empty

20

room, if Hess had already fled (but no, the key was still in the lock) or thrown himself from his window (surely it was barred). Still nothing, except Rotheram's own pulse, like a wingbeat in his ears. Perhaps all he'd heard before was a particularly stentorian snore from the corporal. And yet he couldn't quite shake the conviction that the room was empty – not as if Hess had left it, precisely, but as if he'd never been there. Rotheram must have leaned closer, shifted his weight, for the floor beneath him gave a dry groan. He stifled his breath, counted the seconds. Nothing stirred, and yet the silence seemed subtly altered now, the silence of another listener, as if Hess were behind the door or under the covers or crouched in a corner listening to him, Rotheram, wondering about his intentions.

Rotheram felt his legs start to tremble, as if a chill had risen from the cold floor through his bare feet, and he stepped away. He was halfway to the stairs before he thought to turn back and aim a kick at the sleeping corporal.

One

It's a close June night in the Welsh hills, taut with the threat of thunder, and the radios of the village cough with static. The Quarryman's Arms, with the tallest aerial for miles around, is a scrum of bodies, all waiting to hear Churchill's broadcast.

There's a flurry of shouted orders leading up to the news at six. Esther, behind the lounge bar, pulls pint after pint, leaning back against the pumps so that the beer froths in the glass. She sets the shaker out for those who want to salt their drinks to melt the foam. Round the corner to her right, her boss, Jack Jones, has his hands full with the regulars in the public bar. At five to six by the scarred grandfather clock in the corner, he calls across for Esther to 'warm 'er up'. She tops off the pint she's pouring, steps back from the counter and up on to the pop crate beneath the till. She has to stretch for the knob on the wireless, one foot lifting off the crate. Behind her, over the calls for service, she hears a few low whistles before the machine clicks into life, first with a scratchy hum, then a whistle of its own, finally, as if from afar, the signature tune of the programme. The dial lights up like a sunset, and the noise around her subsides at once. Turning, the girl looks down into the crowd of faces staring up at the glowing radio, and it seems to her for a moment as if she has stilled them.

The men – soldiers, mostly, in the lounge – sip their beers slowly during the broadcast. She looks from face to face, but they're all gazing off, concentrating on the prime minister's shuffling growl. The only ones to catch her eye are Harry Hitch, who's mouthing something – 'me usual' – and Colin, who winks broadly from across the room.

Colin's one of the sappers with the Pioneer Corps building the base near the old holiday camp in the valley. They've been bringing some much-needed business to the Arms for the last month, and for the last fortnight Esther and Colin have been sweethearts. Tonight she's agreed to slip off with him after work – he's got 'something special' to tell her, he's promised – a date that seems destined now. She says the English word in her mind, 'sweethearts', likes the way it sounds. She listens to Churchill, the voice of England, imagines him whispering it gravely, swallows a smile. She concentrates on the speech, thinks of the men on the beaches, and feels herself fill with emotion for her soldier like a slow-pouring glass of Guinness. There's a thickening in her throat, a brimming pressure behind her eyes. It's gratitude she feels, mixed with pride and hope, and she trusts that together this blend amounts to love.

The broadcast ends and the noise builds again in the pub. It's not quite a cheer – the speech has been sternly cautious – but there's a sense of excitement kept just in check and a kind of relief, as if a long-held breath can finally be released. All spring the whispered talk has been about an invasion, and now it's here, D-day, the beginning of the end. The suspected secret the whole country has silently shared for months can be talked about openly at last. Everyone is smiling at the soldiers and calling congratulations, even the locals clustered behind the public bar. Constable Parry, the blowhard, goes so far as to mention the huge floating harbours glimpsed off the coast to the south ('Now we know what they was for'), raising a glass, clinking it sloppily with one of the sappers, who winks back ('No pulling the wool over your eyes, ossifer'). And the constable, egged on, launches into the rumour about Hess being held in Wales. Esther steps up on the crate once more and turns the radio dial through the catarrhal interference until it picks up faint dance music, Joe Loss and His Orpheans, from the Savoy in London. She hears something like applause and, looking round, sees with delight that it's literally a clapping of backs.

There's a rush for the bar again. People want to buy the men drinks. They're only sappers – road menders and ditch diggers, according to her father – but they're in uniform, and who knows when they could be going 'over there'. Suddenly, and without doing a thing, they're heroes, indistinguishable in their uniforms from all the other fighting men. And they believe it, too. Esther can see it in Colin's face, the glow of it. She stares at him and it's as if she's seeing him for the first time; he's so glossily handsome, like the lobby card of a film star.

The crowd in the lounge is three deep and thirsty, and she pulls pints – 'Yes, sir? What can I get you? Yes, sir? Who's next, please?' – until her arm aches, and froth fills the air like blossom. But when she turns to ring up the orders, she sees the public bar is emptying out. It's shearing season, after all. Invasion or no, farmers have to be up early.

She glimpses her father, Arthur, shouldering his way to the door, shrugging his mac on over the frayed dark suit (Sunday best before she was born) and collarless shirt he wears when out with the flock. Cilgwyn, their smallholding, lies a couple of miles above the village; he'll be sound asleep by the time she gets in, milking the cow by the time she rises. He jams his cap on his head, fitting it to the dull red line across his brow, and gives her a nod as he goes, but no more.

She's been working here for almost three months now, since she turned seventeen, but she's never once served him. He sticks to the public bar, the Welsh-speaking half of the pub, while she, with her proper schoolroom English, works in the lounge serving the soldiers, locals like the constable who mix with them, and the motley assortment of other new arrivals. Not that her father's English, his spoken English at least, is so bad for all his thick accent; it's just beneath his dignity to use it.

She would stand Arthur a pint or two if he ever ventured into the lounge (Jack wouldn't mind), but that too would be beneath him. She's been in charge of the housekeeping money in the old biscuit tin ever since her mother died four years ago, but only since she started working has he shown her the books, the bank account, the mortgage deeds. Of course, she had her own ideas of how bad things were all along, but guessing and knowing are different and now she knows: knows why they've taken in their young English evacuee, Jim (for the extra ten-and-six billeting allowance); knows why they've been selling off ewe lambs as well as wethers the last two seasons. Between the national subsidy and the demand for woollen uniforms, the war is quite simply holding them up. Her father is a proud man, the kind who stands straighter in hard times than good, and she's grateful that poverty in wartime is a virtue, something to be proud of. It reminds her of the epic stories he tells of the Great Strike at the quarry, though he was only a boy then. But she wonders sometimes, also, what it'll be like when the war is over, and it crosses her mind that the same thought has sent him out into the night early.

Still, she's not sorry to see him go, not with Colin here too. She doesn't want to face any awkward questions, from Arthur or anyone else (she knows how local tongues wag), and she doesn't want to tell the truth, that she's stepping out with an Englishman – *a Londoner!* she reminds herself. Beneath the national betrayal is an obscurer one to do with her pride at taking her mother's place beside her father, a sense of being unfaithful somehow. She catches sight of Colin through the crowd, the tip of his tongue tucked in the corner of his mouth as he dips his shoulder to throw his darts – one, two, three – then strides forward to pluck them from the board. He catches her looking, puckers up for a second, and she turns away quickly.

Colin says he loves her English, and she's flattered, though when she asked him once what it was he loved about it, he said, 'You know, it's so proper. We all reckoned you were stuck up at first. You talked like an actress, a toff almost.' He laughed, but she must have frowned because he tried to take it back – 'apart from the accent, I mean' – though that had only made it worse, of course. He likes it, he's insisted – 'sounds like singing' – but she's been trying to use more contractions of late, to flatten her enunciation, even asking him to teach her some slang.

'No need to call us "sir," for one thing. Makes like we're in the officers' mess.'

'Well, what should I say?'

'I don't know. Try, "What's yours, luv? What's your pleasure? What's your poison?" And if someone's hurrying you, tell him, "Hold your horses, keep your hair on!"'

She's used the phrases when she remembers, though she can't quite bring herself to say 'luv' without blushing. 'It don't mean anything,' Colin reckons – when she looks for him now he's chalking up scores, grimacing over the sums – but it still feels funny to her.

Pretty soon the pub is down to just soldiers and diehards, the Welsh voices behind her wafting over with the smell of pipe tobacco. They're quieter tonight, slower, sluggish as a summer stream. The talk for once isn't politics. This is a nationalist village, passionately so. It's what holds the place together, like a cracked and glued china teapot. The strike, all of forty-five years ago, almost broke the town, plunging it into poverty, and it's taken something shared to stick back together the families of men who returned to work and those who stayed out.

The Quarryman's Arms is the old strikers' pub – the hooks for their tankards, her grandfather's and great-grandfather's included, still stud the ceiling over the bar – a bitter little irony, since most of its regulars, the sons of strikers, are sheep farmers now. Their fathers weren't taken back at the quarry after the strike, blacklisted from the industry, and for a generation the families of strikers and scabs didn't talk, didn't marry, didn't pray together. 'Robbed our jobs,' Arthur always says, though he never worked a day in the quarry himself. Even now the sons of scabs are scarce in the Arms, only venturing up the high street from *their* local, the Prince of Wales, for fiercely competitive darts and snooker matches, games the soldiers have cornered since they arrived.

To Esther the old scores seem like so much tosh, especially after the cutbacks at the quarry, where barely one in ten local men work now. But the old people all agree that the village would have died if not for the resurgence of Plaid Cymru, the Party of Wales, in the twenties and thirties, reminding them of what they had in common, their Celtic race, reminding them of their common enemy, the English. Dragoons were stationed here to keep order during the strike, and in the public bar the sappers are still called occupiers by some. It's half in jest, but only half. The nationalist view of the war is that it's an English war, imperialist, capitalist, like the Great War that Jack fought in and from which he still carries a limp (not that you'd know it to see him behind the bar; he's never spilled a drop).

Arthur, a staunch nationalist, still speaks bitterly about his one and only trip to England, to a rally in Hyde Park in '37 to protest the conviction at the Old Bailey of 'The Three', the nationalists who set fire to the RAF bombing school at Penrhos. 'Render unto Caesar the things which are Caesar's,' he's fond of quoting the reverend who addressed the rally, 'and unto Wales the things which are Welsh!' Esther heard her father give the speech most recently to Rhys Roberts, the gap-toothed lad who helped out at Cilgwyn the past two summers. Rhys turned seventeen in the spring and promptly joined up, much to Arthur's disgust (his work on their farm would have qualified him for reserve status), though Esther is relieved he won't be around pining for her any longer.

Tonight, however, the success of the invasion has stilled such nationalist talk. The few Plaid sympathisers who remain nurse their beers, suck their pipes and steal glances down the passage to where Esther is serving. She takes a fickle pleasure in standing between the two groups of men, listening to their talk about each other. For she knows the soldiers, clustered round the small slate tables, crammed shoulder to shoulder into the narrow wooden settles, talk about the Welsh, too: complain about the weather, joke about the language, whisper about the girls. Tonight they lounge around, legs splayed, collars open, like so many conquerors.

She tells herself that most of the locals are as filled with excitement as she is, even if they're reluctant to admit it. She yearns to be British, tonight of all nights. She's proud of her Welshness, of course, in the same half-conscious way she's shyly proud of her looks, but she's impatient with all the talk of the past, bored by the history. Somewhere inside her she knows that nationalism is part and parcel of provincialism. She has her own dreams of escape, modest ones mostly – of a spell in service in Liverpool like her mother before her, eating cream horns at Lyons Corner House on her days off – and occasionally more thrilling ones, fuelled by the pictures she sees at the Gaumont in Penygroes.

This corner of North Wales feels such a long way from the centre of life, from London or Liverpool or, heavens, America. But nationalism, she senses, is a way of putting it back in the centre, of saying that what's here is important enough. And this really is what Esther wants, what she dimly suspects they all want. To be important, to be the centre of attention. Which is why she's so excited as she moves through the crowd – ''Cuse me!' – collecting empties, stacking them up, glass on teetering glass, by the presence of the soldiers, by the arrival of the BBC

Light Programme a few years ago, by the museum treasures that are stored in the old quarry workings, even by the school-age evacuees like Jim. They're refugees from the Blitz, most of them, but she doesn't care. If she can't see the world, she'll settle for the world coming to her.

She's sure others in the village feel this. The sappers are a case in point. No one quite knows what the base they're hammering together is for, but speculation is rife. The village boys, Jim among them, who haunt the camp, watching the sappers from the tree line and sneaking down to explore the building at dusk, are praying for the glamour of commandos. There's whispered talk of Free French, Poles, even alpine troops training in the mountains for the invasion of Norway. And the sappers listen to all this speculation looking like the cat who ate the canary. Jack is hoping for Yanks and their ready cash.

American flyers, waiting to move on to their bases in East Anglia, do occasionally drop in for a drink. But they're always faintly disappointing. Each time they're spotted sauntering around Caernarvon, getting their photos taken under the Eagle Tower, rumours start that it's James Stewart or Tyrone Power, one of those gallant film stars. But it never is. For the most part the Yanks are gangly, freckle-faced farm boys, good for gum but insufferably polite (in the opinion of the local lads), with their suck-up 'sirs' and 'ma'ams', and ineffably ignorant, calling the locals 'limeys' and thinking Welsh just a particularly impene-trable dialect of English. Once, though, one of them, a navigator from 'Virginny', pressed a clumsily wrapped parcel of brown paper and string on Esther, and when she opened it she saw it was a torn parachute. There was enough silk for a petticoat and two slips. He'd been drinking shyly in a corner for hours, summoning up his courage. She was worried he'd get into trouble, tried to give the bundle back, but he spread his hands, backed away. 'Ma'am,' he told her, and he said it with such drunken earnestness, she pulled the parcel back, held it to her chest. He seemed to be hunting for the words. 'You . . .' he began. 'Why, you're what we're fighting for!' She's dreamed of him since, getting shot down, bailing out, hanging in the night sky, sliding silently to earth under a canopy of petticoats.

But soon now, she thinks, setting her stack of glasses down just before it topples, they might all leave – the soldiers, the evacuees, the BBC – and suddenly she can hardly bear the thought of it. Of being left behind.

She wonders what it is Colin wants to tell her so much. For a second she lets herself dream . . . of a ring, of him on bended knee, asking her to marry him, carrying her off to his home in the East End, to wait for him there in the bosom of his family . . . his sister who'll be her best friend . . . his mother who'll be like a mother to her . . . waiting for the end of the war as if for some decent period of courtship.

It's not so far fetched, she tells herself. Hasn't she already had one proposal this spring, albeit from moony Rhys, one wet Sunday after chapel? She'd been mute, not knowing where to begin. She and Rhys had known each other their whole lives, grown up next door. His mother, now the village postmistress, had formerly been Esther's teacher. But marry! We've never even kissed, she wanted to cry. Oh, she'd allowed Rhys to take her to the pictures, even let him spend the modest wage her father paid him on her tickets, but they never once sat in the back row together. Rhys had pressed on, pointing out how good he was with the flock, how this would keep the farm in the family. She'd had a sudden recollection of him reading in chapel, intoning the passage about the Good Shepherd as if he were interviewing for a job, and asked pertly, 'Who are you proposing to, me or the sheep?'

The next month, the day after his birthday, he'd caught the bus to Caernarvon and signed up. She might have felt bad if he hadn't had the gall to ask if she'd wait for him.

She looks for Colin now, finds him leaning into one of his

fellows, cocking his head as the other whispers something in his ear. Colin smirks beneath his moustache like Clark Gable, taps the side of his nose. She could have easily got him to tell her what the camp is for, she thinks proudly, but she hasn't. He's even dared her to ask, tempted her with the big secret. But she wouldn't take advantage of their love like that. Besides, everyone knows it would be unpatriotic to ask the sappers what they're building: disloyal to Britain (they all know the slogans – loose lips, etc.), but also, more obscurely, disloyal to Wales. It wouldn't do to give the English an excuse to call the Welsh unpatriotic. But whatever the purpose of the new camp, with its long, low barracks and staunch wire fences, there's been a swelling, puffed-up sense in the village over the last month of being part of something (although it's strange, she thinks, that here's the invasion itself, and the camp not occupied). 'We used to burn their bases,' Arthur has lamented. 'Now we're pleased as punch just to have the buggers about, banging in a few nails.'

And it occurs to her suddenly: *Colin and I will have to elope!* A word she's only ever heard at the pictures. And terrible as it is, it sounds so glamorous. *Elope,* she mouths, tasting the odd English word on her tongue. For a second she imagines she and Colin *loping* into the sunset, almost giggles. She's not even sure if there's an equivalent in Welsh, if the Welsh ever elope.

Colin, propped against one of the stained wood beams, is still chatting with his mates. The dark cropped hair at the nape of his neck shows almost velvety below his cap. He laughs at something and throws a glance over his shoulder to see if she's heard, and they grin at each other. Heads turn towards her, and she looks away quickly. She is wearing one of her parachute-silk slips tonight beneath her long skirt; she likes the feel of it against her legs, the way it slides when she stretches for a glass, while her soldier is watching.

The moment is interrupted by Harry Hitch. 'Girlie?' he croons. '' Nother round, eh? There's a good girl.' He's trying to wind her up, and she ignores him as she pours. Harry's with the BBC. He's a star, if you can believe it, a comic with the Light Programme. 'Auntie,' as she's learned to call the corporation from Harry and the others, has a transmitter tower on the hillside above the quarry; the radio technicians discovered the Arms when they were building it, and they've been coming up of an evening with their 'chums' ever since, six or seven of them squeezed into a muddy Austin Princess.

Harry watches her set a Scotch before him and then a pint, what he calls a 'little and large', the glasses sitting side by side like a double act. 'Cheers, big ears,' he tells her dutifully, his catchphrase. 'Nice atmosphere tonight, eh? Lovely ambulance.'

It's a joke of some kind, Esther knows; when no one laughs, Harry chuckles anyway. 'I kill meself.' He's already half gone, she sees, must have had a skinful before he arrived. Esther has listened to Harry on the radio, laughed at his skits, but in the flesh he's a disappointment, a miserable, moody drunk, skinny and pinched looking, not the broad, avuncular bloke she imagined from his voice.

'Ta,' he tells her, raising his glass. 'See your lot are celebrating tonight too.'

'My lot?' she asks absently, distracted by a smirk from Colin.

'The Welsh,' he slurs. 'The Taffs, the Taffies, the boyos!' He gets louder with each word, not shouting just projecting, and as soon as he has an audience he's off, as if on cue. ' 'Ere, you know the English have trouble with your spelling. All them *l*'s and *y*'s. But did you hear the one about Taffy who joined the RAF? Meant to join the NAAFI, but his spelling let him down.' Esther barely smiles, but there's a smattering of laughter at the bar. Harry half turns on his stool, rocking slightly, to take in the soldiers, their shining faces. 'You like that one, eh? On his first day the quartermaster hands him his parachute and Taff wants to know what happens if it don't open, and the quartermaster, he tells him, "That's what's called jumping to a conclusion."'

More laughter, not much, but enough, Esther sees with a sinking feeling, for a few more heads to turn. She catches the eye of Mary Munro, the actress. 'Here we go,' Mary mouths, rolling her eyes. Mary's thing is accents; she can do dozens of them. Once she did Esther's, just for a laugh, and listening at home, the girl had blushed to the tips of her ears, more flattered than embarrassed.

'Oh, but they're brave, the Taffs,' Harry goes on. 'Oh, yes. Did you hear about that Welsh kamikaze, though? Got the VC for twenty successful missions. But he's worried, you know. His luck can't hold. Sure he'll cop it one day, so he goes to the chaplain and tells him what he wants on his headstone.' He slips into the nasal North Walian twang. ' "Here lies an honest man and a Welshman." And the chaplain says he doesn't know what it's like in Wales, but in England it's one bloke to an 'ole.'

The men are all laughing now, stopping their conversations to listen. The snooker players straighten up from the table, lean on their cues like shepherds on crooks.

'Come on, 'Arry,' Mary calls, 'it's supposed to be our night off.' But she's booed down by the soldiers and Harry rolls on unfazed.

'Reminds me of the Tomb of the Welsh Unknown Soldier. Didn't know there was a Welsh unknown soldier, did ya?' He winks at Esther. 'Nice inscription on that one an' all: Here lies Taff So-and-So, well known as a drunk, unknown as a soldier.'

'Takes one to know one,' someone heckles from the public bar, but the delivery is halting, the accent broad and blunt. It's water off a duck's back to Harry.

'That reminds me,' he cries happily, and gestures for Esther to refill his Scotch.

'Haven't you had enough?' She's aware of the silence behind her, the listening locals.

'As the sheep said to the Welshman?'

'Very funny,' she tells him.

34

'Oh, you Welsh girls,' he says, wagging his finger. 'You know what they say about Welsh girls, dontcha, girlie?'

'No,' she says, suddenly abashed.

'Give over, Harry.' It's Mary again, her voice lower this time, warning.

' 'S only a bit of fun. And she wants to know, don't she? You want to know?'

Esther is silent.

'Well, what they say is, you can't kiss a Welsh girl unexpectedly.' He pauses for a second to sip his pint. When he looks up his lips are wet. 'Only sooner than she thought!' There's a stillness in the bar. Harry shoots his cuffs, studies his watch theatrically. 'I can wait.'

He looks up and Esther throws his Scotch in his face.

There's a second of shock, and then Harry licks his lips with his big pink tongue, crosses his eyes, and the laughter goes off like a gun. A cheer rises from the public bar, and she's suddenly conscious of Jack standing in the passage behind her.

'Steady on,' Colin is shouting over the din. He's shouldered his way to the bar. 'You all right?' he asks, and Esther nods.

'No hard feelings,' Harry is telling her. 'Just a bit of wordplay. Don't mean nothing.' He holds out his hand for a shake, but when she reaches for it, he raises his empty glass and tells her, 'Cheers, big ears! I'd love one.'

'Come on, mate,' Colin says. 'Leave it out now.' He lays a broad palm on the dented brass bar rail in front of Esther.

Harry looks at Colin's hand for a long moment and then says flatly: 'Did you hear this one, *mate*? Do you know it? About the Welsh girl? Her boyfriend gave her a watch case? Tell me if you've heard it before, won't you?'

Colin sighs. 'I haven't. And I don't care to.'

'Really? You might learn something. She was right chuffed with that present, she was. I asked her why. A watch case? Know what she told me? "He's promised me the works tonight."'

35

Colin shakes his head, puts down his pint. Esther sees his moustache is flecked with foam.

'Colin,' she says softly.

'The works, sunshine. D'you get it? Penny dropped, 'as it? Tickety-tock. I can wait. All night, I promise you.'

'You're asking for it, you are.'

'All we're doing is telling a few jokes. Asking for it? I don't think I know that one. Is there a *punch* line to it? Is there?'

Jack is there (limp or no, he's quick down the length of a bar), his huge arms reaching over to clamp round Colin before he can swing, but somehow Harry still ends up on the threadbare carpet. He leans back on the stool, trying to anticipate the blow, and he's gone, spilling backwards. It's a pratfall, and after a second the bar dissolves in laughter again. Jack squeezes Colin once, hard enough to drive the breath out of him. Esther hears him say 'Not here, lad, *nargois,*' and then he releases him. Colin rolls his shoulders and takes a gulp of air. He gives Esther a questioning glance, and when she shrugs, joins in the general laughter.

Harry is helped up by Mary and Tony, one of the sound engineers. 'Up you come,' Mary tells him. 'And they say you can't do slapstick. You're wasted on radio, you are.'

'Always told you Scotch was my favourite topple,' Harry mutters.

Mary leans across to Esther and says softly, 'Sorry, darling. They don't let him do that blue stuff on air, and it just sort of builds up in him like spit.' For the rest of the bar, she adds more loudly, 'Never mind, luv. All you need to know about Englishmen, Welshmen, or Germans, for that matter, is they're all men. And you know what they say about men: one thing on their minds . . . and one hand on their things.' There's a round of whistles from the crowd. She grins at Esther. 'Always leave 'em laughing.' Tony turns Harry towards the exit, but at the door he wheels round and lunges over, almost taking Tony and Mary down in a drunken bow.

'Ladies and gentlement, I thank you.' There's a smattering of sarcastic applause, and when it dies out only Colin is clapping, slowly.

'Piss off,' he calls. Esther wishes he'd drop it now. In his own clumsy way, he's trying to be chivalrous, she knows, but there's an edge of bullying to it.

Harry tries to shake himself loose, but Mary and Tony cling on. 'I did see a bloke in here once,' he says, 'with a terrible black eye.'

'Looking in the mirror, was you?' Colin shouts.

'Told me he'd been fighting for his girlfriend's honour. Know what I said to him?'

'Bloody hell!'

'I said,' Harry bawls over him, 'it looked like she wanted to keep it.'

He's redfaced and suddenly exhausted, and Mary and Tony take their chance to frogmarch him out. Over Mary's shoulder he gives the room a limp V-for-victory sign, and over Tony's arm he flashes a quick two fingers at Colin. And then he's gone, dragged out into the darkness.

'Sorry about that,' Colin says, and Esther tells him quickly it's fine. She needs the job. When Jack hired her, he told her not to take any nonsense: 'In this business, the customer isn't so often right, as tight.' But she doesn't need them fighting over her. Her English is supposed to be good enough to talk her way out of situations.

'You shouldn't have to put up with it,' Colin goes on, but she shrugs. Jack's still keeping an eye out. It's a small village. She doesn't want talk.

'Anyhow,' she says, 'thank you, sir.'

'Don't mention it, miss,' he tells her, getting it finally, but still a little peeved.

She wipes down the bar, drops Harry's dirty glasses in the sink. She finds herself feeling a little sorry for the old soak. Mary has told her he's lost his wife. 'Songbird, she was. Big, warm voice. They met on the circuit, but you could see she was always going to be a star. Got her first top billing for a tour of the Continent in '39, but then the war come and she never made it back. You wouldn't think to look at him, but it was true love.' It makes Esther wonder. She's heard Harry telling jokes about his wife on the show: the missus; 'er indoors; the trouble-and-strife. 'Show *biz*!' Mary told her with a grim, exaggerated brightness. 'The show must go on and all that.'

The clock strikes ten-thirty. *'Amser, boneddigion. Amser, diolch yn fawr,'* Jack cries, clanging the bell, and Esther chimes in, 'Time, gents. Last orders, please.'

Two

She rinses glasses while Jack locks up, pouring the dregs away, twisting each glass once around the bristly scrub brush. They come out of the water with a little belch and she sets them on the rack. Normally she'd stay to dry and polish them, but Jack says it's enough. 'Only gonna get dirty again tomorrow.' He reaches over her to switch off the radio, and she realises with a little flush that she's been swaying to the muted band music.

'It's all right,' she says. 'I'll see to these.' But he takes the towel from her and nods at the door. She wonders if he knows.

In the porch, she pauses to check her reflection in the leaded panes, pats the curls that have loosened in the damp air of the pub, reties her scarf around her neck. Colin likes to tease her about the national dress, the scarlet shawl and tall black hat that Welsh women wear on all the postcards. 'Where's your topper?' he asks. 'Why don't you put on that nice red cloak, give us a twirl?' She likes the attention, but she wouldn't be caught dead in such an outfit – the women on the cards look like severe dolls to her, part Red Riding Hood, part Puritan. As a girl she'd asked her father with shy earnestness what the men's national dress was, and he'd snapped there wasn't one. The asymmetry still bothers her obscurely.

She catches herself frowning in the glass, forces a smile and immediately relaxes it. They called her 'big mouth' at school, mostly for speaking up, she knows, but she's always been self-conscious about her strong jaw and too-wide grin. She once begged Mary to show her how to use make-up, but the actress shook her head gently. 'Not with the bloom on you, luv.' It had made Esther blush more than any compliment from Colin or Rhys, and she clings to it now for confidence as she plucks the colour into her cheeks before leaving the porch.

Outside, the threatened storm has blown out over the Irish Sea, and the night is clear, blue-black and speckled with stars above the denser dark of the mountains.

Colin is waiting for her round the corner.

'Eh up!' he calls softly, appearing from the shadows of the hedge and pulling her to him.

He'd been waiting for her here one night last month, when they'd kissed for the first time. He'd lit a cigarette when she'd appeared, his face blooming in the darkness. She started towards him, towards the redness of his cigarette. 'Give us one, then,' she asked, and he offered the pack, pulled back when she reached for it, held it out again, then lifted it almost beyond reach so that she had to jump a little to snatch it from his hand. They'd smoked together in silence then, watching each other's pursed lips flushing and fading as they breathed in and out. She'd been glad of the grown-up feel of the cigarette's light, fragile cylinder between her fingers, and then all too quickly he'd finished his, flicking the glowing stub over his shoulder, and she'd drawn on hers hurriedly, sucking herself into a coughing fit until he had to pat her back. She could still feel the imprint of his hand, the ringing shudder of his slaps. There'd been an awkward moment when he could have offered her another but didn't, and then they'd been kissing. He tasted exactly like the cigarette, except for his moustache, which smelled damp, muddy even. But she'd liked it. They've met here every night since. Tonight she's promised to go somewhere more private with him.

She's been kissed before, of course, though the only boy she's kissed lately is little Jim, a soppy smooch to make him blush on his twelfth birthday. Just seventeen, but she reckons she's acquitted herself well with Colin, even surprised him a little. She was wary of his questions about her age at first, tried to be mysterious and mock-offended – 'You can't ask a girl that! I've my own secrets to keep' – but the way he'd laughed had made her feel small, childish. 'I pull your pints, don't I?' she told him. 'There's laws, you know. Can't have kids serving in a pub.' But he wasn't convinced, and so she kissed him back, the way she's learned from the pictures, lips crushed together. It had been just as she'd imagined, until she'd felt Colin's tongue slipping against her own and she'd pulled back in surprise. He'd laughed and called it French kissing. 'More like English cheek,' she'd told him tartly, sticking her own tongue out for good measure, but then she'd smiled, leaned into him again, pushing up on her toes and opening her lips as if for a morsel.

'Mmm!' Colin says now as they separate. 'There's a girl. You just hold that pretty thought.' He puts a cigarette between his lips, lights it and passes it to her. 'So's I can find you in the dark,' he tells her, stepping back into the gloom.

'Colin?' she whispers.

He leans his face back into the faint light of the cigarette. 'Hang on a sec, luv. Got to fetch the magic carpet if I'm going to whisk you away from all this, ain't I?'

She puffs on her cigarette, imagining she can taste him, exhales. The local girls have started calling her 'the youngest old maid' behind her back, but she's suddenly relieved she's never had much to do with the village boys. The ones her age are mostly off now, joined up or making good money in factories or in the coal mines down south. Even before they left, though, her mother's death had isolated her from the other young folk in the village. She'd had to leave school to help her father – over the pleas of her teachers, who'd always told her she was destined for better things, secretarial college perhaps – and made up for the loss of her childhood by priding herself on being grown up, an air the other girls had been quick to pick up on and resent. In truth, though, she'd never been much drawn to the local boys – her one youthful dalliance had been with Eric, their first evacuee – even when they'd been interested in her. Rhys Roberts was a case in point.

He and Esther had been born within a month of each other, and their mothers had become fast friends, though Arthur viewed Rhys's father, Mervyn, a rockman at the quarry, with a mixture of jealousy and suspicion. The two women had both worked in service in Liverpool during their youths. 'Though Viv was an *upstairs* maid, on account of her fine English,' Esther's mother always acknowledged (her own pronunciation being marred by occasional slips – *umberella* for umbrella, *filum* for film).

When Mervyn had died in a quarry accident ten years earlier, the families had become even closer, Arthur going out of his way to help the widow of the man he'd snubbed, until Mrs Roberts was able to find work at the school. Rhys's mother had always been grateful for the help – Esther was sure it was one reason the famously fierce teacher had favoured her. And Rhys, too, had apparently felt in her debt, protecting her from the taunts of the other children who called her a teacher's pet, even when he was the one, the slow son of the schoolmistress, who suffered worst in comparison. After Esther's mother's death, Mrs Roberts had been at Cilgwyn every day for a week, quietly seeing to their meals and keeping the place going. Rhys had been solicitous too, in his clumsy way, as if he thought the loss of a parent connected them more. But Esther had resented the way he talked about Arthur, saying the words 'your father' reverently, as if in a prayer ('Your father who art in sheep pen,' she used to whisper to herself), and he was always on about his mother, my mam this and my mam that, as if he were dangling Mrs Roberts before her like a carrot. The fact that Esther *was* fond of her teacher, thrilled by her approval, only made Rhys's insistence, with its reminder of the lingering girlish crush she had on his mother, the more embarrassing. Once, Rhys asked her if she thought his mother and her father might marry, a suggestion she recoiled from, even more so than she recoiled from his more recent plan to unite their families.

The ratcheting tring of a bell announces the return of Colin, wheeling a bicycle before him. 'Your carriage awaits!' She'd been hoping for a jeep, but he *is* only a corporal. 'Better than Shanks's pony,' he tells her with a grin, clambering on to the saddle and wrestling the bike around for her to perch on the handlebars. She feels self-conscious raising her bum on to the frame, aware of him watching, but then they're off.

Colin pedals firmly. She can feel the bike vibrating with his effort as they near the brow of the hill behind the pub, and then her stomach turns over as they start to coast down the far side. Soon they're flying, laughing in the darkness. The wind presses her skirt to her legs, then catches it, flipping the hem up against her waist. Her slip slides up her legs, billows in the breeze as if remembering its past life as a parachute, and her knees and then one white thigh flash in the starlight. She wants to lean down to fix it, but Colin has her hands pressed under his on the handlebars, and when she wriggles he tells her, 'Hold still, luv. I've got you.'

She has never been to Sunnyvale, the old holiday camp, but she remembers, as a child before the war, seeing posters showing all the fun to be had there: pictures of cheerful tots and bathing beauties by the pool. Arthur recalls when the camp was the site of finishing sheds for the quarried slate, when the lane leading to it was a track for freight wagons bringing the great slabs off the mountain. The rails had still been visible farther up, beyond the camp, until '39, when they'd been hauled away for scrap. They're probably part of a tank now, Esther thinks, or a battleship, miles away from where they started. The camp itself had opened in the twenties as a hiking base – a favourite pastime in these parts since the Ladies of Llangollen popularised it in their diary – and enjoyed a brief boom after Mallory stayed there while training in Snowdonia. But his disappearance on Everest, coupled with the Depression, had ended the camp's first period of prosperity, and the war had put paid to its second, after it reopened in the late thirties with much-trumpeted improvements, like a children's playground and the swimming pool.

On hot summer days, gathering the flock from the hillside above, running to keep up with her father's long, loose stride, Esther would steal glances at the faceted blue gem of water below her and imagine its coolness. But such places aren't for locals. Even in better days, the most her father could afford was the odd day trip on a growling charabanc to Rhyl or Llandudno. Besides, as he used to tell her, 'Who needs a pool when there's the ocean for free?' But she hates the sea, the sharp salt taste, the clammy clumps of seaweed. She's only ever seen swimming pools at the pictures, but for her that other Esther, Esther Williams, is the most beautiful woman in the world (Welsh to boot, judging by her name). She'd seen *Bathing Beauty* three times that spring.

So as soon as Colin coasts through the back gates of the old camp, she asks him to show her the pool. He looks a little surprised – probably has one of the empty, mildewed chalets in mind – but something in her voice, her eagerness, convinces him. He props the bike in the shadows behind a dark hut and leads her through the kids' playground. She clambers up the slide and swishes down on her backside, arms outstretched.

He studies her from the roundabout, circling slowly. There's a watchful quality in him, as if he's waiting for something, the right moment, and the thought is delicious to her. When she bats at the swings, he calls softly, 'Want a push?' and she tells him throatily, 'Yeah.'

She settles herself, and he puts his hands in the small of her back and shoves firmly to set her off, and then as she swings he touches her lightly, his fingers spread across her hips, each time she passes. 'Go on!' she calls, and he pushes her harder and harder, until she sees her shiny toe tops rising over the indigo silhouette of the encircling mountains. When she finally comes to a stop, the strands of dark hair that have flown loose fall back and cover her face. She tucks them away, all but one, which sticks to her cheek and throat, an inky curve. He reaches for it and traces it, and she takes his hand for a second, then pushes it away. He's on the verge of something, but she doesn't want him to come out with it just yet, not until it's perfect.

'I saw the pool from up there,' she tells him breathlessly and she pulls him towards it. She can see the water, the choppy surface, and she wants, just once, to recline beside it and run her hand through it. But when she gets close and bends down, she sees that what she has taken for the surface of the water is an old tarpaulin stretched over the mouth of the pool. She strikes at it bad-temperedly, as if it spoils everything.

'For leaves and that,' Colin says, catching up. 'So it doesn't get all mucky.'

'But what about the water?'

'Suppose they drained it.'

He can see her disappointment, but he isn't discouraged. He looks like he'd relish making it up to her.

'Come 'ere,' he says, taking her hand and pulling her along to the metal steps that drop into the pool.

He kneels and unfastens the cloth where it's tied to the edge by guy ropes. 'Follow me.' He climbs down, his feet, his legs, his torso disappearing until she can see only the top of his head. She notices a tiny, sunburned bald spot just as he looks up, and she realises he can see up her skirt. She hops back, snapping her heels together, and he grins and vanishes.

'Colin,' she calls softly, suddenly alone.

45

There's no answer.

She crouches closer to the flapping gap of cloth, like a diver about to plunge forward. 'Colin?'

Nothing.

Then she sees a ridge in the cloth, like the fin of a shark moving away from her, circling, coming back. 'What's that?' she says, and, as if from a long way off, comes the cry 'Me manhood.'

Despite herself she laughs, and in that moment grabs the railing of the steps and ducks below the cover.

It's surprisingly light in the empty pool. The tarpaulin is a thin blue oilcloth, and the starlight seeps through it unevenly as if through a cloudy sky. The pool is bathed in a pale, blotchy light, and the illusion of being underwater is accentuated by the design of shells printed on the tiles of the bottom. Overhead the breeze snaps the tarp like a sail. She can just make out Colin, like a murky beast at the far end of the pool, the deep end. She takes a step forward, the world sloping away beneath her suddenly, almost falls, stumbles down towards him.

When she gets closer, she finds him walking around in circles with exaggerated slowness, making giant O shapes with his mouth.

'What are you doing?'

'I'm a fish,' he says. 'Glub glub, get it?' And she joins him, giggling, snaking her arms ahead of her in a languid breast-stroke.

He weaves back and forth around her. 'Glub glub glub!'

'Now what are you doing?' she asks, as he steps sideways and bumps her. 'Hey!'

'I'm a crab,' he says, sidling off, scuttling back, bumping her again.

She feels his hand on her arse.

'Ow!'

'Sorry!' He shrugs, holds up his hands. 'Sharp pincers.'

'That hurt,' she says, pulling away. She starts to backpedal towards the shallow end, windmilling her arms. 'Backstroke!' she cries, clenching her teeth in an Esther Williams smile. But he catches her, wraps her in a hug.

'Mr Octopus,' he whispers, 'has got you.'

She can hear his heart beating.

' 'Ere,' he says. 'Want to know a secret?'

And she nods firmly, composing herself.

'Pee,' he whispers. 'Oh.' He grins. 'Doubleyas!' It takes her a moment to decipher him. 'POWs!' he repeats, like it's a punchline, and slowly, queasily, she begins to smile. 'That's who it's for! And your lot thinking they was part of the war effort.' He laughs, and she sees that this is what he's been holding in all this time – laughter, a bellyful of it. But after a second she joins him anyway, hoping that if they can share this joke, then he won't think her one of *them*, will see her on his side.

He's still chuckling when she takes his head in her hands and kisses him until the laughter is stifled and he starts to respond. She's put all her strength into the kiss, but when he kisses back it's with even greater force, this soldier she's only known for a fortnight. He turns her in his arms, as if dancing, and she tries to move her feet with him, but he's holding too tight, simply swinging her around. She feels dizzy. Her shoes scuff the tiles, and she thinks, *I just polished them*. The pressure of his arms makes it hard to breathe. She moans softly, her mouth under his mouth, his tongue against hers. When they finally stop spinning, she finds herself pressed against the cold tile wall of the pool. Up close it stinks of dank, chlorine and rotting leaves.

'I'll be leaving soon,' he whispers hoarsely. 'Will you miss me?'

She nods in his arms, although what she feels most sharply is not his loss, but jealous of his leaving. She presses her head against his chest, away from the hard wall. *Take me with you,* she prays.

'I'll miss you,' he tells her, his lips to her ear. 'We could be at the front this time next month. I wish I had something to remember you by. Something to keep up me fighting spirits.'

She feels him picking at her blouse, the buttons. She feels a hand on her knee, fluttering at her hem, under her skirt – 'Mermaid!' he croons – sliding against the silk of her slip.

'Nice,' Colin breathes. 'Who says you Welsh girls don't know your duty? Proper patriot, you are. Thinking of England.' Her head is still bent towards him, but now she is straining her neck against his weight. She can feel the bony crook of his elbow pressing against her side, and across her belly the tense muscles of his forearm, twitching.

'Nargois,' she tells him, but he doesn't understand. *'Nargois!'*

'Fuck,' he whispers, as if correcting her. 'Say "fuck".'

There's pressure, then pain. Colin grunts into her hair, short, hot puffs of breath. She wonders if she dares scream, who would hear her, who might come, wonders if she's more afraid of being caught than of what he's doing to her. And then he's covering her mouth anyway, his tongue opening her lips, thrusting against her tongue, entering her mouth, even as she feels him, with a darting suddenness, enter her below. It drives the air out of her like a blow, breaking the kiss. She clenches her teeth, but his face is in her hair now, his neck arched as if to spit. She twists her head against the coarse wool on his chest, trying to shake it, and he says, 'Almost, almost,' and bucks against her. Something jumps inside her, and she lifts her head sharply, catches him under the chin with a crack.

He cries out, stepping back, clutching his jaw, his tongue tipped with blood.

'Oh! Are you all right?' She starts to reach for him.

'Cunt!' he says, snatching at her wrist. She doesn't know the word, it's not in her schoolbooks, but she knows the tone, pulls away, curses him back in Welsh.

'Speak English, will you?' he tells her, turning her loose.

48

She leaves him there, then, wiping the blood from his lips with his sleeve. She recalls a flirty argument they had over the bar one night last week. He'd wanted her to teach him some Welsh, but she'd laughed at his pronunciation and he'd got mock mad. 'Ah, what's the point?' he said. 'Why don't you just give it up and speak English like the rest of us?' She'd turned a little stern then, mouthed the nationalist arguments about saving the language, preserving the tongue.

'Oh, come on,' he hisses after her now. 'Play the game. I didn't mean it. Come back, eh? We'll do it proper. Comfy like. Get a mattress from a chalet, have a lie down.'

But she keeps going, slipping a little on the tiles, tugging her skirt down, shoving her blouse back in, and she hears him start to chuckle again, the laughter ringing off the tile walls. There's a last shout from the deep. 'Who were you saving it for, eh? Who you saving it for, you Welsh bitch?' He spits wetly.

She expects him to come after her then, feels her back tense against his touch, won't run for fear he'll give chase. But before she reaches the opening, she hears shouts, a harsh scrape of feet on the concrete above. It's as if she's willed her own rescue into being, and yet she cowers from it. Torchlights dance over the cover of the pool. Despite herself, she turns to Colin with a beseeching look – *to be found like this!* – but he's already past her, his head in the shelter of the tarpaulin, peering out. She tries to button her blouse, fingers fumbling. 'Shite,' Colin breathes, but the lights and the footsteps are already receding and she slumps against the wall, her heart hammering. The thought of being discovered, the near miss, makes her stomach clench. Her throat feels raw. She looks back at Colin, wanting to share their escape, but he's scrambling up the ladder, and a second later, he's gone.

A clean pair of heels, she thinks; the English phrase so suddenly vivid it's blinding.

She's soaking, she realises: blouse stuck to her back, hair

plastered against her neck, a sliding wetness dragging down her legs. Her body feels heavy, waterlogged, her arms shaky, too weak to pull her up the metal ladder, and she clings to the cold rail as if she might drown. It's a few moments before she can climb out of the pool. There are shouts at the other side of the camp, where the barracks have been built, but she hurries the other way, back over the playground, the tarpaulin ruffling behind her. The seesaw and roundabout are still, the swings rocking gently in the breeze. She finds the bike where he left it, propped behind a chalet, and climbs on, noticing as she hitches up her skirt that the seam of her slip is torn. Catch-stitched, just as her mother taught her. It will take five minutes to mend with a needle and thread, but she suddenly feels like weeping.

She pushes off, pedalling hard, although she finds it makes her wince to ride. She doesn't care that she's stealing his bike. She'll throw it into the hedge outside the village. He'll never ask about it, and if he does, she decides, staring at her pale knuckles on the handlebars where his fingers have curled, she'll pretend she's forgotten her English.

Three

It's dusk, the summer sky still light, but the sand at their feet in shadow. It slides away as they descend the dune, and ahead of him Karsten sees old man Schiller stumble, struggling to keep his balance with his hands up.

They'd been squatting in the lee of the sea wall, hands on heads, for what seemed like hours before Karsten felt the stiff tap of a muzzle on his shoulder. He'd looked up, opening the arms pressed to his ears, and realised the bombardment had stopped.

No, not stopped – he could still make out the sizzle of shells high overhead – but the targets were more distant. *Retreating*, he thought. Nearer, there came the thin chatter of small-arms fire, then nothing. He heard his knees crack as he stood.

'Think they mean to shoot us?' Schiller had hissed as they moved out, and young Heino muttered, 'We deserve it.' Karsten had told them to shut up.

Now, as they round the bluff and see the makeshift stockade before them, he notices their pace pick up, Heino's bandaged right hand glowing like a lantern held up before them.

From a distance, the stockade looks as if it's built of driftwood, the barbed wire wrapped around it like seaweed, but close up Karsten recognises the fence posts as the blackened stumps of their own shore defences, shattered in the bombardment. Inside, he slowly lowers his arms, feeling the tight ache in them, the unaccustomed strain.

It feels like freedom just to put his hands down.

He stays close to the wire, walking the perimeter until he's at the eastern end of the enclosure, nearest the sea. Between the hulks of beached landing craft, he watches the white lines of surf advancing one after another, listens to the gravelly draw of the tide on the sand.

His father's trawler had been lost at sea twelve years earlier, the body never found, and his mother had moved them as far inland as she could, but Karsten never stopped missing the water. His father had been a submariner during the Great War, and Karsten had joined the Kriegsmarine hoping to follow in his footsteps, only to be told he was too tall for a U-boat. He'd had to settle for the field-grey uniform of the naval infantry and a life overlooking the Channel from shore defences.

The squad had swum out there only last week, draping their uniforms over the tank traps and wire like washing on a line. What he'd give to run into the surf now, strike out through the waves, blinking in the salt spray. He shouldn't have encouraged the men, of course. They were late back to barracks, but he was self-conscious of his new stripe, didn't want to seem a tyrant. Besides, it was the first truly hot day of the year, and now he's glad he let them.

When he turns back into the stockade he sees what's wrong at once. He, the boy, and Schiller are the only ones here. *We're the first,* Karsten thinks, sinking down. The sand, when he touches it, still holds the silken warmth of the long summer day, but when he pushes his fingers below the surface, the grains are chill and coarse.

He had thought himself such a good soldier these past four months, had taken to the army as if his whole life, all eighteen years, had been leading up to this. Already in their initial week of basic training he knew he could carry more, march farther and faster than the rest. He'd been working as a guide for hunters and hikers in the Harz Mountains since the age of fourteen, and once he'd mastered the cadence of drill, the rest came easy. He'd hauled heavier loads for dilettante hikers – yards of coiled rope, ice axes in April, and once the head of a buck, a hunter's trophy, the antlers gripped over his shoulders and the neck dripping blood down his back with each step. He'd hurried back alone before nightfall to skin the carcass and lug home forty pounds of venison for his mother.

Even the petty disciplines of army life came naturally to him. He was used to taking orders. He'd been helping his mother run her pension in Torfhaus, at the foot of the Brocken, since his father's death. Officers, to Karsten, were just demanding guests to be placated with good service. The pension was small and poor, the furnishings more threadbare each season – a great comedown for his mother – but it was always her proud conviction that so long as they were sticklers for cleanliness and neatness, the place could preserve a kind of rustic charm. She taught him to polish the silver, and then to iron and make beds with starched precision, all before he was ten, and he thanked her silently each morning at inspection.

He'd feared it might make him enemies, how easily it all came to him, but in fact it made him friends, admirers. It helped that he was generous with his comrades, teaching them his mother's tricks: dipping a rag in hot water before polishing shoes, kneeling rather than bending over to make a bed, ironing only the inside of shirts. They told him he should be an officer and he smiled shyly, though in truth he lacked the arrogance for command, was a natural NCO, the kind who fiercely mothers his men. They actually took to calling him *Mutti* for a time, and he told them, in return, they'd all make excellent chambermaids.

His barracks mates prized Karsten for one more skill as well. He'd picked up a smattering of French and English before the war. The latter from a season in Hull, where his father had taken a job with a family of fishermen he'd worked with as a POW in 1919, until his mother, miserable among the enemy, as she called them, demanded they move back to Lübeck. The language had come back to Karsten in later years, chatting with skiers staying at his mother's place – from whom he'd also picked up some serviceable French – and he'd kept it up watching American movies, Dietrich's especially, until the ban in '40. It was French his comrades wanted to learn, though – France was where they all yearned to be posted – in order to 'meet the mademoiselles'. He hesitated at first, until they accused him of holding out on them, of wanting all the girls for himself, so he'd taught them *Je t'aime,* pronouncing it hoarsely, then covering his embarrassment by making fun of their accents.

Schiller – he'd been one of their drill instructors then – had caught them at it and shaken his head. He'd been in France in '40 and '41, and they were still a little in awe of him, but someone had plucked up the courage to ask him if he knew any good pick-up lines.

'*Combien?*' he'd snorted, and left Karsten to translate.

As the dusk deepens, Karsten watches a line of British troops file up the beach into the darkness of the dunes. The column bunches near their stockade, those in front slowing to stare, those behind bumping into them. There's some pointing, some laughter at their expense, some hissed name-calling. Karsten rouses the other two, dusts the sand from his uniform and steps close to the wire. Several of the men glance away quickly, as if suddenly shy, and it gratifies him, this flinch.

'Almost have to pity them,' Schiller mutters beside him.

'Pity them?'

'We're out of it, after all.'

It's a shameful thought, and Karsten recoils from it. 'They might shoot us yet.' He knows it's unlikely – the stockade is proof of that – but at least it silences Schiller, the older man sagging back against one of the fence posts, sliding down until he's sitting in the sand. And yet Karsten can't quite shake the notion. Amid all the hundreds of men on the beach, only the three of them are no longer in the war. They, and the dead, gently nodding in the surf. He looks down the column of pale faces, counting heads. Every fifth man? he wonders. Every fourth? Every third? He's a prisoner, their prisoner, yet for a moment he's buoyed by an almost godlike sense of immortality.

He glances around, abruptly guilty, but Heino is still slumped on the sand, cradling his hand, his back to Karsten and the British.

The boy is underage, signed up at a recruiting station by some myopic or cynical veteran. There's less than eighteen months separating them, yet Karsten sees him as a child, divided from the rest, not least by the virginity they'd guessed at and made fun of so mercilessly. The second of three sons, Heino joined up the day he heard his older brother was dead, killed by partisans in Yugoslavia, enlisting under a false name so his family couldn't find him. Karsten had taken him under his wing, reasoning that by the time the boy was shipped back, it would only be a matter of months before he could enlist again. But he did make Heino write home (in return for an extorted promise to get him laid on leave), adding a note to his mother, at the boy's bashful begging, pledging to look out for her son. Karsten had even interceded with Schiller on Heino's behalf, back when Schiller was still sergeant. *Wunderkind,* Schiller dubbed the boy, but in his economical veteran's way he hadn't bothered to report him, and Heino had gone on to become something of a mascot for the unit.

They never did get the boy laid, it occurs to Karsten now. And he hopes this is what Heino is brooding on.

He'd ask Schiller's opinion, but beside him he sees that the other has his eyes closed. Not sleeping, though, Karsten is sure.

He wonders what Schiller's thinking behind those lids. Probably wondering where his next drink's coming from.

In training camp, Schiller had been a morose despot who'd never shown enthusiasm for anything except finding fault and cribbage (nagging them to play, gloating when he won, nagging them again when they quit in disgust). The men had been delighted when he'd been caught drunk one night, puking on the major's roses, and stripped of rank. But they'd been dismayed when he'd been shipped out with them to France.

In a sense, Karsten owes his recent promotion to Schiller's disgrace. After the sergeant had been demoted, another corporal had been elevated in his stead, creating an opening. Karsten had only sewn the stripe on the month before, tongue tip pressed to the corner of his mouth. Heino had raised his arm, posed it, flexing as if showing off a new muscle, and the men had given a little cheer, though Karsten knew they meant as much to jeer Schiller. He tried to shrug off their congratulations, tell them it was just one stripe.

'Maybe so,' Schiller growled. He was slumped in his bunk, drunk again, though no one knew where he got his booze, and he never offered to share. 'It was the Führer's rank, for all that.'

To his surprise, Karsten has become wary friends with the older man. Contemptuous of them as he was in training, Schiller has always grudgingly admired Karsten's soldiering, even using him as an example to the others, and Karsten, for his part, secretly envies the older man's experience. He's the only one in the squad, after all, to have seen action, though Karsten has never been able to push him for the details – has he killed, and if so, how many? He'd tried to bring it up once, in a bar on leave, and Schiller had raised his glass in a mock toast: 'To innocence!' And yet the older man has quietly taken it upon himself to complete Karsten's training these past weeks – teaching him 'all the things they don't tell you in basic', how to handle officers, the men's dodges.

And I listened, Karsten thinks now, crossing his arms and fingering the stitches on his sleeve, *and never said anything about his drinking.*

It had begun before dawn with the naval bombardment, the shells flung from somewhere over the grey horizon, missing them mercifully but spitting gouts of sand through their firing slits with enough force to sting their faces. They'd crouched down, cradling the guns, emptying their canteens over their faces to clear their eyes while the explosions walked overhead, white cement dust jumping out of the low ceiling, sifting down on them until they looked like bakers. Then came the planes, tearing by so loud Karsten thought the noise alone might kill them, rip them to shreds. Finally the landing craft, a long line of them pressing through the surf, throwing themselves on to the beach like spent swimmers at the end of a race.

It wasn't hard to kill the men in them, he found. He'd been so hungry for action, desperate for it after all the weeks of training. He'd actually hoped for an invasion, worried he'd missed his chance. And now here it was, and he felt, more than anything, relieved as he gunned down the distant figures, relieved and vindicated, jerking his sights from target to target, clutching at the trigger. Beside him Heino, feeding him the ammunition, was frowning with concentration, his fingers dancing over the belt as if over piano keys. Karsten felt a sudden uproarious pity for him, wanted to yell at him to look – *look!* – out the firing slit. *You're missing it!*

At least Schiller was getting into the spirit of things, roaring with excitement. Willi, the other gunner's mate, was screaming right along with him, even though he detested Schiller, had been begging Karsten for a new assignment. But now it felt as if they were all coming together, their petty differences burnt off. He could see Willi sheltering behind Schiller's fury, taking comfort in it. Why, Schiller looked as if he might drive the British off the beach with his contempt alone.

But they'd kept coming, of course. Wave after wave, too many for them to keep up with. Karsten's arms had begun to ache, a dull pain spreading from his hands, gripping the juddering gun, to his wrists, his forearms, all the way to his back, a hard pinch between his shoulder blades. It was heavy work, this slaughter. He began to feel an odd sympathy for the exhausted men slogging through the sand, envied them as they lay themselves down before his fire.

And then Willi had been hit, his slack face suddenly looking like a child's. Heino knelt beside him, and in quick glances Karsten watched him apply a tourniquet to Willi's arm, stab him with an ampoule of morphine. It was a neat job, Karsten thought, Schiller would have approved, and only when Heino looked up, proud of his first field dressing, did Karsten lift his feet from the oily pool spreading behind Willi's head.

The end had come quickly then, the hitch in their fire when Willi went down, enough to let the British close to within grenade-throwing distance. Karsten recalls the sound of them hitting the walls of the bunker – he'd thought, for a moment, they were throwing rocks – and then one had flown through the slit and Heino chased it around the concrete floor like a mouse. He heaved two more back while Karsten wrestled with a jam in the breech, before the first bright spear of the flamethrower lanced through the firing slit, boiling across the ceiling.

A moment later a second shot unfurled down the passageway to the rear of the bunker. Karsten heard the breathy roar of it first, felt the warm gust of oily fumes, and just had time to push Heino aside, knock Schiller down before the flower of flame bloomed in their midst. He and Schiller lay there, one atop the other, even after the fire washed back down the corridor, watching the flames dance on Willi's head. They looked so lively, licking his ears and temples, it was hard to believe he was dead, until they smelled the singed hair.

Schiller had clutched him then, started screaming. Karsten stared at his lips, trying to make out what he was saying, deafened by the stammering guns. And then Schiller had put his lips to Karsten's ear: 'You have to tell them. You're the only one. With your English. You have to tell them we surrender.'

Karsten had tried to shove him away when he understood, but Schiller hugged him like a drowning man.

'If not for me, for the boy!'

Heino was huddled in the far corner, shaking. Karsten thought he was wounded, crawled to him. 'Where is it? Where?' He tried to pull apart the boy's arms, wrapped tight around his knees, and then he saw Heino had soiled himself. The boy's face was dark with smoke below his close-cropped fair hair; the tears rolling down his blackened cheeks looked like oil.

There seemed to be a lull outside. Maybe the enemy thought the last burst had killed them all, maybe they were summoning up their nerve to rush the bunker. In the stillness, Karsten heard the thought distinctly: *I can save him.*

Climbing to his feet, sagging against the blackened doorway, he tried to call out, but broke down coughing in the stink of gasoline from the charred walls. Schiller was there at once, pushing their last canteen on him with fumbling hands, making him gulp the water down. Karsten tried again, hanging his head a little farther into the passage this time, the English thick as paste on his tongue. 'Can you hear me?' But there was nothing, no reply, though no flame either, and he knew he was going to have to go down the passage to make himself heard, down the narrow concrete tunnel in which there'd be no way to dodge the fire.

He put a hand out to steady himself and jerked it back. The walls were hot, and when he sucked his fingers he tasted soot.

He looked back at Schiller, saw he was gripping his rifle, and for a second Karsten thought he was going to force him out at gunpoint, until Schiller shook his head, a sick expression on his face. 'For me,' he mouthed, and Karsten knew he meant to put his lips around the barrel, to kill himself rather than face the flames.

Karsten stumbled down the passage then, every second expecting the rush and flood of flame to wash over him, calling out as he went, wondering if they could understand him. The slit of light ahead, tinged red by the sun, looked like tensed lips. Finally he heard something from the end of the tunnel: 'Come on then, if you're coming!' And it seemed miraculous to speak the same language as men he had just been trying to kill, who might kill him any second, the words passing between them faster than bullets.

He hurried the last few steps into the light, remembering at the last moment to raise his hands.

It was so bright after the dimness of the bunker. It made him think of those long summer evenings when he'd come out of a theatre, shocked to find the day still blazing, as if it should have somehow ended, faded to black, with the film. The light made his eyeballs feel swollen and raw, and he blinked and squinted until he could make out half a dozen men, rifles trained on him, and at their centre a burly fellow in motorcyclist's goggles with a tank on his back, and before him the blunt black muzzle of the flamethrower, the delicate blue bud of the ignition flame at its tip.

There was a long moment of silence. Karsten must have imagined it, but he could have sworn it was possible to make out the hiss of gas, the ticking of the fuel cylinders. Standing, swaying slightly in the scarred portal, it seemed as if something more were required of him, something more formal. But under the scrutiny of the several pairs of eyes trained on him, he found himself tongue-tied, like those times in front of class when he'd forgotten the lesson he was supposed to have by heart. He felt himself grow hot, and he realised that beneath the sweat and grime he was blushing. And then it came to him, the correct phrase, rising out of memory.

'How do you do?' he asked, and the rifle barrels trained on him began to bob and weave, and he saw the men were laughing, shaking with it.

'Oh, that's a good one, Jerry! That's priceless, that is. How do you fucking do yourself?'

He had to lean back into the entry, clinging to the scorched camouflage netting, to call the others out. Schiller fairly ran to him, but Karsten had to order Heino out when he hung back – ashamed of having shat himself, Karsten thought. The boy appeared at last with his hands up, his right raw and bleeding. He'd tried to beat out the flames on Willi's head.

It's lightening faintly on the beach, the posts of the stockade becoming visible against the sky, and Karsten thinks it must be dawn. Nearby, he hears the rasp of a match and a guard's face flares in the gloom, then vanishes as if blown out, the light shrinking to the smouldering tip of the cigarette. Enough to draw a bead on in the darkness, though, and Karsten finds himself holding his breath, waiting for a shot. But there's nothing. When he looks back at the sky, he realises the red glow to the east is fire.

In the immediate aftermath of their capture, after they'd seen to Heino's hand, one of the Tommies had offered a cigarette, holding it under Schiller's nose, and when Schiller reached for it, closing his fist and yanking it away.

'What's he want?' Schiller muttered out of the side of his mouth.

They were squatting, fingers laced behind their heads.

The Tommy proffered his hand again, whispered something then, pointed at Schiller.

'What's he saying?' Schiller hissed, almost losing his balance. 'What the fuck's he saying?'

'Trade,' Karsten told him dully. 'He wants to trade you for the cigarette.'

'Trade what?'

'Your cap.'

'*My cap?*'

'He wants it for a souvenir,' Karsten said, looking at his feet. 'To remember this by.' *You're going to get a medal,* he wanted to shout in the Tommy's face, stabbed with sudden envy.

Schiller was already pulling out the cap folded under his epaulette and handing it over.

He offered to share the cigarette. 'Go on. That was a good deal. A souvenir! Who'd want to remember this shambles?'

The victors, Karsten thought, but after a second he took the cigarette and then held it out to Heino. 'Take it,' he barked when the other hesitated. 'You don't know when you'll see another.' And the boy had reached out his good hand.

Throughout the night, they're visited by more souvenir hunters. Heino gives up his prized pack of dirty playing cards for a couple of squares of chocolate, which he gobbles down at once. Karsten trades his lighter for a cigarette and then waits stonily for the Tommy to light it through the fence for him. Karsten assumes they'll run out of things to offer before long. But he's wrong. The Tommies want everything and anything – epaulettes, belts, even buttons – and when the prisoners shake their heads, the Tommies stop asking, stop bartering, start demanding at gunpoint.

Faced with the muzzle of a gun, Schiller gives up his watch, dangling by its strap like a fish by the tail.

'Spoils of war,' he says, shrugging.

'It was your father's,' Karsten says. He has almost nothing of his own father's, everything having been sold after his death to raise the money to move.

'Should have buried it in the sand,' Heino says.

'And ruined it!'

'At least the Tommies wouldn't have got it.'

'That's easy for you to say, you little shit,' Schiller hisses. 'All you've got to lose is your fucking virginity.'

'Enough,' Karsten tells them, though privately he agrees with Schiller. The boy's bravado rankles.

But Heino does have something more to lose, it turns out. Later, when they're told to turn out their pockets by yet another 'collector', the boy baulks at undoing the button on his breast pocket. The Tommy stands over him, nudging him first with the flat of his bayonet, and when the boy bats it away, with the point, pressing it to his chest until Heino gradually lies back in the sand under the force. Karsten waits until he sees the boy holding his breath, nostrils flared, eyes staring, before he reaches across him gently. The bayonet point picks at the brass button, then withdraws with a scrape, and Karsten undoes it, pulls out a couple of sheets of folded paper, hands them up.

'A letter,' Schiller says afterwards, shaking his head.

'It was to my mother!'

'And that's worth dying for? How many times do you want us to save your life today?'

'Don't use me as an excuse!' He pulls away from them, shoulders hunched and shaking.

Schiller rolls his eyes, but Karsten lets the boy cry, and only when he is quiet, goes over and lays a hand on his shoulder.

'I just never thought I'd surrender,' the boy murmurs. 'Killed maybe, wounded, but never that I'd surrender. I wasn't even afraid of that.'

'Well, you didn't, did you?' Karsten takes a deep breath. 'You were just following orders.' It seems to him as if it's the only order he's given since his promotion.

The boy glances over quickly, then away, but nods to himself.

A little later, he looks up at the guards beyond the stockade. 'You don't think they know German, do you?'

'I doubt it.'

'Only,' he whispers, 'there was some, you know, soppy stuff in my letter. I wouldn't like them to laugh at it.'

'They won't.'

'We killed loads of them, didn't we?' the boy asks, brightening. 'How many do you think?'

But Karsten is thinking of his own letters from home, the bundle of them tied together in his locker at the barracks. She's proud of him, his mother has written. The first time she's ever said so, he thinks. No matter how helpful he'd been around the pension, she thought it women's work, beneath him. Even his labours for hunters and hikers were tainted by an air of servitude. 'I used to *stay* in hotels when I was a girl,' she told him once. But now she boasts to the neighbours about his prowess on the range. She's nagged him for photos, and when he sends them, she tells him how smart he looks, how handsome. She has them all lined up along the mantel, as if on parade. *Good for business,* she's written, *if there were any business.* She's just written to him about his promotion. *If only the war lasts long enough, perhaps you'll make leutnant.* It was his father's rank during the last war, his highest station in life, and achieving it, Karsten knew, would be a kind of redemption in her eyes. She was the daughter of a *vizeadmiral* herself, had travelled the world with him as a child. She'd met Karsten's father at a navy ball in 1914 and married him a year later. He was from an old naval family too, and although only a junior officer, already making a name for himself in the new submarine service. 'He'd have made *kapitan*,' she told him once, 'if he hadn't got in trouble in 1917. He didn't agree with the order to attack passenger ships.' She shook her head. 'They wanted to court-martial him, except my father pulled some strings, had him reassigned to the surface fleet.' They'd both been at Scapa Flow in 1919 when the interned fleet scuttled itself. Karsten's grandfather had gone down with his vessel, and his father had spent almost a year as a prisoner of war.

Karsten wonders how she'll feel when she hears he's a prisoner himself, what she'll tell the neighbours. And then he wonders when she'll be notified, and he quails at the thought of what she'll think in the meantime.

His own turn to get fleeced comes a little later. He'd already given up his folded postcard of Torfhaus and the scallop-edged photo of the French whore, Françoise, the men liked to say he was in love with. 'Who's this *fräulein*, then?' the sergeant who'd taken it had asked. 'Look forward to making her acquaintance, I will.' But Karsten had kept his head, not rising to the bait, submitting to it all calmly, with dignity he hoped, locking his eyes on Heino's, showing he could take it.

But then the sergeant returns, moving among them by the flame of a cigarette lighter, until he finds Karsten, pulls him to his feet, makes him stand at attention while he picks at the stitches of his corporal's stripe with a bayonet.

'A sergeant wanting corporal's stripes,' Heino says, shaking his head.

It comes to Karsten slowly that their surrender wasn't that one moment already past, at the mouth of the bunker, but somehow will go on and on. He wonders what more they'll have to give up before it's over. Everything but their lives, probably.

They're silent after that, the three of them, pretending to sleep in the darkness, though Karsten knows none of them are. They're still, but it's not the stillness of sleepers – he's come to recognise the slow, flaring sighs of sleeping men after four months in barracks – but of listeners, their breaths shallow, punctuated by sniffs. The stillness of sentries, he thinks bitterly. He wonders what they're waiting for, what they're hoping to hear. He listens with them, straining to catch the sounds of battle, of a counterattack, but as far as he can tell the rattle and crump of the fighting is growing more distant, faint beneath the lap and suck of the tide. What he hears instead are the sounds the sand makes

– the creaking near the waterline where it's densest, the soft patter of the dunes where it's finest – and the heavy breathing of the columns of men slogging through it, their occasional scuffs and curses. Even now, every few minutes he'll hear the dull clout and scrape of a landing craft's door slamming the wet sand, catch the hooded green glow of muster lamps. If he listens hard enough he can make out the slight sleigh-bell jingling of dog tags, of pack straps, of belt buckles.

He wonders if the others hear it too, or if perhaps they're just attending to the faint sounds of themselves, their hearts, their stomachs, their throats, listening to their own breaths and feeling grateful for them.

And then, in the watery half-light of dawn, with the salt rime already beginning to crust their uniforms, they see what they've been waiting for all along: a line of men, mostly regular infantry by the look of them, hands raised, coming towards them over the flattened dune grass. They hurry to the fence, straining to recognise faces from their own unit. There's a sense of safety, if not strength, in numbers, Karsten supposes, and despite himself he feels his spirits rise. It's as if they've been marooned, the three of them, and now glimpse a sail in the distance. Even another wreck is to be welcomed, apparently. But as he watches, the line keeps coming and he begins to wonder how far back it stretches. It seems a skinny, ragged parody of the British column moving the other way.

Heino starts to wave his bandaged hand, but Karsten pulls it down. There are no familiar faces that he can see, and beyond that gnawing disappointment, he's suddenly wary of these strangers, the way they eye him stonily as they file in – thirty or more in the end – and gather at the far side of the stockade. Several of them fall to the sand, exhausted. The British pass in canteens, but no food, and Karsten and the others sling them over their shoulders, hand them out among the new men.

'It's not so bad, mates,' Schiller tells them.

'That so?' A burly figure detaches himself from the crowd and faces them. 'Maybe we wouldn't be here at all if not for you.'

'What's that supposed to mean?' Heino asks, a little shrilly.

'Leave it,' Karsten whispers, taking his arm. There are no officers, he realises – the British must be holding them separately – and the group has the desultory surliness of enlisted men when no higher ranks are present.

'It means,' the fellow says, setting himself, 'if you hadn't saved your own skins, we'd have had a better chance.'

The boy makes to lunge at the man, but Karsten holds him.

'Leave it!' he repeats, and then more loudly: 'These will be answering the same question soon enough to the next bunch.'

'Defeatist!' the burly man snaps. 'That's the kind of talk put us all here.'

Karsten feels sand grind between his molars, tastes salt. He wants to spit, but doesn't. Instead, he and Schiller pull the struggling boy away, the man's voice following them, taunting: 'How much ammunition did you have left, you shits? How many bullets, how many grenades?'

'Let me go!' Heino snarls, and when at last they do, he jerks away, glares at them as if he'd strike out, but finally throws himself on the sand.

Karsten feels the burden settling over them. This is what it is to be the first; all the rest can blame them. And they, in turn, can blame him, who led them in surrender. Schiller won't meet his eye, and Karsten sees Heino edging away in the sand. He hisses the boy's name but Heino won't look at him, and eventually Karsten stops, not sure who is more ashamed, he or the boy.

Over and over he pushes his hands into the sand, clenching them and pulling them out, watching the sand drain from them however hard he squeezes.

Finally, at full dawn, Karsten notices the guard being changed, and jumping to his feet, he hurries along the fence after a lieutenant and his sergeant, his boots sinking in the light sand. 'Excuse me. Excuse me.'

Without breaking stride, the ruddy-faced lieutenant looks over at his sergeant wearily. 'What's he want, Sergeant?'

'What do you want?'

'The men could use some food,' Karsten tells him uncertainly, adding a 'sir' in the direction of the lieutenant. 'Some of us haven't eaten since breakfast yesterday.'

'Jerry's a mite peckish, sir.'

'Really.' The lieutenant looks thoughtful. 'And what does Jerry eat, do you think? What do you think he'd *fancy*, Sergeant? Humble pie?'

'Or a nice bit of crow, sir.'

Karsten pulls up and watches them go, kicking up sand.

When he slumps down beside Schiller, the other tells him, 'I don't have any English, my friend, but if you want to talk to their officers, do me a favour. Do it far away from me.'

Karsten turns to stare at him, and Schiller glances away over his shoulder. Karsten waits until he looks at him again.

'You were happy enough I spoke English when it saved your neck,' he says tightly.

'I'm still thinking of my neck,' Schiller tells him.

Karsten keeps to himself after that, though in truth none of them talk much that morning, just watch the long columns of Allied troops march past them, the second and third waves of the invasion. The enemy are so many, Karsten thinks, through the night and now the morning, still marching out of the sweeping surf. The prisoners drowse and wake and drowse and wake, and no matter when they awaken, no matter how many hours have passed, there is the enemy column moving up the beach. And offshore the smoke of countless ships; overhead, hour after hour, the drone of planes. It's astonishing, Karsten thinks, a staggering sight, the kind of manpower that built the pyramids or the Great Wall, the wonders of the world.

All these men, he thinks, and yet if he could, if he'd had the ammunition, if the pillbox could have held out, he'd have slaughtered them all, wouldn't he? Hundreds, thousands. For as long as they'd have kept coming. Until their bones covered the beach like rocks. The thought makes him sway with exhaustion, and for the first time he feels a flicker of relief to have been captured, shudders as if to shake it off.

Yet another landing craft disgorges its men. His eyes follow them up the beach, past the stockade, towards the dunes, and he feels an odd pull, a tug towards the horizon. All those men flowing in one direction. He yearns to look over the dunes, as if he has no idea, no recollection, of what's there. It comes to him that he's behind enemy lines, but the shifting geography seems unreal, as if the earth has turned under his very feet. This was German territory and now it's British, but he can't see how it has changed. He pictures the maps he's seen, imagines the fields beyond the dunes tinged the faint dawning pink of empire. And he wishes he could follow that column of men, feels powerfully as if he's falling behind, he who could march faster and farther than anyone.

Four

Her father's acreage includes the steep slope above the camp, but by bike it's a long ride round the mountain and through the village to the farmhouse. Esther pedals hard for the first mile, keen to put the camp behind her, but before long she's labouring. She makes it up the slope to the pub, her breath coming in short, hard pants, but leans over the handlebars, spent, to coast through the quiet village. At the foot of the last long hill home, she squeezes the brakes in defeat, steps down and wheels the bike. Its spokes tick quietly beside her, holding the rushing silence of the night at bay. Her father turns in early, but tonight she wants to be sure he's asleep. She doesn't want to face him, to answer any questions, at least not until he comes stumping into the kitchen with the morning's pail of milk and she can put his breakfast, two thick 'doorstep' slices of bread and butter, in front of him.

She tries to think about Colin, to order her thoughts, make sense of what's happened, but finds each time her mind darting off, turning instead to Eric, their first evacuee. He'd just turned fourteen when he arrived in 1940, a year older than she, but a townie, so clueless in the ways of the country (the first time he watched the milking, he blanched, asked her shakily, 'Milk is cow's *piss*?') that she felt his equal. An only child, she'd been thrilled at the prospect of another youngster about the place –

even a boy, as her father insisted it must be, 'so he can earn his keep'. She pulled on her mother's arm all the way down to the station, only to grow shy when they entered the waiting room, where the new arrivals were lined up as if for inspection.

Her mother nudged her ahead, but she was too nervous to look at any of the strange boys in their brown blazers and corduroy shorts. She hurried down one row after another and only halted when a boy knelt down in front of her to tie his shoelace. She stopped and waited, and he whispered, 'Pick me,' so softly she thought he was talking to his shoe. 'Pick me,' he said again, looking up and meeting her gaze. He reached out and grasped her hand, and when he released it, left a balled-up stocking in her palm. She turned crimson when the crumpled nylon began to spring open like a grey flower and she saw what she was holding.

'All right, Ess?' her mother called.

'Pick me and I'll give you the other one,' Eric whispered.

He didn't take his eyes off her hand until it closed into a fist.

'Mam,' Esther called over her shoulder. 'What about this one?'

He'd been as good as his word the next day when they'd found themselves alone in the kitchen. 'A deal's a deal,' he said. 'I'm no welsher.' He grinned to let her know he was joking. 'Don't tell your mother, mind,' he made her promise. 'Mum said they were supposed to be for her, a gift like, only . . .' He paused and then Esther started to giggle, unable to imagine her mother ever wearing such things, and slowly his grin widened.

Later, he said, 'Will you wear them for me one day?' and she stared at him.

They were inseparable that spring. Rhys had tried to befriend Eric too, but he could never keep up with their rapid exchanges in English. When he kept asking her what they were saying, Eric would bleat at him, *'Baa-aa!'* To her parents she said Eric was teaching her English (though she was perfectly fluent, thanks to

72

Mrs Roberts and all her time at the pictures). In fact, he was teaching her to kiss – teaching himself, she realises now, since they never got as far as French kissing. Her parents seemed to turn a blind eye, although in retrospect Esther knows that summer was the start of her mother's illness. She has felt guilty for the way her preoccupation with Eric caused her to ignore the early signs of decline, the weariness and lack of appetite, and for the comfort she drew from him in the final, wasting days. And maybe that guilt, she thinks now, is why, the month after the funeral, when his own mother wrote from Coventry to say that she wanted her Eric back, that she was missing him so much, Esther told him, 'You should go.' He hadn't wanted to. He still resented his mum for sending him away in the first place. On the train to Wales he'd reached into his pocket and pulled out his brown school cap – his name stitched along the headband by his mother – and sailed it out the window, watching it curve up and back over the line of the train. But Esther made him go. He should be with his mother, she said, feeling selfless, and he didn't know how to argue with her on that score.

She'd seen him off on the sooty platform at Caernarvon station, listening to the carriage doors clattering shut around them – bang bang bang bang bang – like a firing squad. She remembers the engine coming to life: wisps of steam floating up, twisting towards the station's glass and iron roof, and then a stream of smoke, like a kettle coming to the boil. They waited together for the rip of the whistle, holding hands through the lowered window, and then she stepped back to join her father and watched the train move off, the couplings taking up the slack and the carriages jolting forward one by one, just like the toy set she'd seen with Eric in the window of Nelson's the Christmas before. And then the last clacking carriage twisted out of sight.

Two months and six letters later, she heard from an aunt of his that he and his mother had died together – their shelter had

73

received a direct hit – and more than anything she had envied them.

She finds herself turning on to the path to Cilgwyn now, the house a dim shadow before her in the darkness, her steps ringing back off the stone walls of the lane.

They'd kissed first in the last row of the cinema one Saturday morning, she and Eric, but all she can think of now is a joke of Harry's:

'I hear they're putting a swimming pool in the back of our picture palace.'

'*A swimming pool?*'

''Sright. On account of everyone back there's always doing the breaststroke!'

The pedal catches against the back of her calf and she winces, loses her grip, the bike clattering to the ground, its bell clinking dully. Frozen for a moment, praying the commotion hasn't woken Arthur, she stares at the bike lying there dumbly, lets herself down beside it, and weeps dry, choking sobs. *He* was her first, she thinks fervently. *Him*. Eric. Her first love.

It takes her long minutes to collect herself, and then she clambers to her feet, pulls the bike upright. Having brought it so far, it seems she's going to keep it after all. *I earned it,* she thinks viciously.

She heads first to the privy at the bottom of the garden – she hates to sit there in the dark, but she's suddenly desperate – then lets herself in by the kitchen door, tiptoes to her room, holding her breath, and crawls under the covers fully clothed.

She hugs herself, panting softly, listening to the house, the rise and fall of her father's steady snores.

How much later she doesn't know – she seems to wake and yet to have barely caught her breath – there's a knock at the door, a pounding, and she presses her back to the wall. It's Colin, she's sure. He's come for her, and it's only the sound of her father's cursing that stops her crying out. 'I'm bloody coming!' he shouts, and it thrills her, the prospect of him turning his rage on Colin. She hears him shuffling down the passage, the rattle of the matchbox, the rasp as he strikes a light, followed by the slosh of the paraffin lamp. And then he's calling out in Welsh, 'Who's there?' and the answer, in English, 'It's me, Evans, and you can keep a civil tongue. I've brought you something of yours.' For an insane moment, she thinks, *The constable, thank God, he can arrest Colin!* and then it dawns on her: Colin isn't here, never was.

In her relief, she misses the start of the exchange, climbs out of bed and makes her way on trembling legs to the glowing frame of her door.

'—wouldn't tell them where he lived,' Parry is saying, 'so they dumped him on me.' She peers into the passage, sees her father, his back to her, at the front door, Parry before him with his hands on Jim's shoulders. 'Wouldn't tell them anything, as a matter of fact – just his name, over and over, to all their questions.'

'I'd have given them a rank and serial number if I had one,' Jim tells them, and Esther, coming forward and catching his eye, puts a finger to her lips. He's in enough trouble already, and for a moment the thought of someone else's problems steadies her, and she smooths a hand down the front of her rumpled skirt.

She should have known, of course. The disturbance at the camp, the interruption that drove Colin off. It must have been the local boys. They'd been watching the camp ever since the sappers first pecked out the perimeter of the site with mallets and surveying stakes – stakes that had started showing up thrust through boys' belt loops like cutlasses, brandished in high-street duels ('Errol Flynn!' 'Douglas Fairbanks!'). The boys were the ones who'd kept the village informed of the sappers' progress, fuelling speculation about the base's purpose, growing more and more impatient with the mystery. 'It's top secret,' Esther told

Jim when he begged her to ask one of the sappers at the pub, but the way his face fell, you would have thought it was *the* top secret, out of all the many adult things he wasn't old enough to hear or understand. Parry, with whom the boys have a running feud (their favourite trick: reporting a naked light during blackout and, when he comes running, mooning him, the gang of them, arses hanging out of their drawers), had said they were up to something. And she should have known Jim would get mixed up in it. He isn't well liked by the local lads – few of the evacuees are, but Jim is small for his age, and his fiery temper makes him easy to goad (his last name, Leadbetter, has earned him the nickname Bedwetter) – but it doesn't stop him from trying to ingratiate himself by getting into trouble.

'They thought he was Welsh,' Parry is saying now, shaking his head, though Esther can believe it; Jim's picked up a bit of the language in his time with them. 'An arsonist, if you please!' the constable goes on, chuckling, but Arthur is stone faced. He's never been fond of the constable, on account of his insistence on doing all his official business in English.

'What happened to his head?' Arthur asks, still in Welsh, and coming into the light she sees a welt on Jim's forehead, the bruise already turning waxy like spoiled meat.

'Kept putting his hands up, apparently. Surrendering. One of them thought he was taking the piss, gave him a little clout.'

'One of them "heroes"?'

The constable is silent.

'Well, obliged to you for fetching him back,' Arthur says, reaching for the doorknob.

Parry leans in a moment. 'Just so long as it doesn't happen again, eh? He's your responsibility—'

'*Nos-da,* now.' Arthur swings the door to.

'And goodnight to you,' Parry says from the other side, his tone perfectly conversational, as if he can see right through the wood. Jim starts to say something, but Arthur raises a finger and the boy flinches. They listen to the scrape of the policeman's feet in the yard, the creak of the gate.

'POWs!' Jim bursts out as soon as it's quiet. 'That's who it's for!' He looks at them triumphantly, as if the news somehow excuses everything.

'What happened?' Esther asks.

'We broke in,' he says, 'and we found a cell block. You know, for solitary confinement. That's how we knew the secret!'

She tries to look suitably surprised, but she can see he's disappointed. He looks over her shoulder. 'POWs, Mr Evans.'

'But how did you get caught?' Esther insists.

His face clouds for a second. 'Oh, the others,' he says, trying to sound breezy. 'They locked me in one of the cells for a joke and forgot to come back.'

'*Duw!*' She crouches down to get a better look at his head, but he twists away.

Behind her, Arthur has started to laugh thinly and she stares at him.

'Prisoners of war,' he says, and she knows it's taken him a moment to work it out in English, too proud to just ask. 'And all those happy fools down the pub,' he goes on in Welsh, 'hoping for some glorious part in the English war. What a slap in the face!' He shakes his head. 'Glad you could join us,' he adds, looking her up and down, taking in her rumpled clothes.

'I thought I should be decent,' she tells him awkwardly.

He's in slippers and a nightshirt himself, his calves below the hem corded with muscle, the veins binding them like blue twine. The nightshirt is so old it's gone grey, and Esther, so rarely up in the morning before him, can't remember the last time she's seen him in it.

'I could boil that for you,' she blurts out, and he gives her a puzzled look.

'You just see to his head,' he tells her, suddenly weary, pushing past on his way back to bed. 'That's your job.'

She sits Jim at the table, puts water on to warm, fetches a towel, then sets the lamp beside him. 'It doesn't hurt,' he tells her, but pulls back when she reaches for him.

'Hold still.'

She lifts the matted hair off his forehead – 'Ow!' – and clucks her tongue. It's not a bad wound, he's come back with worse from the schoolyard, but there's a nasty-looking scrape at the centre of the bruise where the skin is broken – by a ring? she wonders, a watch? – and moving his hair has opened it again. She stands swiftly, drawing in her breath as a dotted line of blood begins to well up. She feels her tears brimming, turns quickly and stretches for the shelf above the sink, for bandages and the bottle of Mercurochrome.

'Do we have to?' he asks as she drapes the towel round his neck. Then, picking up on her solemnity: 'I'm wounded, aren't I?'

She nods, unable to speak. The boy eyes the bottle warily, takes the corner of the towel and draws it across his mouth.

'For the pain,' he says, biting down as she begins to clean the cut.

She hadn't wanted another evacuee when the Blitz had started and there'd been a second wave of them, though Arthur had said they could use some help around the place. She'd resisted until the summer of '41, after Liverpool had been shattered and a belated trickle of kids began to arrive. Arthur had shaken his head in disgust when she'd come back from the station with Jim in tow. At nine, he was too small to be much use on the farm (the reason why Rhys had been hired the next summer), but at least Arthur wasn't hardhearted enough to make her take him back. 'Don't know what you were thinking. He's like a stray,' he told her. 'If you want to take pity on him, well and good, but he's your lookout. You'll have to see to him and make up for what he can't do about the place.'

She pauses in her cleaning and tells Jim to stop pulling faces. 'It can't hurt so badly. I'm being very gentle.'

He opens his eyes. 'Shows how much you know,' he says. 'It's agony.' Then, hopefully, 'Is it finished?'

She shakes her head, reaches for the Mercurochrome, and he bunches his face again. And all the time she's tending his wound and wrapping his head, she wants to ask, *Which one? Which one did this to you?*

But when she's done and pinning the bandage, he says, 'I didn't tell on the other lads. The constable kept asking who was there, but I'm no rat.' His eyes are alight beneath the white strip, as proud to have kept a secret as uncovered one.

'You might as well have,' she snaps, suddenly as angry at the other boys as at the sappers. 'That lot!'

His face falls, and when she asks him at last – 'Now, Jim' – which of the sappers hit him, she sees his face close. He couldn't tell, he says stubbornly, and when she presses him, 'But you must know,' he raises a fist to his eyes, a gesture that always makes her think he wants to punch himself for crying, and she tells him quickly, 'Hey, hey. I almost forgot. I've got something for you.'

'What?' he asks grudgingly.

'Only if you stop crying. It's only for a brave boy.'

'I wasn't crying.'

She leans forward and puts her mouth to his ear.

'A bike,' she whispers, and he looks at her with amazement, and then with such joy that for a second she thinks it's almost been worth it. He throws his arms around her, and she finds herself standing abruptly, brushing him off, saying lamely, 'Your bandage will come loose.'

Later, when she tucks him in, she tries to make up for it, bending down to kiss him, but he struggles up under the sheets. 'Hey,' he says. 'Does this mean I'm the camp's first prisoner?' And she nods, and leaves him, although a part of her thinks the title rightly her own.

Before she blows out the lamp, she'll hurry to the privy again, sit on the cold wooden seat, drowsing to the fizzing drone of a bluebottle. She'll look out through the half-moon in the door and then down at her drawers in the yellow oil light and see a thin exclamation mark of blood. By the time she goes back inside, the clock over the hearth will read two o'clock, and she'll wonder dully what they call the day after D-day.

Five

Looking out of the window the morning after the invasion, she sees it's just another day, only a pale sickle moon in the blue-white sky to betray there'd even been a night before. Esther forces herself to get up to prepare Arthur's breakfast. Just like normal, she tells herself, if a little sluggish. She sets out the chipped plates with deliberate care, then the yellowing bone-handled cutlery, the bread and butter. Everything in its place. She thinks herself through the movements, conscious of them for the first time in years, as if she's never done them before.

But then, the loaf still clutched in her hand, a slice half sawn, she has to sit, her legs rubbery, shaking. It must be the unaccustomed exercise of the bike ride, she thinks, suddenly breathless.

When Arthur comes in from milking, he takes one look at her and asks if she's all right.

'Fine.'

'You're as pale as milk.'

'I'm fine.'

He knows it's a lie, she's sure, but something in the way she says it – so flatly, without appeal – leaves him unable to challenge her, as if the lie is so nearly naked that to uncover it would be cruelty. He slurps his tea, crams down a slice of bread and butter, and stamps out. At the door, he pauses. 'Boy all right?' he asks, and she can only nod. 'Quite a night he had.' She just shrugs, not trusting herself to speak. She watches him go then, feeling an urge to call him back, but instead shouts for Jim to get up, at once grateful and oddly resentful for the distraction he provided her the previous night. Besides, he's been late to school the last few days and she's newly determined to put an end to it.

There's a scuffle of feet in the corridor, and Jim stumbles into the kitchen, dishevelled and bleary from his late night, the bandage a bright halo around his head.

She butters a slice for him, and for a treat scatters half a teaspoon of rationed sugar over it, watches out of the corner of her eye as he gobbles it down, the smile spreading on his face. She's never seen him in such a hurry to get to school, but he has stories to tell. Absently, he strokes the dressing at his temples as he chews.

'Let me change that for you,' she says, and he submits, still chewing, but once she unwinds the bandage, and he sees the coppery bloodstain like a penny at its centre, he insists on keeping it, and she has to settle for washing the wound, gently dabbing around the scab. He's cheerful, fidgety with happiness, and when she wants to know why, he wonders shyly – not quite sure if he's dreamed it – whether he can see his bike now.

'You're sure you can ride one?' she asks, and he nods so emphatically she worries the bandage will slip.

'Course!'

At first, watching him weave across the yard on the bike, she can't believe he knows how to ride one, is sure he'll end up with another knot on his head or worse, half raises her arms to catch him. But he refuses to let her adjust the seat or the handlebars. He loves the height, though it means he has to mount the bike from the bottom rung of the gate. He wobbles back and forth and then gets the measure of it, swooping around her, laughing gleefully, the dogs racing after him, barking, even Arthur coming to the barn door to watch. 'See!' Jim cries. Then he's gone, flying down the lane, legs spread, feet off the pedals, his bandaged head a blur. *Fearless,* she thinks as the echo of the last bark dies away, and she suddenly wishes she'd kept the bike, could throw herself headlong down the hillside.

'Where'd he get that, then?' Arthur asks, and she calls over her shoulder that he found it.

'Found it?' The village boys, he knows, are not above a bit of thievery.

She shrugs. 'Someone lost it. He found it.'

She stares after Jim until he rushes out of sight, and when she looks round, the dogs and Arthur have disappeared and she is alone in the cobbled yard, apart from a couple of hens pecking in the dust. She goes back inside and fetches the black kettle to the pump, fills it brimful with six sharp cranks of the handle, carries it slopping to the stove. She sits and watches the faint wisps curling from its forked spout slowly braid themselves into a taut line. She watches the windows fog with condensation; the claw feet of the kettle begin to smoke and glow. It looks as if it's standing on tiptoe, shrieking, and she thinks, *If I can stand it, so can you.*

She levers it off the plate finally, allows herself to cry only until she's sure the kettle must be cool, so that she can fill it again without risk of cracking the cast iron. Then she washes every piece of linen in the house – the sheets, the tablecloth, Arthur's nightshirt, her drawers – boiling them with soda. She works them against the zinc washboard in the scarred wooden tub, just as her mother would have, her hands red as berries in the sudsy water, and then she puts them through the mangle, watching with grim satisfaction as the grey water wells up around the rollers and falls away. She hauls the load up to the garden above the house, shakes the linens out piece by piece until they *snap,* hangs them on the line. It's a good day for it, bright and blustery, though the wind makes her eyes run. The cold corners of the damp tablecloth lick her ankles in the breeze, and once a whole sheet rises up before her, pressing itself to her lips and nose until she can smell the faint tang of soap, but she holds on tight, pegs clenched in her teeth, and waits for the wind to drop. Arthur, spying the wagging white sheets from the yard, calls, 'Who are we surrendering to?' And she yells down to him fiercely that the clothes are filthy.

The kettle's rarely off the hob the rest of the day. She scalds the table, scrubs the slate floor, then the whitewashed walls, even the ceiling, losing herself in work. She shuts the doors and windows and swats every fly in the house.

'Bit late for spring cleaning, isn't it?' Arthur asks her at supper, as if she's lost track of the seasons. When she ignores him, he nudges Jim. 'Never mind D-day, lad, it's wash day!' She gives him a sharp look, and he tells her quickly the place hasn't looked cleaner since . . . he doesn't know when.

Although she does, she thinks: since her mother passed. Arthur used to tease his wife for keeping the house spotless in case her old mistress came for inspection, and she'd tap her heart: 'I's me own mistress now.' Esther has to clutch the back of one of the chairs for balance, so overwhelmed is she by the memory.

'Declared war on dirt,' she hears Arthur whisper to Jim. 'And she's not taking any prisoners, mind.' It's rare that he deigns to speak English, let alone joke with the boy, but Arthur's been in an odd, giddy mood ever since Jim told them that the local lads haven't wasted any time spreading the word of the camp's purpose, and the village is in an uproar. She can't remember when Arthur's paid as much attention to Jim's prattle.

'You keep away from those lads,' she tells him, but he just smiles tightly. 'They're all right,' he says. She passes him her portion of meat, and he wolfs it down as if she might change her mind, before belatedly thanking her.

'How's your head?' she asks.

84

'Good! I mean *sore*. But I can take it.'

'Doesn't sound like it knocked much sense into him,' Arthur tells her in Welsh.

'What did he say?' Jim demands, and Esther looks at her father steadily and tells him, 'He said you're a brave lad.'

At a quarter to seven Arthur pulls on his mac and offers to walk her down to the village. It's not his usual evening for the pub, but he gives her a wintry smile. 'I'd not miss tonight for the world.'

'I was thinking of stopping in with Jim,' she says, 'keeping an eye on him. Jack can manage for one night.' She puts a hand on the boy's shoulder, but he shrugs it off.

'Don't mollycoddle him,' Arthur tells her. And to Jim, 'You're not her baby, are you?'

Looking down, she sees the plea in Jim's face, and understands that if she stays now, she'll shame him. Her hand is shaking when she takes down her coat, and she makes Arthur wait while she hurries back to her room to pocket the scissors from her sewing kit.

He's leaning on the wall when she comes out, peering at the sheep. He'll start the dipping tomorrow, and the shearing as soon after as the weather allows. She looks at the placid sheep and wonders if they know what's coming. It doesn't hurt them, the men say, yet every year she sees them buck and roll their eyes as her father pulls them to him. She has a sudden image of herself sorting fleeces, her job each year, the occasional bloodstains on the wool where the shears have nicked flesh.

Arthur starts to warn her about Jim as they walk down the lane. 'Don't get too attached to him. He'll be off soon enough now if this invasion goes right.' It reminds her of what he used to tell her as a girl about the orphaned lambs they hand-reared. Arthur's never warmed to the boy, but he's always been reluctant to punish him, too, unwilling to step into the shoes of his absent father.

The closest he's come to laying a hand on Jim was after Rhys joined up. Arthur had pronounced him a fool over supper one night – 'more sheep than shepherd' – and Jim flew to his defence. 'I only hope the war lasts long enough for me to join up and fight alongside him.' He called Arthur a pacifist, which made her father strike the table so hard the salt had leapt from the cellar. 'Pacifist I might be,' he said in his deliberate English, 'but with the accent on "fist", mind!' He'd heard that somewhere, she thought. His grasp of English was rarely so subtle, but she could see why the phrase would have been memorable to him, the way the English word contained its own rebuke.

Afterwards, he'd turned his anger on her, hissing in Welsh, 'Can't you do anything with him?'

'You never liked him,' she says now, which ends the conversation, the truth sometimes stumping him this way, as if it's a dead end. She wants him to be quiet so she can think about what she'll do if Colin's at the pub, but as soon as the silence falls between them she regrets it. This might be the last chance to tell him, she thinks. To tell him herself, not have him find out. But she can't conceive of the words. She doesn't even know the Welsh for rape, wonders fleetingly if there *is* a word. Even in English she can't quite bring herself to call it rape, what Colin did to her, not now, not even to herself. In the midst of it, yes, the word had filled her mind, buzzing and crackling like a lurid neon sign in a gangster picture. But not afterwards. Rape, as she understands it, is a particular form of murder, when a man kills a woman. It's connected to sex, but the main thing is the murder. No one – in the films she's seen, the books she's read, the whispered stories she's heard at school – no one survives rape. She is still unclear if the sex itself is so violent that it just kills you on the spot, or if the man has to actually strangle you or shoot you or stab you afterwards, and she had thought in the midst of Colin's roughness, the blunt, searing pressure of him between her legs, that she was about to find out. But then he left her, and

86

she felt such relief. She had survived, clambered out of the pool as if from a grave. And this is how she knows she hasn't been raped. The idea of being forced doesn't enter into it – hadn't she gone along willingly enough? Besides, what was it to be forced to do something she didn't want to do? She'd been forced all her life by one circumstance or another – by poverty, by her mother's death, by the needs of the flock. Being forced to do things is such a part of her daily life, and as for this, she'd at least wanted some part of it – the kissing, her hand in his. If she's been raped, she thinks, then she'd wanted it more than most things in her life, although that isn't saying much. And as for the pain, it hadn't been much worse than the time she'd been pinned against the stall wall and the cow had crushed her foot. The blood made her think of a wound, but only a small one, a barked knuckle, a scraped knee.

If she had to call it anything, she thinks now, groping for the word, she'd call it a misunderstanding. He meant one thing, she meant another.

Beside her, Arthur stops for a second, his boots grating in the lane, and when she glances back, she sees him cupping a match to his face, lighting up. In the brief flare his eyes are hooded beneath his cap, and then he shakes the match out. He'd never think to offer her a smoke, reckons it unladylike. As if she were ever going to be a lady! Her, a farmer's daughter. After her mother's death, she'd started to nag him with all manner of questions about the flock. She'd thought Arthur knew every-thing she'd ever need to know – about lambing, about tupping, all the business of breeding – and she took it in solemnly, not giggling as she might have a year earlier in school, even as Arthur blushed scarlet to explain it. And then in the midst of all this information, which seemed so male to her, he told her about *cynefin,* the flock's sense of place, of territory.

She'd heard the word before, of course, but the importance of the concept had escaped her as a child. Now Arthur spelled it out. How it would be impossible to farm on the open mountain if the flock didn't know its place. The sheep would scatter to the winds otherwise. It was why farms hereabouts were only ever sold along with their flocks. No one would buy a patch of land alone. What use would it be? You could try to put new livestock on it, but they'd be gone in a season. 'They're not as dumb as they're made out, sheep,' Arthur likes to joke, but mostly he speaks of *cynefin* with a kind of reverence, with pride even – not least, as he's told her several times, because the English don't have a word for it. As if it's an essentially Welsh quality.

But how, she demanded, did the sheep know where they were supposed to be? 'It goes back to olden days,' he began (though each subsequent time he tried to explain, it became 'medieval times' or 'the Stone Age', so she knew he wasn't really sure). 'Back then, shepherds stayed with their flocks all year – there were more of them or better paid. They even followed the sheep up into the mountains in winter. And those shepherds kept their beasts in a certain patch, until over the years the flocks learned where they belonged.'

But how do they *still* know, she asked, and Arthur had shrugged. 'They remember,' he said awkwardly (he hated humanising the flock, thought it soft). 'They teach each other, I suppose. From generation to generation like. This flock, our sheep, are connected all the way back to those sheep in past times.'

She didn't say it, but she knew what that meant. The male lambs, the wethers, were sold off for meat each year; only the females, the future ewes, were kept. Whatever was passed down, then, however *cynefin* was preserved, it was from mother to daughter.

And the thought of that had been enough to make her, at thirteen, burst into tears. She had to tell the startled Arthur that she was just scared about what it would mean for a flock to be destroyed. He could believe that easily enough – they had both seen, dotted here and there on the hillsides, the shattered empty stone cottages of failed farms – and in his panic at her tears he launched into a bleak tale of the scabies epidemic in '34, how he and several neighbours had helped Dewi Thomas destroy his own flock to stop the spread. 'He shot them, one by one, in the head like, and then he burned them with kerosene. The stink hung about for days. But before that, he had us shear them. He wanted to make what he could, so we took their wool. Not that it was much, you know, it being only November. But you could see the beasts knew something was wrong. They shivered so. I'd have preferred to do the shooting.'

He'd looked at her expectantly, as if this terrible story were somehow meant to make her feel better. And, in his gruff male way, it was, she thinks now, as they trudge down the lane side by side. He'd been so embarrassed for her tears, ashamed for her really, that he'd told a story that he thought justified them. At least he'd not suspected that she'd been crying for her mother. That very month she had her first period, and she managed to get through it without breathing a word to him. (She did appeal to Mrs Roberts, though only after she'd sworn her to silence.)

The thought reminds her that she's had some practice keeping secrets from Arthur. But also of the secrets her mother might have passed on to her, had she the time. All Esther has now are scattered memories. A freckled arm flashing in and out of a beam of sunlight as her mother churned butter, or tipping an old beer bottle filled with milk for a slavering calf. Once they found a lamb snagged on the wire of the fence, its mother bleating fiercely at a crow that had settled itself on a nearby wall waiting for the lamb to tire. The bird had already pecked out one of the lamb's eyes. The crow had been insolent, flashing its oily black wings at them, until a resounding clap from Esther's mother saw it off. Esther, with her small fingers, had had to tease the lamb's short, soft coat off the barb – although she quailed from the ruined socket – and she recalls her mother's stern 'Go on, Ess!' and cluck of approval when the fleece came free.

Esther still sees the lamb, now a full-grown ewe, among the flock. The animal stands out, her head cocked to one side, her good eye looking forward. She turned four that spring, 'broken-mouthed', as they called the older ewes, an age when she might not survive a winter or reliably bear a lamb, but Esther had already persuaded Arthur to keep her another season. 'She's a survivor,' she told him, and he nodded.

She thinks of the ewe now as the pub comes into sight. With one hand she grips the scissors in her pocket, presses her thumb to its point. With the other she takes her father's hand and squeezes it.

'What's that for, then,' he asks, flustered.

She shrugs. 'I don't know. Just be kind to the boy. For me?'

In reply, he flicks his cigarette into the lane ahead, grinds it out without breaking stride.

Six

It feels like a reprieve when she looks into the pub and there's no sign of the sappers. But it's early yet. Many of them don't get off duty until nine. The lounge is quiet, just the BBC gang (Harry putting on a brave face, despite looking a little the worse for wear), but the public bar, where she sees Arthur forging through the crowd, is seething with resentful locals.

'PO bloody Ws,' Bertie Prosser is fulminating. 'It's an insult, is what it is.'

'All right, luv?' Mary asks over her gin and tonic. 'You look like you could use one of these. Put a little rose in your cheeks.'

'What?' Esther is staring past her, towards the frosted glass doors.

'She's just a bit anxious, ain't you, girl,' Harry chips in, and for once she's almost glad for his interruption. He raises his voice to carry down the passage. 'No need to be scared of POWs. They're all innocent men, after all, locked up for something they didn't do.' He pops his eyes. 'Didn't run away fast enough!'

'We're not bloody scared of them!' Bertie hoots, craning over Jack's bar to jab a stubby finger at Harry.

'Maybe you ought to be,' Harry says moodily into his drink. Esther wonders if he's thinking of his wife. But Bertie doesn't hear him.

'We don't give a toss about no Germans. It's bloody English liars we're on about here. I swear, Jack, I don't know why you're even serving these English.'

Jack shrugs; Harry has deep pockets.

'And just whom, my good man, are you calling English?' Harry cries, rallying.

'Well, what is you if you ain't?' Bertie wants to know.

'Why,' Harry says, dropping into brogue, 'I'm your Celtic cousin, to be sure be sure. Isn't that so, our Mary Kate?'

'Aye and begorra.' Mary crosses herself. 'Irish as stew!'

'Codswallop!'

'Och! But we've a wee doubting Thomas here, lassie!'

'Fair dinkum, ocker,' Mary agrees, slapping the bar.

They're all laughing now, except for Arthur, who sips his pint. Even Esther smiles, and Harry leans in and confides, 'Can't be the butt of a joke if they don't know where you're from, see. Only your straight man has a country; patriots got no sense of humour.'

'Very bloody funny,' Bertie calls, shaking his head. 'All right! The League of blooming Nations can stay.' He slips into Welsh. 'I'm serious, though, Jack. You shouldn't let those bloody sappers in here again.'

There are murmurs of agreement and Esther looks over at Jack, sees him weighing it: the cost of breakages if there's a bar fight, against the thirsty business of outrage.

'They'll not be here long enough for another payday,' Esther offers, dropping into Welsh herself, but when Jack glances over, she goes back to drawing her pint. 'So they say.'

'Oh, what the heck,' Jack says finally. 'Let 'em go to the Prince of Wales. They're banned!' And Esther feels herself go weak with relief, clings to the beer pump.

Bertie leads a little cheer, thrusts his chin out. 'Enough of the English buggers.'

'Not to mention a few Welsh fools,' Arthur calls drily.

Bertie whips around like a dog after its own tail. 'Well, Arthur Evans,' he sneers, 'I'm surprised at you taking their part.'

'I'm just saying they never actually told you what that base was for.'

'They led us on, man! They led us up the bloody garden path.'

'They might have left the gate open,' Arthur tells him. 'But I'd say you strayed through it yourself, Bertie.' There's some laughter at Bertie's expense and he colours, and Esther feels a twinge of pity for the old windbag. Arthur turns to the room at large. 'I thought we should have learned our lesson by now. This is what comes of trusting the English!' He sees Esther staring, gives her a thin smile of triumph, but she turns away.

'What're they on about now?' Harry wants to know.

'They're feeling cheated,' Esther mumbles.

'Cheated! Ha! That's a good one. Hey, hey,' he calls gleefully, 'don't tell me you lot are feeling welshed on?'

'Welshed on!' Arthur thunders from the other bar. It's one expression in English he's always quick to pick up on. He looks furious, but Esther can see he's relishing this. Harry, without realising it, has ended up as her father's straight man, setting up one of his favourite speeches.

'Do you think he even knows where that perfidious phrase comes from?' Arthur asks the rest of them in Welsh, dismissing Harry, who sits back and flaps his fingers and thumb together at Mary like a gabbing mouth. It's true, though, Esther thinks; her father, so taciturn in English, is a different man in Welsh, especially with an audience.

'You won't find it in the dictionary,' Arthur is saying. 'Not even your *Oxford English Dictionary*.' He says the last in English, rolling the *r*, drawing it out to four mocking syllables so it sounds like *Dick-shun-Harry*. And in fact, Esther knows this to be true. She asked in class once where the phrase came from, and Mrs Roberts went to the huge volume she kept on her desk like the Bible, poring over it for long moments, until she had to admit, blushing even, that the derivation was obscure. It was the first time Esther had ever seen her teacher stumped, the first time she'd glimpsed that there might be a limit to what was known, not just by her, but by adults, and it worried her. She brought it up with Arthur and he grimaced. 'Typical! Stands to reason your *English* dictionary don't explain it.' 'But—' she began, and he clapped his hands together under her nose. 'It's *their* language,' he said. 'Theirs, see!' He has his own theory, of course, which is what he's regaling them with in the bar.

It goes back to the last century, Arthur explains, when the use of Welsh was forbidden in schools by the English authorities. The rule then was that if a boy was caught speaking Welsh, a placard would be hung around his neck saying, 'Spoke Welsh' – 'bit like a dunce's cap' – and at the end of the day the headmaster would strap him. The real devilishness, though, was that if the boy caught another lad speaking Welsh, and informed on him, he could hand the sign on. The placard would be passed from Welsh speaker to Welsh speaker, the one betraying the next, until a last unfortunate was left wearing it at the final school bell. 'So, your bloody English, see here,' Arthur concludes, 'they call us welshers, cheaters, deceivers, make like the very word "Welsh" means to lie, to betray, when all along they was the ones, with their vicious rule, made our boys act like that.'

It's an old story, and Esther's sure others know it as well as she, but there's something about Arthur's unveiling of the inexorable English logic that's still compelling. She sees heads nodding along the bar, watches Arthur, satisfied, light a cigarette. He should have been a reverend, she thinks. When he first told her the story, she was doubtful. 'Why wouldn't Mrs Roberts know that?' she asked, and he looked at her as if she were a fool. She saw then that Rhys's hope of their parents marrying was fantasy; Arthur was betrothed to the country. 'Maybe she does,' he sneered. 'Maybe your *English* teacher wouldn't want to tell you that truth, eh?' And Esther thought, *That's why she blushed*. Her teacher had lied to her.

His own father, Arthur is saying now, completing the lesson, fell foul of the rule on his very first day at school, told on another boy, and escaped his beating. 'Or so he thought,' Arthur notes with relish. 'When my *grand*father heard of it, he gave him the thrashing of his life, called it a "Welsh hiding".' And here he glances at Bertie, offers him an opening, and the little man volunteers, as if on cue, 'They corrupted our bloody children.' And Arthur nods, draws deeply on his cigarette.

Bertie is starting up a chorus of '*Mae hen wlad fy nhadau*,' the Welsh anthem, and Esther translates to herself: 'Land of my fathers.'

The moral of Arthur's story, she supposes bleakly, is that there's no reason to fear the English, at least not when the Welsh can do worse, and she knows, as if a door has closed in her face, that she'll never be able to tell Arthur about Colin now.

There's only one brief scuffle, later that night, when a few of the sappers – not Colin, Esther sees with relief – try to defy the ban, but Constable Parry bars the door and sends them packing. 'Did your duty there,' Jack tells him, giving him one on the house, and Parry grins and tells him, 'But I'm off duty, Jackie,' and takes a long draught.

'Can't take a joke!' the sappers call from the street, over the jeers of the locals. 'Don't go forgetting who the real enemy are!'

'You are!' Bertie bellows back, and Esther, despite herself, flinches.

Arthur, she sees, never leaves his stool during the melee, a fixed grin on his face. Jack glances into the half-deserted lounge. 'Might as well have an early night, Esther.' He raises his eyebrows, and she nods. 'Arthur! Walk your lovely daughter home, won't you?'

They walk in silence, Arthur setting one foot in front of the other with such deliberate dignity, it reminds her of the newsreel of the coronation she'd seen as a child, almost her first memory: the new king pacing steadily up the long nave of Westminster Abbey.

She must have seen it with her mother, she thinks.

Arthur's performance in the pub reminds her he's always been sniffily suspicious of her English, as if she were putting on airs. He's never seen any reason for her command of the language to be more than 'good enough'; it was her mother who always wanted it to be *proper*. Her heroine was George Eliot – *real name Mary Ann Evans,* she told Esther, *a Welsh girl made good* ('as an English man!' Arthur scoffed) – and her prized possession a massive copy of *Middlemarch,* which she seemed to have been reading all of Esther's life. Towards the end of that last summer, while Eric sweated over her chores, Esther sat on the bed and read it to her. Her mother hadn't managed more than a couple of pages a day, stealing the moments when her work was done, while the floors dried or supper simmered on the stove, and now they were flying, covering twenty, thirty, fifty pages at a time. 'Slow down,' her mother used to beg, gripping the sheets as if they were handlebars. 'Are you sure you're not skipping?' But Esther knew she was proud. There were fewer than a hundred pages left at her death, and Esther had rationed them out, a page a night, then a paragraph, a sentence, reading them silently to herself for the rest of that autumn until, impossibly, they were all gone.

She hasn't missed her mother so much in years, she thinks as Cilgwyn comes into sight, and she finds herself hating Colin for reviving that old hurt almost more than for the new one.

Seven

*D*EAR MUTTI, Karsten writes, and stops, wondering what to tell her. *Since my last letter,* his pencil sighs, *I have been captured by the British.* He looks at the words on the page and they seem baldly ridiculous, a bad joke. Both banal and implausible, even to him.

Someone walks past the mouth of the tent and reflexively he curls an arm around the page laid out before him on the bunk. He watches the man's shadow cross the canvas. The tent must be Great War issue. His first night under it, sniffing the musty air and peering up at the blotchy continents of mildew, the parchment-coloured walls rising to the long ridge above, he'd felt he was sleeping under a water-stained book.

One with blank pages, he thinks now, returning to the letter before him. He's writing in the back of the pamphlet of German phrases and their English equivalents that the Red Cross passed out to them yesterday. Some of the men threw theirs away immediately, but Karsten has kept his, not to learn the phrases – he's glanced at them and knows most – but for the paper. The Red Cross representatives, in their dark, mournful suits and plummy Swiss German, had also explained that they'd shortly be issued official postcards to notify their next of kin. Karsten, the back cover of the phrase book folded open before him, is trying to work out what to write to his mother.

He starts again. *Dear Mutti, It has been a week now since I surrendered to the British.*

More truthful, at least. He looks at the thick, dark pencil marks against the white. They're not allowed pocketknives, so he sharpens the lead by furiously rubbing the blunt point at an angle against the paper, steadily obliterating what he has written.

He expects the Red Cross cards will be plain, like the coarse army-issue stationery he's used to. But he finds himself wishing he could send her a picture postcard like the kind she sent him from home, something that might convey more than mere words. He might have wished for longer letters – she was always too busy, if not with the pension, then with her patriotic activities, food drives, clothing drives, scrap-metal drives – but he loved the scenes she sent, pinned them to the wall above his bunk in barracks like so many narrow windows. In his last letter to her he'd complained about the spring heat in France, and she'd sent back by return mail a postcard of the Brocken draped with snow: *Hoping this will cool you down!*

As a boy, one of his jobs around the pension had been to carry the guests' mail to the post office. He liked to practise his reading skills with the cards, trying to recognise the town and the landscape, which he took for granted, in the exuberant descriptions. *Glorious weather. Spectacular views. Charming locals.* He wondered if he would see his world this way if he was at leisure. *Wish you were here,* they wrote, and he did. There was something so cheering about postcards. When the odd injudicious or arrogant guest complained about the pension or his mother's cooking, he had no compunction about throwing the card away, less out of loyalty to her than a sense that such grousing somehow failed the form.

He'd only sent her one postcard himself, from Paris, where he'd gone on a two-day pass shortly before his promotion. He'd bought two cards – unable to decide which to send – the first of the Ritz, the lobby of which he'd sat in for thirty reverent minutes. If asked about his ambitions, he might have admitted to hopes of a modest addition to the old pension, perhaps a bar, so that they might call themselves an inn, but privately he dreamed of managing a grand hotel with liveried staff and a ballroom. And a suite for his mother. But he couldn't confess that to her. Instead, he sent the other card, of the Arc de Triomphe. They'd seen it together four years earlier in newsreels, and she'd applauded as the long grey column of troops passed beneath it. 'That's that,' she'd told him, leaning over. 'The war will be over now.' His own teenage dejection at the thought of missing his chance to fight had been in such contrast to her relief. It was the first time he'd ever seen her clapping, the soft beat of her gloved hands (she still dressed for the cinema) keeping time with the marching. He wrote that he'd walked through the arch himself, though he'd done it shyly, hands in pockets.

He wonders what he would send her now – a picture of the white cliffs of Dover, he thinks, and at once rejects it. As if he were on holiday, as if he were a tourist!

Dear Mutti, he tries again. *Dear Mutti. Dear Mutti.* Then, *I am safe.*

And after a moment that seems all there is to say. The one thing that will bring her comfort. He lays his pencil down, exhausted.

In truth, he had been relieved to see the white cliffs looming over the hold of the landing craft. More grey than white, they were the first sight of land over the high metal sides of the boat since the ramp had been drawn up, dripping, on the shore at Normandy, and the men welcomed it with a thin cheer, those few of them not bent over and heaving on their boot tops.

They'd sat in the beachhead stockade in France for two long days until, on the evening of the seventh, a lone Messerschmitt, the first they'd seen since the shelling began the previous dawn, dipped out of the twilight and strafed the beach. The slumped prisoners leapt to their feet with a roar, watching the twin plumes of cannon fire stitch across the sand, baying themselves hoarse, until the neat dotted lines had begun to leap towards them. The plane had pulled up at the last moment, only the fine grit thrown up by its fire pattering over them, but not before the cheers had died in their throats and they'd flung themselves to the ground.

The near-miss had galvanised the British into getting them off the beach. They'd been reluctant to waste manpower on the prisoners, but it wouldn't do to have them die in Allied hands, whatever the poetic justice of deaths under German fire.

So on the morning of the eighth, they were assigned to one of the empty landing craft that had already disgorged its men. They started gathering their few remaining possessions, but then a column of Tommies carrying stretchers came over the dunes and made for the ramp. 'Hey, we saw it first,' some wag called, but then they noticed the arm of one of the men on the stretchers swing free, a grey uniform sleeve appearing from the blankets, and they pressed forward to the wire, calling names. A couple of the prone figures stirred, and one raised his bandaged head. The figure seemed to study them for a second, the gaps for his eyes the only dark spots amid the white bandages, and then lay back, silencing them. Karsten, watching from over another man's shoulder, suddenly wanted to find Heino, who'd long since melted into the crowd, find him and shake him. *That could have been us,* he'd tell him fiercely, squeezing the boy's bandaged hand until he yelped.

They had to wait most of the rest of the morning until another landing craft lurched on to the beach, and they looked on impassively as barbed wire was strung around the edge of its hold and the machine-gun mountings altered to allow them to overlook the cargo space.

'Off to invade England, lads,' someone quipped, but none of

them laughed. A newsreel crew hurried up as they were embarking, and Karsten watched the men ahead of him, Heino among them, bow their heads. He nudged those on his left and right, coaxed them into wheeling round, marching backwards up the ramp to spoil the shots. 'They won't know whether we're coming or going.' Only a few – the most exhausted and dazed – went along; Schiller, when Karsten called to him, just shook his head, less in refusal than disappointment, it seemed. Still, Karsten felt a small flush of victory as the cameraman threw up his hands. But then he was inside the stinking landing craft, the floor awash with the days-old vomit of the invasion troops. Gulls pecked at it, flying up screaming only when the men kicked them away.

'What guts!' someone cried, to laughter. But elsewhere, Karsten saw, the men were disgusted and fearful. He looked up at the machine guns. 'We could all be slaughtered here and our bodies dumped at sea,' a man next to him whispered, and Karsten, reminded of their own hot guns pouring fire down the yawning throats of these craft, told him to shut up. 'Oh, yes, *sir*!' the man mocked.

And then the ramp swung closed on the littered beach, and the engines churned into life, sucking the craft back off the sand and starting its slow, wallowing turn, the waves slapping against the steel. With no view of the horizon from within the deep hold, their own vomit was soon mixing with that of their enemies, washing in and out of the oily bilges. They'd been too sick to be afraid after that. A queasy blessing, Karsten thought, a welcome distraction from the guns leering down at them.

The fear had returned soon enough on dry land. They'd been marched up from the docks under heavy guard, and for the first time Karsten felt himself truly in enemy territory. This was England. The guards even seemed more foreign than those in Normandy. There, at least, they had all, German and British alike, been strangers to France. Outside their bunker, the medic who had come to bandage Heino's hand had passed around his canteen – the water tasting like champagne, so glad were they to be alive – but Karsten couldn't imagine sharing a canteen with these guards, couldn't think of anything he had in common with them. And beyond them he felt the crushing, suffocating sense of a whole nation's hatred. He'd felt the raw edge of French resentment of *les Boches* before, of course – that insolent blankness – but there had been a place for them in France, albeit one made by money, in the cafés he'd frequented, or in the warmth of Françoise's arms. Here he couldn't imagine any place for himself, felt that each step he took into England was making him more hated.

After they'd disembarked, on the march up from the docks, he had seen figures in the distance, on rooftops, on ships in the harbour, walking the ragged clifftops. They were just specks really, distant, barely distinguishable figures, but he'd hunched over at the sight of them as if they were snipers, flinching from walking sticks and raised arms. As they passed through the steep, narrow streets, there was some booing, and he found himself looking down, unable to meet the eyes of those watching.

The transit camp they were marched to was ten trudging miles outside the town, at an old racetrack. Rows of tents had been set up in the infield, and barbed wire laced around the rails. Jeeps circled the course where horses had once run, and instead of the flash of binoculars in the grandstand, there was the glint of fixed bayonets.

They had been herded into a long barn, divided into pens for the horses, judging by the stink of manure. Karsten was separated from Schiller and Heino, shoved into an enclosure with an assortment of men from other units. He'd kept himself to himself, squatting in one corner, ignoring the rest, but after a while one of them sank down cross-legged in the dusty straw beside him.

'What I'd give for a smoke,' the fellow muttered. 'Don't suppose you've got one?'

'Sorry.'

'Just as well, probably. I'd burn this whole shambles down, if I had a light.'

'How'd they get you?' Karsten asked. It was the inevitable, ever-present question; he'd already learned to ask it first.

Except this time the other fellow said, 'Surrendered.' He ran a hand over his close-cropped head. 'Never would have thought it.'

Karsten nodded miserably.

'You too, then?'

'Me? No. Knocked cold by a chunk of masonry during the shelling. Woke up with a gun in my face.' He could barely recall whose story it was, just how much he'd envied the fellow who told him.

'Lucky you.'

'Captured is captured.'

The other shook his head.

'Surrendered is the worst. You sure you . . . ?'

'No.'

'Only, I heard.'

'Sorry. Wrong man.'

'Too bad. I don't mean to . . . It's just that it's a little lonely, you know. There must be a thousand men here, and you'd think you were the only one surrendered.' Karsten studied him then, the long pale face under a dark widow's peak, the eyes searching the crowded cell.

'Like I say,' he replied softly, 'we're in it together now, all the same.'

'Appreciate that,' the other said. 'If I had a smoke, I'd give it to you.'

Karsten smiled. 'How'd it happen, anyway?'

'Don't ask.'

'No, really. I'd like to know . . . Can't be that bad.'

'How'd it happen? How do you think? How does anything happen in the army?' He spat. 'Fucking *officers*! My leutnant shat himself, or he'd have used his drawers for a white flag. Ordered us to put our hands up.'

Karsten shook his head.

'*Fucking* officers! Should be shot, the lot of them. You know, I could swear I saw him here someplace, among the enlisted men.'

'Who?'

'My fucking leutnant! Wouldn't put it past him to strip the uniform off one of our dead boys.'

'But why?'

'Wants to pass as a regular soldier, avoid interrogation. Coward twice over. What chance did we have with that kind leading us, I ask you?'

'Not much,' Karsten whispered.

'See any of yours – officers, I mean – mixed in with us?'

Karsten shook his head.

'Pity. There's a bunch of lads wouldn't mind giving some of them a few licks. They could hardly pull rank! Really, you haven't seen any?'

'No,' Karsten said. 'I told you.'

The other man had been scanning the crowd, as if for officers, but now he looked at Karsten.

'No need to cut up so. Unless you're one yourself. Are you?'

'No!'

'All right, I believe you. Just let me know if you see any, would you?' He got to his feet. 'Fucking officers. Course' – he smiled gapingly – 'I'd be dead right now if mine hadn't given up.'

Crazy, Karsten thought. Mad with shame. He watched the fellow move off among the rest, asking the same questions, looking for someone to blame, to hate, to fight.

There'd been a scuffle at last – someone objecting to his

accusations, or to his admission? Karsten wondered – and the guards had leapt in and dragged the fellow out.

'Anyone know that man?' a barrel-chested corporal had called afterwards. 'Anyone vouch for him? You? You?'

'Said his name was Steiner,' someone offered.

'Never met him before,' Karsten said when the man pointed at him. 'What'd he do?'

'Anyone know *you*?' the other demanded. 'No? Well, don't go asking any more questions!'

They'd sat in silence then, the group of them, staring at one another warily until the guards had ordered them out and thrust them back into the flow of men shuffling out of the barn.

Next, they'd been made to strip in the dank concrete corridors below the grandstand. Even in June it was cold down there, chilling the soles of their feet. They were hosed down, then dusted with clouds of bright yellow disinfectant until it clung to their body hair and they coughed it up, their tongues bright and bitter with it.

' 'Ere, are these Jerries or Japs?' the guards hooted to each other.

Still naked, they were run across the grass to stand in long lines in the paddock, shuffling forward towards a brief doctor's inspection. Yellow dust rose off them like fog.

'Tongues, dicks and arseholes,' the men who'd gone before whispered. 'Stick it out, hold it up, spread 'em.' When it was Heino's turn to bend over, he'd let out a long, spluttering fart and the doctor stepped back quickly. A guard brought up the stock of his rifle between Heino's legs with a fleshy crunch, and those in line, to a man, cupped their own balls, as if suddenly modest.

The others stepped around Heino where he lay, writhing and gasping like a caught fish, but Karsten knelt beside him, shaking his head. 'What you gonna do, kiss it better?' one of the guards mocked, but Karsten ignored him. 'Here.' He helped the boy to his feet, but when Heino wiped the tears from his eyes and saw who it was, he shook him off. Karsten let him go, Heino hobbling ahead, bent almost double, one hand pressed to his groin. *Going to get himself killed to spite me,* Karsten thought, watching him fall into one of the lines working its way towards the British intelligence officers, sitting at card tables on the grass.

The rumour, passed through the ranks, was that the interrogators, with their accentless German, were Jews, refugees from Germany. The first Karsten heard of it was someone ahead of him muttering, 'Traitors.' He'd been so preoccupied, glaring at the back of Heino's head, he'd cried out angrily, 'What do you mean?' Too late he'd realised his mistake. Men around him were looking at him strangely.

'I mean, they can't be traitors, can they, the Jews. They weren't proper Germans to begin with.' He glanced around. 'Besides, I'm not afraid of them.'

And the fellow ahead snapped back, 'Fuck off! I never said I was afraid.'

'You should be,' a voice called. 'I heard they're putting them in with us to spy.'

'Whoever said that probably was one,' someone else yelled. Karsten thought of Steiner, found himself twisting his neck to look about him. But wouldn't Karsten have known him for a Jew? The ones in the newsreels, their appearances greeted with boos and laughter from the stalls, were always unmistakable, he thought – craven faces, shrinking forms, the stars on their chests gaudy redundancies. But Steiner didn't look the part, nor did the interrogators awaiting him. He didn't believe it.

Besides, when he'd got closer to the head of the line and could overhear the questions being asked, there were just the usual three – name, rank and serial number – repeated over and over like a litany. Karsten, braced for an interrogation, had felt faintly disappointed. The British seemed mostly interested in finding officers passing themselves off as enlisted men, though they hardly needed spies to do so. They pulled one out of the lines while Karsten waited; the fellow's moustache had given him away among the clean-shaven noncoms and privates. The men watched him go in silence, sorry to see him caught, yet glad to be rid of him too. Only a few saluted, the officer returning the gesture red faced, looking more naked than the rest in that moment. Karsten caught sight of Heino, looking back as the man passed, but the boy looked right through him.

It was the last time Karsten had seen the boy – the camp's big enough to avoid each other – but it hardly matters. The damage is done. He's sure Heino has already told others the story of their capture, proclaiming himself innocent of surrender, as if it were a crime.

Karsten's not quite a criminal, but he notices the others keeping their distance. The only one who doesn't shun him entirely is Schiller. Karsten tolerates his company – it's decent of Schiller, he supposes – but in truth he doesn't want the other to feel he owes him anything. Karsten can't help thinking that he saved their lives at the cost of his own honour, and if he had it to do again, he isn't sure he'd bother.

But then he thinks of his mother, of her running the pension alone, and tries to tell himself he did it for her. He's all she has left, after all. Karsten's father's loss has always had about it an air of desertion. 'I told him he shouldn't have gone out that night with the weather worsening,' his mother has often maintained, in a tone as much critical as sorrowful. His parents had fought all the time, mostly over money, it seemed to Karsten. But once his mother had sneered, 'You might have had the decency to go down with your ship too!' There'd been a long silence – Karsten, supposed to be asleep, had held his breath – and then his father said coldly, 'I would have. Your father ordered me not to.' Which is why it seemed, after his loss, as if Karsten's father might have finally got his wish.

*   *   *

It's coming on for evening, the day's heat lifting, the sinking sun tingeing the tents pink. At the end of the row of them, he sees men filing on to the makeshift parade ground at the centre of the encampment. As he watches, a barking sergeant puts them through their paces.

The drilling began three nights ago, led by a handful of NCOs, the self-appointed camp leaders. The men had rolled their eyes at first, called them zealots, 150-percenters. Why drill if you didn't have to, if there were no officers to make you? It had started with a group of U-boat men. They'd been sucked to the surface in a bubble of air, their sub's last gasp, when it had been split in two by a depth charge in the Channel, and pulled aboard a British minesweeper. They were men who'd been at sea for years, men who'd won victories. And they left the rest in no doubt that, had they been on the western front, the invasion would have been beaten back, or they'd have died trying. Only a couple of them were NCOs, but even the seamen among them acted as if they outranked the other men. They looked at Karsten and the rest – healthy, whole – and flashed them their scars, their burns, and laughed when the others looked away. They made Karsten think of old whores showing their wares to choir-boys, and indeed, among the least offensive names they called them was virgins.

Not that they stopped at name-calling.

Several fellows had fallen foul of them, for criticising the high command mostly. One mechanic had been beaten unconscious with a tin mess tray by a thick-necked ensign for having the temerity to blame the Leader. Karsten remembers the streaks of blood and gravy on the man's face, and the tray, rocking gratingly on the floor, as warped and twisted as a piece of shrapnel.

To think that Karsten had hoped to be a submariner like his father before him, had once, for the price of a round of drinks, bribed his way on board one of the long, dark vessels in port just to get a feel for it.

During the day, the 150-percenters can be seen polishing their boots, brushing their uniforms, and for each of the past three nights they've led the drill. There'd been only a dozen men that first night, but now, as Karsten watches the formation wheel and turn, he sees rank after rank of men, perhaps a company's strength. They look smart enough from where he stands, although it's strange to see them come to attention, their feet stamping down in silence on the turf, no ringing parade-ground echo.

'Enjoying the show?' It's Schiller. 'Looks like you want to fall in.'

Karsten shakes his head. The camp leaders have called for all noncoms to assemble their men for drill, but he's kept silent about his stripe. Now, he realises, he's tapping his foot in time to the cadence. Yet he can't quite see himself falling in when he should be leading. He looks down at his scuffed, scarred boots and wonders when he last polished them.

'Maybe you should,' Schiller says softly.

'I suppose Heino has.'

'Him? Haven't you heard? Shipped him off to a youth camp, the Britishers did. For the underaged.'

'How did they know his age?' Karsten begins, and then he sees the other's wolfish grin.

Schiller starts to saunter on, down the alley of tents, but turns back, fishes in his tunic pocket. 'Almost forgot. They were issuing these outside the mess.' He holds out a bright square of paper, and after a second Karsten takes it. It's a Red Cross postcard.

He watches Schiller amble off, then turns the card over in his hands. It's already preprinted with a curt message:

Dear _____:

This is to inform you that I am a prisoner of the British / American / Soviet forces.

My health is poor / fair / good.

Sincerely / Love, _____

He's furious at these words, thrust in his mouth like a gag. But then, he realises, he's hardly been able to think of much more to say for himself, despite his agonising. He's reminded again of those postcards of his mother's guests – *delightful, lovely, charming* – their repetitious, interchangeable sentiments, and he's suddenly relieved by the anonymity of the card before him, the impersonality.

He looks down the row of tents, over their yellowing peaks and ridges, in the direction Schiller has gone, towards the drilling men, still going through their paces. He does want to join them, feels the pull, like gravity, yet he's not sure he belongs. Too ashamed? he wonders. Perhaps also too proud, in his own stiff-necked way. Not ready to be forgiven.

And it comes to him then that he had noticed a change in the guests' postcards as the years went by. The views were no longer lovely or charming, but *awesome, imposing, majestic*. The Brocken was an 'indomitable peak', according to one guest, a comment that puzzled Karsten mightily since he'd led the fellow up it not two days earlier. More baldly, one young man, who'd appeared at breakfast on his first morning in shining, squeaking lederhosen, wrote that it was 'a truly Aryan landscape'. Karsten had actually held that one up, studying its glossy picture, then staring at the familiar slopes above him, straining to see it.

Eight

E sther steers clear of Arthur as much as possible in the days
following the invasion. It's not so hard. June is a busy time
on the farm, between the dipping and the shearing, and during
the days he's mostly on the hillside with the flock. As for the
evenings, she keeps out of his way by spending more time with
Jim, helping him with his homework – he's slogging his way
through *Great Expectations* – chatting with him at supper in the
quick slangy English her father has trouble following.

The boy's generally impatient with her concern, but he
tolerates her checking his wound each evening with preening
stoicism. When, after a couple of days, she tells him he's healed
and doesn't need the dressing any more, he tugs it back down
firmly. Arthur says he looks a proper fool, but Esther indulges
him, studies the small scab carefully, and says, well, yes, maybe
they'd better keep it covered for one more day. 'In case of
gangrene,' she says, po-faced. And so it goes for a week.
Somehow the shared fantasy has brought them together. She
knows Jim reckons his bandage a badge of honour, a reminder
of his bravery, but to her it's a token of her care for him,
however frayed and dirty. It slips off when he's sleeping, but she
smiles watching him fiddle with it in the mornings, settling it at
a rakish angle over one eyebrow.

'Who are you supposed to be,' Arthur asks, 'the Mummy?'

And for a moment Esther blushes, not sure whom he's talking to, until he raises his arms before him and does the stiff-legged walk.

Arthur's always thought her a fool for bringing Jim home, but she knows why she did it. She'd been late to the station that time, reluctant to go, as if she were somehow being asked to replace Eric. When she arrived other families were already leaving with their evacuees, the children's faces bright as new toys.

'You missed all the good 'uns,' Jim said later with a grimace.

He'd hated all the picking and choosing, he told her, the pointing fingers, and 'I'll take that one'. He took one look at the purse-lipped women lined up to receive them and pulled his gas mask over his head. 'All the pretty girls went first, then the plain ones, then the boys who combed their hair, who stood up straight and answered "sir" or "missus".' When Esther got there, all that was left were what Jim called the 'liquorice allsorts' – the spotty kids, the snotty kids, the fat ones who looked like they ate too much, the ones who scratched, the ones who smelled of piss or sweat or, in Jim's case, fags and booze.

Along with his pyjamas, his spare vests and his Sunday best, his mother had packed the boy off with gifts for his host family – 'swaps', she called them, for their love. But as soon as the train had pulled out of the station, Jim rummaged through his dented cardboard suitcase until he came upon the hard chill of a pint of J & B and the stiff angles of a Players carton. Esther pictured him drawing these treasures out like rabbits from a hat and turning to the others in his compartment: 'Who's got a light, then?' They'd had a time of it, all right, he'd told her, half boastful, half querulous, until one by one they'd lurched to the door, as the train hammered through the wet green countryside, let down the window, gulped a lungful of the burnt air billowing back from the engine, and heaved over the side. Jim had had the misfortune to throw up as they entered a mountain tunnel, covering himself, the window and the dusty livery of the GNWR in puke.

When Esther arrived he was glaring through the steamy portholes of his mask, as the local women worked their way down the rows, asking questions: What's your name? How old are you? Where are you from? The last answer, whether Liverpool or Toxteth or Bootle, gave them pause. 'Slum kids,' the women complained. 'No better than urchins.' It was taking an age for them to pick, a few even leaving alone, shaking their heads at PC Parry, the billeting officer. Mrs Lloyd, moving down the aisle ahead of Esther, asked her daughter, Hattie, 'What do you think, *cariad*? Shall we take this one?' The girl, so spoiled she was known round the village as the Princess of Wales, examined the tear-stained child in front of her and crinkled her nose. 'Crybaby.' She shook her head. 'And, she pongs.'

Jim was refusing to answer any questions, letting the women finger the little luggage label pinned to his lapel. All the children had them, their names and addresses on one side, and on the reverse, 'Further Information': faith, date of birth, ailments. When Mrs Lloyd and Hattie stopped in front of him, the girl seemed puzzled by his gas mask.

'Take it off,' she commanded, but Jim shook his head, the snout of the mask swinging back and forth, the charcoal granules rustling inside.

'Why not?'

He leaned towards her, lifted the rubber seal. 'Your mam farts poison gas.'

There was a bark of laughter from the other evacuees, and Esther covered her mouth. But then the constable appeared, peeling the mask off Jim's head, the straps yanking at his hair, giving him a clip around the earhole.

'You'll be last if you're not careful, sunshine. By then the only bed will be in my cell at the station.'

The Lloyds hurried out and Esther found herself standing

beside Jim, close enough to smell him – the sugary scent of boys' sweat that she recalled from the schoolroom, mixed with the chemical odour of the rubber mask.

She looked at his label and saw, beside 'Mother,' the word 'None', scored in heavy black letters, and took his hand.

They've never been close, though, despite her best efforts. His mother wasn't dead, in fact; he just wished she were. He'd never known his father, knew only that he was a sailor his mother had met on shore leave – '*Sure* to leave,' as she put it. She'd been seeing a new fellow lately, 'Uncle' Ted, her boss at the factory, a civilian who called him Jim-lad and sneeringly referred to his father as 'the seaman', despite Jim's assertions that he was probably a lieutenant or a captain by now. 'Come to think' – Ted winked – 'seems I did hear he was first mate.' Jim had prayed Jerry would get Ted, but when they'd come out of the shelter one morning, it was Ted's house that was in one piece, and their place that was a hole in the ground. 'So she moved in with him,' the boy told Esther, 'but there weren't room for me.' As if he were a giant, Esther thought, and not a tiny boy. Esther's heart had gone out to him, of course, but he'd always resented her mothering, submitting to it under duress at best. It had been that way from the start. She took one look at the bedraggled boy in her kitchen and insisted on a bath. She'd made up the bunk in the boxroom just that morning, and she wasn't having him put himself between her clean sheets without a good scrubbing.

He declined, gruffly at first, 'Not likely,' and then, as she went about filling the kettle from the pump in the yard, with increasingly desperate politeness: 'I'd not want to be a bother.' Finally, thinking perhaps she didn't understand his English, he tried being firm, as if talking to a dog: 'Missus? No, missus. No!' But she ignored him, carrying in the sloshing kettle and easing it on to the stove. Beads of water skittered over the hot plate. 'You can't make me,' he yelled, taking a step back down the passage as Esther pushed her sleeves up. He'd fought her tooth and nail, but she'd grappled with too many oily sheep, helping strip them of their fleece, for him to have a chance. The steam was billowing from the kettle when she marched him back into the kitchen in just his vest and drawers. She poured a steaming, silver stream into the tub, added cold from a jug, and told him to hop in, turning away demurely, though not without catching a glimpse of his bone-white flanks before he sat down with a quick splash.

She started to move towards him with a brush and he flushed, cupped his hands between his legs, and bawled, 'You're not my mother!' and she stopped as if slapped.

Instead, she scooped up his clothes where he'd thrown them and bent over the fireplace, feeding them to the flames as he yelled from the tub, half rising and then sinking back beneath the water. *'In-fes-ted,'* she shouted, turning back to him. 'I can hear their little bodies popping in the flames. *Uckavie!'* She gave a shudder. How dare he bring lice into her mother's house!

Tonight, after a chapter of Dickens, she reads the newspaper with him, helping find the towns and villages on the map of Europe tacked to his bedroom wall.

'Caen,' she says. 'Cherbourg.' She points them out and he bats her hand away. 'I can see.' She lets him use the pins from her sewing kit, moving them east across the map with the Allied advance. She's always forgetting who they represent – Monty, Patton, Bradley? – or pretending to, at any rate, because he enjoys telling her.

'Who's this, then?' she asks, pointing to a pin still stuck near London.

'Rhys,' he says, with an edge of accusation, and for a second she wonders, *Who?*

It's been less than three months since his proposal, but it seems a lifetime ago. Esther went along with Jim to see Rhys off at the station after his last leave despite, or perhaps because of, turning him down. The village was too small for hard feelings. His mother was there, fussing about, picking lint off his uniform collar, then smoothing it down. 'Quite grand, isn't he?' Mrs Roberts asked Esther, speaking in English, as if they were still in class. 'I thought I'd always have to iron and polish for him.' She gave a wobbly smile. 'At least until he found a wife. And here the army's gone and taught him how.' Esther and Rhys both glanced down, and his mother followed their eyes. 'And would you look at his *boots*,' she breathed in wonder, but when she looked up, Esther saw the tears standing in her eyes, like pearly pinheads, and it occurred to her that his mother was terrified for him. Rhys was so placidly confident about returning, Esther had never imagined him not, and even when she considered it now, it was almost impossible to imagine anything as interesting as getting killed ever happening to him. And yet the sudden fear of it must have made her weaken, because when Rhys leaned out of the train window and whispered, 'Can I at least hope?' she nodded slightly and promised to write.

And she has. Only a couple of brief, dutiful notes, to be sure, but Jim has written too, and all they've had back is a measly picture postcard of the Empire Cinema in Leicester Square, addressed to 'Mr Evans, Esther, and Jim', saying how friendly the English were, how dingy London was, and that he'd been assigned to the kitchens – news that managed to disappoint or annoy all three of them.

Not that his mother has heard much more herself. 'It's embarrassing,' Mrs Roberts confided to Esther with a little laugh, over the counter at the post office. 'Here I am, the postmistress, and my own son a poor correspondent. Not that he was ever much good at his English when I was his teacher, as you know. And it's because he has to write in English, you see. The censors can't read Welsh.' She shook her head. 'Can you imagine! Strangers reading a boy's letters to his mother.'

It's just as well that Mrs Roberts is a talker, Esther thinks.

She's always a little tongue-tied around her former teacher (still scared that Mrs R, as they called her in school, will criticise her grammar), but more so when the subject is Rhys. The first time she saw his mother after the rejection, she kept her hands clasped behind her back, as if afraid she'd get a rap across the knuckles with a ruler. Thankfully, though, it seems Mrs R doesn't know of the proposal.

'Last known location,' Jim is saying now, resting a finger on the head of the pin representing Rhys, twisting it back and forth to press it home. Esther's eye wanders to Rhys's postcard of the picture palace, propped up between two lead soldiers on the deep windowsill that serves as Jim's desk. The last word Mrs R had from him, over a fortnight ago, was that he was awaiting orders. But to Esther, it's almost as if he might still be inside the grand cinema, sitting in the stalls.

It miffs her, that one postcard. She's wanted to share Rhys's escape somehow, or better yet, have it instead of him, if he's too cloddish to enjoy it. (He told her when he left he'd be back just as soon as the war was over. 'But why?' she asked crossly, thinking him a mother's boy, and he blinked and coughed and told her, 'For you.') Esther has promised Mrs R, good student that she is, that she'll write regularly – faithfully, she almost said. But whenever she starts another letter, her own news about the village or the farm – the gathering, the washing, everything the same as every other year – seems so drab she can't go on. Besides, it makes her feel foolish, as though she's encouraging him, or worse, chasing him.

And once she'd started stepping out with Colin, she could hardly write to Rhys.

'Course, he could be anywhere by now,' Jim says. 'Probably not allowed to tell us.'

'I'm sure he's safe.' But she's misread the boy.

'Safe!' he scoffs. 'I bet that was a cover, about being a cook. He couldn't very well say if he's a secret agent or something. He's probably already behind enemy lines.'

She tries to seem serious. 'Sounds dangerous.'

'Not half!'

She sees how much he misses Rhys then, how his longing, too, is etched with envy, his desperation for an escape of his own, from childhood. From her, she thinks with a start. Rhys and Jim shared this small boxroom when Rhys worked at Cilgwyn, and the two of them became thick as thieves – Rhys as patient with Jim's childishness as Jim was with Rhys's ponderous English. Rhys had even taught the boy to whistle. She remembers them, last summer, bouncing around the barn like a pair of mad things, trampling down the hay pile.

'Why don't you write him another letter?' she suggests. 'I bet he'd like that.'

'If he can even get letters where he is,' Jim says, but after a moment he gathers paper and pencil, bends over his desk, and she leaves him to fetch another lamp.

Rhys, a spy? Rhys dangling under a parachute? She wants to laugh, but for a second the romance of Jim's vision seduces her. The boy loves him, she thinks, and she feels a pang of envy. If only she could. It seems so suddenly attractive, a way of turning back the clock. She thinks about writing to Rhys herself. Could she still accept him? Could she just pass it off as a mistake, a confusion. 'Oh, you mean you want to *marry* me!' He looked so smart in his uniform. *Well groomed,* she thinks, turning the words over in her mind, as if she's just understood something.

And yet when she imagines kissing him, her tongue flinches from that dark gap between his two front teeth.

When she checks back later, Jim is staring at the line of marbles running along the edge of the window, each balanced in a little scallop of putty.

'What have you got?' she asks, leaning forward to look at the paper, but he hunches his shoulders.

'Come on,' she says, and reluctantly he pulls away and she sees that the paper is blank, the whiteness stumping him.

'Why don't you let me help,' she says, her voice taking on a teacherly tone.

He shakes his head.

'You could tell him about the bike.'

'I was gonna!' He glares at her reflection in the dark window.

'I'll check your spelling if you like.'

He ignores her.

'Well, tell him I say hello.'

'He's *my* friend,' Jim rounds on her with sudden heat. 'Not your boyfriend.'

She chokes out a laugh. 'You can have him!'

Lying in bed later, she thinks of the nights last summer when she heard them, down the hall, chattering away in their mongrel mix of Welsh and English, whispering and laughing. About her? she wondered.

'Shh,' she'd hissed at them. Rhys was no better than a child, she'd thought. Yet now it occurs to her that perhaps she'd been jealous. Not of Jim, but of Rhys and his easy rapport with the boy.

She stares into the darkness, tossing and turning. She feels so . . . full somehow, filled with feeling, throttling on it, but with no way to let it out. The words lie curled and heavy in her belly. She can't write to Rhys: if she put pen to paper, she doesn't know what would come out, how she'd ever control the words. She has an urge to confess, feels it pressing behind her teeth, swallows it down, but also gnawing on her is the desire to blame someone – Colin, of course, but also Rhys. If he hadn't been so . . . *dull*, she might have fallen in love with him, mightn't she? So wasn't it his fault as much as hers?

Now that she thinks of it, she pictures him home on leave after finishing his basic training, coming into the pub the evening before she saw him off at the station. He'd been with a group of other young people, including a couple of local girls, Mair Morris and Elsie Pritchard, all of them underage. Esther refused to serve them at first, but Jack had intervened, smiling. He glanced over at the constable in his accustomed corner, who nodded indulgently, and told her, 'I think we can make an exception just this once.' Esther had watched Rhys get drunker and drunker, Elsie braying with laughter at his jokes, Mair running a hand down his uniformed arm. Esther had had to wave Jack away when he asked if she wanted to knock off early and have a drink with her pals. It had dawned on her that Rhys was right, that people – Jack, PC Parry and, if those two, then half the village – thought him her swain, and a furious shudder swept through her.

And that was the first night she'd talked to Colin, it seems to her now.

Nine

In the last week of June, Esther pulls a cardigan on to go down to Williams the butcher with the new month's ration coupons. She's been stretching the meat portion out all week, day after day of *lobscau,* the thin, salty stew of mutton, leeks and swedes that she serves with onion cake. Arthur tolerates it with a kind of grim pride – it's a national dish – but Jim hates it with an expressive passion, making faces, claiming it's made of some unholy mixture of lobster and cow, hence the name. *If only!* Esther thinks. She pines for the old days, when during the shearing or haying the men of the village would descend on each farm in turn for a day, and the woman of the place would feed them lunch in exchange. It was a fierce competition among the wives to see who could set the best table. Esther's mother had been a famous hostess – the old-timers would tell her so on quiet nights at the pub, licking their lips at the memory of her mother's stewed blackberries – and Esther wonders now if, in her own clumsy efforts to emulate such hospitality, despite rationing, she might not have encouraged Rhys when he worked at Cilgwyn. She'd certainly practised her baking on him, and he'd swallowed down the sourest rhubarb crumbles, the tartest gooseberry pies, with a fixed smile. Mistaking her pride for love, she laments.

At any rate, she determines to bake Jim one of his favourites, a curd cake, for tonight, though for some reason the thought of the sweet, gelatinous dessert makes her momentarily queasy.

She's still at the door when she spies Jim below her, cycling up from the village. Even through the hawthorns that line the lane, she can see he's labouring up the slope, standing on the pedals, doggedly refusing to dismount and push the bike, though it would probably be faster. He only left for school, feet up on the handlebars, fifteen minutes ago. He must have forgotten something. She tries to picture the bully-beef sandwich she made him, still sitting on the kitchen table in its greaseproof paper; but no, she remembers giving it to him. A book, then – he hates lugging the Dickens tome around – or maybe some new treasure he wants to show the others. Whatever it is, she thinks, ducking back inside, he'll need help finding it if he's not going to be even later for school – a thought that makes her flush with annoyance.

But when he swoops into the yard, scattering hens, dropping the bike with a clank on the cobbles, he runs past her, past the house, heading for the gate to the meadow.

'Jim!' she calls, 'Jim!' and he stops on the last bar, glances back at her briefly, and then ahead up the hill, where she spies half a dozen boys racing through the long grass. More are cutting across the field behind the barn, a flock of starlings rising before them.

What mischief are they up to now? she wonders. Jim has finally given up his bandage, but only because it's served its purpose. He's become more popular in the last fortnight, a bit of a hero even to the Welsh lads. And all because he's been struck by an Englishman. But now he has something to live up to. Just last week, when there was a spate of shoplifting, he got caught trying to smuggle a marrow out of Thomas's under his jumper. 'Looked like he was in the family way!' the grocer told her, too amused to be angry, although he added ruefully that some other lads had made off with five pounds of strawberries. Esther suspects Jim was a decoy, but she hasn't pressed him on the other boys involved. What she fears is that the incident at the camp has taught him something – that getting caught and keeping your mouth shut are how you prove yourself.

'Come back here!' She takes a step towards him, trying to smile despite her raised voice.

He's redfaced, gulping for air, and waves her off until he catches his breath.

'Nasties!' he finally yells. 'The nasties are here!'

'What?' She shakes her head. 'What did you say?' But he's already dropping down into the meadow on the other side of the gate, charging off through the bracken after the rest, his satchel bouncing wildly on his back.

It strikes her that he's making for the camp by the shortest route, over the ridge, and she's suddenly fearful. Didn't he get enough of a fright the last time he was there? For her own part, she's not ventured anywhere near it in two weeks. She just knows he's going to get into more trouble. He's already clambering over the mountain wall, halfway to the ridge. The boys are far ahead, and she feels a flash of irrational anger at them for not waiting for him. But then she sees they're not alone on the hillside. Several small knots of people are working their way up the slope from different angles, and on the brow above she can make out other figures now, too large for children, silhouetted against the white clouds. And then it comes to her, what he shouted from the gate, and she sags back against the doorjamb.

At last, she thinks. *They're here.*

It means the sappers must be finished. It means Colin must be leaving.

She only comes back to herself when one of the hens struts over and starts pecking at her feet, expecting to be fed. She kicks it away impatiently, watches it totter off haughtily, as if on high heels. She focuses again on the figures climbing the hillside. She should tell her father: the flock is in the summer pasture over the ridge, and he'll be worried about the new lambs. They can be sensitive creatures; a bad scare can stunt the newborns, make the ewes dry for a season. The flock has been dangerously reduced over the past few years – the combination of a cold snap during the last lambing and a particularly vicious fox abroad this spring – and they can hardly afford more losses.

She finds Arthur in the barn, grinding a pair of shears on the whetstone. He always likes to put away his tools in good order. As a child she sometimes thought he loved them more than her, even his father's old quarry chisels, which he oils every year.

'Hallo, luv,' he calls, as her eyes adjust to the gloom. The only light in the barn is the sun coming through the door and the gaps in the plank walls. 'Can't understand how these lost their edge,' he says, running a finger down one blade. Esther's overheard Parry down the pub saying the boys snipped through the wire fence at the camp with shears, but she keeps her mouth shut.

'So, what's the palaver?'

'Better come see. The upper pasture's turning into a grandstand.'

'No!'

She nods, and behind him she hears more running, sees the shadows of hurrying figures flowing along the back wall of the barn, flickering through the chinks in the wood.

'Bugger,' Arthur swears – in English, as is his habit. He rises from the shearing bench he's been straddling, yanks his cap off the nail behind him and calls for the dogs. They'll be in the hay somewhere, napping in the heat, and sure enough, a moment later they trot into the yard, yawning pinkly. Arthur is already past the gate when he turns and looks for Esther, who is hanging back. 'Come on, then.' It's the same brusque tone he uses on the dogs, and she finds herself following automatically. He sets a fast pace, making a beeline for the ridge, kicking up sparks of dew. Esther weaves a less direct path behind him, picking her way around the rough ground. Mott, the older dog, stays close to her, leaping from tussock to tussock, while Mick, the youngster, scurries ahead of Arthur, glancing back anxiously. This is how they work – one dog to push the sheep, one to steer them. She can feel Mott trying to press her on, tacking back and forth behind her, but she's in no hurry, only putting one foot in front of the other out of alarm for Jim, the mischief he might get into.

She wonders whether she'll see Colin, what it'll be like. He's become almost an abstraction to her lately. She can barely recall his face, but then the moist brush of his tongue comes back to her – not his lips, not the prickliness of his moustache, just his flickering, probing tongue filling her mouth. She has seen a few of his mates in the street, sappers she recognises from the pub, and felt their eyes, heavy, on her. He's talked, she's sure, but she's less certain what he might have said. Not the truth, she thinks. Something more colourful, boastful. And if he's told his friends, she wonders how long before someone in the village hears something. It's this she fears more than anything, dimly sensing that what he did to her can't in the end be rape if no one else knows. She suspects that what kills the poor girls raped in films and books, finally, is shame. All those hands over mouths, all those horrified looks. But the sappers will leave soon – today, tonight. Everything will be in the past then, able to be forgotten, provided no one else knows.

Above her, she makes out Jack by his limp, picking his patient way along the crest and then gone, down the other side. A moment later Arthur crosses the ridge. There's a sharp gust from the valley below, and she sees his jacket billow like black wings, hears the cloth snap, and then he, too, is down off the edge and out of sight until she crests it herself, minutes later, hair flying in her face. The wind has blown the sky clear, and from this height she can see the Llyn Peninsula angling away all the way to Caernarvon, the old castle walls shining palely in the sunlight. But then another gust batters her legs, pressing her light summer dress against her. She feels a sudden ache in her breasts and pulls her cardigan, an old one of her mother's, tighter around her as she descends.

Half the village seems to be scattered below – everyone from butcher Williams, still in his starched white coat, to Blodwyn Parry, the constable's dowdy daughter ('Blod Plod' to the local boys), even the Reverend Morris, who must be wondering what he has to do to get this kind of turnout of a Sunday. Esther notices her father slowing as he reaches the crowd, reassured to see the flock farther down the slope, perfectly content, drifting over the lower pasture. Arthur nods to some on the fringe of the crowd, shakes hands with others. People move out of his way – it's his land, after all – and his progress reminds Esther of how the dogs part a flock. *Sheepish*, she thinks. The villagers feel sheepish. The word appears before her in her own flowing copperplate. She's been having these spells lately when words, English words, seem newly coined, as if they're speaking to her alone, as if she's seeing the meanings behind them. She's conscious of her lips, her tongue, forming them. It makes her feel like a child again, learning the words for the first time.

Entering the crowd herself, she finds it still, quiet. The villagers stand around, the men smoking, the women with their arms folded on their aproned chests, some of them still breathing heavily from the climb, and the children nudging each other as if at chapel – everyone looking, but no one pointing, downhill, beyond the quietly grazing flock, to the men behind the fence.

It is the first time any of them have seen the enemy.

The Germans – the very word means something different now, something *more,* Esther thinks – are standing in loose ranks. The only ones she's seen before have been at the pictures, in newsreels – the famous ones, like Hitler and Göring, Goebbels and Hess, and then the others, marching by like so many extras. The makeshift parade ground where they're gathered fifty yards below includes the former holiday camp's playing fields, and from the hillside the touchlines of the old football pitch are still faintly visible, like scars. To Esther the fences around the camp look like the markings for some new game.

A Union Jack – twin to the tiny one flickering from the turret of the distant castle – crackles from the blazing new flagpole rising above the camp, like one of the pins in Jim's map.

Beneath it a British officer, the light flashing off his glasses like a semaphore, is standing on a box calling names from a list – 'Schiller. Schilling. Schmidt, Dieter. Schmidt, Hans. Schneider' – and the Germans are barking '*Ja,*' one by one, the words, clear but distant, carried up the hillside by the crisp breeze. *Ja,* she whispers to herself experimentally. Once in a while one of the Germans will repeat his name, and she realises with a little start that they're correcting the pronunciation.

'Weber?'

'*Veber! Ja!*'

She glances at the new soldiers, the guards. They have the black-and-white armbands of MPs, and their officers wear smart red bands around their caps that distinguish them from the sappers. A group are walking the perimeter fence, checking the wire, pulling on the posts with all their strength. She sees them stop at one point for several minutes, and a stocky private throw himself against the fence, bounce off, throw himself again. To her left and lower down, some of the lads are pointing to the MPs. This must be where they cut through the wire, she thinks; the MPs are inspecting the repairs. She sees Jim in the knot of boys and starts to make her way down to him. He's standing next to one of the ringleaders, Stan Robinson, one of the few evacuees to hold his own among the locals and a nasty piece of work, though he's not much to look at. A skinny albino who goes by the nickname Pinkie, he seems as breakable as china, and Esther wonders whether this is why boys submit to his bullying without fighting back.

Jim is rapt when she stops beside him, his eyes wide as if they can't take enough in. 'Come on,' she tells him quietly. 'Come and see Mott.' The dog, curled up and panting at Arthur's feet, is a favourite of the boy's, although her father doesn't like him making a fuss over a working dog. But Jim doesn't even turn to her, just nods downhill and whispers, 'Nasties.' He must have picked up the pronunciation from her father.

Pinkie makes a sharp gesture. 'Nazis,' he hisses, and there's such roughness to his voice that the smile dies on Esther's face.

'Don't talk to him like that.' But Pinkie just pushes past with his cronies, and after a glare at her, Jim follows. She hears him muttering, 'Nat-sees, nat-sees, nat-sees,' with precisely the same air of impatience.

The boys drift down the hillside, hanging around the lower fringe of the crowd, then are led away by Pinkie until they form a little island of their own below the adults. To get to Jim now, Esther sees she'd have to cover open ground, and she moves back towards her father.

She looks into her neighbours' faces as she slips by them, wonders how they're feeling. The Lewises have a son, Denny-Jon, in the desert, and their expressions are flinty. Lona Lewis claws the air, swiping at a fly. But in the eyes of others Esther sees something else. Mrs Roberts, for instance, who waves her over.

'I can't help thinking,' she whispers. 'Perhaps these fellows were captured by my Rhys, do you reckon?'

'You've heard from him, then? He's over there?'

She shakes her head in disappointment, just like in class. 'Not a word. But he must be over there, don't you think? Where else would they send him? He couldn't tell me even if he did write, but I'd still like to know if he's looking after himself, getting enough food, if it's cold.'

'I'm sure it's summer there too,' Esther says, confused.

'Oh, I know, I know. Only I was thinking of knitting him a scarf and gloves, and I should make a start now if he's going to have them by the autumn, allowing for the pace of the mails over there.' She says this last with a hint of disdain. They stand side by side, staring silently at the Germans. 'I bet they know,' Mrs Roberts says after a second, and Esther could swear she'd like to go down and quiz them.

The older woman sighs heavily.

'And they call it the fatherland,' she says, as if to herself. 'I wonder how the mothers feel about that. How did they ever let the men get away with that one?' She laughs wryly, turns to Esther. 'You know, when I watch the newsreels, I keep thinking I'll catch sight of Rhys in a parade or something. Wouldn't that be a turn-up for the books. Our Rhys on the silver screen.' She grins at Esther. 'You'd like that, I bet. He was always saying what a film fanatic you are.'

Esther keeps her eyes on the Germans. There's a trace of disapproval in the older woman's voice, but whether it's to do with Esther and Rhys, or whether it's just that Mrs Roberts thinks Esther should be reading more and going to the pictures less, she can't be sure. She still has the copy of *Tess* that Mrs R loaned her when she left school. Esther was supposed to borrow a book every few weeks, to keep up her reading, but she'd never finished *Tess,* sensing within twenty pages that its tale of rural poverty would grate on her, and Mrs R eventually stopped asking about it. Since then, all Esther's read is Margaret Mitchell and Daphne du Maurier. 'Escapism!' Mrs R would say.

'I should get back to my father,' Esther says after a pause, and Mrs R nods absently.

When Rhys proposed and Esther said no, he'd looked non-plussed for a long, slack moment. 'Mam would love it,' he tried, and she'd snapped, 'You've never told her!' He shook his head mournfully. 'Wanted to surprise her.' Esther forced herself to maintain a stony silence until he added, 'Everyone else already thinks we're walking out together.' As if that were an argument! Wishful thinking, more like. Besides, she'd told him, she didn't care what everyone thought, though now she wonders, did she really say that?

She finds Arthur at last, waits beside him for the roll-call in the camp to stutter to its end. A clipped English voice calls, 'Dismissed,' followed by a sharp command in German, and the ranks, so orderly a moment before, dissolve. There's a rush towards what Esther guesses is a mess hut, where a queue begins to form. She studies the Germans – a crew of submariners captured in port, if the rumours are to be believed. They're not what she's imagined; many are young, as far as she can see, some so fair they seem to gleam in the sun. Mostly, though, they look thin and a little tatty, their uniforms the colour of wet sky.

'A sorry shower,' Arthur sighs.

It's odd, she thinks, to see the enemy like this after years of hearing their planes droning high overhead. She's seen the concrete blockhouses built as shore defences. She's seen the ribbed wreckage of one of their bombers on the beach like a dead whale. But it wasn't like when the training aircraft from the local base went down last year and she cried for the three young crewmen burned to death who had drunk at the pub. She hadn't been able to imagine the men who'd died in the German plane. Even after Eric's death she couldn't feel anything towards the pilots who dropped the bombs; they seemed so far above her, beyond the range of her emotions. She tries to decide how she feels about Germans now. It seems important. She ought to hate them, she thinks, and she supposes she does, but she can't quite muster the heat of anger. She doesn't know them, after all; whatever they've done, it doesn't feel like they've done it to her.

She catches sight of Colin suddenly. He's coming along the lane, kitbag over his shoulder. She's actually surprised she still recognises him, that he hasn't grown a beard or gone grey, that he looks the same. She watches him join another of the sappers she knows from the pub – Sid, she thinks his name is. The two of them carry their bags out of the gates, toss them up into a waiting lorry. They loiter, chatting, Colin throwing a glance, then another, up the slope before they set off, strolling along the wire, peering in at the men they've built the camp for. She feels an almost overpowering urge to spit, the tiny ball of saliva fizzing and bubbling on her tongue, forces herself to swallow it. Whatever she feels about the Germans, she realises, seems pale compared to what she feels about Colin.

A thin blue cloud of cigarette smoke rises above him, and Sid dips his head to take a light. A group of Germans waiting in the breakfast queue notice them and the straggly line drifts towards the fence. She sees Colin and Sid pause; one of the Germans calls something, but she can't make it out. Colin plucks the cigarette from his mouth, seems to wave it for a second, twirling his wrist like Basil Rathbone, then tosses it over the fence. There's an almighty scramble among the prisoners before a stocky man leaps out of the pack. He holds his prize aloft, like a salute, before pulling it down for a deep drag. Sid flips his fag over the fence too, snapping it off his fingertips, and the same thing happens. The unlucky Germans start shouting and gesturing, and after a moment Colin and Sid light up again, take a puff and flick another pair of cigs over the top.

'Like feeding ducks,' Bertie Prosser cries from somewhere in the crowd, and there's laughter. The joke passes down the hillside until the boys pick it up and start quacking. Esther sees Jim flapping his elbows and then hurrying after Pinkie and the rest as they creep downhill, through the starved-looking newly shorn sheep, into the copse of trees across the lane from the camp. Their laughter and shouts of encouragement begin to mingle with those of Colin and Sid. *Don't!* she wants to call to Jim, but she knows it wouldn't do any good. The crowd of scurrying, diving prisoners has swelled now, but the whole affair is brought to an abrupt end by a tall fellow who comes flailing into the scrum of prisoners, knocking them down, shoving them out of the way. He's shouting something, and Esther sees him raise his arms, waving the others back, smacking the cigarette from one man's happy face, stamping it into the soft mud.

'Come on,' she hears. It's Colin's voice, suddenly quite clear. 'Play the game.' Perhaps it's the breeze carrying his voice – the appeal in it, whiny, demanding – that chills her, makes her hug herself.

The boys are at the fence now too, forming a loose circle behind the sappers, and they take up Colin's cry until the lanky German turns and begins to stride towards them as if the fence weren't there. Colin lights another cigarette, holds it out to him as he advances, then throws it over the wire, but whether as a peace offering or a taunt, Esther can't tell. She sees the boys fall back a yard. Arms are pointing from the nearest tower, a whistle blows, and then she sees, trotting from between the huts on the other side of the compound, a group of MPs in two short columns, their white truncheons drawn, pulled along it seems by a pair of huge dogs at their head.

At the last second, the big man bends and scoops up one of the cigarettes, flings it back over the fence in a wobbly arc. But before it lands, he's surrounded by MPs and prodded back with truncheons, the dogs snapping and leaping against their leashes whenever he raises his arms to gesticulate towards the fence. Colin and Sid, she sees, have made themselves scarce, but the boys are still there, scrabbling for the cigarette thrown back their way. She sees Jim squirm his way clear and run off down the wire, whooping, holding up the still-smoking fag like the Olympic torch.

Within the fence, the faces of Germans and MPs turn up the slope to where the villagers stand. Hands are angled to shield eyes against the sun; arms are lifted, pointing. Esther finds herself blushing, embarrassed to be caught staring, but even as she turns away, Mott, at her feet, lifts his head and offers a long howl of reply to the snapping dogs below.

MPs are hustling down the lane towards the gang of boys, and the crowd starts to melt away, the villagers – the reverend, Bertie Prosser – not running, exactly, but drifting off over the ridge towards the village, as if on some just remembered business. Even Mrs Roberts is beating a retreat back to her post office counter. Esther looks at Arthur, but her father has his feet planted. It's his land, and he'll be damned if he's chased off it, but he does send Mick and Mott down to move the sheep, whistling and calling commands, as if this has been his intention all along. She's conscious of the men in the camp watching the dogs' work with interest. The boys are scattering before the soldiers, and she looks anxiously for Jim, runs down a little way until she spots him, heading uphill.

She waves and waits as he hurries towards her, beaming, while behind him the guards pull up and return to the camp. 'Did you see?' he says breathlessly when he reaches her. 'Did you see?' He brandishes the smouldering cigarette, puckers his lips around it for a moment and pulls it away with a smack, and Esther, before she can think to stop herself, gives him a wallop that sends the glowing butt flying and makes him stumble to one knee. 'Haven't you got into enough mischief down that camp?' she begins, but then she stops. There's a faint cheer – from the other boys, she thinks – but when she looks round wildly, she sees it's from the men below.

When she turns back, Jim is staring at her, clutching his cheek and ear.

'Well, you deserved it,' she says, but more gently, offering her hand. It's still warm from the blow, and as she opens it she expects it to be red, as if she's the one who's been struck. 'Oh, come on.' She hadn't hit him that hard, had she? 'Look at it this way. You'll be able to wear your bandage for another week.' But he shakes her off, pushes past her. 'Not funny!' She feels his hand on her hip, moving her. 'Broody cow,' he breathes, and then he's past. 'And you can keep your bloody bike, too,' he shouts from above her. The cry rolls down the hillside. She sees the sheep stir.

And for a long moment she freezes, unable to move, to look up. Her dress, she sees, is muddy where he's touched her.

She thinks of the first time she gave him anything, after burning his clothes. She'd dressed him in an assortment of her father's things – the trousers rolled up until the cuffs were fat as sausages. He looked so forlorn, she'd run back to her room and returned with a jumper. 'This was Eric's,' she said – they'd used it as a blanket once to sit on the hillside, and she still liked to press it to her face sometimes – and he asked, 'Who's Eric?' and she told him. 'And he was an evacuee and we loved him,' she said, trying to win his trust. But something in Jim's eyes, a slight recoil, had told her he didn't want to be loved, or more importantly, not by her, and something in her had answered his flinch. And now she knows: she picked Jim because he wasn't Eric; she picked him because he was as different as a boy could be. She picked him because she could be sure she'd never love him.

She glances back at the camp furtively for a last sight of Colin. She's sure now it wasn't he who hit Jim – the boy would never have gone so close to him otherwise – and she tries to decide if she hates him any less. But she can't make him out down there in the crowd of men, finds herself focusing instead on a couple of the Germans. They're standing, hands on hips, looking up at her, and all at once she feels very exposed on the hillside. She turns and pulls her cardy around her, hurries to join her father.

'Well,' Arthur says with a grim smile, jerking his head back to where Jim has disappeared over the ridge, 'at least he didn't get caught by them this time.' He gestures to where a lorry is pulling into the lane, and she realises it's the sappers, leaving.

She takes a deep breath. So it's her secret, she thinks. As if it never happened.

Ten

It must be the new bunk, Karsten thinks, his first few nights in the new camp, the cloying scent of freshly sawn timber, and the thin mattress, through which he can count the slats beneath his back, buttocks, thighs and calves.

He can't sleep.

It's not fear, at least. This new camp has come as a relief to the men. Karsten feels it himself, this slackening. It shames him, but he understands it.

The journey by truck from the transit camp at Dover had seemed interminable. Twelve hours? Fifteen? He'd lost track some time in the night, the dread growing with each mile. The worst moment had been just after dusk, when the column had pulled over in a dark culvert and they'd been ordered out. Not a man had moved. Karsten had listened to the latches on the tailgates being snapped open, so like the sound of a rifle bolt being drawn back, and seen the fear in the faces around him. He'd finally slapped his own thighs and climbed down, pushing the tarpaulin aside like a curtain. Others, though not all, had followed, and they'd been herded to one side, lined up facing a low stone wall . . . and ordered to piss. Back in the truck, Schiller had leaned over and whispered, 'Haven't you had enough of leading?' but then Schiller hadn't gone when given the chance, and within an hour, his bladder aching like a wound, he'd had to beg the guard at the back of the truck to let him go over the side, clinging to a rib of the roof with one hand, his dick with the other, his piss a jumping silver stream in the headlights of the truck behind.

Karsten might not have been worried about being machine-gunned in some field – at least it'd be quick – but he wasn't without his own fears as the men jounced along. The watery dawn light seeping through the truck's tail flaps revealed, when the wind lifted them, fiercely rugged mountains, jagged peaks cutting across the sky like a piece of paper torn in two. He stared at the boulder-strewn hillsides, the cascades of grey scree tumbling into lakes like mirrors, and thought, *A thousand years' hard labour*. Though when someone gave out a low whistle at the view, he called out staunchly, 'It's nothing compared with the Harz.'

'At least you're loyal to landscape,' someone else had yelled from the other end of the truck, and before Karsten could reply, Schiller had hissed, 'Shut it,' though whether to him or the other man, Karsten wasn't sure. He'd spent the rest of the trip in grim silence, though even he couldn't resist the general air of giddi-ness when they'd disembarked at the new camp.

The barracks certainly looked more comfortable than the mouldering tent town at Dover, and even the distant audience of locals on the hillside, so disquieting in their stillness, were easily driven off, like so many sheep. Karsten had exulted in throwing back their filthy cigarettes, though he'd got dirty looks from the rest, and Schiller had pulled him aside in the mess line and demanded, 'What are you trying to prove?'

They'd set out to explore the camp as soon as they'd eaten, mapping it minutely, discovering which showers had the best flow, which bunks were in a draught, which latrine seats were the least splintery. And like explorers (like conquerors, indeed, Karsten thought bleakly) they'd named everything they found: the barracks after the grand hotels of Europe – Savoy, Adlon,

Ritz; the guard towers – Eiffel, Pisa, London, Babel. The barracks *were* palatial compared with the tents they'd come from, yet the men fretted over them, bouncing on the thin striped mattresses, opening and closing doors and shutters, tut-tutting about the rough finish. 'I hope everything's to your liking?' Karsten, no stranger to picky guests, asked sarcastically, looking down at Schiller, perched on the lower bunk, and the older man grinned and told him, 'I'll take it!' Schiller even persuaded the others to name their barracks after Karsten's mother's place, the Pension Simmering – a joking kindness, Karsten supposed, though the reference made him more, not less, homesick, and he had to force himself to smile.

He'd written of it to his mother that evening – they'd all fallen to letter writing as soon as they'd been issued stationery after dinner – telling her that he was still in the family business and pointing out at least that every bed was filled with a long-term guest. And then he'd crossed that out, sucked on his pencil. Around him men were scribbling away, the barracks as silent and concentrated as an exam hall at the *gymnasium*. 'What are you writing?' he'd asked Schiller, and the other had said, 'Just about the shitty weather, the lousy food.' The weather had turned, a persistent drizzle settling over the camp like a mountain mist, and the offerings in the mess had been poor – better than Dover, but much worse than their own mess in France – but Karsten told him, 'You can't write that.'

'Why not?'

He'd searched for an answer, aware that men in the nearby bunks were waiting too.

'Who's that to, your wife? What's she going to think, reading that? It's going to worry her, make her cry. Is that what you want?'

In truth, it occurred to Karsten, it probably was what Schiller wanted – sympathy, pity – but not even he would admit that.

'So what should I write?' he asked, half impatient, half humouring.

'I don't know. Tell her they feed you decently, that the camp's humane.'

'Propagandist! Is that what you write? You should be ashamed, lying to your own mother.'

'What else?' Karsten told him sharply. 'It's all we can do, isn't it? The only way left to protect them.'

Schiller stared at him for a long moment, and Karsten realised that he'd crossed a line. The men around them were watching carefully. And then he added, 'As if you never lied to your wife,' and Schiller's tight face broke into a crooked grin.

He listens for Schiller's breathing now, tries to decide if he's asleep, but he doubts it. Judging by the sounds from the other bunks, they're not alone. He imagines them all lying awake, waiting for the last light of the summer evening to fade from the cracks around the windows. The heavy silence is punctuated by the men's frustrated sighs, or the sighs of their farts. Here and there too, as Karsten listens through the night there is, amid the sporadic thumping of pillows and rustle of blankets, the quietly insistent rhythms, the short smothered breaths and creaking bunks, of masturbation. Karsten's heard it before, back in basic training or in the barracks in France. Yet it shocks him now. Once, he hears someone hiss gruffly, 'Come, if you're going to!' and there's a snort of laughter. But he's silent when he feels his own bunk tremble, thinks he's giving Schiller his dignity, what little he has left. It's the inevitable male remedy for sleeplessness, he thinks, and he feels a sullen envy when Schiller stills.

He touches himself experimentally, but there's nothing. He tries to think of Françoise. Fifi, as Schiller liked to call her, the whore he'd been half in love with in France. She'd been his first, though only Schiller had guessed (after seeing Karsten emerge so quickly on their first visit and whistling 'Blitzkrieg!'), and he'd sworn to keep it a secret. The rest would never imagine it,

Schiller reassured him. 'You're their hero, remember. You're good at everything.'

Still, Schiller had made ribald fun of him over Françoise, encouraging the others to tease him – not about his inexperience, but his devotion. 'Camouflage,' Schiller had whispered to him once. 'If they make fun of one thing, they'll never guess the real joke. Besides, it's good for you to have an Achilles' heel. They'll like you more for not being perfect.' So Karsten had tolerated the jokes. Besides, he'd been such a fool for Françoise, he actually liked to be mocked on her account. As if the jokes made her more his, even when some of the jokers had probably had her themselves.

But then he didn't want to have her like the others. He'd lost his virginity to her, but afterwards it felt like an anticlimax. As if he still needed to *find* something.

And so he'd set about wooing her, doggedly faithful, as if, having paid for her that one time, he had to prove he loved her. How he strove to prove it! He used to wait for her, for hours if he had to, while the rest took their turns with other girls. Françoise would come halfway down the bowed stairs, see him sitting there and greet him wearily. 'No rest for the wicked, *hein?*' And all he'd do is take her for a drink, or if it was early enough, for coffee. Once he'd persuaded her, besought her really, to have dinner with him. 'You have to eat, don't you?' She'd been taken aback, as if it were an indecent suggestion, but that glimpse of real emotion, the thought that he'd finally touched her, had only made him redouble his efforts, until she'd relented, calling him a nag, *mon mari* – my husband – which, even in jest, filled him with hope (though she'd also been sure to make him promise to buy her dinner *and* her time). But when he thinks of her now, all he can see is her pouty picture in the hands of the Tommy on the beach.

They used to call their trips to the brothel 'manoeuvres.' Going on manoeuvres, they told each other with a wink when it was their turn off-duty. Trench warfare. Bayonet practice. It was the language of victors, Karsten thinks now, of conquest. Back then, of course, the girls were the ones who surrendered.

The truth, he tells himself, making himself exhale, is that he never loved Françoise. It was the waiting for her in the brothel, the scrape of feet overhead, the opening and closing of doors as he sat in the parlour. The whispery bustle of a full house. Once, he turned to find Schiller staring at him, and he realised he'd been straightening the antimacassar on the arm of the sofa.

He rolls over in his bunk and lights the candle on the bedpost, pulls out another sheet of paper and sets to writing his mother another letter.

At least in the morning there's something to take his mind off his sleepless night. Someone wandering over the parade ground has found the hard-packed remnants of painted white lines, the traces of a football field. Karsten watches as men follow the marks hastily through the scrubby grass, dragging their heels through the dust until they meet at a corner, then another, until finally an entire pitch is unearthed. For a second, they stand around stunned, marvelling as if they've dug up the remains of Troy alongside Schliemann. Football, here! And then there's a flurry of calls to the guards for a ball. In the end, it's the 150-percenters who secure one, appealing to the commandant – a grey-haired, florid-faced veteran who'd lost his right arm above the elbow – and cementing their position as camp leaders in the process.

A game breaks out at once, and Karsten finds himself in the midst of it, nudged forward by Schiller. Karsten's not a skilful player, but his size and strength allow him to acquit himself respectably and as the game wears on, men who've hardly spoken to him since their capture are passing him the ball, calling him by name. Schiller, on the sidelines, takes bets and bellows encouragement, claps Karsten on the back during a pause when the ball flies into touch.

'Played.'

The ball comes to rest against the fence, and the men stare at it – the players and those gathered to watch the game. There's a single strand of wire, a foot off the ground, that runs inside the fence, set back ten feet. They've been warned not to cross it.

'Let someone else,' Schiller says softly. Karsten hasn't even been aware of the thought, but as soon as Schiller says it he can't *not* run forward, stand at the wire, squinting up at the guard towers, a hand to his brow. They see him, he's sure (the guards have been hanging out of the towers watching the game), but they make no move, and he's damned if he's going to ask their permission. Instead, he takes a deep breath and steps over the wire.

'Oi,' someone shouts, 'stop right there.' But Karsten strides forward, pretending he doesn't know English – 'Halt! Bollocks, what's German for "Halt"?' – his head down, intent on the ball. When he bends for it, he can smell the damp grass in the ditch on the other side of the wire, and as he rises again – 'Halt!' 'Yeah, what's the German for it?' *'Halt!'* – he looks up at last at the land beyond the fence, the trees and then the bright steep slope of pasture. He's been here for more than a day, he realises, but he's barely dared look beyond the camp, over the tar-paper roofs of the barracks, through the scribble of barbed wire topping the fences, and then only in glances, as if the outside world were too glaring to look at for long.

'No, idiot. The German for "halt" *is* "halt".'

'Fuck it is!'

Above and behind him there's the dry snap of a rifle bolt, and he stands very still, staring at the view.

A shiftless, slovenly lot the guards seem to him, more jailers than soldiers. Karsten knows the kinds of men who draw such duty – shirkers and backsliders, the dregs of an army. There'd been one in his squad in basic training, Voller, the broad arse of the platoon, always bringing up the rear. He'd eventually been transferred to some sort of cushy guard duty. There'd been grumbling among the men, but Karsten had told them, 'It's for the best. You wouldn't put a fellow like that in the front rank of a parade any more than you'd put him in the front lines. You wouldn't want us judged by the likes of him. Stick him in the rear where he'll be invisible.' He'd been relieved, in truth, to see the back of him, as if Voller were some shameful secret.

And what does that make me, he thinks, *to be guarded by the likes?*

He takes one more look through the fence, glances back over his shoulder at the guard tower and the other prisoners lined up silently. And then there's Schiller, clapping impatiently. 'Come on, it's not half-time. Let's get on with it.'

This is the form his gratitude takes, Karsten finally understands as he heads back. Looking out for him, vouching for him with the other men. All the little jokes to show that Karsten can be a good sport. All the little warnings.

He's distracted during the rest of the game, letting the ball slip under his foot and then lunging into tackles. One clattering collision ends with the other player springing up, shoving Karsten – '*Now* you want to fight, eh?' – the foul escalating into a dusty, panting tussle until the other man's teammates pull him off. Karsten looks up from under his brows, hands on knees, and sees his own side standing back, watching. None of them have come to his aid. Even Schiller is silent.

The next time the ball flies out of play, Karsten jogs to the sidelines and tells Schiller to take his place. He doesn't wait for the other's reply, just turns away from the game, back towards the fence.

The camp is at the high end of a valley, he sees, spread out across a deep shelf. There are the remains of a slate mine to the north, the hillside scraped back to the purple stone, a pile of waste slate like a burial mound beside it. The slope to the east, craggy cliffs interspersed with steep spills of scree, isn't much less barren. But to the south, separated from the longest side of the parade ground, by a narrow lane and a stand of hawthorn trees, a grassy hillside rises to an angled ridge. It's here the locals gathered, and it's here that Karsten finds himself drawn. What's over that ridge? he wonders as he drifts back and forth along the wire.

He's there, one evening later that week, when he spots the local boys, hiding in the trees, spying on them. Something about their furtive scrutiny enrages him, almost as much as the oblivious-ness of the other men. They've been prisoners for less than a month, and already they've relaxed their guard to the point of being ambushed by children.

He glares into the trees as if to say, I can see you! And when that elicits nothing more than a shivering of leaves, a shifting of shadows, he cries out, 'Show yourselves. Little cowards!' Cries out in German, as though speaking to himself, not them.

In the mess he complains to the others, but they shake their heads. 'They're just boys,' Schiller says with a note of impa-tience. 'What do you care about boys?'

'It's like you're on duty,' he adds when Karsten goes back to the fence, what Schiller teasingly calls 'the front'.

Schiller himself has joined the evening drill organised by the 150-percenters. It's proudly rumoured that they've even im-pressed the commandant with their smart precision. The 150-percenters have gone so far as to offer him the Heil Hitler; the gesture is officially banned, but the major has overlooked the audacity. *Makes him feel like a general,* the men say. The joke is that he's returning the salute with his phantom limb. At any rate, he seems content to turn a blind eye to the 150-percenters' excesses – one fellow, rumoured to be homosexual, has had both hands smashed in a door frame so he can't even fuck himself – in return for an orderly, disciplined camp.

'You'll join us if you know what's good for you,' Schiller tells him darkly.

Karsten knows he's right, yet he can't tear himself away from the fence, even when he feels the ground beneath him tremble with stamping feet. On the march from the Dover docks they'd run a gauntlet of schoolboys perched on a railway bridge who spat down on them, heads jerking back and forth, as the column passed below, until the men's shoulders and hair shone with saliva. 'Filthy British weather,' the fellow beside Karsten had muttered. At the time Karsten had been too shocked to feel much more than despair, but in memory the moment makes his scalp crawl. These boys aren't spitting, of course, but he feels their eyes on him. And he thought he'd bested them by throwing back the cigarettes!

The first letters from home start to arrive at the end of their second week in the camp.

A bowlegged sergeant conducts the mail call, appearing from the guardhouse one afternoon, a sack over his shoulder and a wooden crate in his other hand. After all the weeks of waiting, the last few moments are the worst. The sergeant, perched on his crate, seems to have no grasp of the concept of alphabetical order, delving into his sack and pulling out letters at random, as if he's Saint Nicholas himself, or drawing names for a raffle.

But perhaps that isn't such a bad idea, Karsten thinks, pressing close; a letter is a prize. And besides, the sergeant's method gives them all hope until the very last, straining to make out their names in his terrible accent, and even then they make him turn the sack inside out and shake it before the tight circle hemming him in loosens.

There's nothing for Karsten that first day, but he's buoyed nonetheless. *Not long now*. Besides, a letter to a barracks mate is almost as good as one to yourself, since you share everything in camp. Karsten listens to the lucky ones reading their letters that night and the next. But on the third night, the third day of mail with nothing to show for all his letter writing, he wraps his arms around his head in the darkness, distraught with jealousy.

At least he's not alone in that. Astoundingly, one of the letter readers has received a sausage in the first shipment, and later that night, when the men find him gnawing at it under his blanket – the smell gives him away – they make him sit at the table and saw at it with a blunt penknife so they can all have some. In the candlelight, it looks to Karsten as if the men are lined up to take the host. And indeed the shavings peel off, thin as paper, and dissolve on the tongue like communion wafers, a sacred taste of home.

The fourth day, and no mail.

The fifth, nothing.

Karsten has written more letters than anyone – has begged for the stationery ration of men who don't want to write – and yet day after day he turns away from mail call empty handed. He keeps it up, though, writing almost daily now, as if it's his duty.

He can tell from the replies that several of the men have taken his advice about not complaining in their own letters. *I'm glad they're treating you fairly*, one wife writes. And yet gradually, hearing the letters they get back – *we're coping well, spirits are high, everyone has faith in our army* – it becomes impossible for Karsten to quell the suspicion that these loved ones might be lying to them in return. What is it really like at home? How are they truly managing? The camp commandant has posted a newspaper – a two-day-old copy of *The Times,* ironed flat by one of the guards – on the side of the mess to keep them apprised of the course of the war, but the camp leaders have denounced it as propaganda and forbidden the men, especially those few with a little English, to read it. And now love seems to be further obscuring the truth from home. Even the others begin to doubt it, and resent Karsten for inadvertently putting the thought in their heads.

'I know, I know,' Schiller says one evening. 'We're "protecting" them. But do you ever think perhaps we shouldn't have told them we're prisoners at all? Said we're still on the front lines, or better, told them we're sitting in a café in Paris. Wish you were here!'

Karsten ignores him, but listening to the letters, he realises he can't say for sure any more who is protecting whom. Another couple of days without mail and he hardly cares. Now the men read their letters softly, not looking in his direction, while he scribbles another.

'What have you got left to tell her?' Schiller asks once, though not unkindly.

He still can't sleep, his thoughts turning to his mother over and over. He's grateful, as if for mercy, when there's finally something else to distract him. One evening shortly after lights out, he becomes aware of a stillness spreading over the barracks. Something other than the slow transition to steady breathing. It's almost as though they've been waiting for something, Karsten thinks. He can't make anything out himself yet. And then there it is, at the very edge of hearing, carried on the breeze, drifting in and out as on the tide, the distant drone of engines overhead.

'Heinkels,' someone breathes, and Karsten wonders how the fellow knows – they're all navy here. But he doesn't ask, no one does; they want to believe it. 'Heading up the Irish Sea,' another voice adds. A third: 'Turning for Liverpool or Manchester.' They listen, rapt, as if to a radio, Karsten thinks, picturing his mother's boxy Volksradio, her first set, the two of them kneeling before it.

The windows of their barracks are shuttered and bolted from outside, but the sound sifts down to them through slatted vents under the roof. The throb of the engines might as well be a serenade, and long after the tune has faded, they lie still, hoping for the distant fanfare of bombing. There's a long pause and then a scrape of bunks being pushed together, the soft grunts of men clambering up, one on the shoulders of two others. They can't quite reach, so they call on Karsten, the climber. He pulls himself up, yanks at the louvre until it comes loose, lowers it, pushes his head into the dark space. He can hear no more, but he hangs there for a moment smelling the air – he can just catch a tang of the ocean – taking deep huffs of it until someone else demands a turn. Men balance there all night, though they hear nothing else, craning for a glimpse of light at the horizon, of fires. When they do catch sight of something, it's only the dawn, and they have to scramble to replace the louvre before reveille.

It's all they can talk about the next day, the planes overhead. Every barracks has heard it. The camp leaders are smiling, strutting a little. The men, for once, can't wait for nightfall, as if the sooner they go to bed, the sooner the planes will come again. Except this time they don't, not the next night nor the one after that, and when, on the third, they do return, the men catching the pulse of the engines for a few moments, like a snatch of some favourite tune, Karsten finds himself thinking not of the bombs the planes carry but of the men inside, of how they're only a few hundred feet above, and of how by morning, if they survive, they'll be miles away.

When he finally drowses, he dreams of pulling himself through the louvre, climbing out on to the barracks roof, of reaching his arms up into the sky and catching hold of the undercarriage as a plane sweeps overhead. His uniform snaps like a flag in the wind. He imagines the sensation in his stomach as the plane unloads its cargo and bobs up, lightened. He watches the stick of bombs fall away beneath him, a curving line of fence posts, and as they drop behind, he watches the landscape dip and rise in waves until the plane crosses the white line of cliffs at Dover, like a halo around Britain, and there's the sea itself glimmering between his feet. In his dream, dawn breaks, a flock of gulls scuds beneath him, and there are the beaches of France, flashing golden with shell casings. His arms should be tired, but they're firm, not even shaking with effort, as if, rather than holding on, he is gripped in the talons of a huge bird. He pulls himself up, doing chin-ups for the sheer joy of it. Any minute now, he thinks, they'll land, but no, the plane keeps speeding along over Alsace, the corduroy patches of vineyards, and then north-east until he knows where they're headed by the mountains rising before him. Then they're banking, dropping lower and lower until he can make out rivers, roads, Bergenstrasse, on the outskirts of town. He starts to windmill his legs, and then his feet touch in a puff of dust and he's sprinting down the lane, running faster than he's ever run, not home, not yet, but to the post office, to intercept his letters, to carry them home himself, smiling at how he's outstripped them.

He could escape, he tells himself in the morning. He should. What better way to redeem himself? He's heard rumours the camp leaders are working on a plan, but when he tries to approach one of them, an older corporal called Sulzer, the man just shrugs.

'But it's our duty,' Karsten tries.

'Don't you tell me my duty,' the other sneers.

'I've heard talk of a tunnel.'

Sulzer stares off, shakes his head. Karsten studies him, unsure whether to believe him or if the fellow simply doesn't trust him.

'Come on, boy,' Sulzer says finally. 'Does it look like I spend my time digging in the dirt?' His uniform is immaculate, from the starched points of his shirt collar, like a pair of scissors at his neck, to the steely gleam of his boot tops.

'Besides,' Sulzer goes on, 'our duty is to have faith in the Leader, to remain loyal. Why should we escape when victory is at hand? We need to sit tight, maintain discipline, and wait for the panzers to plough down that gate.' Karsten recalls that Sulzer has boasted about being in the SA from the start, working on the first autobahns, even claimed with a straight face that he'd been in *Triumph of the Will*, marching past the Leader with a shining spade at shoulder arms.

'I heard a rumour that Hess was being held in Wales,' Karsten blurts out. 'One of the guards was talking about it. Did you ever meet him?'

'That turncoat? Fuck him! And what are you doing talking to guards?'

'I was eavesdropping. Trying to learn something. To help us escape.'

Sulzer sighs. He still has the submariner's pale, almost translucent skin from living under artificial light for weeks on end, made all the starker against the dark wave of hair combed severely across his brow. It's a pallor Karsten recognises from old photographs of his father in uniform, on the mantel at home.

'What's your problem, son? Don't you believe in our final victory?'

Afterwards, Karsten tells himself he'll go alone if he has to, but each morning he thinks, *Perhaps there'll be a letter today.*

He takes out his frustrations on the boys at the fence. In desperation, he hunts along the ground, scrabbling in the dirt for pebbles, and starts to fling them into the trees. They clatter off the trunks, crackle through the leaves. There's nothing for a long moment – behind him in the silence he can hear the drag and crump of marching – and then the youngsters break. It's as if the undergrowth is coming to life, rising up, and then they're running, charging away uphill in panicked flight. Karsten, watching them flee, finds himself suddenly breathless. Most of them are just kids, ten-, twelve-year-olds by the look of them, but the others he sees are teenagers, not much younger than Heino. Or himself, for that matter.

He thinks he's driven them off, walks away from the wire

with his shoulders squared, writes to his mother about it – his third letter in a week – but the next night they're back, more insolent, showing themselves, darting out of the trees to shake their fists or offer the men a two-fingered salute, before he charges the wire, roaring at the affront, and has the pleasure of seeing them fall back in fright. *'Renn!'* he cries. *'Renn!'*

'You're making a spectacle of yourself,' Schiller warns him that night. The drill, he knows, had been interrupted by his outburst. 'Besides, you'll only encourage them. Why would you do that?'

'Why would you put up with it?' Karsten asks. 'At least I'm doing something.'

'Frightening children.' Schiller snorts. 'The war's over for us. Too late to fight it now.'

By the next evening the boys have mastered their fear, greet him with a shrill chorus of their own: 'Run, run!' And Karsten shakes his head, smiling grimly despite himself.

And then at last he hears his name at mail call, shoves through the crowd, arm raised as if in the Heil Hitler. 'Here! Here!'

'My dear son,' he reads to the others; he can't wait but tears the letter open on the spot, proclaims it as if it were some vindication. 'Thank you for your letters – a third has come this very morning – and thank God for your life. I had heard nothing for so long, I confess I had begun to entertain the worst.'

There's a pause while Karsten takes a deep breath, and the others look away.

'Can you forgive me my faint heart,' he reads on, 'or at least my tardy reply? I should have responded earlier but for a bout of cold or some such, brought on surely by my fears, but from which I am now on the mend, in no small part thanks to your fine medicine. To be sure, I hardly know how I might have survived these past dark days but for the kindness of our neighbours, many of whom, as you know, have also lost sons and husbands, and who comforted me greatly in my trial. Herr Florian, our postman – you'll recall he lost a boy in the East last winter – was particularly solicitous, seeing me at the window and assuring me, even as he passed by, that there might yet be word. I could scarcely believe it, but then there he was last week with a funny little smile on his face, holding out your letter at arm's length (I had warned him I might be contagious), and he's been back each morning since. "Well, we know he wasn't wounded in his writing hand!" he told me today.'

'I should say!' Schiller laughs, but Karsten is frowning at the letter. 'Well, what else? Go on!'

'It's nothing,' Karsten says. 'Foolishness.'

Someone makes the wet smacking sound of kissing.

'Oh, my boy, my boy!' Schiller cries in falsetto, plucking the letter from Karsten's hand. 'Come on! We've been waiting for this as long as you.' He waves the white page before him, lets Karsten snatch for it once, twice, and gives it up at last only when Karsten holds out his hand.

'I should confess,' Karsten reads stiffly, 'as you might guess from Herr Florian's joke, that I have let it be understood – not so much a falsehood as an assumption I've not contradicted – that you are injured. And who's to say not? You have spared me the details of your capture, and I think I know my boy well enough to say if you were wounded you'd spare me that worry, too – don't even begin to deny it.'

'Ha!' someone cries. Karsten doesn't look up. 'You will think your mother foolish or frightened to imagine such heroic scars for you, but it is more pride than fear. There are those, you see, who blame our men in France for the invasion, call you and your fellows names I will not repeat here. I assure them that knowing my son as I do, you must have fought until your last round, until things were hopeless, or until you were ordered to set down your gun. But try not to think too ill of such folk. It is their despair and fury that speaks, and I must confess I have myself cursed those who lived while I thought you died.'

He can feel the silence around him now, the stillness of the men.

'But now I can tell them all, the doubters, the faithless, *Never fear!* I thought my boy lost, and he has been returned to me. Just so will France, which some fear lost, be ours again, I'm certain. The Leader himself has assured us of our eventual, destined victory, a day made all the sweeter to me now for knowing it will reunite us.'

There's a long pause and then Karsten reads, 'Your loving mother,' and the men melt away as if ordered to dismiss.

Only Schiller pauses as he passes. 'Tell me again. Who are we protecting in these letters of ours?'

They don't hear the planes that night, or the next, or the next. Before long the barracks begins to fill again with the furtive sounds of sleepless men.

Karsten doesn't talk to anyone, or anyone to him, for days after the letter. But it's his mother's rebuke that stings him most. He finds himself focusing especially on her faith in the Leader – an echo of Sulzer's – and his failure to share it. He knows why. She'd let slip once – though she vehemently denied it later – that his father, the former *leutnant,* thought Hitler a jumped-up windbag: 'A corporal? Might as well be led by a cinema usher, a bus conductor, a park warden!'

'That was before the Reichstag fire,' his mother insisted. 'Your poor father didn't live to see it, but everything changed after that. That was Herr Hitler's true election. That's when he really became Leader, even to those who didn't vote for him.'

Another time, she accused his father of being a snob.

But really, Karsten knows, her own favourite until '41 had been Hess, Hitler's grave deputy. She'd been crushed when he'd flown off to England. *That traitor,* she would spit in later years, but to Karsten it always seemed as if Hess had betrayed her personally, as much as the country.

He wishes he could talk to someone about this, suspects it's just as well that he doesn't. As it is, listening to the other men, he realises how little they actually say to one another.

There's been no mention of the absent planes, for instance, he realises as he stands at the fence one morning and stares up at the high hillside, watching the flock drift across it like a cloud across a clear sky. He's been fascinated by the sheep ever since he saw the shepherd gather them once, marvelling at the way he whistled commands to his dogs, sending them racing in long curving arcs to flank the flock, head it off. Like a general running a campaign, he told himself at the time, almost picturing the arrows of attack and retreat laid over the grass. And then he understands why the men don't talk about the planes: they know what it means. The lines are being pushed east; the front is moving farther and farther from them. They're falling out of range of their own air force.

Now when he watches the shepherd working the sheep, the flock pressing together, rippling over the hillside, he can't help thinking of a great white flag. He tries to call the dogs himself, putting two fingers in his mouth to whistle, others around him taking it up, but even the nearest dog only stops for a moment, cocking its head, and then, with a flick of the ears, dismisses them, races on.

Eleven

Constable Parry sternly warns them all at the pub the week after the Germans arrive that they're not to gawp at the prisoners. He's paid a courtesy visit to the camp, met with the CO. 'Prohibited by the Geneva Convention,' Parry tells them, swelling with pride. It's not every day he gets to enforce international law. 'The major's required to protect the men in his custody from violence, vigilantism and injurious public curiosity such as might serve to make them subject to scorn or ridicule.' The grave effect is reduced by the constable's smile of triumph at the end of this speech, like a child who's just recited a lesson from memory.

'Bloody hell,' Harry says. 'Hear that, Mary? The buggers have only gone and written a law against making fun of someone.'

Parry ignores them, asks Jack to lift the ban on soldiers and invite the major and his men to the pub. 'This is a new bunch, after all. Got to let bygones be bygones.'

Esther's resigned to it. She knows that Jack needs the cash.

'They're still English,' Arthur points out.

'I'll vouch for these,' Parry tells him. 'They're policemen themselves, after a manner of speaking. Brother officers.'

'Just so long as the long arm of the law reaches into their pockets,' Jack says.

Parry ushers the major and a captain, the camp medical

officer, into the lounge the very next night. The doctor is a rumpled heap of a man, but it's the major who draws the eye. He's missing an arm, his right, below the elbow, a polished swagger stick clamped under the stump, the brass ferrule at its tip winking in the lamplight. Jack, the constable is politely explaining to this personage, was also wounded in service of his country, and Jack slaps his leg.

'Where was it, Jackie?' Parry calls, and Jack tells him, 'The Somme.'

'How about you, Major?'

'County Mayo,' the major says flatly, and the bar stills, the long silence measured in the drip of the pumps.

'He's a Black and Tan,' Esther hears someone murmur behind her in Welsh. Even she's heard of their bloody exploits in Ireland. Arthur and some of the other nationalists, she knows, have a grudging admiration for the IRA, some of whom were held in Welsh prisons in the twenties.

'What can I get you, gentlemen?' she asks stiffly.

The major glances past her at the bottles lined up against the wall. 'Would you happen to have a drop of Madeira?'

There's a faint ripple of laughter through the bar, and he glares around balefully while Esther glances at Jack in confusion, mouths, 'Madeira?'

'Somewhere round here,' Jack tells her, feeling under the bar and pulling out a dusty bottle. He waves her over, whispers, 'I only keep it for the ladies on Boxing Day.'

Esther sets out two glasses, starts to pour, but the major holds up a finger – 'If I might' – lifts the bottle in his one good hand and carries it over to the corner table, the captain following with the glasses. They proceed to drink their way through the entire bottle, the locals looking on with mounting interest, less at the stolid captain, who seems unaffected, than at the major, who rapidly becomes the worse for wear, red faced and listing, and yet never relinquishes his hold on the swagger stick tucked in his armpit. 'It's like a death grip,' Harry marvels. Even when the major, having called for another bottle and been told apologetically by Jack that he's just drunk the only one, staggers to his feet and calls for their driver, the swagger stick stays impressively erect, as Mary notes.

It'll be the last time they see him in the Arms. 'Drunk us dry,' Jack laments when he hears the major's taken to frequenting the Prince. By the end of the week, the story has gone the rounds and is already a local legend. Esther even sees Jim marching around the yard with a sawn-off broomstick under his arm.

'Good riddance. Bloody Black and Tans,' Bertie grumbles.

'Oh, I don't know.' Harry twinkles. 'He seemed 'armless enough.'

The major's absence is a boon for business at least, since his men make it a point to steer clear of their officers when drinking. They're all right, Esther supposes, but it's odd to have the pub full of strangers again, to hear so many English voices drowning out the Welsh. She serves them with lowered eyes. They seem to press upon her, arms stretching for their pints or proffering their money (she prefers them to leave it on the counter rather than have their fingers paddling in her palm). The lacquered oak bar seems suddenly flimsy – she can even smell them across it, the pong of Brylcreem – and the passage behind it feels narrow as a pen. At least on the walk to and from the pub she still has the reassuring weight of the scissors bumping against her hip, though the point has worn a hole in the lining of her coat pocket. She takes to standing behind the pumps, or near Mary when she's around, even if that means spending time with Harry, too.

Actually, she's been grateful for his blowsy presence on a couple of occasions. She's become uncharacteristically clumsy of late, slopping drinks, letting the pumps overflow, fumbling with glasses, twice in one night letting full pint mugs slip through her fingers, shattering on the slate flagstones behind the bar. What she hates is the moment of stillness after the smash when everyone turns to her, the stares of the men, and then the outbreak of catcalls and whistles. But Harry somehow makes it all right, turning it into a joke, raising a long stiff arm (she thinks for a second it's a Heil Hitler salute, until he puts a curled fist to his lips), pretending there's a bottle hidden behind it. The idea is she's sneaking a few in the back, but at least everyone turns to look at Harry. Except Mary, who's probably seen the act a thousand times. Mary, in fact, is the one she's most afraid of, Mary raising her plucked eyebrows quizzically.

'What's up, luv?' she asks one night in late July, when Harry's in the gents. 'You can tell your Auntie Mary.'

And in truth Esther has thought of telling Mary – she's a woman of the world, after all, she won't be shocked – but there's never a chance with Harry around. Esther sits up Monday nights listening to the radio for the opening bars of 'There'll Always Be an England', the signature tune of their show, *The Finest Half Hour*. They have a recurring skit, a bawdy little routine called 'Lil and Bill', in which Bill keeps pursuing Lil and she keeps fending him off. When Bill brags about his manhood or his romantic exploits, Lil drops into a Churchillian growl: 'Nev-ah have so many heard so much about so lit-tle!' Bill even told her once 'to think of England', and, holding her breath, Esther heard Lil come back, 'I am, I am. No surrender!' It made her yearn to tell Mary about Colin, blurt it out, but now, facing her, something about the way Mary leans a little drunkenly across the bar makes Esther stop, fearful of being laughed at: *You what, luv? With who? Col-in-out-shakeit-all-about!*

Mary sees her hesitation now, wags a long finger. 'That's no way to keep a secret!'

'Secret?' Harry asks, coming back. He always has a banty little bounce to his stride after going to the gents, ready for action again. 'What secret's that, then?'

Esther holds her breath, but Mary gives her a wink.

'Yours,' she tells Harry. 'Esther was just asking where you're really from.'

'Where I'm from?' Harry splutters. 'You know, I think I've forgotten. Twenty years on the music-hall circuit will do that for you. Anyway, best way to keep a secret is that. Forget it! Besides,' he says, leaning closer, 'my big secret is the Secret of Comedy.' He looks left and right. 'Be honoured to share that with you. You just have to ask. Go on!'

'All right,' Esther says gamely. 'What's the secret of—'

'*Timing!*' Harry bawls in her face, and starts laughing so hard he begins to cough. The punchline smells of hops.

'Sorry, luv.' Mary pats her hand. 'Let you walk into that one. But how else you gonna learn? Listen,' she whispers when Harry's distracted again. 'The only way to keep a secret is not to let on you've got one, see. Soon as someone knows you've got one, pretty thing like you, they'll come up with all kinds of ideas! Like about you and that nice young Rhys.' Esther flinches, and Mary laughs. 'And the moral is, choose your secrets carefully.'

Mention of Rhys makes her think of Mrs R. It's been almost two months since she's heard anything from her son, and at the post office she tosses others' letters back and forth across the counter brusquely, as if touching them offends her. For her own part, Esther has noticed couples fall silent when she joins the end of the queue for the cinema. It infuriates her. Rhys is just failing again, she thinks, the way he failed all through school. He should be ashamed of himself. But all the same, she stops Jim from asking Mrs R about him at every chance.

Rhys's silence may be why Jack has been so decent about Esther's clumsiness in the bar, all the breakages. He'd be within his rights to dock her wages, but he's patient for the first couple of weeks, happy to see the pub full again.

'Chalk it up to busyness,' he tells her when another glass slips through her hand, and Harry roars, 'Bombs away!' Jack bends down to help her pick up the pieces, plucking the shards out of the foam as she stammers an apology. She smiles then, and he tells her, 'There's a sight hasn't been seen around these parts for a while.' He winks and inclines his head towards the bar. 'And I know a few other folks wouldn't mind seeing it, I bet. Smile never hurt in this business.'

She knows then she's been letting him down, and she stands up, tucks the hank of hair that has fallen forward behind her ear, and decides to make an effort.

There's been a young, hangdog American flyer nursing a beer at the corner of the bar all night, chewing gum between drinks, his jaw working away as if in angry conversation with himself. When he orders another, she sees his hands shaking and he makes a wretched face. 'Steady as a crock.'

She sets the beer before him gently, and asks him about himself. He's a belly gunner in a B-something-or-other, waiting to fly on to a base in East Anglia. What's that like? she wants to know, and he tells her morosely, 'You know what they say about not looking down when you're scared of heights? Well, I can only look down.'

'A flyboy afraid of heights!' She laughs, and he mumbles glumly, 'Among other things.'

She asks him why he's there alone, and he explains that his crew aren't much interested in him. 'There's no percentage in it. Belly gunner's average life expectancy is two and a half missions.'

She thinks he's joking. 'You can't have half a mission, silly,' and then he looks over and it dawns on her. 'Oh.' She's been hanging around Harry and Mary too long, she thinks. Everything seems like a gag.

It touches her, his loneliness, and to change the subject she asks where he's from, and he says, 'Rhode Island,' and she leaps on this. 'Where the chickens come from!' she cries, excited to recognise the name. They have a half dozen of the rusty pullets with their rumpled feathers at the farm. But Harry, beside her, bursts into laughter – 'Oh, you're learning, girl!' – and the airman grimaces: 'Funny.' She's instantly sorry, the more so because Harry has started clucking and crowing on his stool, and the guards, jealous she's never given them the time of day, are laughing uproariously.

Harry takes it as his cue to launch into a joke about a fellow who goes into a bar and orders three pints every night. 'One for himself and one each for his two brothers, fighting in Burma and France, see.'

But Esther can't take her eyes off the poor young American, his furious chewing. She begins to explain the misunderstanding, imagining that if she can just ask him about the chickens seriously – how *did* they get that name? they *are* awfully red, aren't they? – she might convince him of her sincere interest in poultry. But then she stops, simply astounded that she can hurt him, this fighting man.

Harry prattles on beside her: 'And then one night he just orders the two pints, and the barmaid says, "Oh, I'm so sorry for your loss, sir. Can I ask, was it your brother in Burma or your brother in France?"'

It seems so unlikely, the stricken look on the American's face, almost a joke, that she smiles to herself. She sees him swallow hard, and even this is funny, and she starts to laugh out loud, watching him pull his cap on and flee, his beer unfinished.

'You've heard it,' Harry says in a hurt voice, looking round. But she shakes her head, waves him on.

'Well, he just looks at her and says, "Neither, luv. I'm just on the wagon."'

And Esther laughs even harder.

'There you go,' Jack says, slipping past her down the bar, and she understands that as far as he's concerned she can break any number of glasses, and hearts too, so long as she keeps her own intact.

She isn't much friendlier to the guards afterwards, but at least she stops dropping drinks. She tries to feel guilty about the airman, but she can't. Any hurt she could have caused him seems so trivial, yet she also finds herself feeling the smallest thrill when she recalls it.

Twelve

At Cilgwyn, Esther and Jim are barely talking since she slapped him. Arthur looks from one to the other, more baffled by their silence than their previous chatter in English. The boy's bike lay in the yard where he dropped it for two days, before Esther picked it up one night, late for work, and rode it to the pub. He doesn't need it anyway, she tells herself, now that the school holidays have started. She uses it whenever she goes to work now, or to the pictures – always riding it as fast as she can, pell-mell up and down the hills.

A few nights later, Jim doesn't appear for supper. They wait for five minutes, then ten. Esther asks Arthur if he's seen him since the afternoon, and he shrugs – 'He'll come when he's hungry' – spears a floury potato, starts to eat. She sits still, as if she were a part of the table setting along with the knife and fork. Jim's made himself scarce since school ended, but she knows where he is. She's seen the white glow of the camp lights over the ridge each evening, like a moon that never quite rises.

She leaves Arthur at the table, his mouth full, shaking his head, and she strides over the hill in search of the boy, calling Mott for company. On the climb, she imagines all the trouble he could get into; on the way down, all the trouble she'll give him. She gets as far as the trees above the camp, slipping into them unobserved in the deepening dusk, before she spots the boys on their bellies in the ditch running alongside the lane. Something about their wariness makes her slow and then stop, leaning up against a tree. It takes her a moment to find Jim at one end of the line. He has his fists pressed to his eyes, and for a moment she assumes he's crying, starts from her hiding place, but then she realises, *Binoculars, he's pretending they're binoculars.* And she finds herself turning to look where he's looking, at the men behind the fence.

They seem so aimless at first, drifting across the parade ground. Then gradually she sees others scattered around the buildings, sitting or standing, talking or writing letters. A group squat in the dust – playing cards, she guesses from the way they move their hands. Some are even dozing in the heat. Perhaps it's their idleness – a novelty to her, brought up around farmers who always have too much to do – but she finds it oddly peaceful watching the men, her heart slowing after the steep climb. She feels so observed behind the bar, it's a relief to watch for once. It's the same way that the darkness of the pictures relaxes her, and from the gloom of the trees the men moving across the still, bright square of the parade ground seem like figures on the screen.

They've all surrendered, so she's overheard the guards saying, their contempt barely concealed. 'No danger of any of you lot doing that,' Mary had teased them, and they'd bristled at the dig. 'Have you know, I've seen action,' one of them retorted. 'In Malaya. Be there now if it weren't for the malaria!' Harry had slapped his neck resoundingly, 'Ugh! He got me!' and feigned a swoon. 'It's a wound, too!' the guard blustered, but by then the laughter was general. 'Blokes!' Mary whispered to Esther. 'Sensitive about their bloody honour as any girl about her virtue.'

The boys Esther notices now out of the corner of her eye are pointing at the men, one after another – counting? she wonders – but then she sees Jim blow on his fingertips and she realises he's miming shooting, picking them off one by one.

She should go down and fetch him home, but now that she's here she doesn't have the nerve to creep closer to the fence. She sees the flash of a match, and the face of the guard in the nearest tower is momentarily lit up against the fading sky, and she holds her breath.

Soon the boys grow bolder – or perhaps, in the way of boys, simply restless with keeping still. They start to sing, of all things, Pinkie leading them, crouching and waving his hands like a choirmaster. She cranes forward to catch the words. 'Oh, give me land, lots of land under starry skies above,' they trill, 'don't fence me in.' She recognises the Gene Autry tune from the Saturday morning serials. They break up in giggles before they can get much farther. The dog beside her stirs, and she says softly, 'Settle.'

She thinks of the constable's warning, of the Geneva Convention, but suspects the boys relish the idea of breaking the biggest rules they can.

One of the guards in the tower finally rakes his searchlight along the treeline, and the boys fall silent. It's barely dusk, but in the gloom of the trees the leaves flare green, as if a breeze has turned them. Esther blinks, the light dancing before her, and when she can see again, the boys are flat to the ground. She thinks of Jim's washing, the grass stains on his clothes. The searchlight swings back for one more desultory pass and then tips up against the sky, reminding her suddenly of the Twentieth Century–Fox icon. In the echoing silence after it snaps off, she can almost hear the brassy trumpet fanfare.

The Germans for the most part ignore the boys – they mustn't understand the words of the song, she thinks, and it seems like a mercy – though a couple stare hard into the trees. The rest start up a game of football. Do Germans even play football? she asks herself. It seems so mundane and yet intimate to see them at play. She almost expects the guards to intervene. Surely prisoners shouldn't be allowed to play games. She studies them intently, wondering if she can tell anything about the kind of soldiers or sailors they might make from the way they dribble the ball, slide in for a tackle, but all she can think of is how young they look. The thudding of their boots on the hard earth as they chase the ball carries to her clearly.

Below her, Pinkie starts up in a hoarse stage whisper, like a commentator on the radio: 'Fritz now, playing the ball forward to Fritz on the wing, he cuts inside, crosses to the big centre forward, Fritz, who sends a header into the arms of the keeper—'

'FRITZ!' the other boys chorus.

Esther shakes her head. She looks at the guard in his tower, but he's hanging over the railing watching the game, his back to the dark drum of the searchlight.

It's a warm night, pleasant in the shadow of the trees, and she finds a dry spot, dusts it of leaves, and sits, hugging her knees to her chin. One team has taken their shirts off, or knotted the arms of their overalls at their waists, their chests glowing pale in the dusk beneath tanned faces and necks. She watches one fellow – fair-haired, so different from the dark-haired local boys – barge another off the ball, then dribble it away. He's a strapping lad, but his flying hair makes him look delicate somehow.

After the roughness of the collision, he's surprisingly graceful with the ball at his feet. It looks to her as if he's dancing with a partner. She pictures each step-over and turn as if it were printed on a sheet from Arthur Murray. And then he shoots, destroying the illusion, and the ball flies wide of the goal, skidding off the hard earth and rolling up against the fence. He stands with his hands on his hips for a moment, then trots towards it, pausing at a thin line of wire a few yards inside the fence and glancing up at the guard tower. 'Yes, yes,' someone calls impatiently, and the German steps over the wire, gathers the ball, and kicks it back into play. He stops at a water bucket on the sideline on his way back, drinking from a tin cup, pouring the dregs over his head until his hair darkens. A breeze steals up the slope from the camp, ruffling Mott's coat as he dozes, and Esther strokes the dog as she watches the men run back and forth.

She doesn't know where the time goes – the ball runs up against the fence over and over – but suddenly it's nine, the men turning towards their barracks. She waits for the boys to leave first, so that at home Jim gets to ask where *she's* been. 'Never mind me,' she says, slamming a cold plate of food in front of him. 'You've been at that camp.' He begins to deny it, and she tells him, 'Don't lie. You've been bothering those prisoners.' And he tells her scornfully, 'They *are* the enemy, you know.'

The major, the constable announces to the pub, has complained about the boys' shenanigans, threatened to send his men after them. Esther feels a fleeting fear for Jim, and yet some part of her thinks he might deserve to be caught this time. By the end of the week, the constable has extended his own rounds to include the camp. 'The major appreciates the benefits of greater co-operation between the military and civil authorities.'

'Means it's beneath our dignity chasing kids,' one of the guards mutters.

Parry just shrugs. He has no intention of driving the boys off himself. 'They'll only be back in the village making mischief,' Esther hears him confide to Jack. 'No, I've got other fish to fry.' He means the Germans. He reckons they'll think twice about escaping now they've seen him on his rounds.

'Escaping!' another guard scoffs. 'This lot? Not likely.' He waves his white hanky. 'Don't have the balls, do they?'

'Ladies present,' Parry coughs, and Esther lowers her eyes.

'Wouldn't have surrendered if they did.' The guard sets his elbows on the bar. 'You only have to look at them – one half thanking their lucky stars, the other too ashamed to look you in the face. Hardly know which to pity more.'

Still, the constable's not to be put off. He makes a point of conducting his rounds promptly each night, proud of his punctuality, as if it shows backbone. 'I might not know German, see, but I'm speaking their language. Look at their trains, man.'

Arthur rolls his eyes. 'He's just jealous. There the army is with five hundred prisoners, and what's he got? One little cell, not much bigger than a pantry, and all he's ever locked up in there is taters.'

'It's me duty, I reckon,' Parry tells them pompously. 'Protecting the local citizenry.' There's been talk of the Germans working on local farms, like prisoners in the last war, he confides. 'And if that's so, I want 'em to know I'll be keeping my eye on them.'

Esther can hardly imagine the idle men she saw the other night working.

'Work!' Harry says grimly. 'Shooting's too good for them.' And there's an odd silence while they wait for a punchline. (Esther doesn't hear it until the next radio show: 'Saw Heinz herding cows, and I says to him, "Were you a farmer back home, then?" and he goes, "*Nein,* but it's easy for a German soldier to herd cattle. I'm just following udders!"')

On her next night off Esther tells Arthur she's going to the pictures, cycles to the bottom of the lane, then doubles back on foot, up the slope. She tells herself it's to catch Jim, to make sure he doesn't get into any more trouble, but she crouches behind a tree when she hears the metallic grind and rattle of the constable's bike and sees Parry ride into view. Seven o'clock, she thinks; he'll be off home soon for the tea Blodwyn's making him. She watches him cycle by slowly, his eyes on the camp. A couple of the Germans give him a wave, but Parry just glares at them.

Before he's even out of sight down the lane, Esther sees the boys, Pinkie leading them, saunter out of the trees below her. On another of their 'recce missions', as they call them. Jim brings up the rear, swinging from trunk to trunk as he hurries down the steep slope, yodelling like Tarzan.

Most of the men ignore them as before, but she sees a small knot – three or four of the younger Germans – advancing on the fence and finds herself standing, as if to run. Pinkie has his fists up and is bouncing around, throwing out shadow punches. 'Wanna fight?' he calls. 'You don't look so tough.' He jabs the air in front of him, his stark white fists shining in the dusk.

Little coward, she thinks. She hears Jim's thin voice: 'Seconds out. *Ding ding.*' And then one of the Germans, a stocky fellow, marches up to the wire, shrugging off his shirt, and the boys fall back a step. He grins, pops his muscles, warms up with a few swift combinations, bobbing his head and shuffling his feet, then drops into a stance, fists raised. He beckons impatiently, and Pinkie, after a second, takes a tentative swing, but the prisoner just slaps at his cheek like he's been bitten by a flea, shakes his head.

There's a burst of laughter from his friends, and she can see Pinkie blushing from here. He starts to windmill his arm, winding up for a haymaker, but the German's lost interest in him. He walks along the wire, feinting at the boys, making some of them jump, and stops in front of Jim, the smallest, and crooks a finger. The boy looks down the line at the others, some of whom are waving him on, and she sees him throw out a small fist. The German reels, falling back into the arms of his comrades, who hoist him up, push him forward. Esther watches, perplexed by the performance, and then it occurs to her that they're humouring the boys, *playing with them.* Jim seems puzzled himself, but throws out a combination to the gut, and the big man doubles over, sags to his knees, amid laughter from both sides of the fence. One of the boys holds Jim's hand up. The winner.

The light is fading, but the evening is still warm, the slate hillsides radiating the heat they've been absorbing all day. A wasp brushes her ear, its loud buzz making her flinch, and she shakes her hair violently. She leans against a trunk, it's cool and rough against her neck and cheek, and studies the boys. They're trying to talk to the Germans now, Pinkie thrusting himself close to the wire, pointing at himself, then the Germans. She slips a little lower through the trees, trying to make him out. He seems to be hurling curses at the fence, but as she listens more closely she hears a grotesque kind of English lesson taking place.

'This'll help you talk to the guards,' Pinkie is saying, but all the words offered for simple greetings are obscenities. 'Alfweeder-sane,' Pinkie enunciates, waving goodbye, 'means "Bugger off!"' A man's voice repeats the words slowly after him, to the accompaniment of giggles. 'And when you meet someone, you say, "Pleased to fuck you!"' Pinkie says cheerily. Esther feels herself redden, with embarrassment then anger, and swats at the wasp, which has found her again. Another man, she sees, is urgently miming eating. 'Oh,' Pinkie says. 'What do we say when we're hungry?' He grins at the others. 'What you ask is, "May I have some cock, please?" Go on, try it. "More cock, please!"' The German repeats it and the boys howl with laughter. It's suddenly too much for Esther. She can't bear to see it go on, and she finds herself pushing through the undergrowth, the brambles pulling at her legs.

'Stop it!' she shouts, stumbling into the midst of them, arms raised, and they scatter like sheep. For a moment she has Jim's arm, and then he breaks free and she chases them into the trees, listens to them crashing through the brush.

'Hey,' she hears Pinkie call in the darkness. 'Was that your mam, Bedwetter?' And Jim howling, 'No!'

She stares after them, stung by their laughter, but when she turns, the men at the wire are watching her silently, their eyes wide. Somehow she imagined that they'd bolt too. They're not laughing at least, but after a second this makes her more, not less, uncomfortable.

She looks from one to another, quickly turns.

'Don't go,' someone blurts in accented English, and she stops for a second as if she can't quite believe it, as if it's some trick. She searches their faces in the gloom, then starts to back away once more.

'Thank you,' the voice calls, and this time she sees it's the tall, sandy-haired one at the edge of the group who has spoken. She thinks she might have seen him playing football.

'You're welcome,' she responds automatically.

There's a hurried exchange in German, and she looks from man to man until the tall one raises a hand like a boy at school. She nods, curious about what he could want to ask her.

'What's your name?'

She stares at him open mouthed, finally shakes her head, staggers back into the trees, stands there for a long moment in the deep shade. She's out of sight, but the men stay where they are, searching the shadows, and she keeps still, her breathing shallow.

'Come back,' the tall one calls, and she looks at his beseeching face, marvelling at it. One of his comrades tries to pull him away, and as he turns something occurs to her, and she calls softly, 'If you know so much English, why don't you tell your friends they're not learning what they think they're learning!'

'I will,' he says quickly, nodding towards her voice. 'I will. We were just playing with the boys. I'm sorry for any offence.'

And he *is* sorry, she sees, with a kind of wonder – he actually blushes – and what's more, he's afraid of her leaving. She sees the fear on his face, the disappointment as she stays silent, sees his hand on the wire, and she thinks, *He can't touch me.* And the thought warms her through.

Thirteen

His conversation with the girl – his *tête-à-tête,* as the others start to call it in coarse French accents, his *rendez-vous* – brings Karsten a new notoriety in the camp. A better one, he supposes. At least the men are talking to him again. They all want to know what she said to him there at the fence, what he said to her, and when he hesitates – he knows the truth will disappoint them, and besides, he's embarrassed, ashamed to admit he kept silent while the boys mocked them – they tease him, call her his 'Welsh girl' and him her 'lover-boy'.

Karsten denies it all, of course, knowing as he does so that this is part of the game, part of being a good sport. He recognises this taunting – they're the same ribald jokes he endured about Françoise – knows his role.

'You're learning,' Schiller tells him with a little nod.

Karsten stands at the fence the next evening, hoping for a glimpse of her. Pure foolishness, he knows. It was hardly a romantic encounter, nor is the girl precisely a prize. She'd not even been wearing a dress, but rather breeches and a bulky sweater; the guards had probably mistaken her for one of the boys. A tomboy, and young, too, seventeen or eighteen. Françoise had been seventeen, or so she'd told him over dinner, but he'd never believed her. In her make-up and experience she seemed so much older. And yet there was something about this girl. The way she'd looked at him, with anger, contempt, pity even, but also as if she expected something better of him.

It's the first time in almost two months that he hasn't cursed his knowledge of English, wished in fact that it were better, quicker.

Still hoping forlornly for her to appear again, he hears a rustle in the trees on the last day of July, and as he watches, a stray sheep emerges from the undergrowth, daintily leaping across the ditch. She ambles across the lane and begins nosing in the sweet, lush grass on the other side of the fence. A crowd of men gradually gather beside Karsten to watch, drifting along with her as she crops her way back and forth. For the first time in a fortnight or more, they actually respect the warning wire, line up along it, not wanting to scare the animal, as if they are watching in a zoo.

Karsten ignores the whispered jokes about his 'girlfriend'. Someone runs to the mess, comes back with a handful of furred carrots, a greenish potato.

'It's not a goat,' Karsten hisses. But he creeps towards the fence, proffering the vegetables as if they are a peace offering. The ewe wisely ignores him and the food, nibbling at the grass. The tearing sound of her teeth is so loud it makes Karsten flinch. He reaches out a slow hand, touches the wire, and then stretches through to stroke her back, and for a moment she submits to it. The wool is tightly sprung and, as he pushes his fingers into it, greasy with lanolin. But what astonishes him is how warm it is. He looks back at the others with a smile of wonder, but that sets the men hopping over the wire, and the sudden movement makes the ewe shrug him off and jump away, breaking into a loping trot.

The men watch her go.

'You could use some work on your technique, lover-boy!' someone drawls, and Karsten shrugs, grins lopsidedly. He can still feel the wiry warmth of her fleece, the trembling tick of her heart. He can't remember when he last touched another live thing.

It makes him ache for escape. But when he asks Schiller if he's heard any more rumours about a tunnel, the other rolls his eyes. 'Only tunnelling around here,' he says, making a pumping gesture, 'is fellows into their fists.'

By the end of the week, the girl seems an apparition, too improbable to believe in. Karsten must have imagined her. Still, he lies in his bed and thinks of her stepping out of the trees like a spirit, touches himself, guessing many of the others are doing the same. But at least in *his* dreams, he can speak to her.

He wonders what his mother would think of his talking to the girl. He has not written to her since her letter, nor she to him. Fraternisation, she'd probably call it. Of course, he hadn't told her of Françoise either, but then they'd never talked about girls, his mother and he. He supposes that fathers and sons, mothers and daughters, have such awkward conversations, but mothers and sons? What could they say to each other?

Perhaps she thought he'd simply absorb what he needed to know. It was hard to be an innocent in a guesthouse, especially a cheap one, not with all those bedrooms overhead. His mother never turned away business, not even those couples who, the next morning, when addressed by name, 'Herr Schmidt, Frau Schmidt,' blinked at her in bafflement across the breakfast table. They used to make him burn with anger, these people lying to his mother. Sometimes he would try to catch them out, addressing them by other names, just to see if, confused, they would answer. Other times he would use their false names to their faces over and over, drilling them sarcastically. He wanted them to know he knew they were lying. Once, though, when the couple in question had hurried to check out, his mother had slapped him a ringing blow, slapped the smile of triumph right off his face. 'It's not your business,' she told him. 'Learn to look the other way.' He'd stood there dumbfounded. *Why, she'd known all along.* 'But they're lying,' he'd begun, and she'd raised her hand again. 'If I can put up with it, so can you!'

He learned after that to recognise a slight change in her tone when she talked to these couples. He could be sitting in their cramped kitchen and hear her welcoming guests in the hall, and even without seeing them – their stiff faces with the twitchy smiles they gave each other when they thought they were unwatched – he'd know, just from the way his mother said *'Wilkommen, Herr und Frau.'* There was a hollowness to it, a kind of resignation – not a welcome, truly, just a weary acknowledgement. Every time such a couple checked in, more so even than the married couples, the families with children, he thought of his father. He missed him for himself, of course, though he could hardly remember him, thought of his father more as a role, an empty place at the head of the table, than as a person. But those were the moments when he felt his mother's loss most keenly.

Perhaps that, he thinks, is why they never talked about love. Why, even when there had been girls – respectable girls, local girls, German girls (and he'd had his share of crushes) – he hadn't spoken of them to her. On his last night before the army took him, he'd made a plan to meet a girl – Eva. She was a little older than he, twenty maybe, a rosy, round-faced thing with plump little hands. He'd watched her from afar for years, it seemed, always on the arm of some fellow in uniform, but he'd only had the nerve to ask her out, to the cinema, after he'd joined up. It was the bravest thing he'd ever done, he thought at the time. He stared into her dark pupils while she thought about her answer, and then he'd told her, 'I'm shipping out tomorrow,' and she'd pursed her lips and said, 'Well, then.' She called him a patriot. She said that there was no higher love than the love of one's country, and he nodded mutely. Her own patriotism was well known among the local boys, who called her the Recruiter.

Karsten had laughed along with the rest, thought her a gullible romantic at best, at worst a slut for the swastika, but now he saw what she felt most was pity. Knowing it, he still planned to use it against her, pitiless himself. But as he'd gone downstairs that evening, he'd found his mother alone in their cramped kitchen and he knew she'd been crying, and so he'd stayed with her. Perhaps, he'd thought, squeezing her hand, there was no distinction between pity and love. That's when she'd told him his father would be proud of him. She squeezed Karsten's hand. 'Don't disgrace us,' she said, and he'd nodded and sworn.

He wonders now if his mother still thinks him a virgin – the very worst thing a soldier can be, other than a coward, he thinks bleakly. And yet he finds himself, despite himself, hoping she does.

As for Eva, he'd written to her to apologise, but of course she'd never written back.

Karsten consoles himself that the Welsh girl's fleeting appearance at the wire at least scared the boys away, but before long they're back, and to his surprise he's actually pleased to see them. He recognises the one she grabbed, asks his name, but the boy ignores him. Ignores him yet lingers, as if fascinated by Karsten's English, as if the language issuing from him were as improbable as a talking sheep or dog. The boy is slightly built, with a watchful look about him, and seems always on the fringe of the crowd. A follower, Karsten intuits, a tagger-along, tolerated by the others, perhaps bullied by them.

'Where's your sister?' Karsten tries again the next night, but the boy bristles.

'She's not my sister! I'm an evacuee. My dad's in the navy!'

He sticks his chest out as if for a medal. There's a challenge in his voice, but Karsten doesn't want a fight.

'You must miss him,' he says kindly, but it's a mistake. The boy's face clouds, and Karsten sees too late how he's trapped him. The boy can't admit he misses his father in front of the others, can't say he doesn't for fear of seeming disloyal.

'Shut up!' is all he can cry, and his shrill belligerence only makes the older boys laugh.

The gang as a whole is losing interest in the camp. Fewer boys come each night, and when they do, they chat among themselves, bored by the prisoners. *No longer afraid of us,* Karsten thinks.

He's reduced to entertaining them to maintain their interest. When he sees one of the older toughs, an albino by the look of him, lighting a cigarette, he brings two fingers to his own mouth, raises his eyebrows.

'You must be joking, sunshine.'

'Not to smoke.' Karsten struggles for the word. 'For a . . . trick, you know. Magic.' He cuts his eyes towards the slight boy, the one he's really doing this for.

The tough frowns, but Karsten can see he's intrigued, and in his own good time he strolls over, offers a cigarette jutting from his pack. 'You're really not going to smoke it?'

'No matches,' Karsten tells him, pulling his pockets inside out.

'Fair enough. I'll go along.'

The albino waves the others over like an impresario, and they stand before Karsten as he twirls the cigarette in his fingers. He has a modest repertoire of sleight of hand, with which he used to entertain his mother's guests as a boy, but he's rusty, his knuckles stiff, and on his first attempt the cigarette slips through his grasp. He has to fumble to catch it.

'Oooohh!' The older boy rolls his eyes. 'You're good, you are. Know any others?'

Karsten ignores him, trying to still the sudden panic he feels. He used to have a line of patter to distract his audience, but he's so gripped with stage fright he can't think to translate it. He pushes his sleeves up, concentrates on his next pass, one hand slipping over the other, and to his own mild surprise the cigarette vanishes. He turns his hands back and forth before them, smiling in triumph.

Even the albino is impressed. As for the little lad, his eyes are huge. He's surely never seen anything like it before.

'Where is it?' he asks in hushed tones, looking at the albino as if he might know.

'Gone,' Karsten says. He puts his two empty fingers to his lips in a suave smoking gesture. 'Unvisible!'

'*In*visible,' the tough snorts, but the little one, enraptured by the trick, breathes, 'Unvisible,' as if it's the magic word.

Instinctively, Karsten reaches out to him with a twirl of the wrist. He means to produce the cigarette from behind the boy's ear, but for once he's forgotten the wire and has to let his hand fall quickly to hide the cigarette.

'Come on,' the tough says, suddenly suspicious, as if Karsten intends to keep the cigarette. 'Where is it?'

Karsten mimes forgetfulness, rubs his face thoughtfully, and then draws the cigarette from his nostril, to the delight of the younger boys.

'Oi!' the albino cries. 'That's disgusting.' Karsten holds out the cigarette but the other shakes his head. 'I ain't putting that in my mouth!'

'You can't always believe your eyes,' Karsten says, smiling.

He holds it out again, but the boy isn't having any of it.

Besides, the others are clamouring for him to do it again, and Karsten obliges, running through the routine twice more, three times, balancing the smoke on the back of his hand, making it vanish with a clap, then pulling it from thin air with a flourish as he gets his feel back.

He slips the cigarette between his lips as he saunters back to the barracks that night, wondering if the boy will tell her about the trick, if she'll believe him. And abruptly he hopes not. That she'll want to see it for herself.

But the next night brings only the boys again, and by the end of the evening they've seen all his tricks a dozen times.

He'd feared the little one would vanish with the rest, when they lost interest, and yet there he is, one day all by himself, looking around as if for company. Perhaps the others haven't deigned to tell him of a new meeting place.

It's the chance Karsten's been hoping for.

He pulls a pair of toy planes from his tunic. He's been working on them all week, fashioning them from a couple of bed slats with a blunt penknife. They're crude things, not much more than crosses of wood lashed together with twine and painted with boot polish, but each has a golden propeller, cut from flattened shell casings he's begged from a guard. They're not much, but he's proud of those propellers, has polished them to an oily shine, the first thing he's polished since his surrender. He's bent the soft metal blades at an angle, so when he swings the planes through the air before the boy, they swirl with a soft ticking sound, glittering in the sunset.

Karsten can see the desire in the boy's eyes. He can't take them off the planes, one in each of Karsten's rough palms now. He lifts them towards the boy, but the lad hops back like a bird.

'Would you like them?'

The boy nods emphatically.

'The girl,' Karsten says cautiously. 'The girl who fetched you. Tell me her name and you can have them.'

The boy stares at the planes, their propellers winking. He's torn, Karsten sees, but finally he shakes his head.

'Come on.'

The boy's shoulders drop and he turns away, and Karsten finally relents. She'll just have to remain the Welsh girl. Much as he wants her name, there's something about the boy's loyalty that moves him.

'Here, then.' He pushes the planes through the fence before he can change his mind, and the youngster snatches them out of his hands, darts off.

For a slow moment Karsten feels bereft, as if he's given up a treasure. The boy wanted them *so* much. Karsten's hands, which cradled the toys for days, feel abruptly empty. But when he sees the boy running uphill, the planes whipping over the long grass, banking around tree trunks, sailing towards the crest, it comes to Karsten that this is what he has wanted all along, for the planes to go where he can't. Into a home. He thinks of them crossing the threshold like the flights he'd watched in France racing across the coastline; he imagines them roaring around the kitchen, flashing past whitewashed walls; pictures them diving through the steam from a kettle as if it were a low cloud skimming over the lake of the sink, shooting across the long, flat field of a dining table, past bucolic scenes on the china ranked along a dresser. He thinks of them buzzing through the dimness of a hallway, banking sharply, gradually gliding in for a safe landing on the broad, smooth strip of a well-made bed. And he thinks of the girl finding them there, or among the plates on the dinner table, or on the boy's desk. Thinks of her reaching for them with surprise, wondering where they're from.

Perhaps she'll ask the boy; perhaps he'll tell.

And he realises, *They're for her.* Somehow, he's made them for her.

He dreams of her coming to the wire the next day, but he's still pleased to see the boy, even alone, hurries to meet him at the wire, smiling. But the lad is grim faced, empty handed. Karsten feels a brief pang that the planes have already lost their appeal. Or perhaps he's simply lost them, or had them taken from him by some bully at school, and the premonition fills Karsten with indignation.

The boy won't look at him at first, pacing back and forth before the wire, staring at his own scuffed boots.

'Those planes,' he blurts out eventually. 'Those planes you gave me.'

'Yes.' I'll make more, Karsten thinks. A whole squadron. Enough for the boy, for a whole village of boys, if need be. Anything to make him look less distraught.

'They were *German* planes, right?' He looks up sharply into Karsten's face as he says – spits – the word.

Karsten searches for an answer, his smile curdling. A part of him has forgotten the war still going on somewhere.

'Not really,' he says at last, guardedly. 'They were just planes.'

'But *you* made them,' the boy insists.

'You didn't think they were German planes when I gave them to you.'

'At school they said I joined the wrong air force.'

'They're any planes you want them to be.'

'No! You *made* them. What did you mean them to be? It doesn't matter what I think; it's what you meant them to be. You were thinking of German planes, I bet.'

Karsten begins to deny it, and stops. Of course he'd been thinking of German planes. But what he really wants to say is that he'd been thinking of freedom. The freedom he'd heard in the planes overhead, the freedom he'd felt thinking of the toy planes, something from the camp, something he made there, existing outside of it, outside of his reach, his sight.

'Anyhow, they're gone now,' the boy says with a sigh. 'I chopped them up with the hatchet and stuck them in the fire.'

Karsten pictures the brass propellers twisting in the heat, blackening, falling through a sooty grate.

'They called me a traitor,' the boy chokes out.

'I'm sorry,' Karsten says softly, overwhelmed by a wave of grief. He begins to say he'll make him something else, but he can't think what.

He lies in his sagging bunk that night, long after the barracks grows still, staring up at the coarse timber joists of the roof, impatient for sleep to ambush him, yet constantly vigilant. He was never this alert on guard duty. The hut stinks of men, of sweat and feet and damp wool and arseholes, and he rolls over to catch the sporadic scent of the sea. He can make out the smell of the damp trees on wet days, or of dry heather on fine ones. *Nights are the worst,* he thinks. He dreads nine o'clock, when they're ordered off the parade ground and herded back to their barracks. The evenings, once it gets too gloomy to play football, once the dusk deepens and the white dots of sheep on the hillside vanish, are a slow, anxious prelude to this confinement. It makes him feel like a punished child, no older than the boy, sent to bed early, and he dreads the winter when the days will get shorter and they'll be locked in even earlier.

He wonders if his mother is punishing him by not writing. She considered it unladylike to strike a child – that was a father's place. Not that she didn't hit him on occasion, but more commonly she would give him the silent treatment if he disappointed her.

Recalling his childhood and her punishments, he's reminded that he did once see her turn away a suspicious couple from the pension. He'd have been just seven or eight. This was before he understood the nature of trysts. He remembers it because he overheard her telling them there was no room, and when they mentioned the Vacancy card in the window, she said her son must have forgotten to take it down. He'd thought it was a mistake and hurried out to tell her that no, there were vacancies, but when she persisted, he grew indignant, as if he were being blamed unfairly. The man, he remembers, became impatient.

'Are there rooms or not, madam?' And his mother shook her head adamantly. 'The boy is mistaken.'

'But *Mutti,*' he'd cried, and she snapped at him to shut up, and he burst into tears, the injustice of it too much to bear. 'It's not fair,' he sobbed, and the young woman had crouched down beside him, taken his hands in her soft ones. 'There, there, little man.' Her head of brown hair was as glossy as a fresh chestnut, and he'd reached out for it. But then he felt his mother's hand on his shoulder, pulling him to her. 'Don't you touch him!'

The woman had stood stiffly and told the man they should leave. 'Otto, please.' She put a hand on his arm, and as Karsten watched from his mother's skirts, the woman stroked the man's sleeve lightly. 'Don't make a scene,' she said softly, as if it were just the two of them, and the man turned to her then, and without another word they'd left.

His mother had gone to the parlour window and snatched up the Vacancy sign, as if she'd rip it in two, and then stood there trembling, just behind the curtain, until they were gone.

'But there *are* rooms,' Karsten growled accusingly, actually stamping his foot. And she nodded curtly, slipped the sign back in the window. 'Not for them.'

'You lied!' It was the first time he'd ever caught her.

'They lied to me first,' she said. 'Herr and Frau *Wagner*, indeed. Very funny! As if I was a fool, a bumpkin! They'd never have tried it if there was a man about the place.' She hadn't spoken to him for the rest of the week.

They were Jews, of course, he thinks now – probably married, in truth, something about the way the woman had touched the man told him so even then – but trying and failing to pass. Except, as a child he'd not known them.

The next evening, the boys are back, all of them, even the little one. He'd not expected to see them again. As he approaches the fence, they hold out their hands through the wire as if for a toy, a gift. But when Karsten raises his own hands, empty, they hurl abuse, and the night after they're gone again, the little loner too, and Karsten feels oddly abandoned.

In the dusk, the full moon opens above him like the mouth of an impossibly distant tunnel.

He wonders how his father handled his own captivity all those years ago. He never spoke of it much, or of the war in general. Indeed, when Karsten thinks of him, he can barely remember his voice. His father had been gone so much of his young life, sometimes for days at a time if the fish were running, and then gone for good before Karsten turned seven. All he recalls are glimpses – his father bent over the model of a ship in a bottle at the kitchen table, patiently explaining what he was doing. Karsten had asked him how he'd learned all that, and his father had told him a fellow prisoner had taught him. His last model had been unfinished at the time of his death, and Karsten had whiled away the long, still hours of mourning finishing it.

Fourteen

Esther can hardly believe it was her, running down to the wire like that, scattering the boys, confronting the Germans. The thought of it, in retrospect, makes her heart race. What had she been thinking? What was it about the boys' mean joke?

And it comes to her that it wasn't what they said, but what she thought they might say next. She'd imagined it rising in Pinkie's throat, forming wetly on his tongue. That's what she'd had to stop. That word Colin called her.

Cunt.

It's such a furious-sounding word, so low and guttural, like a grunt. She rolls it around her mouth like a salty pebble, saying it, harsh and fast, under her breath. It's a word you can rush through, over almost before it's begun. It starts to slip out of her now in moments of anger or pain. When one of the hens pecks her foot, when the axe jars her arm as she splits kindling. It reminds her of Colin, but each time she says it she feels a little stronger, as if the odd male power of the curse accrues to her with each utterance. When Pinkie jeers 'Jerry-lover!' in the queue for the pictures the next week, she leans close and calls him the name, and when she steps back, he's beet red under his shock of snowy hair, as though she's bloodied his face.

She had feared he might call her it, but she's struck first, the word like a fist.

She has no idea what it means, of course. What it actually means. Just its emotional meaning – fury, contempt. She has never heard anyone else use it, and not only, she thinks, because it's an English word, but perhaps also because it's a secret word, unspeakable. She's so used to the secrecy of Welsh, the cloak of it that the villagers draw around themselves at the pub, or in the high street if a stranger passes, that it thrills her a little to know a secret English word.

She thinks of the great dictionary in Mrs R's classroom. Is it still there? she wonders. But the way Mrs R handled it, carrying it into class at the start of a lesson like the tablets of the Ten Commandments, letting it topple with a slam on her desk to silence them, Esther guesses it must have been Mrs R's own volume. More likely it's in her house now, behind the counter of the post office, or perhaps in the parlour, where all the ladies in town kept their best things – stuffed songbirds under bell jars, burled mahogany mantel clocks, and the massive dictionary with its winking golden spine and tissue-paper pages. Esther imagines looking up the word, but would such a profanity be there?

She pictures a blank space on the page, a gap in the record. She has the idea, fixed from the schoolroom, that Mrs R knows all the words in the dictionary, but she can't imagine her knowing this one. Not that her old teacher hasn't been known to swear. 'Dash it all!' she would cry if the chalk broke, or sometimes, more softly, 'Dash it, girl,' if Esther disappointed her. It seemed at once so unladylike to curse, and yet the phrase had a kind of tough elegance, so much less crude than her father's 'blast's and 'bloody's. Looking up the word one night, when she had stayed behind to clean the board and Mrs R had been called to see the headmaster, Esther was pleased to see the meaning. To smash, to throw down. She pictured a teapot, for some reason, swept on to the slate flags of the floor, shards flying in all directions. She'd snapped the book closed on the rest of the definition before Mrs

R had bustled back into the room. Her teacher had dismissed her then, thanking her solemnly, and in this way Esther had known the headmaster, Dr Lock, had told her that Rhys was failing in another class. She only stayed behind in the hope of walking home with Mrs R, talking to her about some book she'd borrowed (something by the Brontës, say, whose works she devoured her last year in school, fascinated by the doings of the English gentry, though she knew Arthur would disown her if he knew). But on days when Rhys had got into trouble, Mrs R would send her on ahead, sit in the schoolroom for a while, and walk home alone. She looked so beaten down those evenings – a mother suddenly, no longer a teacher – Esther wanted to hear her swear, 'Dash the boy!'

Only months after leaving school, reading one night, she came across a passage of dialogue, a character cursing, the line printed only as '——!' and it dawned on her. *Of course!* What a dashed fool she'd been to miss it. Suddenly it seemed the most literary of swear words. Not a word at all, really, but the absence of words, words too awful to print, to speak.

Except now, she thinks, she knows some of those words, those awful English words.

And then, at the start of August, Esther misses something else. It must be the second time, she thinks when she works it back, the weeks, the months, and yet somehow she had ignored the first time, missed the missing, like a dash in her own life. The absence of blood.

I should have known.

She'd count herself cursedly unlucky – pregnant her first time! – if it didn't make her feel such a fool. She pictures herself: the pregnant girl sent to sit on the stool in the corner with the dunce's cap on, 'Spoke English' round her neck on a loop.

Her whole life living on a farm, her family's whole livelihood dependent on breeding and birthing, tupping in the autumn, lambing in the spring, and it's taken her weeks to realise she's pregnant. She's seen her father mix the raddle, the oily red pigment he daubs on the belly and legs of the rams every September, watched him take the count each night of ewes with red tails, smeared rumps, where the raddle has transferred. And like a ewe in heat, no better than a dumb beast, she's taken the tup at the first time of asking. A fool, she thinks hotly. She would laugh if it were anyone but herself.

And then too, finally, she feels as if she might really have been raped. All this time, thinking she's escaped Colin, thinking she's escaped with her life. Yet she'd been right to start with, when the word had sprung to her mind as he'd pressed her against the mildewed tiles of the pool. He had wounded her, she thinks, and not a small wound, the drops of blood in her drawers, but something deeper and stranger. *What a wound it is that stops you bleeding.* And in her heart there's a morbid fear that what he's given her is a lingering death, nine months long, that she won't survive childbirth, that she'll die and he'll have raped her after all.

She takes the heavy scissors out of her pocket at last and sets them back in her sewing basket, impaling a ball of wool. She'll be needing her knitting and sewing soon enough, she thinks. But in the meantime, there's nothing to be protected from any more.

She's subdued for days. Even the pictures, where she goes to escape, no longer feel like a refuge. Outside, the marquee's lights seem to wink at her, 'Now Showing, Now Showing'. Inside, she sits at the very front of the stalls, shrouded in the blue fog of cigarette smoke that settles beneath the stage, as far away from the courting couples in the back row as possible. But with the screen looming over her she finds herself dreading a glimpse of Colin in the newsreels, finds her eye drawn to a shock of curly black hair, a trim moustache, a certain rakish angle to a forage cap. This close she can feel the rumble of the Allied tanks rolling through French or Dutch or Belgian villages; she recoils from those girls on the screen throwing flowers and beaming, dancing in the streets.

Afterwards, she can barely recall the news when Arthur asks her. She has thought of writing to Colin, telling him, but she doesn't have an address for him, and even if she had, she can't imagine how to put it. *I've missed*, she tries, but all that comes is *I've missed . . . you.* And she recoils, first from the lie of that, and then even more from the truth within the lie, the truth that if she tells him, she'll be asking him to come for her, to put it right. So is it shame that's stopping her writing, she asks herself, or pride? Both, perhaps? Either way, she refuses to give him the satisfaction of an appeal. Better by far not to ask than to be refused.

Instead of going to the pictures, she takes to spending her free evenings, and then any time she can escape from her chores, in the trees above the camp, smoking to keep the midges off, staring at the men.

She wonders what will become of the Germans now. The war has gone on so long – her whole life, it feels to her sometimes – it's hard to imagine it ever ending, despite the victories. They'll be there for the rest of their lives, she thinks, studying the men, until they'll have lived here longer than they ever did in Germany.

She finds herself wishing it were Colin down there behind the wire, a prisoner himself. She thinks of him surrendering, hands raised, pictures him in solitary confinement, curled up in a dark cell. But even as she smiles grimly to herself, the very word 'confinement' turns on her. It's as if the language is coming to life, talking back to her in its slippery English tongue. For she's the one, she thinks suddenly, she's the one who'll be in her confinement soon enough. The word itself seems a cell to her, pressing in on all sides, inescapable. She watches the grey men trudging across the dusty parade ground, wonders what the wire feels like clutched in a fist. She wants to run down there, press her face, her breasts, her stomach to the fence, feel it pressing all over her, the metallic tang of it between her teeth. She'd bite down on it, just to stop screaming.

And then she wishes Colin not a prisoner at all, just dead, slaughtered by one of these very Germans if possible. Him, or him, or him.

She hasn't seen the gang of boys at the camp again – most likely bored by the prisoners at last – but one evening Jim returns alone. He's had some falling-out with the others (over her? she wonders, over what she said to Pinkie? but he won't talk about it). At first she thinks he's come looking for her, and she presses against the tree she's leaning on, but he only has eyes for the camp. By rights she should send him home, but there's something so plaintive about the way he kicks his scarred leather ball down the lane alongside the fence, then sits on it, bouncing slightly, staring in at the Germans' game, that she doesn't have the heart.

She holds her breath when one of the Germans drifts over to him – the one she talked to, she's sure – strains to hear what they say, but there's no shouting this time, no name-calling. The German just crouches behind the fence, pretending to be a goalkeeper, while Jim fires his ball over and over against it, making the wire ring. Jim's back the next night and the night after that, talking with the prisoner, about what she can't imagine. Once she sees Jim slip his small hand through the wire, and later, as the German walks back to his barracks, she sees him lighting a cigarette. It makes her want one, but looking into her pack – she's taken to buying her own now – she pauses, trying to remember how many there were the last time she had one. She has a vision of Jim going into her bag, stealing one, the very one the prisoner is smoking now, and she's instantly affronted, not at the prisoner – she'd not begrudge him – but at Jim. *She* wants to have given the German the smoke.

What on earth can they be talking about anyway?

The next night, she sees the German pull something from his tunic, shielding it from the guard towers. It glints in the dusk as he slips it through the fence into Jim's open hands.

She's waiting for him later, sitting on his bed in his room when he comes in, and she holds out her palm.

'Give me.'

She expects him to bluster, but he seems almost relieved to show it to someone. A thin green beer bottle – she recognises it from the pub; they sold a crate to the guards recently – and inside it, when she holds it to the light, a tiny ship, a fishing boat made of matchsticks, with a square scrap of grey cloth for a sail. Sailors, she recalls, submariners. The glass is still hot from the boy's hand.

He looks at her expectantly.

'How do we get it out?'

She's thinking of a grey shirt with a small square hole in it.

'How do we get it out?' Jim repeats, and now she sees why he's offered it up so eagerly, but she shakes her head. He takes it back, tries his fingers in the neck one by one, but even the longest won't quite reach the prow.

'You can't,' she says gently. 'Not without breaking it. That's the whole point.' But she can see it's lost on him. The prisoner has given him a toy he can't play with.

'Well how'd it get in there?' he asks, concentrating on his little finger, waggling behind the glass, like a worm on a hook.

She shrugs, stumped. 'Some trick.' And the boy nods heavily, as if he'd expect no more from a German.

'You'll get that stuck,' she warns, and he pulls his finger out quickly.

'What do you two talk about?' she asks.

Jim holds the bottle up, squints down its neck. 'He wants food, fags.' He tilts the glass to his lips as if to drink, then blows experimentally, and she sees the little sail flutter. 'And he keeps asking your name.'

'You didn't tell him!'

'Course not!'

She smooths her hands down the front of her skirt.

'Well, you're not to go back there. Ever! You hear me?'

He sets the mouth of the bottle to his eye, peers at her through the thick glass, as if through a telescope.

'Aye-aye, Cap'n.'

She nods, satisfied, but then she can't resist. 'What's *his* name, anyway?'

'Hans.'

'Hans,' she begins, and then Jim cracks up, '*Hans up!* Get it?' She recognises it as one of Harry's gags.

She drifts off that night wondering about him, the German, wondering what he misses most in his captivity. He'll miss that square of shirt come winter. She wonders where it's from. The small of his back? Under his arm? She leans in to study it. *I could patch that.* Suddenly a finger pokes through, crooks as if beckoning.

She looks for the bottle the next day when she's making Jim's bed, marvels at the workmanship. The rigging, which she'd taken for button thread at a glance, is too fine. Hair, she thinks. *His?* And there, at the prow, the curve of the anchor, a pared crescent of fingernail. There's even a figure, face pinched out of candle wax, in the little wheelhouse. When she looks down the neck – wrinkling her nose at a meaty reek of fat, the glue perhaps, lingering beneath the old-beer stink – she's amazed how much smaller the ship is when not magnified by the glass. In the miniature cabin, the tiny wheel rocks back and forth. It startles her somehow, the shrunken enclosed world, and she lowers the bottle, rests it in her lap. She wonders how the German made it, wishes she could ask him.

The following morning, when she's alone, she hard-boils a couple of eggs – all that won't be missed. Fresh eggs would be too risky, she's decided, too easily broken. She listens to them knocking in the pan, looking over her shoulder the whole time, then picks them up, still hot, and juggles them into her coat pockets for later. She thinks of them there, cooling, the whole time she's preparing lunch.

She tells herself she's just being magnanimous. The latest news from France is good. Jim needs more pins for his map. Cherbourg has fallen, Caen, the Allies have pushed twenty, thirty, fifty miles inland. Orléans is next, Paris in sight.

And then abruptly the news is bad. Mrs Roberts comes by the house, interrupting the three of them at lunch, red faced and flustered, a telegram gripped in her hand. *Who could be sending them a telegram?* For a clenched second, Esther thinks it's from Colin, or from one of his mates about him. That her wish has come true.

'I just left,' Mrs Roberts says, sinking on to the settle. 'Didn't even lock the door. There's terrible, I am. Left my post. But I couldn't think what else to do. You were so good, Arthur, when I lost Mervyn.' She looks from Arthur to Esther, and takes her hand. 'And you deserve to know too, love.' She holds out the telegram, and when she sees Esther hesitate, she flaps it impatiently.

'Go on!' Jim hisses.

She scans it silently – *I am directed to inform you, with regret . . . notification has been received . . .* – offers it quickly to Arthur, who bats it aside. 'What's it say?' he hisses, and she tells him softly, 'It's from the War Office. Casualty branch. Rhys is . . . missing.' She can't take her eyes off the word – missing – runs her finger over the ridges of the heavy black type where it's pressed into the onion skin. She thinks of her contempt for Rhys, her dull fury at him for failing to write, and she almost gags.

'There it is.' Mrs Roberts nods, for all the world as if Esther has just given the right answer in class. Arthur stares at his former neighbour for a long moment and then sits beside her, grasps her hands in his – 'Vivian' – and to Esther, stunned, it seems weirdly as though Rhys has got his old childhood wish, uniting them at last. 'I'd just finished knitting him a nice scarf,' Mrs Roberts begins, and somehow the thought of this breaks her. She sobs against Arthur while Esther and Jim look on. The scene reminds Esther vividly of her own mother's funeral.

'Missing?' Jim whispers to Esther. 'What's that mean?'

'Missing in action,' she tells him weakly, but she can see he doesn't understand the gravity. She suddenly can't bear his innocence, and she bends towards him, whispers, 'Presumed dead.'

'He can't be.' The boy recoils. 'He can't be, Mrs R. Not Rhys.'

They're all staring at him now, and he looks from one to the other.

'It's not true,' he says, and Arthur motions Esther to take Jim out, almost as if he doesn't want to parade a child in front of the bereaved woman.

'You don't think so?' Jim asks her outside, and Esther looks at him. They've been so distant these past few weeks. She wishes she could tell him something. In the hedge nearby a thrush is singing, the same two notes, over and over.

'He could be on a mission,' Jim says with desperate enthusiasm. 'Something top secret.' She shakes her head, more in wonder than denial, but she sees the hope drain from his face and something else take its place. 'Bastards,' he says. 'Those German bastards!'

And before she can reach out to stop him, he's gone, haring up the slope. She would go after him but Arthur's at the door, motioning her inside. 'She keeps asking after you. Come and see what you can do with her, eh? I've to go and see about locking up the post office.' He shakes his head. 'Says she won't have a moment's peace until she knows it's done.' Esther casts one more glance after Jim, yearns to outrun him, and then Arthur touches her arm. She looks at his hand on her sleeve, nods mutely, and goes in to Mrs Roberts.

'Oh, my dear,' the older woman calls, wiping her eyes. 'I'm sorry. I know this must be hard for you, too.' And hesitantly, Esther takes her hand. It's not the time to debate how much she felt for Rhys, certainly not to say that she's turned him down, and even as she thinks of it, thinks of him gone, she feels the tears coming, though whether for him or herself she doesn't know, and the doubt suddenly stills them. Her eyes prickle but the tears draw back. To where? she wonders, blinking.

'Second of August,' Mrs Roberts is saying shakily. 'That's when they say it happened, more than a week ago. I can't get it out of my head, what was I doing then? I can't remember for the life of me. Nothing, probably, nothing special at any rate. And all the days since then. Just living. It's really true what they say, isn't it? Ignorance is bliss.' She claps a hand tight to her mouth, as if to trap the words, and Esther wraps an arm around her, holds her, shyly at first and then more firmly as she shudders.

'You know,' Mrs Roberts tells her when she's calmer, 'I always thought you'd be the one to go places. Even after you left school, I told myself: When the war ends she'll do some things.' Her voice wavers. 'So I knew my boy doted on you, but I discouraged it, you see, warned him you were meant for better. There's a terrible mother, I am, but I had such hopes for you. I didn't want to see his heart broken.' She pinches her lips together. 'I thought we'd be reading *your* letters from London or someplace like that.' She fumbles for Esther's hand. 'But I'm awfully glad you're here now.'

Esther can only nod, over and over.

'There's still some hope,' she says at last, and after a watchful moment Mrs Roberts pats her hand and tells her, 'Of course there is.' And Esther thinks, *Neither of us believes it.* For his mother, she sees, the news is the confirmation of her worst fears, built up these months. She almost seems relieved, vindicated.

197

And for me? Esther wonders. It feels like a punishment, for doubting him, for thinking the greatest danger he faced was his mother's angry impatience for a letter. Yet even now there's a part of Esther that grates at the fool for getting himself killed. It's as if he's vanished into the dark gap between his two front teeth.

She sits with her former teacher for another hour and then walks her home via the pub, where she makes Jack open early and pour Mrs Roberts a brandy on the house. When she comes back, after seeing the woman into the care of her neighbours, she finds the pub sombre. People are trading memories of Rhys. The guards have started it, asking about the lost man, and she sees that he's claimed by both sets of drinkers, the soldiers and the locals, fostering a new rapport between them. The soldiers order their drinks from her so softly, almost demurely, that she knows they've already heard about her and Rhys.

'D'you remember the time . . .' the constable says, and people nod, even Esther, though she doesn't. She listens to her father describing Rhys as a strong back, a fine boy, and she looks in his face for a trace of a lie, but can't find one. 'Always good with the dogs,' Arthur is saying. 'Small wonder,' he used to add, 'with that space between his teeth he should have the loudest whistle in the county!' But tonight she waits in vain for the punchline. It reminds her of Rhys's father, how Arthur had never missed a chance to vex Mervyn Roberts, calling him all manner of names, belittling his job in the quarry – rockmen being less skilled than slate splitters and dressers like Arthur's father and grandfather – and envying it at the same time. Yet as soon as Mervyn was dead, Arthur had gone round to the house and set about helping his widow, and Esther never heard him speak another ill word about the dead man. It's a matter of honour for him, she thinks, but it requires him to forget Rhys, the real Rhys, the Rhys who once tossed a cigarette in a haystack, the Rhys who liked to sleep in the sun, the dogs curled against him. *Rhodri Rhys Roberts,* the telegram named him, and for a second she'd thought it meant someone else. She'd never known him as anything other than Rhys. Now it's as if he's been rechristened in death, as if Arthur and the rest have created a Rhys they can mourn.

And what about me? She tries to feel something, but she finds where her grief should be a kind of impatience that Rhys's troubles should intrude when she's in the midst of her own, and a jealousy, too, that in death – if he is dead – he's been scrubbed clean, even by the constable he tormented as a boy. *They want to believe he's dead,* she thinks. *They like him better this way.* That, and the fact that he's the first village boy lost. They're a proper part of the war at last, just as they'd hoped when the camp was being built. They can hold their heads higher and stiffer on market days now that there's a name to add to the plaque in the chapel listing the losses of 1914–1918. At the end of the evening, Jack gives the bell a strike, and in the silence afterwards, rather than announcing last orders, he asks them to join him in a toast, 'For a local hero.' Even the English drink.

She walks home, hands in pockets, gripping the cold eggs waiting there.

That night she sits up with Arthur, mending clothes and listening to the radio. When they came in and went to check on Jim, she found him awake, red eyed, his hands clutching the white sheet, filthy, his nails bloody. She fetched a basin and washcloth and sponged them, and he told her he'd been prying stones out of the lane to throw at the Germans. 'They just watched me,' he said. 'Stepped back from the fence where I couldn't hit them.' She thought of the one she'd planned to throw the eggs to, pictured his face. Jim had gone on hurling stones, and mud, and sticks, whatever he could lay his hands on, cursing in earnest this time, until they'd gone indoors. 'But I never cried,' he told her fiercely. Her eyes drifted to the map on the wall, trying to see if the pin for Rhys was still there.

When she comes out, Arthur sets a cup of tea beside her, and when Jim's sobs start, he puts a hand on hers, turns the radio on low. Harry and Mary are doing one of their 'Lil and Bill' numbers.

BILL: I just met an old soldier, told me he'd not had any since 1930.
LIL: Poor dear!
BILL: Oh, I don't know. It's only twenty-one hundred hours now.

Esther stares at her lap, blushing, but it's not clear Arthur has even got the joke. When she looks up, he's staring at her, as if waiting for something, and she thinks how dry her eyes are.

'I'm very sorry,' he tells her awkwardly, and she nods.

'For you, I mean, love. I know you were friends, like.'

'He's just missing,' she tries, not out of any real hope, but to deflect his sympathy, and when she sees the look of pity cross Arthur's face anyway, she reminds him sharply, 'You thought he was a fool to go,' and she can see he's stung.

'Perhaps,' he says after a pause, 'you were a bigger one to let him go.'

'What's that supposed to mean?'

He shrugs. 'Maybe you could have stopped him, is all.'

She picks up her sewing basket and leaves him then, but lies in her bed, eyes wide, the tears tumbling from them at last.

In the days that follow, the queue at the post office, whenever Esther passes it, seems to stretch out the door. Everyone wants to admire how well Mrs R's holding up, assure her that Rhys will turn up. 'Like a bad penny,' the postmistress braves. Esther keeps her company for the first day or two, then withdraws, queasily embarrassed to be included – 'you too, dear' – in the sympathy.

At first Mrs R nods at the hopes expressed, but increasingly she hitches her shoulders, shakes her head brusquely. Before long she's stooped from shrugging, but still she puts up with the well-wishers, murmuring 'No, no word, thank you' as often as she licks stamps and with the same sour face. And then, one sweltering afternoon in the last week of August, the little PO packed with bodies, she finally loses patience with their pity. 'I'm a mother, not a fool,' she snaps at yet another hushed assurance, and Esther, waiting in line, winces almost as much as the unfortunate customer. In her mind's eye, she pictures Mrs R furiously smudging the heel of her tiny fist across the board, changing 'console' to 'condole' as if it were a stupid spelling error.

The next morning Rhys's mother takes to wearing black.

Fifteen

Esther can't bring herself to return to the camp after the news about Rhys. The boys are back, she hears in the pub, joined by some of the local men, even a few women, hurling abuse or simply booing the prisoners. Jim, she guesses, is there with the rest, shouting himself hoarse. She found him jabbing a stick into the ship in a bottle the day after the telegram and snatched it away from him. But he'd already knocked the mast askew with his poking, smashed the little wheelhouse. 'What are you doing?' she'd cried, straining for calm, and he'd told her defiantly, 'Getting it out!'

'Does it make you feel any better?' she asks one night when he returns from the camp, and he tells her, 'Yes!'

'You could come,' he adds more softly, but she shakes her head.

Arthur is right, she realises. She could have stopped Rhys from going to war. And that's why she can't go back to the camp with Jim. It's hard to escape the feeling that she, more than any of these Germans, is to blame for his loss. If only she'd accepted him, he'd be alive, and Colin would never have been more to her than another customer. And it seems to her that if she's to blame for Rhys's loss, she's just as culpable for her own woes.

Without the camp to escape to, and shy of the village, where she's still the object of a cloying sympathy, the house begins to feel very small, as if the walls are closing on her. Or as if she's growing, she thinks in a panic. Each morning she tries to gauge the change in herself in the small hand mirror she inherited from her mother, sucking her stomach in and studying herself in its bright oval. At lunch and supper she picks at her food, but stuffs herself hungrily with bread when the others are out, sometimes not even waiting for it to rise fully, but burning her fingers on the still sticky dough. In one week, she eats half the pickled eggs in the jar behind the bar, until she catches Jack staring at her, shaking his head: 'Never could stand the things meself.'

At least Arthur doesn't seem to notice anything, but he's been distracted of late by the prospect of work at the quarry. Old Twm Tudur is retiring – lumbago finally getting the best of him – so there's an opening for a new dangerman and Arthur covets the job, sees it as his great chance, a foot back in the quarry. He's already been down there, learning the ropes, nagging the old fellow to put in a word for him. 'Twm got his start as a young rubbler on my father's bargain, so he owes us that much.'

It isn't much of a job, in Esther's opinion, tramping through the dark galleries with a little torch, but at first she encourages him. Anything to keep him out of the house, anything to draw his attention off her.

'It's a serious business,' Arthur assures her proudly after he gets it. 'Checking the shafts for flooding, gas, signs of cave-in.' When the men went on strike all those years ago, Tudur had stayed on and the strikers hadn't objected. He was keeping the place safe for when they went back, as they saw it. Arthur's father, who never saw a scab without crossing the street, would always give Twm the time of day.

It's only when Arthur brags to her about going up the long, lashed-together ladders, forty or fifty feet into the moist blackness at the roof of the caverns to dislodge the loose slates that might in the past have fallen on the men below, or now on the crates of artworks, that she starts to have second thoughts. He tells her of swaying through the chilled dark, touching the black sky of the roof, chipping slates out as if they were stars. It's the moisture leaching down through the mountain that erodes the caverns. She can smell it on his clothes after his stints in the quarry, the dankness of rain that fell on the hillside above, where their own sheep now graze, a thousand years earlier.

She's always known Arthur wanted to get back underground, to reclaim his father's place. He's never put chisel to slate, and yet on black days when he's lost lambs, or when the debts are due, he sees Cilgwyn the way his father did, as a form of exile. 'Slate's in the blood,' her grandfather used to say, and Arthur's always maintained that the farm killed the old quarryman, ever since he found him slumped in the pasture, surrounded by cropping sheep. 'In the lungs, more like,' her mother had suggested once; the only time Esther ever saw her father raise a hand to her.

Esther's mother had always been impatient with his dreams of the quarry. 'King Arthur,' she'd scoffed. 'You and your blooming birthright!' Perhaps she took it personally when he grumbled, 'Slave to sheep, I am. A flock of females, at that.' As a child Esther had once asked if the quarry was her birthright too, but her father had just laughed. *Quarry's no place for girls,* he'd said, and something about the way he'd looked at her had made her burst into tears. *You wouldn't want it,* her mother told her, drying her eyes with the frayed hem of her apron. *Dark, dripping place.* But since her mother's death, Esther realises now, Arthur has been talking about getting back to the quarry more and more. Without anyone to mock him, it's stopped being a joke.

Rhys's loss has reminded her of how precarious the lives we take for granted are, and she's suddenly terrified of losing her father. He works nights in the quarry, reasoning, 'It don't make no difference, day or night down there,' and claiming that this way he can still put in his time with the flock, but she can't sleep for worry. She's more solicitous towards him than she's been in months – makes his favourite, milk jelly, for Sunday breakfast – though she knows that somehow this care is calculated, a hoard of love she's storing up in the hope she might draw on it later, if he finds out about the baby. Not that her concern seems to soften him any. If he's not expressing impatience with it, she suspects he enjoys it, the look of fear on her face when he tells his stories. And yet she knows she's not the only one who's afraid. He stops in the pub every night before he goes down the quarry, and though she begs Jack not to serve him, please, he's taken to enjoying a shot with his beer. Arthur says it helps him relax, find his balance on the ladders. That if he's too tense, he's more likely to take a spill than otherwise. 'Nothing to fear,' he tells her expansively. 'Slate's in my blood too.' Dutch courage, she thinks it, though she could never tell him that. Instead, she reminds him that all he's protecting are some crates of artworks from the National Gallery. He's said it himself: National bloody Gallery? How many Welshmen in there? And when even that fails to move him, she tries to assure him they don't really need the few shillings he makes. But that's a mistake. He bridles at the mention of money. 'All I mean is, the war will be over soon,' she says. 'Paris liberated and all. Things'll get better.'

'But that's just it,' he tells her. They're in the kitchen late one warm August afternoon. 'You mark my word, before we know it, the quarries will be producing again, and there'll be proper work for Welshmen once more. You didn't think I was going to go running up and down those ladders like a monkey for the rest of my days. That's just a start.' She's relieved, yet he must see some scepticism in her face because he presses on. 'It's the war, isn't it? Someone's got to put new roofs on all those houses smashed in the Blitz. Hundreds of thousands of homes, in England and France, now Germany. Think of it! It'll be a heyday for them 'as got a foot in the door. My father always said a slate roof will last a hundred years, but that was the very problem. They put a roof on the world from these mountains and then the demand dried up. Until now. It'll be over soon, and when the rebuilding begins they'll need Welsh slate again. Why, the nation will rise right along with those roofs!'

He gives a little nod, as though he's won some argument, but he's mistaken her look: she isn't sceptical, not any longer, just appalled by his logic. Thinking of Eric, of Jim. Too late, he senses her dismay. 'It's an ill wind,' he offers, shrugging on his mac, but when he sees her hardening, he withdraws even that hint of concession. 'And all thanks to the war. To bloody Hitler and his cronies.' He pauses, framed in the door, and all at once she sees his nationalism for what it is, selfishness, and more than that, a kind of licensed misanthropy.

'And the farm?' she wants to know. 'The flock?' What'll become of them if he's working full time in the quarry? He's already begun to neglect his duties, lying in while she milks the cow in the morning, catnapping in the late afternoon stillness of the barn.

'Them?' He squints at the distant white bodies on the hillside. 'Know what they look like to me sometimes? Maggots.'

She shudders as she watches him stride out, his long shadow stretching up the hill.

She remembers how he's always talked about the *cynefin*, with a kind of solemnity, which she recognises now as resentment. Preserving the flock, preserving the *cynefin* passed down through the ages, the weight of all that time, is more responsibility than he wants. They're a burden to him, the flock, the land. Maybe even her.

Isn't this *my* birthright, she wants to cry, watching him leave. But the word sticks in her throat.

Sixteen

K arsten faces the blank page again, once more unsure what to write to his mother. No word from her since that first letter, but he's decided to swallow his pride. And yet, what to write? The problem, he thinks, is nothing ever happens in the camp. There is simply nothing to report. He squints at the white page fluttering in his hand, its blankness dazzling in the late August sun, the only marks on it the translucent smudges of sweat left by his thumbs.

The heat has lasted all week.

He sets the paper aside, lies back, propped on his elbows, staring up beyond the trees to the distant green hillside, imagining his body pillowed by that lush meadow grass. He still suffers from insomnia, the sleeplessness itself a kind of nightly prison, his bunk a narrow cell. His eyes, in the clouded mirror of the latrine, are shadowed by bruised circles of fatigue. Karsten glances around at the other men, stretched out on the coarse scrub of the parade ground. For just a second, it seems to him as if they could all be back in a public park in Munich or Berlin, picnicking on the grass, except that as far as he can see in each direction, it's only men. They're laid out like so many wounded, casualties of the battle of boredom, the 'Sitzkrieg', as Schiller has dubbed the grinding dullness of camp life, each day as unvarying as the rows of identical barracks behind them.

It's been less than three months, Karsten thinks – and he has to calculate the dates a second time in his mind before he can quite believe it – but already time hangs heavier on them than a field pack.

The other men, he knows, have been fitfully energised by the new weekly film show that the commandant has instituted at their pleading. They've had two shows so far, a frothy aquatic musical and an ancient horror movie. They watched the former nonsense with rapt awe, so long had it been since most of them had seen a woman. Esther Williams was all they could talk about for days – Karsten even found himself picturing his Welsh girl in a sleek swimsuit – until the 150-percenters began to sneer, 'What kind of a name do you think *Esther* is, anyway?' *Frankenstein,* shown the next week, drew a still larger audience, probably because the story was easy to follow without knowing the language, though also, Karsten suspected darkly, because it allowed the men to be afraid, gave them licence to experience those fears they could never talk about to each other. It's escapism, he knows, rather than escape, but he's gone along with all the rest, if only to watch the newsreels.

They're the price of the films, of course. Propaganda, the camp leaders have warned, encouraging the men to talk back to them, or over them, to throw Heil Hitlers up on the screen, or shadow puppets – yapping dogs, snapping crocodiles. The men greet the Pathé cockerel with sounds of frenzied clucking and shotgun blasts, like a crowd of schoolboys. When Churchill appears, or the long-faced King, they boo; when it's de Gaulle, they hum the cancan. As if the war were some vaudeville show, Karsten thinks. He doesn't believe the newsreels any more than the rest do, but they're a forceful reminder that he's only an audience for the war now, no longer an actor in it.

He picks up his letter again, touches the pencil point to his tongue. It's a whole month since he's last written. Not that the other men are any better – after the initial flurry of letter writing, they've all fallen off. Still, he feels dogged about it.

He might write to her about the boy, he supposes.

Karsten hadn't expected to see him again after the little planes had proved such a failure, but he'd been back within the week, hanging around the wire. So lonely, Karsten thought, even we're company. Poor company at that. At least the boy had told him his name – Jim – if not the girl's. Even as he'd slipped him the ship in a bottle, which he hoped might make the boy feel a little closer to his own father, he'd feared it wasn't much of an offering. He'd watched Jim carry the bottle away with a sinking sensation, and when he didn't return for the next couple of days, he presumed the worst – smashed to bits.

But then there he'd been, running to the wire, right up against it, shaking it so hard it rang, beads of rain flying from it. And he'd been shouting, bawling. Karsten had started forward before he'd made it out. 'Murderers. Filthy bastard murderers!' He paused then. It was clear this time the curses were in earnest. *His father,* Karsten thought. But he went on nevertheless, and the boy actually backed away from him, though the wire stood between them, as if Karsten might somehow strike him dead anyway.

'What is it?' Karsten asked, and the boy told him, spitting it out, so breathlessly Karsten could barely follow.

'And you killed him,' Jim cried. 'You lot.'

And then he'd started flinging stones, mud, and Karsten had been driven back out of range, shamed as much as anything by his initial relief that it wasn't the boy's father, at least. But then it came to him, watching the boy's fury, that perhaps one death was a harbinger of the other.

Karsten had felt so terrible he tried to talk about it to Schiller in the mess the next morning.

'You didn't kill him,' the other told him between mouthfuls of porridge. 'Can't be guilty for something you didn't do.'

Karsten nodded, though somehow the very awfulness of it was that he felt guilty for something he hadn't done. 'Not guilt, then,' he tried. 'Pity perhaps? Sorrow?'

'For the enemy?'

'For them. For us. I don't know! Sometimes it feels like they're all linked somehow, the losses, like a chain, one death coupled to the next, and the next, whichever side they're on.'

Schiller sipped his coffee, made a face. 'I often think how when Willi went down, he spilled his coffee. It must have been on the ledge below the firing slit, until I felt it splash me, you know, the warmth soaking my sleeve. The tin cup bounced across the floor. You don't recall?'

'No.'

Schiller nodded. 'Because it wasn't coffee, of course. There was no cup. I only imagined it.' He stared into the oily blackness of his mug, gave a little shudder. 'I don't want to be a link in a chain.' He leaned forward, lowered his voice. 'That's why we surrendered, isn't it?'

Jim had been back that night, joined by the rest of the boys, one of the gang again, standing right next to the albino, the crowd of them hurling abuse, mud balls, fallen branches. The men had hung back, weathered the storm until the guards had finally ordered the lads off.

Jim had kept coming, though, night after night, with the others and eventually alone again, growing quieter, glowering rather than raging, but still bright with hatred. It had been a week before Karsten could approach close enough to call out what he'd been thinking for days: 'But you said he was missing. You don't know he's dead.' The boy blinked. 'He could be a prisoner like us. My own mother thought I was dead when she didn't hear. My own mother.'

Jim's face had stiffened, grown masklike. He'd said nothing, but he left earlier than usual, and the next afternoon he'd been back at the wire, waiting.

When Karsten got close this time, he saw Jim had a black eye, a real shiner.

'Who did that to you?'

'Some lads,' Jim said sullenly. 'At school.'

'But why?'

'Because.'

'Because of what?'

'Because I told them about Rhys, about him maybe being a prisoner.' He looked down at his feet, twisting in the dirt of the lane, and then up at Karsten. 'What you said.'

'And they didn't believe you?'

'No, they did. They believed it.' He glared at Karsten. 'I didn't say *you'd* told me.'

'But why did they hit you?'

And Jim said fiercely, '*I* started it. "A prisoner?" they said. "Doesn't that mean he surrendered?" They said being captured meant he was a coward. So I fought them.' He raised his small bruised fists, and for a second, before waving them aside, Karsten felt a thrill of pride in the boy.

'And they gave you that?'

'You should see them.'

Karsten put a hand on the wire. 'You know, I only said your friend *might* be a prisoner.'

'But it's the only explanation,' the boy said. 'The only hope.'

The way he said it – like a general – Karsten knew he believed it. Maybe there had been moments of doubt. Maybe others had tried to change his mind. But fighting for it, being beaten for it, had convinced him somehow, proved it.

On the other side of the wire, the boy was looking around, past Karsten, to the men on the football field, the barracks behind.

'What's it like being a prisoner?'

'Dull!'

'What do you do?'

'As you see. Play sports, write letters, walk.' Karsten shrugged.

'Aren't you planning an escape?'

He laughed. 'Escape? I don't think so. Where would we go? Who would help us?' But the boy, he saw, wasn't laughing. If anything he seemed disappointed, and it moved Karsten to add, 'Besides, what makes you think I'd tell you about it?'

'So you *do* think about escaping?'

'Are you trying to trick me?'

'*Tell me!*'

Karsten leaned down and whispered, 'All the time.'

He wasn't sure what to expect. Perhaps that the boy would be frightened, but instead he beamed. They were silent for a minute, not looking at each other.

'Are you,' Jim asked shyly, 'a coward?'

Karsten hunched his shoulders, as if for a blow that had already fallen.

'What?'

'You heard.'

He was serious, Karsten saw, the answer deeply important to him. For just a moment, he wanted to cry yes! and have done with it. For just a moment, he could feel the cool relief of admitting it, even to this child. He was almost certain the boy would rather have his friend alive and a coward than brave and dead. All he had to do was say it. Yet something inside him recoiled. Some pride, some recollection of those dreadful steps down the passage out of the bunker. He recalled Schiller, of all people, back in training when he was still their sergeant, saying once that the thing cowards were most afraid of was being found out: 'Which makes them act like fucking heroes.'

The boy was still waiting, an almost pleading look on his face, and finally Karsten told him, 'I hope not.'

Jim nodded.

'I'm glad.'

And Karsten felt a lightening inside himself, though he knew the sentiment was more for the other man, the boy's friend. 'Cowards don't get taken prisoner, do they?' he added. 'It stands to reason. A real coward just runs away.' And for a second he actually believed it.

Of course, he can't write any of this to his mother, he thinks, glumly. Funny how he could say such things to a boy, a stranger, the enemy, and not to his own mother. She's as much as told him she doesn't want the truth, but having not told it to her, he doesn't know what else to write. One thing you could say for your enemy: there was no danger of betraying him. The paper in his hands is wilting in the heat, still blank, but looking as if it could hardly support words any longer.

Behind him some fellows have started a football game; others to bet on it. In short, it's desultory business as usual. He's asked to play, but shakes his head. Twice the ball bounces through the crowd where he's sitting. To his right, a group of men talk about the upcoming film. They've been promised *The Invisible Man* this week, and anticipation is high after seeing a clip of it in the coming attractions – that bewitching image of a man, head swathed in bandages, slowly unwinding the white gauze, gloved hands passing around and around his head to reveal nothing, no hair, no features, just those glasses hanging in space above a bandaged jawline.

What an image for prisoners, Karsten thinks. What they wouldn't give to be invisible, to just walk out of the gates.

The fellows beside him are speculating about whether such a thing is possible, and he can't help eavesdropping. The 150-percenters have put about rumours – secret weapons, armies in reserve – to keep their spirits up. Were such things so much more unlikely than the astounding flying bombs raining down on London? What if the Führer's scientists had discovered how to make a man disappear? someone asks. Mightn't there be secret armies of invisible men waiting in special camps to be unleashed, hundreds, thousands of men made to disappear by the science of the fatherland?

Childish hopes, Karsten thinks, turning away, though he wishes he could share them. Those pictures of the bandaged man only made him wonder what kind of terrible wound the fellow had suffered. What kind of hideous disfigurement could only be healed by making its victim invisible? It makes him think of the flame-thrower casualties, the bandaged wounded they'd seen carried past them on the beach at Normandy. That could have been him, or Schiller or Heino, if he hadn't surrendered. He's wondered what lay beneath those dressings – melted, scorched flesh – but he's never imagined emptiness, nothingness. It's an odd kind of healing, he thinks, that makes both wound and man vanish.

The ball bounces into their midst again and Karsten sets the letter aside. He folds the paper into his pocket, relieved, and goes after the ball. But when he turns to kick it back to the players, he sees they're looking the other way, towards the guardhouse, where a crowd is forming. Somewhere he hears a radio playing, a tune he recognises. Slowly it comes to him: *La Marseillaise*. It was banned in France, but more than once, on patrol, they'd heard it faintly in the village, clattering through the streets after its fugitive strains, trying to determine which house it was coming from, never finding its source.

Still holding the ball, he starts to follow the other men, hurrying towards the guardhouse, the radio playing inside it. *Something has happened*, he thinks, his heart racing. But before he gets there, the news spreads towards him, called from men on the fringe of the crowd. Paris has fallen, and as he hears it, he slows to a walk, a stop. Paris has fallen. He pats the pocket of his tunic, feels the paper there, crinkling. At last, he thinks, news. Something to write to his mother. But then, by the time it reaches her, she'll already know, of course.

*   *   *

It's just more propaganda, the camp leaders insist the next morning. Paris? Impossible! But if it is a lie, a fiction, the men see that their guards believe it. The Tommies, who themselves have seemed stunned by the drudgery of camp life, are cheerful for a few days, giddy even, suddenly generous with their cigarettes and chocolate. The men accept them hesitantly, as if they might be tainted, but eat and smoke them anyway, scowling.

Karsten can barely believe the news himself. All his dreams of escape have been of France, of getting to France, and now it's not enough. He tries to imagine the fall of Paris, but all he can think of are the images of German forces taking the white city. He thinks of his mother, her words as she watched the newsreels of the conquest in '40. *The end of the war.* They thought they'd won. So now what does it mean? He remembers the Arc de Triomphe, standing beneath it, the marble bright but cool, almost chilly on a warm spring day. *Our triumph. Their triumph.* As if the stone itself were fickle. When he pictures the arch, only the direction of the marching men is different, as if the newsreels he remembers have been run backwards through the projector. He hopes it'll be as easy to reverse again.

And then there it is, at the end of the week, on the Pathé News. The raucous, cheering crowds in the familiar, flickering streets. Smiling, waving Tommies astride their tanks, and the girls throwing garlands, kisses. He feels a pang of jealousy, but what haunts him afterwards, what he sees most vividly in his memory, are those other images, not of celebration but revenge, the pictures of the French women shorn in the streets. The women who slept with Germans. *Les collaborateurs horizontales.* He thinks of Françoise, of the dinner he pleaded with her to join him for. The meal, he hoped, would make their relationship normal, like a courtship. Proper. And for the first time he sees that she had taken pity on him when she agreed. Pity on him, the conqueror, the occupier! He'd insisted on the finest food, the best wine. Called for music, left a generous tip.

'I'm in love with you,' he'd told her, and she'd nodded perfunctorily, not even looking up from her dinner.

'Do you think you could ever love me?' he'd asked.

She'd chewed and swallowed. *'Jamais!'*

'But why?'

She'd searched for the words. 'We are enemies, *hein*? Anything other' – she rubbed her finger and thumb together – 'would be surrender.'

He cringes at the thought, but makes himself imagine her, the hair tumbling around her ears, the locks bouncing off her narrow shoulders, wafting to the floor like feathers. He hears the women have been stripped in the streets, but it's this nakedness, the nakedness of her head, a nakedness he never imagined, that appals him. To be *seen* so! 'Forgive me, but she's just a French whore,' Schiller tells him. 'She's had worse done to her.' But the shame of it seems unbearable, intolerable to Karsten. He can't imagine how she'll possibly survive it. It makes him think of basic training, the way they'd all been shorn that first day, their heads looking so shrunken, so white, as if the skulls beneath them had been revealed already in all their thin fragility.

And he'd been worried about her in the arms of a Tommy! Such selfishness. He hopes now that she has a Tommy, a big, loving one, that she clings to him, drapes her tresses around him, sweeps them across his chest in the night. Someone who can save her hair.

Karsten had once begged her for a lock of it. They'd been in the corner of a bar, and she'd reached a hand beneath her skirt and pulled out a single pale loop, held it glistening before him, laughing at his stricken face.

It was the only thing she ever gave him for free.

In the night, when he can sleep, he dreams the smell of Françoise's hair. It's there, faintly, though he can't quite inhale it, can't quite capture it. He dreams of holding her, aches to

218

protect her, cradling her head, feeling its hard ridges instead of curls, the scabs from the scissors, the raw, torn places. Her crown is hard under his chin.

He lies there then, rigid, feeling his erection subsiding in tiny staggering flinches.

Just a French whore, he tells himself. But that's exactly what terrifies him. He can't even protect her. The thought of a single hair on her head being harmed shakes him.

And then he finds it's not Françoise he's thinking of, but his mother. He's never felt more imprisoned.

The boys, who've been gone for a couple of weeks, appear again in the wake of the news from France, inspired no doubt by the newsreels. Karsten studies them with a kind of dull fury, Jim among the rest, but does his best to ignore them. He feels like a fool for trying to befriend the boy.

They're not interested in him anyway. Since the fall of Paris, the camp leaders, the NCOs, have been trying to set an example, polishing their boots and buckles, brushing their uniforms, and resuming drill each evening, bullying as many of the others into joining as they can. It's this spectacle the boys are transfixed by, watching the massed ranks file by on the parade ground, and then seeming to join, forming a column of their own that marches up and down the lane as if the fence were a mirror, in emulation, it seems at first, and then gradually in shambolic parody, bumping into each other, kicking each other up the backside. When the men give their Heil Hitler, the boys all offer another salute, putting a finger to their upper lips, a ragged line of dirty-kneed Führers.

It's too much for the camp leaders. They've put up with the boys thus far, considered their presence beneath notice. But now they've gone too far. It's a criminal offence in the fatherland, after all, to make fun of the Führer. They go to the major, demand that something be done.

The next evening when the boys appear, goose-stepping, the searchlights swing down on them like huge white clubs. They stand frozen as if stunned by the blow, almost two dozen of them, like actors stricken with stage fright. Karsten sees Jim's white face among the rest. And then there's the scrape of boots on the lane, and a party of guards appears, double-timing it towards them. The boys bolt like rabbits into the trees, the men behind the fence jeering their flight. The guards press after them, but they're slowed by the heavy undergrowth, the low branches snatching at their caps. Karsten sees one man get caught by his epaulette, as if run through at the shoulder. By the time they emerge from the trees, the boys are far ahead up the slope. The guards watch them go, hands on hips, while from the camp below there's a smattering of applause.

And yet the next night, too, the boys are back, mocking the prisoners, but now also the guards, waving up at the searchlights. The Tommies give chase again only to be outpaced once more, the boys careening away, but only until they know they're out of reach, and then they slow, as if taunting the guards to come on. A couple of boys use the flock as a shield, and the guards seem reluctant to push through the sheep. 'They don't bite,' someone cries from the camp, but as the shout goes up, a guard is bowled over by one of the startled beasts, and there's a burst of laughter from the prisoners. Now, Karsten notes, their jeers are for the guards, as they trudge downhill, making their clumsy, cursing way through the trees, mopping their brows.

The following day brings a change of tactics, the guards going out into the lane in the late afternoon, an hour or so before the boys usually appear. They hurry into the trees and take cover to left and right. There's a murmur among the prisoners; nods and smiles are exchanged. After a long, dull day the air is heavy with anticipation. When the boys appear at dusk, the guards in the towers ignore them ostentatiously – one even spreads a newspaper over the wooden railing before him.

The boys straggle out of the trees and into the lane, calling abuse, coming closer and closer to the wire. Jim, among others, Karsten sees, has blackened his face with mud or shoe polish – like commandos, he supposes, though the effect is to make the boys seem more like urchins. He pushes himself towards the front of the crowd pressed against the wire, but when Jim sees him, he moves down the line, and after a moment Karsten doesn't bother pursuing him. When the searchlights play down the lane, the boys don't flinch, their shadows wheeling around them. A tiny lad plays a game of chasing the light, running along in it as it moves, until he stops, panting, not more than a yard from the fence, close enough that Karsten can see his little chest heaving.

The boy's cheeks are glowing red, the fine damp hair plastered to his brow, but it's the look of exhilaration on his face, of joy, as if he's forgotten where he is, who they are, that Karsten can't take his eyes off. He crouches down. The youngster can't be more than six or seven, and for a moment he actually beams at Karsten. It's just a game to him. And suddenly Karsten is leaning close to the fence. 'Run,' he breathes, but still the boy smiles. 'Run!' Karsten says more loudly. 'It's a trap.' The boy frowns, as if puzzled that he can understand Karsten, and then his eyes widen.

There's a shout from the trees, and the guards rise out of the underbrush. For just a second, the boys are stock-still, and then Karsten is bellowing at them, 'Run! Run!' Jim appears beside the little boy, grabs his hand and yanks him away, though not before leaning close to the wire to whisper something. 'What?' Karsten calls after him, but by then his shout has been picked up by the other men – though whether in warning or in derision, Karsten can't be sure – and the boys are off, pumping madly, arms and legs flailing, racing for the gap in the trees where they came from as the guards close in from either side, cutting off their escape. Half of them make it, surging uphill; the rest – *is that Jim among them?* – turn and scatter.

'No!' Karsten calls, pointing. 'The lane, the lane. They won't be coming up the lane.' He clings to the fence, pointing, scales the first few rungs of wire to get a better view, watches the children scatter, the guards chase after them, the searchlights weaving. And Karsten finds himself climbing higher and higher to watch them go.

Seventeen

R otheram is racing the sunset, the old staff car careening
through the Welsh countryside as if he's the one escaping,
not hurrying to investigate an escape. Perhaps that isn't so far
from the truth, though, he reckons.

He's working his way north-west, following the Wye into the
hills of mid-Wales. Twisting and turning with the road, he's
caught flashes of the river through the trees, and once the distant
roar of falls, but as he's climbed higher towards its source, it's
dwindled to a coppery stream glimpsed only dimly under stone
bridges.

He'd been making good time until, barrelling round one tight
bend, he'd almost ploughed into a flock of sheep filling the road.
For a second he thought he'd driven into the river itself, the
rippling white backs flooding the narrow lane like water rushing
over rapids. He'd stamped on the brakes, fishtailed to a halt,
tearing a spray of grit from the verge. In the abrupt silence of the
stalled car, he heard it patter through the grass, watched it skip
towards the advancing sheep eyeing him blankly. He'd leaned on
the horn then, but they just bleated back at him, and he'd had to
sit for long minutes while they broke around him, their flanks
brushing the car, rocking it gently. He watched them go in his
mirror, until the last bobbing back rounded the bend, then
belatedly roared onwards.

He grits his teeth now as he jounces over a pothole, and the broken-down suspension of the Humber jars his bandaged ribs. Beside him on the passenger seat, the silver film canisters jingle-jangle like a giant's loose change.

He'd come down to breakfast late that morning, surprised that he'd finally been able to sleep after his call to Hawkins and the vigil at Hess's door in the small hours.

He found Lieutenant Mills and one of the corporals – not the one he'd woken the night before – lounging at a long wooden table in the kitchen, washing down charred toast with cups of tea from the largest china teapot he'd ever seen. The doctor, his mouth full, pointed to it, and Rotheram nodded.

'There you are,' Mills said, swallowing and setting a cup before him. 'So what's your plan for today?'

'I'm leaving,' Rotheram said simply. 'Appears I was wasting my time. Perhaps everyone's. New orders should come through this afternoon.'

Mills nodded for what seemed a long time and finally nudged the toast rack.

'Go on,' he said when Rotheram hesitated. 'The butter's local, and we've also got this.' He slid a crystal jar across the table. 'Honey. Special rations on account of our guest. Not that he eats half of it – afraid of poisoning!'

Rotheram lifted the lid, dipped his knife and studied the honey before he spread it thickly on his toast and took a bite. The rich sweetness was incredible. He wondered that he could have forgotten the taste. How long had it been since he'd had honey? 'Good, eh?' Mills said, and Rotheram nodded as he chewed.

'No hard feelings about last night?'

Rotheram took a mouthful of tea, shook his head. 'It's just that I'm not Jewish,' he said.

'Course not, old chap.'

Rotheram detected a hint of the bedside manner in the way Mills said it, but the mere thought of explaining his history to the lieutenant was exhausting.

Mills was silent for a moment, then brightened. 'If you're waiting for orders this afternoon, your morning's free, yes?'

Rotheram looked up slowly.

'Why not come along with us, then?' He gestured to the corporal. 'We're taking Hess for a Sunday drive. He likes a little fresh air every so often.'

'I don't need another crack at him, you understand.'

'I know,' Mills said, grimacing slightly. 'It's not just for you. The thing is, he asked if you'd come.' He laughed awkwardly. 'Seems he's bored with our company.'

And so, thirty minutes later, Rotheram found himself in the front seat of an open-top staff car, the corporal, whose name was Baker, at the wheel, and Mills with Hess beside him in the back seat. The car reminded Rotheram uncomfortably of Hitler's tourer in the previous night's film.

The drive seemed to restore Hess. He'd been subdued when he climbed into the car, pausing on the running board to tuck his red woollen scarf into the collar of his sweater and wrap his greatcoat around his knees before sitting down. But now Rotheram, half turned in his seat, saw the colour return to the older man's cheeks. Hess noticed his scrutiny.

'How do you like my gift from Mr Churchill?' he asked jovially, indicating the car. 'It's just the thing for the beautiful Welsh countryside, wouldn't you say?'

'Why do you think you're in Wales?' Rotheram asked blandly, but Mills broke in with a shrug. 'No need to be coy. We ran into some locals at a crossroads on one of these jaunts last month and he recognised the lingo. Bit of a cock-up, really, but at least they didn't recognise him.'

It was still chilly, but the sun had come out, and Hess slipped on a pair of dark glasses.

'He recognised Welsh?' Rotheram asked sceptically. He was addressing Mills, but Hess answered, sounding impatient.

'Where else in the British Isles do they speak another language? In fact, it seems a peculiarly apt place for my confinement.'

'How so?'

'Isn't Wales where the ancient Britons retreated to? When the Romans came, I mean. Wasn't this their last redoubt? Aren't these' – he waved an arm around, but the country was deserted apart from sheep and cattle – 'their descendants? Your Mr Churchill, I gather, had plans to pull back here if we had invaded.' Hess smiled thinly. 'We'd have made you all Welsh. Instead, it's me who's a little Welsh now.'

'Hardly the party line, that,' Mills sneered. 'To think a few months' stay in a country is a claim to nationality.'

'Months? No, I suppose it takes – what would you say, Captain – a few years?'

Mills gave a wincing smile, but Rotheram wouldn't rise to the bait.

'Wales,' Rotheram considered. 'The land of retreat? Or defeat?'

'Of last stands, perhaps,' Hess offered, turning away.

They rode in silence after that, driving uphill along a tight lane hemmed in by high stone walls. Rotheram, gripped by a sudden claustrophobia, staring ahead, flinching as startled rabbits bolted before their wheels. At the brow of a ridge the track opened into a small dirt yard. The view, tumbling hills speckled purple and yellow with heather and gorse, spread before them.

They climbed down to admire it, while the corporal steered the huge car through a five-point turn, so laboriously that Mills felt compelled to direct him.

'You never said what you made of our film, Captain,' Hess suggested companionably.

'I thought it was vile lies. Rabble-rousing propaganda.'

'You think so?' Hess mused. 'That it incited the mob?'

'You don't?'

'I suppose so. But the mob was only a small number, really. A few thousand out of millions who saw the film. Not so efficient if its goal was to rouse. You saw it in Germany?' he asked, and Rotheram, caught off guard, nodded slightly.

'A film like that,' Hess went on, 'does something more important than stir the few, don't you think? It makes the rest an audience. Passive, you see? You watch a film, you sit in a cinema, you see things, you feel things, but you do nothing.' He leaned closer. 'That film made our actions a drama to be watched, talked about, as if it were only happening on a screen, on a set. Forget incitement. That's the power of film, to draw a line between those who act and those who watch.'

Rotheram shook his head. He looked for Mills, who was helping Baker wrestle the canvas roof of the car into place.

'You disagree, Captain? It had some other effect on you?'

'Tell me something,' Rotheram said, turning to him. 'Let's grant, for the sake of argument, that you have no recollection of why you came to Britain. Why do you *think* you came? You must have wondered.'

'I was on a secret diplomatic mission, as far as I can determine.'

'Yet you can't recall the details, and no one else from Germany has tried to fulfil the mission since.'

'I imagine you have other theories.'

'Some say you were crazy before you crashed. That you were already unstable when you decided to fly here.' Hess was impassive. 'Others, that you'd fallen out of favour with Hitler, that you felt your position, your life, threatened. They say you ran.'

'Would you like me to be an exile, is that it, Captain? Another refugee? Should we sympathise with each other now? Is that the form this takes? Why yes. It's all coming back to me. I'm remembering, remembering. *Mein Gott,* I'm really a Jew. How could I have forgotten?'

He started to laugh, then saw the blunt fury in Rotheram's face.

'Why won't you believe me when I tell you I'm not a Jew?'

'Why won't you believe *me* when I say I do not remember things?' Hess smiled. 'But for the sake of argument – yes? – let's say that you are not a Jew. But if not, why do you hate me so?'

'Why?' Rotheram exclaimed. 'Why!'

'Please. There's no need to raise your voice.'

'Because,' Rotheram pressed, 'because you and your kind drove me from my home, accused me of being a Jew—' He caught himself, suddenly conscious of Mills's approach.

'But don't you wonder, Captain,' Hess whispered, leaning close and slipping into German, 'what that says about the way *you* feel about Jews?' He pivoted to Mills, and Rotheram felt his face flush. 'Ah, Doctor, I was just suggesting a stroll to the captain.'

Mills nodded. 'If you're up to it.' He looked quizzically from Rotheram, gazing off, to Hess, who raised his eyebrows.

'It's downhill, after all. If the corporal would be so kind as to meet us at the crossroads?'

Mills gave a wave to Baker, and the car rumbled back down the lane while Hess led them through a rusty kissing gate onto the hillside.

Rotheram watched him go, still stunned by Hess's question.

'You're sure this is all right?' he roused himself to ask as Mills stepped through the gate ahead of him.

'Quite. We've done this walk before. It's the bugger's favourite. The locals are all at chapel this time of a Sunday morning, and believe me, he isn't likely to escape.' He gestured at Hess, who was gingerly lowering himself down the path. His limp was more apparent now than in the house. When they drew level with him he was already breathing hard.

'We can go back,' Mills said, putting a hand on his shoulder. 'If you're unwell. Don't want you getting a chill.' He grinned at Rotheram behind the other man's back.

'The *herr doktor* is worried about my health,' Hess told Rotheram, shaking Mills off. 'He watches me well, so that I won't catch cold, or stub my toe, or fall downstairs.'

Mills coloured at this reference to the latest suicide attempt.

'I just want what's best for you.'

'Yes, yes.' He paused before a steep stretch of the path that had been washed out by rainwater.

'Perhaps?' Hess raised his hands, and for a second Rotheram thought it was a gesture of surrender. Then he saw Mills duck under one arm, and he bent to let Hess lay the other across his own shoulders. In this way they eased down the slope, silent apart from Hess's panting, now that they were so close. The old man was surprisingly heavy, Rotheram thought, despite his gangly frame. He felt his arm weighing on the back of his neck. The faint scent of cologne wafted from Hess's collar.

When the slope was more gentle, the older man lifted his arms, and Rotheram was glad to step away, pressing a hand to his bruised ribs.

'Thank you, gentlemen. Where were we?' Hess asked. 'Oh, yes, the doctor. He does take fine care of me, but Doctor, don't you find that difficult?'

'Well, you're not always the most cooperative patient.'

'No. Forgive me. Don't you find it a . . .' He searched for the word. 'A conflict?'

Mills shook his head gravely. 'My oath as a doctor—'

Hess held up his hand. 'Forgive me again. I didn't mean this conflict. Your *hippokratischer* oath, I know. We have this in Germany. Every doctor has this. No. I mean, is it not a conflict that you are keeping me alive in order for your government to kill me?'

'What makes you say that?' Rotheram asked.

229

Hess looked at him.

'*You* know, Captain Roth. It's why you're here. To decide if you can try me. Let's see. Can we, can we?' Hess held his palms out before him like an unsteady pair of scales. 'But I ask you, why bother? You want to kill me, just kill me.'

Mills, put out, had walked ahead.

'Doctor! I've shocked you with my talk. And on such a beautiful morning. Please. Of course I don't mean *you* should kill me. Besides, I'd do it for you, if you'd let me.'

'You want to die?' Rotheram said.

'Does that seem mad to you? In which case, does that mean you shouldn't try me and kill me? Or does it seem sane, under the circumstances, which would mean that you should?'

Rotheram had pulled up beside Mills, a little below Hess on the slope, and now he found himself looking up at the speaker as if he were on a stage. A shadow crept over them and Hess glanced up at the clouds. When he looked down again his smile had faded.

'I have no one left, you understand. I do not remember my wife, my children. I do not remember my country. My life has already been taken.'

Mills sighed and shook his head, but Rotheram was rapt.

'You are still trying to decide about me,' Hess said.

Rotheram nodded.

'You really shouldn't trouble yourself. It doesn't matter in the end.'

'It matters to me.'

Hess shook his head. 'All those signs you look for, dilating of the eyes, for instance.' He took his dark glasses off, folded them away, gazed at Rotheram. 'Those only matter if the subject cares about being believed. I don't care, because whether you believe me or not . . .' He shrugged. '*Kaputt!*'

'Oh, now,' Mills began, but Hess didn't take his eyes off Rotheram.

'You want the truth about me? First you tell me – am I right or not?'

It occurred to Rotheram that he had been the last to know this truth. Even Hess was there before him. He found himself nodding slowly.

'So,' Hess sighed. 'I thank you for this honesty.'

'Your turn,' Rotheram said.

Hess studied him. 'Indulge me. One last question. Then I promise to tell you what you want to know.'

'What question?' Rotheram asked tiredly.

'You know already.'

As if from a long way off, Rotheram heard the scrape of a match beside him as Mills lit a cigarette. He took a long breath and shook his head.

'Some think I'm a Jew, but I'm not. Not to myself at least. Still, perhaps that doesn't matter, the way I see myself, not compared to the way others see me. Not when the way you see me is a matter of life and death.' He shrugged. 'Is that an answer?'

'An answer? No.' Hess gave a crooked smile. 'But maybe the truth.'

Rotheram looked up. 'Well, then, I believe we had a bargain.'

'Quite. So, am I unbalanced? Am I faking my amnesia?' He leaned close and Rotheram could feel Hess's breath against his cheek. 'The truth is – I don't remember any more.' He stepped back, smiling apologetically. 'We have something in common, you and I. The same dilemma. Are we who we think we are, or who others judge us to be? A question of will, perhaps.' He glanced over Rotheram's shoulder, and then back, meeting his eyes. 'How can you hope to judge me, Captain, if you can't decide about yourself?'

He held up his hand before Rotheram could answer.

'If you go now,' Hess said softly, 'you may outrun him.'

Behind him, Rotheram heard Mills whisper, 'Oh, bloody hell.'

He turned to where they were looking. A bull had appeared on the hillside below them. Rotheram was stunned. Where had it come from? Had it been hidden in the shadows by the wall or lying in a shallow dell? It trotted steadily across the field, brushing aside frothy blooms of Queen Anne's lace almost daintily, not more than twenty feet below them, and as Rotheram watched, its dark, velvety head swung round – he saw the pale curve of its horns turn – to study them.

'Hell,' Mills said again. The cigarette that was dangling from his lower lip fell to the ground. 'Bloody bloody bleeding hell.'

It occurred to Rotheram that Hess, slightly higher and looking past them, would have seen the beast first. He wondered if all the talk had simply been a way to distract them while the bull approached.

'Come on,' Mills was saying. Rotheram felt a hand on his arm.

'I believe he's seen us,' Hess noted calmly. 'Gentlemen, I am fifty years old, and with a limp, I might add. I can hardly outrun him, but you might. If you go now.'

Rotheram felt himself fill with disgust. What foolishness! To lose the prisoner to a bull.

'Are you coming?' Mills hissed.

'The corporal can shoot it,' Rotheram said, searching beyond the bull, but although he could make out the car, beyond the stile at the near corner of the field, there was no sign of Baker, who might have gone for a smoke or a piss. Rotheram and the doctor were unarmed, standard procedure for interrogators with a prisoner, but even if Rotheram had had his service revolver, he doubted he could stop a charging bull with it.

'Even if the good corporal were to see us,' Hess said, 'he would need to move very smartly to get a clear shot. And,' he added wryly, 'I'm not so confident of his marksmanship. Not on a Sunday morning.'

'Come on!' Mills had already started to edge towards the stile, but as he took a step in that direction, the bull moved almost leisurely to cut him off. Its bulk seemed ponderous, but it was flanking them, Rotheram noticed, shocked by the animal's intelligence, angling up the slope, avoiding charging uphill at them. In a few moments it would be above them. It was already close enough for him to see its dark coat wasn't smooth, but kinked with tight woolly tufts, the black curls licking at the base of its horns. He could smell it, too, a rich smoky scent on the breeze.

'Go now, please,' Hess told Rotheram.

Before he could make up his mind, Mills took to his heels. He'd seen what Rotheram had seen, and spotted also that the route to the near corner was now open. Rotheram felt Hess's hand on his back. 'Really, there is no need to die for me, Captain. It would be foolish, no? To die for a dead man?'

He pushed again, but weakly, and Rotheram stood fast. He was trying to decide if he could carry Hess (he doubted it, given the condition of his ribs) or perhaps draw the bull off. He stared at the creature, and for a second its huge dark eyes appraised him in return, and he was suddenly and profoundly conscious of himself as no more than an animal. For all his learning, his civilisation, he might still be killed by a beast.

'Captain.' Hess raised his voice. 'I really must insist.' Rotheram, glancing away from the bull, saw the determination in his face. He tried to steel his own will, to keep his eyes on the old man's, but he could hear the hoofbeats now. 'Wouldn't this be easiest for all of us?' Hess whispered. He was fumbling with the buttons of his greatcoat, drawing out the bright red scarf that had been tucked into his collar. With a final feeble shove, not much more than a pat on the back, he set Rotheram in motion towards the stile and himself hobbling towards the bull, the scarf flourished behind him on the breeze like a signature.

Rotheram found himself running – it came so easily, instinctively, his legs adjusting to the steep slope of the ground –

chasing the doctor, making headlong for the stile. He couldn't remember the last time he had run. He made a point of walking out of the building during raids in London. He must have run since that time he fled the cinema in Berlin, he thought, but he couldn't recall. It troubled him because, even as his rib seemed to grind in his side, even as he heard the thunder of hoofs behind him, he found he rather liked running, the wind in his face, the blood beating in his head. It made him feel so alive, he couldn't imagine why he had ever stopped.

Sensing the beast closing, he veered sharply for a low stretch of the wall, his arms bracing him as he swung his legs over the top, and tumbled into the soft unmown verge of the lane. Looking up, he saw the bull's galloping momentum carry it past, saw Mills clattering over the stile into the arms of the corporal, as the beast broke off its chase, tossing its great glaring head.

He climbed to his feet, favouring an ankle he must have skinned on the wall, and looked uphill. There was no sign of Hess.

For a sickening moment Rotheram stopped searching for the man and started looking for a prone body, but then he saw him, upright on the hillside, waving. Rotheram felt a rush of relief, and then almost immediately an overwhelming flood of disappointment that left him light headed and sagging against the wall.

He watched numbly as Hess hobbled downhill and Mills scurried to join him.

'Are you all right?' the doctor called.

'An old man wasn't worth his trouble, apparently,' Hess cried. 'The black beast didn't want anything to do with me.'

'But are you all right?' Mills insisted. He sounded panicked, almost hysterical, but to Rotheram Hess looked better than he'd ever seen him. He seemed braced, his eyes gleaming, his cheeks as rosy as his damned scarf.

'Really, Doctor,' he was saying. 'I'm perfectly fine. Your concern is appreciated. Although,' he smiled ruefully, 'I doubt very much that you can actually save me from anything in the long run, you know. Is that the car?'

Mills and Rotheram watched him limp down the lane towards the corporal. They looked at each other and then quickly away, before they followed, Mills staggering a little. 'Awful thing,' he muttered under his breath. 'Running before the enemy like that.' And Rotheram nodded and told him softly, 'It's all right.' And yet for a long, numb moment, he couldn't conceive how the war was being won.

Major Redgrave was waiting when they pulled into the driveway. He eyed them carefully as they got out of the car. 'Everything all right, Lieutenant?'

Mills wouldn't meet his eyes, but glanced around at the others and shrugged. 'Fine, sir.' A light rain was beginning to ring in the trees around them, and the doctor ushered Hess inside while Redgrave stopped Rotheram. His new orders had arrived; the transfer to POWD as predicted by Hawkins, but also a second cable, urging him to a camp in North Wales.

'Been an escape, apparently,' the major was saying. 'Sloppy! Anyhow, you're expected there post-haste to look into it.'

To Rotheram it seemed like a cosmic joke at first. An escape? After what had just happened? But almost at once he felt a tremendous relief, as if given a second chance.

Ten minutes later, he was throwing his luggage into the Humber. He didn't plan to offer any goodbyes; nevertheless, as he climbed into the car, the whole strange household straggled out to see him off. Mills and Corporal Baker even waved, although Hess, between them, kept his arms at his sides. Under their gaze, Rotheram set off down the drive, but then swung the wheel round to circle it, pulling up again, gravel spattering under the wheels. He hurried back inside, ignoring their startled faces, re-emerging moments later with the film cans held before him like an empty tray, the densely wound reels shifting and sliding inside them, making him feel as if they were about to spill.

Apart from the near miss with the flock, he's kept his foot on the gas ever since, turning north and continuing to rise through a layer of cloud, and yet ahead of him now, as the mist shreds, he sees night is starting to fall. The steep grassy slopes to the west are already a velvety black, just the white flecks of sheep like faint stars in the dark. The thought of more sheep in his path makes him ease up at last, slacken his breakneck pace. Where is the escaped man going to go, after all, he asks himself. What chance does he have with hundreds of miles of hostile ground between him and home?

Eighteen

It's a crisp Friday, the first in September, and she's washing eggs, cleaning the muck off them with a stiff little brush. After the heat of August, September has come in damp and blustery. Jim went back to school two days earlier, his face as overcast as the skies, and the night before, Arthur came in off the mountain, his eyes teary from the wind, grumbling that the dampness was going to hold up the haying. Only Esther welcomes the cool weather, pulling on heavy sweaters, swaddling herself in her long winter coat when she ventures out. Arthur set the rams to the flock earlier in the week, and each morning, looking up at the hillside, she can count more of the ewes, their rumps smeared red from the raddle. She's scrubbing the last egg as if she'd scour the speckles off it, wondering what she's going to do, when Arthur bangs out of the bedroom, his hair rising in wispy flames, and snatches his shotgun off the hook above the door.

For a pale second – such is her guilt – she thinks it's for her, that he's guessed her secret. She fumbles the wet egg in her hand, catches it, heart thudding, then watches silently as Arthur cracks the breech of the gun, jams the bright red shells into the barrel. Their brass firing caps stare at her owlishly and then wink shut as Arthur snaps the stock to.

'Loose dog,' he bites out, grim faced. 'What are you, deaf?'

She must have been so lost in her thoughts. But now she can hear the distant barking and, following him to the door, see the flock flying across the fields, rippling over the uneven hillside in the morning sun.

It's happened before, she knows, drying her hands and watching her father hurry uphill. Hikers' dogs have got in among the sheep. 'Worse than foxes,' according to Arthur. But she hasn't seen hikers in years, not with the war on, and the only local dogs are working animals – like Mott and Mick, now snapping at their chains – who know better than to worry sheep, and the guard dogs she's heard baying from the camp. But she can't recall ever seeing them loose before.

And then she's running too, waving and shouting after her father, but her cries must be whipped away by the wind because Arthur keeps surging upwards, alternately dwindling and growing as he crosses ridge after ridge, until he vanishes over one rise and doesn't reappear.

She struggles on, bracing for the sound of the shotgun blast, but there's nothing, just a lone seagull, strayed in from the coast, floating across the grey sky.

At last she comes sweating and panting over the brow and there's Arthur in the hollow below her, leaning into his shotgun as if into a gale, and facing him two guards from the camp, one with his own rifle raised, the other with both hands clenched around the leash of the dog, which lunges and snaps between them.

The guards and the dog all seem to be barking at once; it takes her a moment to make out that one of the guards is shouting at the dog, 'Down!', the other at Arthur, 'Drop it!' By contrast her father is still, intent, only the muzzle of his gun drifting slightly with the bucking of the dog in his sights.

'Stop!' she cries, but it comes out as a croak, so winded is she from the climb. She has to put a hand to her chest to summon her breath, and when she looks up, her throat tensing to try again, they're turning their weapons on her. Arthur flinches away as if scalded, but the guard's aim lingers. She feels her hands rising before her, buoyant as the gull floating overhead, and then she clenches her fists, forces them down, nails biting into her palms. Instead, she calls out in English, calls their names. She knows them from the pub: George, the Malaya veteran, hunched over his rifle; and Les, who waved his hanky when he told them about the Germans surrendering, hauling on the dog's leash. Finally George's head lifts off the sight.

One of the prisoners has escaped, Les explains when Esther joins them – all three men, even the dog with its lolling tongue, somehow calm, abashed – and she can't help twisting her head as if the German might be watching them, just as she might have watched him from the hillside. But which one? she wonders.

'Thought they weren't supposed to have the gumption to escape,' Arthur says.

Les is blotting his brow. 'Dog had his scent before you stuck your oar in.'

'He had a scent, all right.' Arthur gestures towards a clump of gorse in the deepest part of the hollow. The ground around is torn up and muddy, raddle smeared on the grass; the rams have been busy. Then Esther sees the tufts of wool, snared and fluttering on the low branches; makes out the spindly legs tangled in the brush, still and twisted as branches themselves; finally recognises the familiar face with its one ruined eye. Not raddle, it comes to her, but blood.

There's no sign of the prisoner, that day or the next, though the countryside is crawling with guards. 'Poking bayonets into every hedge, and noses into everyone's business,' as Arthur puts it, with a contemptuous smile. Esther had feared trouble after the confrontation on the hillside, especially when her father loudly asserted his right to shoot any dog on his land during tupping season, but in fact the guards have given in without a fight. The dogs are likely useless for tracking, too easily distracted by sheep spoor and the occasional rabbit ricocheting uphill, but Arthur considers it a triumph, as if he's driven the invader off his land (though soldiers can still be seen climbing to and from the uplands along the brow of the hill). He sits in the pub that night, answering Bertie Prosser's questions about the stand-off, like a king in his court.

He's fortunate the guards are all out on the mountains, Esther thinks, breathing on a glass to polish it in the deserted lounge. Even Constable Parry is lending a hand, flying up and down the local lanes on his bicycle, dark cape whipping behind him in the wind as if he hopes to run the escapee down – though he does stop off for a quick pint, and to report that the camp comman-dant has sent for an investigator – from London, no less.

At the end of the evening, Jack tells her she doesn't have to come to work for a few days. 'Not with this desperate fellow about.'

She thinks she might creep down to the camp again instead. She's curious which prisoner has escaped, wonders if it might be the one she spoke to. He seemed bold enough, and with his English he might have more of a chance than most. If she dared go back to the camp, she'd look for him. But the closest she gets is the ridgeline, ducking below it when the searchlight reflectors on the guard towers catch the sun, as if she's the hunted one. Besides, she hears the boys have been warned off: the guards are trigger happy now, according to the constable. Whichever prisoner it was, he apparently scaled the fence while the guards were chasing off the boys.

'Found a blind spot and took advantage of the distraction,' according to Parry. 'Slipped away with the crowd in the dark when the guards ran them off.'

'See!' she tells Jim later, a little too pleased that the taunting of the prisoners has backfired.

'As if it's our fault,' Jim cries. It's not, Esther knows, but after feeling so guilty that the prisoners were being abused for Rhys's death, she feels oddly vindicated (though, to her surprise, Jim has lately confided to her that he thinks Rhys might be a prisoner after all).

The boys, at any rate, keep clear of the camp, more interested in patrolling the village, armed with sticks and cricket bats, at least until called in for supper.

On Sunday, the third day of the escape, a scare sweeps through the congregation gathered for chapel. Esther comes in late – she's tarried at her mother's grave, tidying the blanket of heather transplanted from their own hillside – catches only the scraps of rumour. Someone's clothes have gone missing from a washing line; someone else has lost half a pint of milk left out on a windowsill. Muddy footprints have been found on newly scrubbed steps. The whispers are only stilled when the reverend starts the service. Beside her, Esther sees Arthur holding his head up, family chin out, though whether in a show of staunchness or because she's starched his collar too severely, she can't be sure. For herself, she's been so anxious these many weeks on her own account, it comes as a strange relief to hear the unusual fervour in the hymn singing and prayers, to sense the fear of others. It makes her feel less lonely. And then she catches a glimpse of Mrs R's straight, black back before her, and bows her head.

The last time Esther was at the PO she'd noticed a picture frame above the counter, turned towards the wall. She'd stared at it – some government poster? outdated postal rates? A photo of Rhys, she'd abruptly intuited. Mrs R was in the back fetching a parcel; Esther couldn't help reaching for the frame, twisting it round. The colours were faded, the three jaunty plumes rising from the crenellated crown more grey than silver, but she recognised it from the schoolroom, where it hung over the board: a needlepoint sampler of the Prince of Wales's coat of arms.

'That old thing,' Mrs R sighed, returning. 'I'd have taken it down altogether but the wallpaper's so faded.'

'But why?' Esther murmured.

'Couldn't stand to read it.'

Esther traced the letters scrolled around the banner at the base of the crown: *ich dien*. 'I don't know Latin.'

'"I serve,"' Mrs R translated. 'Only it's not Latin. It's the motto of the King of Bohemia, taken by the Black Prince after he defeated him at the Battle of Crécy, 1346.' She turned it back to the wall. 'It's German, you see.'

Esther stared at the brown paper backing. 'They're just words,' she tried, and Mrs R smiled tightly. 'Did I not teach you any better than that?'

Esther hasn't seen her since, and she seeks her out after the service.

Mrs R is studying the scythes and pitchforks leaning against the chapel wall, the grim-faced farmers retrieving them for the walk home. 'Woe betide any German out for a stroll on this fine Sabbath.'

'You must hate them,' Esther blurts.

'Do I sound so bloodthirsty?'

'It's natural enough.'

'You'd think so, wouldn't you? I did go back, you know, to their camp.' It's only because she looks away as she says it that Esther is able to compose her own features. 'I don't know what I was imagining. That I'd curse the lot of them, probably. But when I got there, all I could think was to ask if they knew where he was.' She shakes her head at the foolishness. 'As if I spoke more than two words of German.'

Esther's about to say that some of them speak English, but bites her tongue.

'Besides, it's pointless. They were captured before Rhys went missing. They couldn't know what's become of him, any more than they could have . . . could be to blame. As for this one we're all so afraid of, all I can think of is his mother.' She sees Esther's face and laughs. 'He must have one, you know! She's probably worried sick.'

Mrs R purses her lips, nods in the direction of the cemetery. 'Well, I should pay Mervyn a visit.'

Esther returns to work the next night, as usual, telling Jack she couldn't leave him in the lurch, though in truth there are hardly enough customers to warrant her presence. Even the turnout in the public bar is sparse, several local men notable by their absence. Esther is ashamed at first, thinking them cowardly, until Jack notes morosely, 'Wives keeping them home, isn't it,' and Harry – doughty, defiant Harry, who's insisted to Mary and the others that no Jerry's going to drive *him* out of his favourite pub – adds in a falsetto, 'Save me, save me!' Esther feels a sudden superiority to the other women, a prickling pride in her own bravery. For surely that's what it is. Arthur, to be fair, has insisted on walking her to work, and Jack accompanies her home. But she doesn't need them.

As if to prove the point, she stands alone in the darkened yard after going to the privy, listening to the night sounds, searching herself for fear. And there's nothing. Not even when she feels a puff of air against her neck, as if someone has just blown on her. The owl from the barn, she tells herself. The draft of its wingbeat. And sure enough, a moment later she hears it *shush* into the long grass. After a vole, probably. But even then she stands fast. *So this is bravery,* she thinks, staring at the stars pinned above her. This absence of fear. Not something you feel, after all, but something you don't.

The following morning she waits with the other women in the queue at the butcher's, watching the scarved heads bend towards one another, listening to the gossip. 'Gives me the heebie-jeebies,' someone is saying, 'to think what he might do.' There's a long pause, during which Esther feels herself stand a little straighter. Then someone else perks up, 'Still, every cloud . . .' and the women smile slyly at each other, cover their mouths to stifle giggles.

'I don't know what you're afraid of,' Esther cuts in, and they shuffle themselves into composure. 'Of course not, luv,' someone says soothingly, but Esther is already hurrying away, even though it's almost her turn and she hasn't any meat for dinner. She knows then why she's so fearless, and it's nothing to be proud of: because the worst has already happened to her.

That night after the pub closes, it's the constable who walks her back to Cilgwyn. 'Don't fancy the thought of a young lady alone with a fugitive about,' he tells her meaningfully. 'Why, I wouldn't let my Blodwyn out of doors after dark.' She tries to tell him the German must be miles away – 'If I were in his shoes, I'd be long gone by now' – but Parry shakes his head doggedly, almost as if he hopes the fellow is still around, about to pounce from behind a tree.

She smirks, recalling a joke of Harry's from that week's show. *D'you hear the toilets at the local police station have been stolen? Police say they've nothing to go on!*

'Best not take any chances,' the constable is saying, giving her a narrow stare. 'You've no idea what he might be capable of.' It comes to her with a flush of anger: *He's trying to scare me.* 'No,' she retorts icily. 'No, I don't. Why don't you tell me?' Which shuts him up for the duration of the walk.

Only later in bed, tossing and turning in the darkness, does it occur to her why she snapped so. As much as the constable wants to recapture the fellow, some part of her yearns for him to have escaped. She falls asleep dreaming of him swimming to Ireland, hair a dark pelt across his brow, shoulders cutting cleanly through white water, a gleaming smile gripped between his teeth.

*   *   *

She's pictured him as Johnny Weissmuller, she realises, recalling the dream with a blush when she wakes. Though wasn't *he* German, perhaps, with a name like that? She lies in bed, still heavy with sleep, until the cow's lowing sets off the dogs. She wraps her mac over her nightgown, stuffs bare feet into her clammy wellingtons, and stumbles out into the dawn. The dogs fly at her, chains clattering on the cobbles, and she whistles for them to settle. The cow's bellows feel like an ache in her own chest. She's halfway to the barn when she glimpses some movement near the chicken coop, chases around the corner, clapping her hands as if to startle a fox, and finds a man crouched there.

For a second she starts to smile – still dreaming, she reckons, still drowsing in bed – and then a hand covers her mouth.

She thinks of Colin, suddenly, thrashes wildly and feels the grip tighten on her jaw, hears a voice in her ear: 'Don't cry.' And strangely something about the heavy accent calms her. Not Colin, of course, but a German.

He drags her back into the shadow of the barn, so swiftly that she feels one of her boots slip free. The cold air on her bare foot reminds her of the danger she's in, but the thought comes to her less with fear or anger than weary recognition. This. Again.

It's only his poor English that helps her keep her head, gives her a sense of superiority even as he holds her. 'Cry *out*,' she wants to correct him; she isn't about to cry. But she settles for nodding emphatically, her chin working against his cupping hand. His fingers smell of raw egg. He hesitates a moment, but she can feel his grip relax and she opens her lips to speak. For a second she can feel his finger against her teeth, and then he releases her, as if afraid she'll bite.

It's their first proper look at each other, and her immediate response is relief – it's him, the German from the fence. She remembers how embarrassed he'd been then, how he'd blushed at the bad language, and momentarily she's actually pleased to see him instead of some other, some stranger.

He smiles slightly himself, then recovers, whispers tersely, 'I have a gun,' a hand jammed in his pocket like a gangster at the pictures. He's lying, she's almost certain (she's heard of no one missing a gun, no pistol to be sure), pretending as if it were some kid's game. Yet when she looks down, she finds her hands tensed over her stomach. It takes an effort of will to unlace her fingers.

From the back of the barn, the cow bellows again, tosses her head. She's terrified, and Esther, trained all these years to treat the beast as well as a person – better – starts toward her.

'Don't move, please.' He jabs the ridiculous 'gun' at her again, and she almost dares him to show it. Still, she has an instinct she might be safer if he thinks she believes him.

'She needs to be milked.' She meets his eyes. 'If not, she'll keep that up until she brings someone else.'

He's silent then, and she moves past him, limping without her boot, pulls up the three-legged stool and presses her head to the beast's flank. The cow stamps once, twice, snorts wetly, finally stills, and now the only sound is the drumming of milk in the tin bucket.

She feels him hovering behind her, then bending close, and she tenses, but when he rises, she sees he's only set her boot beside her. She wiggles her foot inside.

'Thank you,' she calls, but he's silent.

All Esther can see of him from this angle is his feet in the straw. She watches him edge his way around the animal, perhaps looking for a way out of the barn on the other side of the stall, or trying to put the beast between him and the main door, so its bulk shields him. When he strays too close to the hind legs, she snaps, 'I wouldn't. She'll kick.' He's still then, and she stares at his scuffed boots, his muddy trouser cuffs, as the patter of milk in the pail changes to a long hiss as it fills.

The milking will be done soon. And then what? She wonders if she can outrun him to the house, raise the alarm, fetch Arthur. She doubts it. She might scream, yet somehow having waited this long . . . how to explain why she waited? For the sake of a cow? It made perfect sense to her a moment before, but now it seems foolish. She imagines trying to explain it to Arthur, to Constable Parry, imagines Harry getting wind of it: 'Pull the udder one!' She doesn't want to attract any attention, after all, any laughter.

She lifts the pail, backs out of the stall, and he gingerly eases the cow aside to follow her.

'Please?' he calls softly.

'I won't tell anyone,' she hisses, 'if you go now.'

He studies her for a moment.

'My father will be up soon.'

He still has his hand thrust in his pocket. Any harder, she thinks, and he'll wear a hole in it. And then he smiles. 'Thank you . . . Esther.'

Jim! She flushes. *The little liar.*

'It is Esther?' he asks. 'Like the swimming actress?'

She nods slowly, more shocked that he knows Esther Williams's name than her own.

'And what do they call you?'

Hans? she dreads. But he tells her, 'Karsten.'

'Karsten?' The name feels dry in her mouth, and she wets her lips, looks up to see him doing the same.

'Please?' he says again, and it dawns on her that he's eyeing the bucket in her hand.

She stares at him a moment more, then reaches for an old china teacup, its handle snapped, that Arthur keeps on the shelf for when he wants a drink of water from the pump. The German dips it into the pail, puts it to his mouth, rears back slightly.

'Warm?' he says in surprise, and she nods solemnly.

He drinks a long draught, his throat throbbing, then another. He's scruffier than she recalls from the camp, his dark blond hair sticking up on his head, but he seems bigger too, as if he'd been stooping behind the wire.

247

When he's finished he holds out the cup and she sees a thin white line below his nose, and despite herself she starts to smile.

He tenses.

'You've—' She swipes a finger before her own face, and he rubs the residue away with the back of his hand. Only when it's gone does she see that it's the hand from his pocket.

They stare at each other and then she snatches up the pail and hurries towards the house, fast as she can without spilling, as if it were blood. She'd so nearly burst out laughing, but inside, with her back to the door, she finds she's already swallowed the laugh. Instead, she fumbles with the bolt – she can't recall the last time they actually locked their door – skins her knuckles shoving it home. She crouches at the window, sucking the scrape, but there's no sign of him.

She should tell her father, but at his door, her hand raised to knock, the thought of him charging out of the house with the shotgun again gives her pause. He'll not catch the German, and then they'll have soldiers and dogs crawling all over the farm again. And for what? Her breathing slows to match the steady tidal draw of Arthur's snoring. Her fist falls. He'll be long gone by then, this Karsten.

In the kitchen, she slowly drags back the bolt.

She lets Jim sleep in until he's almost late for school, then hurries him out of bed and through his breakfast, watches him run down the lane. When she goes back into the kitchen Arthur is up, drawing on his boots between slurps of tea. She holds her breath while he stamps across the yard to the privy, but there's no cry, no shout, though when he unchains the dogs on his way back and they hare around like they've caught a scent, he yells after them, 'Silly buggers.' She hurries out to sweep the yard, setting them sneezing, and then busies herself strewing fresh straw in the barn, gathering eggs and broken shells from the coop, until she sees Arthur stalking off uphill to inspect the flock, with the dogs in attendance.

Only after she's satisfied that she's covered any traces, leaning breathless on the broom, does she search herself for remorse. What if the German hurts someone, kills someone? Wouldn't she be partly to blame? Yet somehow she can't believe it. He seemed so . . . polite, so contrite. Besides, couldn't he have hurt her, killed her, if he had a mind to? She's put no one else at any more risk than herself. And if he wouldn't attack her, whom would he attack? Frankly, she'd be more worried about *him* if he ran into anyone else; she recalls the glinting collection of pitchforks and scythes propped against the chapel wall after the service on Sunday. No, she tells herself, she has too many regrets already. She refuses to take on another. Besides, the whole country's against him; why should she make one more. She hopes he leads the guards a merry dance.

Still, through the day she checks herself for guilt, as if for a pulse, but there's nothing. Without it, the encounter hardly seems real, as if it were the dream she'd first imagined it to be. *Me Tarzan, you Jane!* But then she remembers his name, Karsten. She's never heard it before; couldn't have imagined it. She says it over and over to herself as she goes about her chores.

She's almost giddy in the pub that night, can't recall the last time she felt so unburdened. Harry winks at her, crosses his eyes and lolls his tongue, but she doesn't care. A few of the guards, George and Les among them, straggle in before last orders and she teases them, asks them if they think their man's in the pub somewhere – 'In a barrel, maybe? At the bottom of a glass?' – makes a little skipping show of looking behind the bar. It's reckless, she knows, yet how are they to catch her if they can't even catch him?

It's a quiet night and Jack lets her go early. The constable offers to walk her home, but she tells him to save his legs, and when he starts to object she simply takes to her heels, hitching up her skirt and running up the lane into the darkness, leaving him to call her name over her ringing footsteps and laughter. When she pulls up breathless around the bend, she can't believe how easy it is to get away. Though for all that, she's caught by a sudden pelting downpour before she gets home.

Nineteen

It's almost a letdown the next morning when she looks into the barn and there's no one, just the cow eyeing her moistly. Esther fidgets as she milks, craning over her shoulder, staring into the shadows, pausing to listen to the rustle of mice. Ridiculous! She'd laugh at herself if there were anyone to share the joke. He must be miles away by now, and moreover, she reminds herself, she hopes he is. Isn't that why she helped him, after all?

She sees Jim off to school and Arthur over the ridge to survey the rams' progress through the flock. Only when she's alone does she allow herself to think of the German again. She wonders if he's thinking of her, worried that she'll raise the countryside or marvelling that she hasn't. She tries to picture his movements. East across the mountains, or west, down to the coast and Ireland? She wishes she'd asked him, but she doubts he'd have told her. The latter, she hopes. East is England, and she shudders at the thought of crossing all that hostile ground.

But when she goes to look for eggs, she finds him crouched in the lee of the barn, as if he never left. She swallows back a scream, less of fear than surprise. She's imagined him so vividly gone, her first thought is that he must have forgotten something. *You're going to be late,* she almost cries, as if for a train.

'Good morning.' He grins.

251

'What are you doing here?' she hisses, though even in the midst of her shock, she thinks, *I brought the dogs in last night.* As if she were expecting him.

He smiles crookedly, touches his stomach. 'Still hungry,' he tells her, with a little wince at the understatement.

'You can't hang around here. What if someone sees you?'

She wants to fly at him, shout *Shoo, shoo,* as if he were a particularly bold or starving fox (the same thing, really, she reminds herself).

'I'll go if you feed me,' he says simply.

Or not a fox, she thinks, but a lamb, one of those motherless ones she's nursed with a bottle who keep following her around all summer. The ones she weeps over when they're sent to market.

She crosses her arms. 'How do you know I won't raise the alarm?'

'You threaten?' He smiles, but tightly, his eyes narrowed as if trying to make out something in the distance.

'Warn,' she says.

He nods. 'You are correct. Perhaps I'm trusting too much.' He thinks for a moment. 'You know, if they catch me they will interrogate me, yes?' He gives the barest of shrugs. 'They will want to know everything. Where I hide. How I ate. Who I meet.'

'Now who's threatening?'

He smiles. 'Warning.'

'At least you didn't bring your pistol today,' she says tartly.

He smiles at his hand, holds it out to her to shake.

'They'd never believe you, you know,' she says.

'You know better than I, of course.'

His open palm hovers between them like a taunt, and just as he lets it fall, she grasps it.

'I do.' She gives his hand one firm, swinging pump and pulls away before he can exert any pressure.

'Wait here, then. And for God's sake keep out of sight.'

252

She returns with a thick heel of bread, a flaky wedge of cheese. It's not much, just all that won't be missed. She bundles it up in her skirts, afraid it won't be enough, that he'll demand something more. She thinks of young Pip in *Great Expectations,* making off with a whole pork pie for his convict, and envies him. But when she spills out her offering on the straw floor of the barn, the German falls on it greedily. She'd meant to make him take it and go, but she can't bear to make him stop once he's started. Besides, he finishes the meagre meal very quickly. He's picking a last flake of cheese off his chest before he thinks to look up at her. 'Thank you.'

And perhaps because it's so poor a meal, and his gratitude so sincere, she takes the pack of cigarettes she has stuffed in her pocket and offers him one. Even in the gloom his eyes light up. He fumbles out a smoke, scrabbles with the matches, and only after he's taken a long drag does he relax. He catches her staring at him, and she looks away.

'Please,' he says, gesturing to the pack, inviting her to join him, but she shakes her head. Something about his face when he drew on the cigarette. It was as if she recognised him, saw him as a young man, a boy, really, like any other, lighting a cigarette at a bus stop, in the queue for the chippy.

'Where did you learn English?' she asks, to change the subject.

'Cinema,' he tells her.

'It's lucky,' she says.

He gives a stiff little hike to his shoulders. 'Lucky for my comrades. There was so much smoke in our bunker we couldn't find anything white enough for a flag. So they sent me out, because of my English. Now some call me *Weisse Fahne* – White Flag – behind my back.' He laughs, as if daring her to join in, but instead she feels a shiver pass through her, as though a distant door has been opened and a draught slipped in.

'I meant lucky because we can talk,' she says carefully.

'I suppose,' he says, and then simply, 'Yes. That's so.'

'So you did surrender?' she asks shyly, and he winces as if she's touched a wound.

'We were overrun. We had no choice. Or so it seemed at the time.' He tips his head back to blow smoke at the sky.

'Do you wish you hadn't?' she whispers.

'I'd be dead.'

She nods. 'But still. Do you wish?'

He sucks deeply on the cigarette, his cheeks hollowing. 'Every day.'

'But now you've escaped.'

He snorts. 'Do I look so free?'

'That's why you must go,' she urges. 'Go and don't come back.'

As if for emphasis, she presses the crumpled pack of cigarettes into his dry hand. But when he's halfway out the door, she runs after him and holds out the matches.

She watches him go then, trotting through the long grass, body bent low, her heart rattling like the box of matches in his shirt pocket.

She spends the rest of the day wondering if he's left, looking up at every flicker of movement, every stirring in the breeze. At lunch Arthur asks her, 'What is it?' and she stares at her plate, waiting for him to read her guilt in the part of her hair, until he goes out again. It comes to her that the German must have been watching them, waiting for Arthur and Jim to leave, and she goes about her afternoon chores, self-conscious as an actress. It's thrilling at first, this sense of being observed, as if she's never alone, but as the day wears on and he doesn't show himself, it begins to feel oppressive, as though he's spying on her.

She should be more worried about the scrutiny of others, she tells herself. That night she keeps her head down as she goes about her work. So preoccupied is she that it takes her a while to sense the change in the place. The local men are back, for the most part.

The German's been loose almost a week and his threat seems to have dissipated, the consensus being that the fellow's long gone. But it seems to her that the new ease in the pub isn't due just to the German's being gone. It's because the guards are largely absent – out on the search still, or stuck at the camp (the major has doubled the guard since the escape) – and for the first time in months there are more villagers in the pub than strangers; Welsh is the loudest language. Looking round, she can see it in the men's eyes. It's their pub again, their local. It's not until her father comes in an hour later – ruddy faced from the wind, but grinning, so that he seems to still glow with the pride of having driven the guards and their dog off his land – that she recognises the same look on the other men's faces. Why, even the constable looks happy, despite the escape, or perhaps because of it, vindicated in his warnings and somehow elevated, better than the guards he's been chumming up to lately, his own man again.

Jack's telling a story about throwing out a soldier who came in late the night before: 'Some joker – a captain, mind you – but he was no captain of mine, I told him when he started banging on the bar for service, and then he got all up on his high horse, said he'd get better service if he was the escaped Jerry himself, or some such rot.'

'Said he was a Jerry!' the constable cries. 'I'd have shown him the door meself if he hadn't taken himself off to the Prince.' And Esther laughs with the rest, as if by some miracle of nerve it had actually been him, here.

Perhaps, she thinks, looking around in wonder, the German's done them all a favour, drawn off the English, freed them in some modest way even as he's freed himself. They should raise a glass to him, she thinks, feeling better about helping him, when another thought overtakes her: *This is what it'll be like after the war ends*. But the sudden glimpse of the future makes her stomach tighten, as if she were seeing it not from behind the bar but from behind a closed window.

The next morning, she goes to the barn with two hard-boiled eggs tied in a hanky, but there's no one, and she thinks, *Well, good for him,* though not without a pang – she'd hopped back and forth while the eggs boiled, as if she were the one in hot water – and immediately hurries to town in case there's any word of his having been captured.

That afternoon, though, he's waiting for her again, and she finds herself beaming as she sees him. She produces the eggs – she's saved them, even thought to wrap a little salt in a twist of newspaper – and he closes his fists on them tightly.

'You know, you really have to go,' she tells him again.

He's rolling one of the eggs gently between his palms, as if afraid to smash it, and he doesn't look up until the white starts to show through the cracks.

'What are you waiting for?' she asks. 'Why stay here?'

He bites down on the shining egg, and she looks away. Between swallows, he tells her, 'To let the search pass.'

It makes sense, she supposes. It's as good a spot as any, wild, remote, and the guard dogs can't track him. But more than anything she feels relieved – he'll come again. As for Mott and Mick, she gives Karsten slivers of bacon rind to feed them until they know his scent.

He sleeps in the quarry, and she realises that he must have followed Arthur home one morning. Now he creeps up on them each day, watches the comings and goings, and then when she's alone, he appears.

One afternoon she's looking out for him when she sees the clothes on the line dancing wildly, bucking and writhing in the gusty wind. As she watches, one of the pegs pops off and her navy dress pulls free, streams downwind, leaping and twisting.

She should hurry to catch it, a breeze like this could carry it, soaring, out to sea, but all she can do is labour uphill, wading through the long grass. Breathless, she makes it at last, buries her face in the bundle in her arms, and when she looks up, he's there behind her, chasing after a billowing scrap of white. He snatches it out of the air, holds it overhead where it snaps like a pennant as he brings it on to her. It flies in his face – her silk slip, she sees – and she grabs it from him, blushing.

'Someone will see!' she cries, not sure if she means him or her slip.

He comes three more times that week, fleeting visits – the first interrupted, along with her heart for a beat, by Arthur, rising early and calling for his breakfast – and each time she resolves to send him away, to refuse him food. If she keeps him here, he'll be caught, she's sure. And yet she can't stop herself.

When she heard Arthur's cry, she pressed her hand over the German's mouth. He was in the middle of saying something, and for a second she felt his breath on her palm, the odd softness of his lips in the midst of his stubble. Then she saw his eyes widen, and she drew her hand away, and they listened together.

'I have to go,' she'd whispered, and he'd nodded, licked his lips.

'Where were you?' Arthur had asked. She looked away at first, but when he asked again, she looked into his eyes, told him, 'Nowhere,' and he just shrugged.

Only later, pouring her father's tea, did she recall the German licking his lips, realise she'd felt his tongue, too, for a flickering second, slipping between her fingers.

The second visit, there are no interruptions, and after she's fed the German there's an awkward, desperate silence until she asks him what it's like under the water.

'I'm not a submariner,' he tells her with a slow shake of the head. 'My father was.'

He's silent for a moment. 'I did go aboard one once. A friend smuggled me on during a training drill. Cold.' He shudders. 'And wet – from all the leaks, I mean! Everything drips, everything tastes like salt and oil.' He makes a face.

'But are there no windows?'

He laughs, and then, seeing her disappointment, recovers himself. 'We heard a whale – singing, you know. My friend said it thought we were another whale. And sometimes, I swear, I could hear schools of fish swim past us, a fluttering sound like . . . stroking the hull.' He halts, embarrassed. 'The others said it was only kelp, or bubbles.'

'I wish it were fish,' she says, and after a moment he nods.

Only at the end of the week, sitting in the gloom of the barn, watching the dust float like stars through the sunlight slipping between the gaps in the wood, does she ask him his plan.

He shakes his head. 'I can't tell you.'

'You don't trust me!' She stares at him. *After all this!* Just that morning Jim had asked for another egg, and she shook her head. 'The guards,' she tells the German icily now, 'have reduced their patrols. They're back at the bar. This is your chance. Isn't it your duty?'

'And your duty?' he asks sullenly. 'Why do you betray your country?'

Why indeed, she wonders. But then isn't it her second betrayal? Perhaps it comes easier. But no, she knows that's not so. It's that the second betrayal, so much larger than the first, overshadows it, almost erases it.

'Would you rather I didn't?' she manages. 'Besides, it's not my country, not in the way you mean.'

He frowns. 'You do not feel this . . . *die Vaterlandsliebe?* Fatherland-love. *Der patriotismus.*'

Patriotism? She's never seen before how love of country is so wrapped up in the love of fathers, but it suddenly seems so typical of the way men would ask for love. No, not even ask. Demand, as a duty.

'Do you?'

'I think so. Yes.'

She feels upbraided somehow, defensive, and then she recalls what Mrs R said on the hillside the day the Germans arrived:

Fatherland! How did the women ever let the men get away with that one?

'And if it were called motherland-love?' she asks.

He stares at her as if she's asked something else, then slowly nods. More in thought than in agreement, she thinks, but what he says eventually is 'I do trust you.'

He still sounds like he's trying to convince himself, but she nods in turn.

'It's just safer for you not to know,' he adds. 'In case of questions.'

'But you do have a plan?'

'Of course.'

She feels a flutter in her stomach. 'It's Ireland, right? That'd be best, I think.' She can't look at his face as she says it. She turns and stalks to the barn door.

'Is that what you'd do?' he asks softly, following her.

She raises an arm without looking at him, points downhill to the lacy fringe of surf along the coast. 'On a clear day you can see the Wicklow Hills from here.' She nods. 'That's where I'd go.'

There's a long silence, and it occurs to her that he might ask her to go with him, the two of them swimming to Ireland, Johnny Weissmuller and Esther Williams, matching each other stroke for stroke. Could he pass as Irish? she wonders. Could she? The thought is somehow seductive. And from there, where? Germany? Could she learn German, act German? She doubts it. America, then – yes! Who knows, in America he might even pass as Welsh, with her help. What did they know of Welshness there? She'd be free to invent it. They'd travel as far as it took, find some place where the people had never heard of Wales. And not to escape Wales, she thought, but to *be* Welsh, him too, because no one else would know otherwise.

She gazes at him, waiting, but the question he asks at last is 'Do you want me to go?' and she breathes, 'Yes.' It's the only answer, though for a second, such is the earnestness with which he asks, she imagines she's replying to that other imagined question.

He stands there for a moment, swaying slightly on his heels as if in a breeze, and then he leaves her, stooping against the dusk as if the descending dark might crush him. She watches him go with a sense of release, as of a secret finally spoken.

That night, she tells herself she'll be glad to be rid of him. Yet there's some misgiving nagging at her, nibbling at the edges of her satisfaction. She tries to concentrate on it, isolate it in her heart, and then it comes to her. She's jealous, of course. She wants him to escape, but most of all she wishes he could have taken her with him.

It makes her remember Rhys, her jealousy at his leaving. Is that why she didn't stop him? she wonders. Did she want him to go, to go for her? And suddenly it seems as if the Rhys who left, the Rhys who went – why, she'd have married that Rhys.

Poor thing, she thinks, he couldn't win.

But then it occurs to her that that Rhys, the Rhys who left, might not have wanted her any more.

The next day, she doesn't see the German, or the next, or the next, and by the fourth day – watching Arthur cutting the rams out of the flock and penning them for another season – she concludes he's gone at last. But instead of filling her with the expected relief, the thought only makes her despair. She dreams of him that night, imagines him on a little boat out at sea. The boat's oddly familiar, and it comes to her that it's the ship in a bottle he gave to Jim, and then she's on board herself, looking up at the frayed grey sail overhead, which reminds her of the hole in his shirt, and she wonders where it is. And then her hands are moving over his chest, his arms, looking for that little hole. He's stretched out before her on the sand now, waves lapping at their feet, and she's kneeling over him, lifting his limp arm, hunting for the hole in the folds and creases of his wet shirt, thinking, *I can mend that for you, I can mend it, if I can only find it.*

Twenty

Escape, it has come to Karsten, is as complicated as surrender. Not one act, one moment, so much as a process. Escape followed by escape followed by escape, just as one surrender succeeds another and another. It's exhausting to think of.

From within the wire, he recalls, freedom always seemed so limitless, so infinite in its possibilities. The men in the barracks would while away the sleepless nights talking of what they'd do after their release – the beers they'd drink, the schnitzel they'd eat, the baths they'd take. Freedom in their minds was silk sheets, pressed shirts, obliging women. Karsten loved to listen to them, imagining them as guests at the grand hotel he'd manage one day. But of course, like his fantasy of a hotel, their dreams weren't of any life they'd lead, but of a life they promised to themselves after release. They were dreams of escape from the camp, to be sure, but also from their old lives. More than that, he thinks, lying in a ditch by a deserted lane, they were the dreams of conquerors, of the spoils of war. None of them had come close to such things at home – only briefly in France, for forty-eight hours at a time.

In fact, escape, the here and now of it, is poverty, not luxury. It's being cold and wet and hungry. Oh, there'd been a brief moment of elation: the breeze in his hair at the top of the fence, the lurch in his stomach as he'd dropped to the ground, the look of naked astonishment on the faces pressed to the wire. And then Karsten had bolted into the night, dodging the guards and following the boys, bumping against them, laughing with them, unrecognised in the night. Around the bend they'd scattered in the darkness and he'd gone his own way. He'd climbed at first, with some idea of getting to higher ground, some faith in his ability to move faster in mountainous terrain than anyone he knew.

There'd been no sign of pursuit, the guards charging after the boys if they could be bothered to go after anyone, and he thought that if the other prisoners kept quiet, he might not be missed until the next morning. But he'd been idle for so long, his muscles felt stiff and tight as he strode up the dark slope, and dropping down the far side, he began to realise that he had no food, no shelter, no idea what he was doing. He might have broken his ankle, even his neck, that first night, sliding down a long slope of scree in the dark, but he'd been lucky, had stumbled upon what he thought was a cave mouth, and pulled himself inside. He'd lain there that night, and only then had it come to him, what Jim had whispered at the wire, a name, her name. Esther.

Why of course! he'd thought, laughing at the perfect dream-like inevitability of it. And then, miraculously, he'd slept, his deepest night of sleep in months, and on a bed of stone at that, only to be woken by the baying of dogs on the breeze, wondering if he'd merely dreamed her name. He'd drawn back into his lair and discovered that the cave he'd imagined was no cave at all, but a tunnel, a mine shaft. Praying the dogs couldn't track his scent over rock, he'd retreated underground, only to get lost in a series of galleries. He'd stumbled around in them for hours, maybe a day or more, until he'd made out a dim light, hurried towards it, to find an old man snoring at the foot of a tall ladder, a bottle beside him.

Karsten had waited, starving, terrified his rumbling stomach would give him away, until the old fellow roused himself, and then Karsten had followed him, trusting him to know the way out. Karsten should have left him then, of course, struck out in the opposite direction as soon as he emerged, blinking, into the grey dawn, but his stomach was now his compass, and instead he followed the fellow to his farmhouse.

It had seemed like fate to find the girl again, the coincidence, more than anything else, making him trust her that first morning. But afterwards, gone to ground again, he couldn't stop thinking about her, couldn't get away from the sense that talking to her was the closest thing to freedom he'd tasted since his escape.

But now she has told him to go.

Talking to her about his father has reminded him that his father never wanted him to go to sea. Karsten had been aggrieved by that; all his friends, sons of other fishermen, were expected to follow in their fathers' footsteps. But when he'd pushed his father, all he'd say was 'Have you ever seen a drowned man?' It had made Karsten think his father afraid, though later, after he was lost but his body never recovered, it occurred to him that his father was trying to spare him something, protecting him even in death.

He's not sure why he hasn't tried for Ireland, but once she says it, he wonders if he is afraid of drowning. If he returns to her, perhaps she'll think him a coward, and he can't bear that.

He leaves the mountains and climbs down to the coast, one foot pulled after the other, not using the lanes but crossing the fields, pushing through clumps of sheep or cattle, once out-running a bull, squeezing himself into hedges to sleep. In the darkness he feels the slope flattening, and an hour later he's on sand again. He hates the feel of it underfoot, the yielding. He retraces his steps to the wrack line, following the dirty path of seaweed and jetsam in the starlight, until up ahead in the watery predawn gloom he sees the jumbled lines of tipped masts.

The boats are beached in the sucking mud, waiting for the tide to lift them, but he knows that with the tide will come their owners. He can't move any of the larger vessels, but he manages to haul a dinghy through the mud, alternately pushing and pulling it to the water, his ankles sinking in the muck.

He shoves it through the surf, and when he feels his feet being lifted from the bottom, he scrambles over the stern and collapses in the bilgy bottom, breathing hard, letting the current pull him down the shore until the boat scrapes bottom again – a sandbar – and he unships the oars, begins to pull for the dark horizon. After what seems an hour, he looks up and sees a streaky brightening. He's heading west, at least, though over his shoulder, where he's making for, is still pitch. And when the sun comes up, he can't see the shore, the beach, just the mountains behind it, rising up smokily into the clouds.

He thinks he's rowed the whole day when the sky darkens again, but looking up he sees storm clouds pressing down, feels the wind begin to pluck at him. He's drenched with rain first, and then the inky black waves start to slap the boat, break over it, the water so dark he thinks he must be stained by it. There's nothing to bail with, and in the gloom he feels his feet, then his ankles, then his calves grow cold.

Finally, in one slow, rising toss, the boat bucking beneath him like a live thing waking, he's in the water, the little vessel snatched out from under him like some joke. He's going to drown like his father and for a fleeting moment he is at peace. Died escaping, he thinks. Died trying. Died at sea. Honour restored. He thinks of his mother receiving the news, wonders if his body will ever be found. A splintered oar flies end over end above him, impales the surface with a great gulp not a yard from his head. It might have killed him on the spot – and in that second, gazing at it bobbing before him, he realises he doesn't want to die, clutches for the oar. He clings to it through the afternoon, and then the night, alone and yet feeling his father close to him, watching him, and some time in the darkness it comes to him: it wasn't drowning that his father was afraid of, but seeing men drown. How many must he have watched over through his periscope. In the morning the misty curtain of dawn lifts over a line of grey peaks and he kicks for them, lets the tide shove him in.

The Wicklow Hills, he thinks, licking the salt off his lips. Relief breaks over him like a wave.

He lies on the beach, where water meets sand, for a long time, letting the surf lift and lower him. He drifts off to sleep like that, and when he awakens he's high and dry, the sand beneath his hands warm from the sun. The last time he went in the water was in France, before the invasion. It tastes the same, he thinks.

From his prone position he seems to see a pair of wide, dark eyes hanging over him, watching him, and then he focuses, sees that they're the firing slits of a bunker cemented into the cliffside. He lies very still, feels the morning sun warm as blood on his brow. Before him, then. To the east.

So, not Ireland after all.

He squints up at the bunker, staggers to his feet. No point in running. He walks towards the emplacement, hands up, waiting for the cry, waiting for the flash. It reminds him of the walk out of his own bunker, the wait for death, and it comes to him suddenly that it was the bravest thing he's ever done, surrendering. Only when he's staring point blank into the slit does he see that the bunker is empty, unmanned, disused, and he sinks down against the concrete and wraps his head in his hands.

Later, shivering in the wind, he lowers himself through the gun slit. Where better to hide while he recovers his strength? No one will think to look for him here. The bunker smells so familiar, it feels like coming home.

Twenty-One

S he's feeding the hens two mornings later, swinging her arm
in long arcs to scatter the grain, skipping slightly to avoid
their pecking, when he walks out of the barn. Her fist tightens
reflexively on the handful of feed in her grasp. He's smiling
through his beard but stumbling a little, staggering – it takes her
a moment to realise he's swaying, dancing, imitating her steps
with the hens. 'Did you miss me?' he asks, reaching for her
closed hand, raising it as if to twirl her, before she jerks away.

'Get off!'

He tries again, smiling, as if she's just a clumsy partner, and
she flings the grain at his feet.

'What are you still doing here?'

She sees his smile waver, sees how forced it is, how fixed. He
looks like he might laugh, but hysterically.

The hens dart between them, and he nudges them aside.

'I've nothing else for you,' she tells him, though more than
once since he's left, she's wished she'd cleared out the pantry
for him. 'No food,' she repeats, enunciating the words slowly
as if the problem is only one of language. It comes to her that
she's somehow keeping him here, as if her helping him to
escape has only bound him more. 'I'll scream,' she tells him,
even takes a deep breath, but he just watches her, shaking his
head.

'Who will hear?' She'd think it a threat but for the way his shoulders slump, as if at the futility.

'Don't you want to get away?'

He gestures to the mountains, the sky. 'Where should I go? With no food, no clothes.' He plucks at his fraying, torn uniform.

'Then why escape at all?'

'I saw a chance. That's all.'

'A chance of what?'

He looks around as if for an answer. 'I don't know. Nothing more than this view, perhaps. Something else to look at other than wire and fence posts.'

'So now what?'

He shrugs. 'They catch me. I give myself up.' He sees her face. 'I'm sorry.'

'No wonder you trusted me,' she says bitterly. 'It didn't matter if I turned you in. I thought you wanted to get away. To . . . to—'

'To where?'

'To redeem your honour!' she cries. 'No wonder you surrendered.'

'*Ruhe!*'

The word rings off the house behind her, a word she doesn't know but understands.

She tries to run then, but he catches her wrist, drags her into the barn. She shakes loose, but by then he's blocking the door. She moves to dart past him and he's before her and she springs back, panting, about to scream. *No!* she thinks. *Not again.*

'Wait!' he calls. 'Wait. Please! I'm sorry.' He slumps down on one of the hay bales, a hand up to placate her. 'I tried. You hear. There is nowhere to go. But I tried.'

She takes in his matted hair, the salt stains on his tunic.

'You swam—'

'Swam! I almost drowned! Might be better if I had.' He shakes his head mournfully. 'You can't know what it is to lose your honour.'

She has taken a step forward at the thought of his dying. 'Yes, I can.'

'How?' he starts, and she cuts him off: 'I just can.'

He searches her face, then slowly nods, not that she's told him something new, but that he's finally understood something. He holds out his hand and she takes it, and he pulls her down beside him on the bale, and for a moment they sit very still between the glinting dusty bars of light.

'You're the only one I've told.'

'Why?'

'Because you're the enemy.'

He presses his lips together.

'*His* enemy, at least. He was one of the ones who built your camp. Left the day you came. Off to France.'

'Then it doesn't matter,' he says. 'No one else knows.'

'They will,' she says. 'Soon enough.'

He opens his mouth, closes it.

'What will you do?'

She shrugs, and he nods as if she's answered, finally bows his head.

This close, she can smell him, and the scent is surprisingly familiar. It takes her a moment to realise, he smells like the mountain after sleeping on it.

'You must be starving,' she says presently, and he raises his eyebrows. She clasps his hand and leads him towards the house.

He hesitates at the threshold as if fearing a trap.

'How do you like your eggs?' she asks.

'Very much,' he says, looking about, and she doesn't correct him, but decides frying would be fastest.

She sets them before him, two lace-edged eggs, looking oddly naked on the plate, and steps back, suddenly shy of him. He falls on them, eating the first methodically, lapping the sluggish yolk

– she'd compromised between hard and soft – with the rubbery white, before he thinks to look up. He swallows hard and gestures to the chair across from him.

He eats the second egg more slowly, smiling and nodding between mouthfuls. Afterwards, she pushes a napkin towards him and he dabs at his beard.

'Thank you!'

'You're welcome.'

They both fall silent, as if overhearing their own conversation for the first time.

'I want you to know, I would never have told them about this.'

She nods.

'How have you been travelling?' she asks, to change the subject.

He rubs his face. 'I just follow the sheep. I thought they would know to keep away from any soldiers.' He laughs. 'I envy them! If only I could live off grass, I could be free.'

'Not so free,' she says, thinking of the *cynefin*. 'They don't stray far.'

'Maybe it's a kind of freedom too. To stay home.'

She gives a short laugh. 'I never thought of it like that.'

He shrugs.

'How much longer do you think until they find you?'

'A few days, perhaps, if I'm lucky. But I think I will give myself up. End my holidays.' He smiles crookedly.

'For me, you mean.'

He purses his lips. 'I don't want to make trouble for you.'

'No trouble,' she says. 'I could feed you, find you clothes.'

'Even if I never escape?'

She nods slowly.

'Thank you,' he breathes. 'But no.'

'When will you do it?'

'Soon. Today.' His face clouds, and she knows he's thinking of it, of surrendering again, raising his hands.

'Surrender to me,' she says suddenly.

He smiles, shakes his head. 'They'd never believe it.'

'You're too proud,' she says, 'to surrender to a woman.'

'And you? Who would you surrender to?'

She studies his face. The beard, she thinks, becomes him. True, he looks a little like a castaway, but also older, as if he's coming into himself.

'It's why you kept coming back, isn't it?' she asks, and he grins.

'I was starving.'

She's silent for a long time and then he raises his arms, palms out, and she steps forward, takes his hands, draws them down around her.

She has led him out of the house, gripped by a sudden claustrophobia – it's her father's house, her mother's – to a sheltered corner of the field behind the barn. Now she lies beneath him, buoyed by the thick bed of uncut grass at her back, staring at the sky, the clouds ebbing across it. She fears she might recall Colin, but instead it's Rhys he reminds her of, with his gentle, gingerly fumbling, and she wonders suddenly if Rhys died a virgin; hopes not, for his sake. She presses her face to his neck, tastes salt – *the sea* – watches the clouds slide together, then slowly and silently tear themselves apart.

Afterwards, lying side by side, staring at the sky, he asks, 'So, did I surrender to you, or you to me?'

'Can't you tell?'

He turns his head in the grass. 'No.'

'Me neither,' she says. 'Not everything is war, after all, I suppose.'

She stretches. 'What would you be doing now if there were no war?'

'The same, I hope. You?'

'Not likely.'

He rolls on to his side and stares at her.

'I'd make you . . . woo me.' She giggles.

'How?'

'Ask me to the pictures?'

'Of course! Would you care to join me?'

'Why, however did you know? I love the pictures.'

He holds his arm up, crooked, and she slips hers through his, and they lie there staring up at the bright screen of the sky, arm in arm. After a few minutes their breaths are so steady they seem to fill the clouds, blowing them away. Like filled sails, she thinks.

'How on earth do you get the ship in there, anyway?' she asks suddenly, and he laughs.

'No, really. I want to know the secret.'

'No secret. You just ask the bottle very nicely!'

She joins him then, the two of them in each other's arms, stifling their laughter against each other.

When she finally sits up she feels lightheaded, as if she's just rolled down the hillside, the way she used to when she was a girl.

'What will you do?' he asks a little later, and she knows from his tone what he means. She may have been thinking of Rhys, but he was thinking of Colin.

'I don't know.'

She feels the tears drawing up from somewhere so deep inside she's sure they'll be ice cold.

And then he breathes, 'I wish I could marry you.'

She stares at him, shoves the tears aside with the heel of her hand as if to see him better, finally starts to laugh.

'What? What is it?'

'Oh, I'm sorry. I'm sorry. It's just that I'm not sure that would help exactly!' Then she sees his face. 'But I wish you could, too.' And she does. Her second proposal, she thinks, stroking the long grass.

And then he whispers, 'Keep it.'

Her fists tighten on the stalks. 'What business is it of yours?'

'I might have shot him,' he says, 'your soldier. If I hadn't been captured, I mean.'

'I wish!'

'Or he me.'

'Don't say so.'

'I'm the enemy, remember. I shot others not so different to him. I don't even know how many.' He looks at her, and her eyes flick away. 'Keep it,' he says. 'For me.'

'For my enemy?'

'Your prisoner.'

She starts to deny it, stops. He's right. These are the very last moments of his freedom. It would be easy to promise him, but instead she turns away, stares down the long slope beyond the house to the wavering shore, the breakers flipping and churning like the sheets of a restless sleeper, studying it all as if she'll never see it again.

They dress in silence, not looking at each other.

'Well,' she says at last.

'Yes, sir.' He comes to attention and she shakes her head.

'Please don't.'

'May the prisoner make a request?'

'What?' she asks warily.

'A last . . . cigarette?'

'Of course. They're in the kitchen.'

'It might be my last for a long while.' It takes her a moment to register his sly grin, and then she shoves him, turns and runs for the house.

She's in the yard, still in the lead just, before she sees the figure emerging from the barn.

'Get away from her!'

It's Jim, shotgun in hand.

She pulls up and Karsten runs into the back of her, grasps her.

'Run,' she whispers. Jim looks like he's about to topple over from the weight of the gun. 'Oh, please run.' But Karsten just squeezes her, whispers in her ear, 'It's better like this. To give myself up to him. I owe him something.' And slowly he releases her, turns towards Jim, his hands rising as if weightless.

Jim is squinting at the bearded figure, then he beams with delight. 'I knew it was you!' and Karsten nods ruefully.

The boy stands guard over him until Arthur appears for supper, and then the two of them lead Karsten away.

She watches them go over the hill together, Karsten in front, his hands on his head; the boy behind, now clutching a pitch-fork; Arthur in the rear, the shotgun over his arm, his cap tipped back, where he pushed it in consternation when he'd first come upon them.

She asked to go with them, but Arthur had shaken his head, and she'd not known how to insist. 'It's a lucky escape you've had, my girl,' he said, his face stricken, when she told him the story of Jim's rescue.

She'd looked at Karsten, but he refused to meet her eye, as he had ever since Jim appeared. What else could he do, she thinks, and yet seeing him square his shoulders as the men left, she couldn't help feeling he was relieved somehow, and she feels cheated. And it comes to her, watching her father's grim face, that perhaps it wasn't escape she's been lusting after these past few days, but capture. Could that be it? Was all her recklessness just a desire to be caught red handed? How many times this past week has her heart raced at Arthur's appearances, how many times has she felt a kind of anger at him for being so dense? Is that why she'd driven Karsten away so vehemently? Because, if she were caught, so would he have been? But now he *is* caught, she thinks, and she envies him almost as much as if he'd got away. He'd been protecting her by not looking at her, not speaking to her, as she paced back and forth across the yard, but now she wishes he'd just embraced her, or she him.

This is what men will never understand, she realises, watching the distant figures breast the ridge, Karsten's hands thrown up against the sky for a final moment, then sinking out of sight, followed by Jim's silhouette, Arthur's. Their dishonour, men's dishonour, can always be redeemed, defeat followed by victory, capture by escape, escape by capture. Up hill and down dale. But women are dishonoured once and for all. Their only hope is to hide it. To keep it to themselves.

That evening the pub is filled again, as if the village has breathed out. The guards are back too. She hasn't seen it so full since D-day.

Even Jim is allowed in, a signal honour. Arthur hoists him on the bar, patiently lets him tell his story in English, while the other lads can only cluster at the doors and windows. Jim's glowing, Esther sees, burning with heroism (or at least the beer Harry's been letting him sip). It's another gift the prisoner has given him, she sees. One man's loss, another's gain.

'Why, I thought he was going to prick Jerry like a sausage with that pitchfork!' Arthur is telling them in Welsh.

When it's her turn to speak up, she plays her part, albeit mutedly.

'Thank goodness for Jim here.'

'Ah, there was nothing to be scared of,' George, the guard, says. He's drunk, Esther sees, making up for his lost nights' drinking.

'It's not like *you* caught him,' she hisses.

'Lucky for him, or he might not have walked back to camp, but been carried. Trouble he put us to.'

'Can't blame him for trying to escape,' Arthur calls from the other side of the bar.

'Enemy sympathiser, is you now, Evans?'

Esther starts guiltily, but the constable is glowering at her father, jealous, she sees, that Arthur is the one to have brought the fugitive in. 'Your enemy's enemy, is that it?' It's an old gibe. The constable likes to needle the nationalists by reminding them that some of their leaders had spoken up for Germany before the war.

'There's no dishonour in serving your country, I think,' Arthur growls in Welsh. 'Wouldn't you agree, officer?' he adds, switching to English, which shuts Parry up. 'Like to think I'd do the same,' Arthur goes on. 'Like to think we all would.'

They carry Jim home, asleep and snoring heavily.

Arthur lays him in his bed, and Esther tucks him in, and the two of them stand over him for a moment, watching him sleep.

Later, as she lies awake in her own bed, she envies Jim his deep, even breathing. She wonders if it's the German's fate that's troubling her. She could have fed him, she thinks, perhaps hidden him for months. But when she thinks of it now, she feels the burden of it, the responsibility, pinning her to her bed. She didn't want his life in her hands, she realises, not even after they'd made love. Otherwise she'd have insisted on concealing him.

Her hands steal over her belly. The escape has distracted her, delayed her. But now she feels her stomach growing heavier, a weight pressing her deep into the mattress, deeper, until it seems like the weight of a man covering her, and she sits up with a cry.

Twenty-Two

The sun, which she'd thought gone for winter, comes out again briefly in mid-September, swelling from behind the clouds, drying out the grass, to Arthur's delight, but making Esther melt beneath her sweater and heavy coat.

She knows there are ways to get rid of babies, but she doesn't know what they are. All she knows, from the farm, is how to save lambs. It frightens her, the thought of losing the baby, but then she looks at Mrs Roberts, back at work behind her counter the very day after the telegram – calmer now than before the news, as if the worst is over – and she thinks, *If she can stand it, a grown child, all that wasted love, so can I.* Esther hasn't seen her cry once since the day of the telegram; the circles under Mrs R's eyes look leathery as scales.

On Jim's thirteenth birthday, the week before, she'd appeared at Cilgwyn with a present for him, a box of lead soldiers. 'Cor!' he cried, falling on them like treasure, and Mrs R gave a twitchy smile and told him they were Rhys's. 'He'd want you to have them, I expect.' Esther had seen the torn look on the boy's face as he fingered the little figures, how much he wanted them for himself. But then he thrust the box out. 'Rhys will want them . . . when he gets back.' It's Jim's latest hope that Rhys has escaped from some German camp. The box had swayed there in the air for a long moment. 'Well, you look out for them until then, eh?'

Mrs R told him softly, and Jim declared, 'I will!' in his new baritone, as if she'd just entrusted him with a life.

Esther has taken her lead from Mrs R's stoicism, trying to be equally brusque with well-wishers offering sympathy after her encounter with the German. Truth be told, she knows she'd crumple at the first hint of kindness over her real woes.

At the pub each evening, she watches Mary across the bar, not listening to her but watching her lips, trying to imagine her saying, 'Oh, luv, I know just the remedy.' Then, in late September, Harry announces they'll be off soon – 'Called back to London, now things aren't so hot' – he and Mary and the whole BBC contingent. Numbly, Esther rings up his order and stares at the pair of cigarette cards from the *Wireless Wonders* series, autographed by Harry and Mary, that hang in frames behind the bar. She can hardly recognise the impossibly young Harry doffing a homburg to reveal a lush head of hair, or the silkily airbrushed Mary in pearls and a marcel wave, wouldn't believe they were the same people if she hadn't seen them sign the cards – 'Cheers, big ears,' followed by Harry's scratchy autograph, and 'Kisses! MM,' the rounded *M*'s, one above the other, tracing the line of Mary's perfect décolletage. She listens to the show that night (Harry doing a skit about two German POWs caught digging a tunnel: 'Ach du lieber, Fritz. Next time, vee need to hide zeh dirt.' 'But vere, Hans?' 'Vee vill dig another toonnel and hide it in zere!'), thinking, *I'll never see them again.* Yet she still can't imagine telling Mary.

And then, on the fifth evening after Karsten's capture, she hears George and Les laughing. When Harry wants to know what the joke is, they tell him, 'Not so much a joke as a pratfall, you might say. Bit of slapstick. Seems our Jerry runner took a tumble, slipped on a bar of soap—'

'Oh, it might have been a banana peel,' Les volunteers to renewed laughter, none of them having seen bananas for months.

'Or perhaps a patch of ice,' George continues. 'Anyhow, seems he broke his leg, snapped like a stick of rock, I hear.'

Esther puts a hand to her mouth. *So this is what it is to be caught.*

'Oh, it's all right, luv. Luckily he wasn't going anywhere for a while.' She's grateful that George seems more interested in Harry's reaction. 'Now don't tell me that don't tickle your funny bone. Don't tell me it don't crack you up.'

But Harry just sits stone faced among the laughing men.

'Thought you'd appreciate it, specially like,' Les says, and the others quieten down.

Harry takes a sip of his drink. 'How's that then?'

'Why, on account of you're a . . . joker, of course. A jester? Ain't that what you are? Harry Hitch? Hairy Itch, more like!'

'Fuck me, if it isn't Oscar Wilde,' Harry says pleasantly.

'All right, gents,' Mary weighs in. 'Amateur hour is over. Don't call us, eh?'

'Don't call you what?' Les leers.

'That's enough!' Esther sticks a finger in Les's face. 'Or *you've* had enough. The lot of you.' She glares around at the guards, who smile, look to Jack and the constable – 'Listen to the lady, lads' – and finally shrug.

'Hecklers,' Mary is saying. 'Radio's made me soft, or I'd have had his guts for garters. But thanks, luv.' She smiles approvingly. 'Grown right up, you have. Anyhow, I owe you one.' Behind her, Harry nods over his beer.

It comes to Esther later, on the slow walk home, that she's been clinging to some shameful, superstitious hope of the German's seed driving out Colin's, of the war being fought in her womb. Of bloodshed.

The next night she summons the courage to follow Mary out to the privy, telling her of the pregnancy in the shadows behind the pub, not ten yards from where she first kissed Colin four months ago. The thought of that somehow makes her laugh, and Mary tells her, 'Oh, luv. That's not one little bit funny.'

Yet perhaps it's the laughter, the hysterical edge to it, that convinces Mary.

'Aren't you the dark horse,' she says sadly. 'So that's your secret.' But Esther shakes her head.

'I'm not saying who the father is, so don't ask.'

Mary gives her a sidelong look.

'You don't know him, anyway, so don't think you do,' Esther snaps.

'Why are you telling me?'

'I want to keep my secret.'

'Just not the baby,' Mary says a little fiercely, and Esther nods, head bowed. But when she replies, it's with steely bitterness.

'It's all right for you. You're free. You'll be leaving soon. The war'll be over and you can go anywhere, do anything. And don't tell me the world's not all it's cracked up to be – *you* stay here!' She struggles to get her anger under control, offers a last tight plea: 'I'll do anything.'

'That's what worries me.'

But after a long, appraising pause, Mary tells her she knows a fellow.

'Doctor in Liverpool. Used to look after girls on the boards if they got into . . . difficulties.' She studies Esther closely. 'Well, luv, "If it were done when 'tis done, then 'twere well it were done quickly."'

Esther nods.

She's restless all the next day, until in the afternoon she calls to Arthur where he's working in the barn that she's going blackberrying. She's halfway there before she realises that the best bushes scraggle along the lane behind the camp. She hasn't been back since the escape, and she's shy now, bending over hedges, concentrating on her picking until she reaches the shadows of the trees. Only then does she let herself look up, tarry. The men below her seem even more lackadaisical than usual. She's heard he's got two weeks in solitary, but there's no knowing how long he'll be in the infirmary while his leg is set. She can make out the cellblock from here – the same cells Jim was locked in the night of her rape, a prison within a prison. Men are playing football in front of it, and she winces as they slide into tackles, imagines the sickening pop of bone, and suddenly she can't bear to look, crouches low over her basket, staring into it at the dark berries and then at her fingertips, stained with juice as if with ink. She gets up slowly and climbs away, never looking back at the camp.

That evening, Mary comes up with some cock-and-bull story about a visit to an ailing friend in Liverpool – 'Old Miss Bunbury' – and spreads it round the pub. Harry makes a fuss about missing her, but Mary tells him to give over. Then she says, ' 'Ere, Esther, you're always on about seeing the big city. Why don't you come along with me. Miss Bunbury won't mind, and I could use the company. Even treat you to a ticket, I will.'

It seems so transparent to Esther, but Jack thinks it's a capital idea – he has a bit of a crush on Mary, Esther realises – and Arthur can't keep up with Mary's rapid English long enough to object. Stubborn as sin, Arthur is nonetheless abashed by Mary, for once in his life embarrassed by his slow English, too proud to let this woman see she knows more than him. He knits his brows in concentration, his shaggy eyebrows curling like fish hooks. 'Forecast's for rain,' he says with a shrug. 'I suppose I can spare her.' And for a moment Esther feels sorry for him, even though every day since she's realised she's pregnant, she's lived in fear of him finding out – not so much that she's pregnant, but by whom, her own private shame suddenly a shared national one.

That night, she lies awake thinking of him at the last lambing, hands red from a basin of steaming water, tying a noose in a waxed cord, telling her to steady the shuddering ewe between them – its breath coming in hot, grassy snorts while he reached into it. But that lamb had lived, she tells herself.

She has a spasm of doubt the next morning, tells Arthur she doesn't think she can spare the time, but he tells her nonsense. 'You've been . . . not yourself lately,' he says, and she looks away. He's sharpening the scythe, following its curve with long, whistling strokes of the whetstone, but he sets it aside. 'Down in the mouth, I mean. It's understandable, what with the news about young Roberts and the fright of that Jerry.' He nods as if agreeing with himself, reaches for the whetstone again, sets it singing back and forth along the blade. 'Do your spirits a world of good, a bit of excitement.'

The hardest part is telling Jim, who's instantly jealous. 'It's not fair! Why can't I go? I'm *from* there!' And when Arthur tries to hush him, the boy cries, 'He was *my* friend. Why does *she* get all the sympathy?' He only shuts up when his newly broken voice betrays him, rising girlishly.

In her anxiety, she arrives too early for the bus to Caernarvon, where she's to meet Mary. She looks up from her watch to see Mrs R beckoning from the post office door.

'Off to Liverpool, I hear.'

Esther nods, unsurprised.

'An adventure! I remember my first time. I didn't want to come back.'

The possibility hasn't crossed Esther's mind, yet it's so suddenly obvious she feels guilty as she hastens to deny it.

'Only teasing. You should see a bit of the world. Here, I've a map of the city about someplace, might come in handy.' Before Esther can object, she's popped back inside. 'Hang on a mo.'

It's chilly in the shadow of the post office, and Esther looks longingly towards the bus stop, the green bench shining glossily in the morning sun. The street is momentarily empty, utterly still. *Like a photo*, she thinks. And then the bus grinds into view around the far corner, its maroon flanks scraping the hedgerow.

She's on the verge of bolting when Mrs R reappears, slaps a yellowing map into her hand.

'There, wouldn't want you to get lost.'

'Thank you,' she breathes, a little too fervently, but Mrs R cuts her off. 'Better run now.'

Esther opens the faded map on the bus, stares at all the streets spread before her, but the tiny type makes her dizzy so she gazes out of the window instead. The trees are still full, she sees, but where they hang over the road, the leaves that flutter against the glass are dull and curling slightly, like hands at rest.

Mary meets her in front of Caernarvon station, a little round valise in her gloved hand, and when she asks Esther if she's all right, the girl nods and smiles nervously. 'I've never been on a train before,' she says, and Mary grips her hand.

Once they're in the compartment, Esther fidgets, craning back and forth, looking around her, her hands stroking the nubbly upholstery. It's all familiar from the films she's seen, yet when the train clanks forward she starts and giggles. 'It's so . . . exciting,' she says, by way of explaining to Mary, and then she hears herself and her face falls.

They pick up speed, the racketing clatter building all the time, and she looks at Mary in alarm. 'Is something broken?' And the other smiles and shakes her head.

When they're settled, just the two of them alone in the compartment, Mary hands her the valise, and Esther, after a moment's hesitation, springs the catch and opens it.

She sees her own eyes grow large in the vanity mirror set into the satin-lined lid.

'Glad rags,' Mary tells her, leaning back on the seat cushions with a lopsided grin. 'For your day on the town.' Esther looks down at herself, her thin gingham dress – Sunday best, though she feels a hypocrite in it – and her long wool coat, too heavy for the season but all she has that's halfway decent.

'Go on,' Mary says.

Esther pulls out a neat tweed suit with a matching hat and gloves, an ivory-colored blouse – 'Silk?' she breathes, and Mary nods – and lastly filmy stockings, a garter belt. She looks up teary, and Mary crosses the compartment, holds her, lets the train rock her through the countryside.

'I thought you might want a . . . a costume,' Mary says at last. 'I don't know. That's the actress talking, eh? I know it's silly, but I bet you'd feel better if you put them on. For a bit of confidence. You'll need a change anyway. Why not put these on now and get into your others after?'

A disguise is what she means, Esther thinks. So she'll look like a city girl. When she fingers the watery blouse, she can't imagine herself in it, but that somehow seems the point. That in it she won't be herself any more, but someone else.

'They're so lovely,' she says. 'I can't – I'd just get them dirty.'

Mary clasps Esther's hands in hers and whispers, 'Put 'em on.'

And she does. Though not without a shy glance at the windows. The compartment is a non-communicating one, there's no danger of interruption, yet there's glass on all sides of her.

'You'll just be a blur.' Mary laughs. 'A beautiful blur!'

Still, Esther waits until they're speeding along the coast, flat drab fields on one side and the flashing high tide on the other. The sea looks so inviting, so alive, the waves breathing in and out, she can't understand why she'd ever preferred a pool. Tawny autumn sunlight glances off the surface, ripples through the carriage, and she pictures herself in one of the gaily striped changing huts along the front at Llandudno or Rhyl, stepping into a new bathing suit, ready to strike out into the waves like Esther Williams. But when she catches a glimpse of her face, hanging ghostly in the window, she sees her own smile is pallid, not the bright bared beam of the swimmer. And what of poor Karsten? He's not going to be swimming anywhere soon. She visualises his leg in a heavy cast, dragging him down beneath the waves, like a movie gangster with his feet in cement.

She steps gingerly out of her clothes, putting out a hand to steady herself against the speed of the train, blushing at the state of her underwear, until Mary hands her the new clothes and then she's lost in the feel of them, the smooth clasp of the silk stockings, so unlike the scratchy woollen ones she's used to wearing, the softness of the blouse at her neck. She thinks of the stockings Eric had given her years earlier, but she'd slipped them on only once, surreptitiously, in the house, just up and down quickly, too frightened of discovery even to look at herself in the mirror.

Afterwards, Mary comes close, tucks Esther's hair behind her ears and smooths rouge into her cheeks – 'War paint!' – pats her softly with the downy sponge from her mother-of-pearl compact.

'There,' she says, and positions Esther by the window as they thunder through one of the tunnels along the coast, for her to admire her dark reflection. 'Chin up,' Mary whispers in her ear, and when Esther straightens, Mary shrugs the rayon macintosh off her own shoulders and drapes it over Esther's like a cape. 'Bravo!'

Later, after the giddiness has passed and the tracks have turned inland towards the city, Mary asks her gently if she's sure, and Esther nods, because she is. She's thought it through. All she can think is that what's inside her is a little piece of Colin. Mary tries to tell her, 'It's not him, whoever he is, not anymore, luv. Whatever's in there isn't responsible.' But Esther just stares ahead, unblinking, at the approaching city, its smoking chimneys like a thousand steaming kettles. England, she thinks, wondering when they crossed the border.

Mary has the cabby they meet at the station drive them around the town. 'My pal's never seen the city,' she says, and he takes them past the docks so that Esther can glimpse the Mersey, the golden Liver Birds glinting dully in the distance. He takes them past the cathedral, detours around streets closed and flattened by bombing, and then Mary has him drive past theatres she's worked at. The Orpheum, the Apollo, the Regency. 'Regency's gone,' the driver says, and Mary slumps a little. 'The old Reg. Got my start there in a dance act, Bean and Bubbles.' She squares her shoulders. 'Well, now they can put in those better dressing rooms they was always promising us.'

Beside her, Esther stares out at the ruins around her, the ruins Arthur is so eager to rebuild. She's seen the newsreel footage of the Blitz, the burning buildings and the littered streets looking as rocky as the slopes around the quarry. But it has never been quite real to her. Now she begins to understand. A single gutted house still stands at the end of one flattened terrace like an exclamation mark, and she suddenly sees the streets as sentences in a vast book, sentences that have had their nouns and verbs scored through, rubbed out, until they no longer make any sense. *All those buildings,* she thinks, *I'll never see.* The boarding houses she'll never sleep in, the cinemas she'll never sit in, the cafés she'll never eat in. And not just here, but in London, in Paris. She has so much wanted to see the world, and now, before she's got any farther than Liverpool, she's beginning to see how much of it is already gone.

Mrs R's map, which she's taken out to follow their route, lies across her lap, but when she goes to close it, she can't seem to work out how to fold it flat however hard she tries.

'There, now.' Mary throws an arm around her. 'There. It'll be OK.'

She has the cab drop them at the Queen Anne Hospital, and she goes in and asks for Dr Trotter. 'Doc Rotter, we used to call him,' she whispers to Esther. 'Just a joke! He started out looking after one of our leading men with the clap – only applause he never wanted, let me tell you! – and then moved up, or down, I suppose.' The doctor looks surprisingly old when he comes out – silvery at the temples – but when he gets closer, Esther sees he's not as old as she thought, just haggard, his tall frame bent over. She can see the outline of his knuckles where his fists are thrust deep into the sagging pockets of his crumpled white coat. It's as if they're holding him up, those straining pockets, and she concentrates on them, unable to look him in the eye.

'Yes?' he says impatiently, and then he sees Mary and his pale face reddens in blotches. Without another word, he strips off his coat and throws it in a wicker hamper by the door, ushers them across the street into a dank pub.

It seems perfectly fitting to Esther that on this strangest of days someone should be ordering her a drink from a barmaid.

'Thank you,' she says shyly when he sets a Guinness in front of her.

He shakes his head. 'Don't,' he says. 'It's medicinal. And don't even ask,' he tells Mary. 'If I'd got your telegram sooner, I'd have sent back you were wasting your time. I'm not in that line any more.'

'Anyone would think you weren't pleased to see me,' Mary says with a little pout, but he's not having any of it.

'I'm not doing it, Mary. It's no use.'

She stares at him, and he leans across the table.

'You're thinking you can blackmail me, perhaps, but in the first place I don't care, and in the second place no one else will either. You know what I have in there? A ward of blokes just brought in on a hospital ship. Pulled out of the North Atlantic. Torpedoed. Know how cold those waters are? Man's lucky to live ten minutes. Know what kept them alive? All the oil burning on the surface. I've fellows in there with the hair scalded off their heads, and frostbitten toes. You think they give a toss what I've done in the past?'

He glares back at Mary across the table, and she takes a sip of her drink.

'Please,' Esther says, but softly, as if she's talking to one of those poor torpedoed men.

'Not a chance, miss. I'm sorry for you, but . . .' He drinks, sets his glass down with a knock. 'I lost four patients overnight. Four.' He's studying her, but she can't take her eyes off his hands, the long fingers curled around his pint. 'They're the ones I pity. Someone's got to. Lord knows the enemy doesn't. Those U-boat bastards never stop for survivors.'

'The enemy!' she starts, but then has no idea what she means to say. Something about his being as pitiless as the Germans, but then it comes to her that they're not all without pity.

The doctor waits, frowns, then adds more softly, 'If you want my advice, you just won't, all right?' He turns to Mary. 'And you won't let her, if you're her friend. Just look at her. She's a slip, anaemic for sure. Undernourished and overworked, I'd say.'

He finishes his beer in two more swallows and rises to his feet. Mary stands quickly and Esther sees her open her mouth, close it, then take his hand in hers. He flinches slightly, but she holds on.

'Look after yourself, all right, Doc?' she whispers, and stretches to give him a peck on the lips.

He seems to stand a little straighter after that, and as his features relax, Esther sees how handsome he is. But then he gives an impatient hitch of the shoulders and leaves the pub.

When she sits down, Mary points at Esther's drink and tells her weakly, 'Bottoms up, darling.'

'He's a grumpy bastard, I know, but he's a good doctor,' Mary says after a couple more sips. 'If he says it isn't safe, it isn't safe.'

Esther stares at her. 'Have you ever . . . ?' she begins, and Mary says, 'How do you think he got into the game?' She takes a swift drink. 'He was married then. She's dead now. Wouldn't leave her. Couldn't, he said. So I told him I couldn't have it, or I'd scream blue murder and make a scandal. And so we . . . unmade it. And a couple of times since, I've brought other girls to him, for his sins. I'm sorry. I suppose the war's changed him. For the better, mayhap.'

She frowns, and after a second Esther asks in a scared voice, 'Did you ever have children, Mary?'

She shakes her head. 'And I'm a bit long in the tooth for all that now.'

'I'm sorry.'

'Don't be. You've enough to worry about, dear.' Mary pats her hand.

'But if his wife's died—'

Mary cuts her off. 'In the war, luv. In the bombing. I couldn't very well . . . It'd have felt like taking advantage. Profiteering, almost.'

Esther studies her drink. She's not sure. It seems neat to her – Mary, the doctor – a tying up of loose ends. She wants something to come out of this trip. 'Besides,' Mary says, 'we've a lot of water under the bridge, I just told you.'

'But if you were in love . . .'

'Hearken to her about love,' Mary cries, but when she sees Esther's face fall, she softens. 'You need to save some of that hope for yourself, sweetheart. Not to mention, I think Harry would have something to say if I ran back to the doc.'

'He could find another partner,' Esther begins, and then she stops herself, conscious of Mary watching with that same patient stillness as when she's waiting for a punchline to sink in.

'Don't look so shocked,' she says, nodding. 'You're not the only one has secrets. He's not so bad, really. When he's not drinking or telling jokes, he's actually quite the darling.'

'I don't believe it!'

'Why do you think he kept stum about this whole trip?'

'He knows?'

'He knows to keep stum.' She studies Esther's face over the rim of her glass. 'I'm sorry, luv, I had to tell him. It's all right. Not everything's a joke to him, you know.'

It feels like such an intrusion to Esther. The thing she's most feared. She imagines Harry's hearty voice announcing her, her name flying through the air, invisible in the night, slipping out through the radios of the village.

'Tell me something, then,' Esther says fiercely.

'What?'

'Harry's secret. Where's he from?'

'From?' Mary looks at her carefully and decides. 'He's from Golders Green, luv.'

'But why's it such a big secret?'

'Because he's a Jew, you little idiot. Harry's Jewish.'

They wait outside the pub, opposite the hospital, for another cab, watching the ambulances pull up. Uniformed men are carried in, and two come out, one on crutches, one with a huge white bandage wrapped around his jaw, as if for a toothache. Mary treats her to cream tea at Lyons, and sitting there amid the tinkling din of china and silver, Esther realises she's going to have the baby. And that she'll have to tell Arthur. There's not much chance of concealing it from him any longer, a man whose business is pregnancy.

In the train on the way back, they don't talk much. Once Esther asks, 'But about Harry. How can he make jokes all the time? Jokes about the war?' And Mary shrugs. 'Hardly know myself sometimes. He says it's how he knows he's still breathing. Life has to go on, I suppose, luv.' Esther leans against the window frame and watches the country flicker past in the long evening like a film strip. When they enter the string of tunnels along the northern shore, it comes to her why so many of the films she's seen show trains racing through tunnels at romantic moments, and she flushes – not at the crudity of the imagery, but at her own denseness for not getting it. She sinks back in her seat and braces herself for each thundering entry, the rushing, pounding darkness of the tunnels. In between, she watches the coast slide past, the sun setting on the shining sand flats, a lone child toddling across the wetness with a bucket and spade in hand.

As dusk falls and she begins to recognise the landscape around them, she stands and begins to undress.

'You can have those,' Mary says. 'Really, luv. They look so much better on you.'

But Esther shakes her head. 'When would I wear them?' She smooths and folds them perfectly and lays them back in the case.

The train begins to brake, a feeling like falling in the pit of her chest, and instinctively she clutches herself, her hands spanning her stomach, *cradling* it, she thinks.

She looks up to see the flags fluttering from Caernarvon Castle, black against the sunset. 'They say it's well preserved,' Mary says absently. 'Is that so? Impregnable? Like our modern shore defences, thank goodness.'

Esther nods, doesn't bother to correct her. She herself had thought the castle, jutting into the straits, was an ancient version of the squat concrete pillboxes along the coast, until her father disabused her of the notion. 'That ain't why they built it. It's for the English garrison, stationed there to put down any Welsh rebellion. Defence against invasion, indeed! We'd already been invaded. That was the first outpost of their empire.' But so what if Wales was the first colony, Esther thinks now. It's still home, *still ours*.

Harry is waiting at the station, and he offers Esther a ride, and she accepts, eager to get home, to get it over with. They don't say much on the drive – Mary next to Esther in the back, Harry up front like a chauffeur – but the silence is companionable. Esther studies the back of Harry's head, his face in the mirror, but it looks no different.

'Did we miss anything?' Mary asks, and Harry shakes his head, then stops himself. 'Actually, yeah,' he says. 'I ran into a soldier while I was waiting for you at the station bar. Captain who came into the Arms, Esther, one night when you weren't on, a week or so back. You remember, Mary. This was when the other guards were all off hunting Jerry, and this one soldier comes in and gets into it with the Welshies?'

'Oh, him,' Mary says. 'Took offence at their calling him English or something, and then made some joke about how he might as well be German.'

'That's the one. Took himself off in a huff. Anyhow, I was sitting at the bar and this captain comes in and we both sort of looked at each other in the way you do when you recognise a fellow but can't quite place him. Anyhow, we got to talking and it turns out he was sent up here to investigate the escape, see.'

Esther leans forward in the back seat.

'Well, seems he was interrogating the prisoner after they brought him in, asking him where he hid and that, when the top Jerries in the camp made a stink and demanded to see their man. Something about making sure he hadn't been ill treated. Only – and here's the part – after they were done with him, his own people, mind, that's when he had his leg broken.'

'What?'

'Yeah, it was them that did it! His own men, not the guards. Those arseholes were just having us on, boasting and that.'

'His own fellows. But why?'

'Exactly,' Harry cried. 'That's what I asked this captain, and what he asked the Jerry himself.'

'And what did he say?'

'Just that they wanted to know what he'd been up to, same as the interrogator, and he wouldn't tell them.'

'Why not?' Esther asks.

'Well, now,' Harry says, warming to it. 'Listen to this. He told the captain he valued his privacy! How about that? *Valued his bleeding privacy!* Actually, the captain reckoned the bloke only escaped for a bit of solitude in the first place – seems it's not unusual. I asked him if he got anything more out of the fellow, but all he said was "What was I going to do, break his other leg?" Fellow wouldn't even say which ones had done it to him, apparently, and they all claim he slipped.'

Mary shakes her head, and Esther sinks back into the upholstery.

'Funny thing is,' Harry chatters on, 'I used to fancy myself an interrogator.'

'Pull the other one.'

'No, really. I thought about it. Back in '39. I was too old to fight, but I speak a little Deutsch and I wanted to do my bit. Besides, what's a comic do but ask a lot of questions. "What do you call a . . . ? What's the difference between a . . . ?" '

'All right.' Mary laughs. 'I'll bite. What happened? You volunteer?'

'Never went through with it. It come to me, see, that comics always answer their own questions. That's what makes it a joke, after all, the way we let the audience off the hook. For just a second they think it's serious, a test, and they don't know the answer. And then we let 'em off, and they laugh out of relief as much as anything.' He shakes his head dolefully. 'I'd have had my prisoners in stitches before I learned anything.'

Mary sighs. 'Talk about your Secret of Comedy.'

'Which reminds me.' Harry brightens. 'Get this. The captain also spilled the beans about that major, how he keeps his swagger stick in place.'

'How's that, then?'

'Turns out he has his batman sew a little loop under there, like a sling, see. Batman says he's got a wooden hand and all, but he prefers not to wear it, apparently.'

'What do you know,' Mary says dreamily.

Harry shrugs. 'Everyone's got their little secret.' He gives a little wince. 'Sorry girl.'

Mary squeezes Esther's hand as the girl weeps silently. 'You'll be fine, luv. You're a trooper!'

At the farmhouse, Harry leans out of his window and tells

Esther to listen to the show that night, and she nods absently, stands at the gate while they turn, and watches the car's headlights glide downhill. A *trouper,* she realises belatedly.

Liverpool, she thinks. A train, a car. A Jew. She can't believe it's been just one day, she feels so changed. The air is filled with the heavy scent of freshly cut grass. Arthur's been busy. She leans over the stone wall that divides the farmyard from the fields, stretching up the mountains behind the cottage, and takes a deep breath of the familiar perfume. She can just make out in the darkness the humped grey backs of the flock speckling the near slope. A couple of the closest sheep, a ewe and a lamb, roused by her presence, clamber stiffly to their feet and move off a few yards before kneeling again.

Arthur is standing over the slate sink when she comes in, scrubbing at a burn on one of the pots, and when he sees her he tries to hide it, but she puts a hand on his arm and makes him turn round. It's strange to find him at such a domestic task, and for a moment she stares at him as if she hasn't seen him for months. Indoors, without his cap, the red line where he pulls it over his eyes seems to divide his face in two. Below, he's tanned an angry red from the summer sun; above, his forehead is an almost sickly white. It's as if the blood has settled below his brows, like a pint that hasn't been topped up.

'What is it?' He smiles, and she reaches up and smooths down a wisp of white hair sticking up on his crown.

'Where's Jim?' she asks.

'Turned in.'

'I'm pregnant,' she says simply, and she sees his smile wither. He lifts his hand to her, red and dripping from the sink. *His own people,* she recalls, bracing herself, but then her father seems to stay his hand. In his eyes she can see her guilt and shame, reflected as fury, yet still he holds back, even as his hand seems bound to leap forward and strike her. It's the innocence of the child, she thinks. He would strike her, but not the child. She's guilty, but not the child. She is composed of nothing but shame and this tiny core of growing innocence. The baby suddenly seems more like herself than herself. It's as if she will give birth to herself and slough off this older, failed version. She feels fiercely defensive, willing to do anything to protect it.

So when Arthur asks, 'Who?' she tells him, 'Rhys,' and watches him lower his arm with a sigh. 'I knew it,' he says, and she realises in a rush – *of course!* – that Rhys would never have proposed to her if he hadn't already asked her father's permission. And Arthur must have given it, she thinks, as if it were back pay for the months of cheap labour, even though he knew how she felt about Rhys, even though he thought the boy a fool himself. It feels to her like a kind of betrayal, a rejection – perhaps he always meant to apply for work underground, hoped to get shot of the flock and her in one fell swoop – and it hardens her in her lie. *It's an ill wind,* she thinks defiantly. His words.

But just when she thinks she's escaped the blow, Arthur tells her, 'You'd best go along and let her know, eh?' Esther must look confused, because he adds, softly, 'His mam.' She baulks then, but he nods his head. 'It'll be a consolation to her, I'd say. And maybe not such a surprise, neither. She knows he was sweet on you.'

She hasn't thought it out; the name came to her so unbidden. It seemed so neat a moment before, so perfect, a way to keep her secret and the baby, a lie between Arthur and her, but now it's starting to seem messy. And yet how to take it back?

'I can't tell her,' she stammers. 'I'd be too ashamed.'

'Might have considered that before,' he says, though not unkindly. 'I'm sure she'll keep it quiet if you ask her – not that that'll be possible for long; it'll get harder before it gets easier – but you should tell her. It'll make the world of difference.'

And so she goes, telling herself it is a kindness. Rhys has already become such a memory for them all, such a fiction, really, like a character in a book, it's not hard to imagine these extra pages for him. What does it matter, anyway, who the father is? She could wait until the morning, tired as she is, but she knows she'll never sleep for thinking about it.

Outside, she heads to the barn and fetches the bike. When she comes out, she finds Jim perched on the top bar of the gate, like a bird on a telegraph wire.

'You're supposed to be in bed.'

'How'd it get in there?' he hisses. 'Was it really Rhys?' All she can do is swallow and nod, but when she looks up, what she sees on his face isn't doubt, but jealousy.

Rhys is hers now.

'You'll marry him if he comes back?'

She leans the bike against her side, nods again, stiffly, feeling as if her head is a stone that might tumble off her shoulders if she moves too much. Arthur hadn't asked the question – unable to utter that 'if' to her face – but she knows it's the unspoken assumption. The very end of the happy ending.

'Because you love him,' Jim says, as if explaining it to himself. 'And he loves you.'

'Yes?' she tells him. 'Yes.'

He purses his lips. 'But what if he doesn't come back?'

She gives a little strangled yelp, shocked despite herself – Jim has clung so tenaciously to the possibility of Rhys's survival, only to give up so easily now that he thinks Rhys hers – and then shocked at her own shock, at her instinctive duplicity. She puts her face in her hands to cover her confusion, and after a moment she feels him stroke her back.

'It's all right,' he says gently. 'If it's a boy, you could call it Rhys.'

Her sobs have convinced him, satisfied him somehow, yet in the midst of her relief she wonders where they've come from. She wouldn't have thought she could cry for Rhys if she'd had to. Doesn't think herself such an actress, no matter what Mary might reckon. Will lies just spring from her unbidden now? she wonders. Is she embarked on a succession of them, a lifetime of them? Because yes, if it's a boy, she will have to name it Rhys, and every day of its life she'll call it Rhys, Rhys, Rhys. She can feel the sobs coming again, but when Jim reaches his arm around her, pressing close, she jerks away.

'You should go to bed,' she tells him, and he glares at her as if to say, *Make me.* In the moonlight she notices a faint down silvering his upper lip. But then he sticks his tongue out and runs inside.

The war will be over soon, she thinks, looking after him, and he'll be gone too. His mother, Esther knows, has written to him recently to say she was finding a new place for them – no mention of 'Uncle' Ted – and that she'd send for him soon.

It comes to her that Colin was a boy once, and perhaps that's why, when she thinks of him now, she feels, for the first time, nothing. Not fear. Not hatred. He's done his worst, to be sure, but his worst seems suddenly so much less than her own.

She straddles the bike, points it down the lane and coasts through the dark village.

Twenty-Three

Waking in the infirmary, staring at his leg suspended above him, glowing palely in its plaster, Karsten wonders fleetingly if he's turning into the invisible man. He can't see his leg, though he knows it's there under the cast, itching fiercely, fragile as glass.

He'd been wary of the interrogator, his excellent German, so much more polished than that of the camp translator, a former lecturer in German literature who spoke an oddly accented brand of High German full of 'thee's and 'thou's, and whom the men called Charlemagne. Rotheram, the captain introduced himself as. He was in his late twenties, Karsten judged, no more than ten years older than him, yet he looked drawn, tired. When he leaned back to run a hand through his hair, he winced, clutched his side, rubbing at some ache, some old wound. His haggard look emboldened Karsten; the man seemed too exhausted to have his wits about him. He offered Karsten tea, and Karsten took it, careful not to let his hands shake. It shocked him that he'd looked forward, back in Dover, to interrogation, as a chance to prove something. But he'd had no secrets then. When Rotheram started by saying 'You surrendered, I see,' Karsten was actually relieved, not insulted.

The captain produced a pack of cigarettes from his pocket,

held it out. 'That must have been hard. Would you like to talk about it?'

It might have been the recollection of Dover or the question about surrender, but all at once Karsten realised he knew the fellow. He reached for the name. *Steiner.*

Karsten drew a cigarette from the pack as gingerly as if it were the pin of a grenade. He hadn't had a smoke for a couple of days – he'd lost Esther's pack when he'd been swept into the sea – and the bitter taste of the tobacco on his tongue thrilled him. He watched Rotheram/Steiner light a match, extend it across the table, and he bent stiffly to the flame. It took him a heady moment to master the darting rush of nicotine, to stop himself from drawing too hungrily on the cigarette.

When he steadied himself, he said, 'Can I ask you a question first? Is that permitted?'

'Not normally, no,' the captain said, smiling thinly. 'But I'll allow it.'

'Well, then, are you a Jew? A German Jew?'

Rotheram sat very still, the smile retreating from his lips. He looked at his hands on the table for so long that Karsten thought he was counting the hairs on them. Finally he said, 'Can't you tell?' And in truth Karsten couldn't. He'd recognised Rotheram as Steiner as soon as he'd offered a smoke, but that seemed less important than whether he should have recognised him at Dover, known he was a Jew. That's why he'd asked. He stared at the captain as if he might divine the other's secrets, and eventually Rotheram asked, 'What if I am?'

'Then I'd ask what it was like for you to leave,' Karsten said evenly. 'To run? I'd imagine that must have been hard, too.'

'Touché,' Rotheram told him. He looked up then. 'I'll tell you, if you tell me?' And Karsten, after a moment, nodded once.

'Then, yes, I am. I used to be a German, but now I'm just a Jew. Is that what you want to hear?'

It shocked Karsten to find that he believed the man. Stare at him as he might, however, Karsten couldn't see anything different about him, any more than he had with the couple his mother had turned away from the pension all those years ago.

'And leaving,' Rotheram went on steadily, 'running, if you will, was the most shameful thing I've ever done in my life. The most cowardly. Sometimes I think saving my life was the worst thing I ever did in it.' He leaned towards Karsten then, gave a gaping smile. 'But we both know that, I think. What we'd give for a second chance, eh, Corporal?'

Karsten watched the ash on his cigarette grow longer and longer, until it seemed that if he moved it would tumble, that he was sitting still in order to save it. Then Rotheram pushed his empty teacup forward. Karsten tapped the ash into the saucer, took a long last pull on his cigarette, and slowly shook his head.

'I'd do it again,' he said quietly, and when Rotheram opened his mouth, Karsten whispered, 'And you would too. It's all right.'

Rotheram had bent across the table, frowning. 'Do I know you? I mean from before, from home?'

And then there'd come a hammering at the door.

'Yes!' he'd cried in annoyance, and a guard hurried in, bent down to him and muttered something.

'The major sent you?' Rotheram demanded angrily. 'The major?' He seemed about to say more, but then glanced at Karsten, composed himself. 'Well, it seems there's going to be a brief interruption to our conversation.'

They'd congratulated him at first, the camp leaders, called him a hero, an inspiration. Schiller was with them; he'd probably begged to come along. *He's my friend*, Karsten could imagine him crowing. He'd actually winked at Karsten at one point, and he'd seen it then: The slate wiped clean. A way back into the fold. Welcome home.

But then they'd wanted to know what he'd seen, as if he'd been out on reconnaissance. He couldn't see how to tell them without talking about the girl, and if he mentioned her, even in passing, he knew it would spread, embroidered with rumours, beyond this little room, beyond these men, to the rest of the camp, and eventually to the guards. So he'd hesitated, and they'd seen it and become suspicious. How had he managed to elude capture so long? Luck, he suggested, but they shrugged it off. He wasn't the lucky kind, was he? It made them wonder, they said, wonder what he'd really been up to. Talking to the British, maybe?

'I'm no traitor,' he said, and they sneered at him.

'Did you really not learn anything out there?' Schiller pleaded, and Karsten nodded.

'Well?'

What *did* he learn out there? Nothing new, exactly, nothing the rest of the men didn't know. He'd realised it in the empty bunker, but it had come to him not as something new but something old, something recognised. He'd known it in France, on the beach, only he'd not been able to face it then.

What had so amazed him there was that the invasion, so vast in scale, could have been kept a secret. He'd heard, and discounted, the rumours of invasion all spring, just like the rest of them, yet still he couldn't fathom it. How had that time, that place, been kept so close? How had those thousands of men been kept secret, training at bases, massing in camps, produced now, as if by magic? He suddenly imagined the whole of Britain – not just the leaders, the soldiers, but the civilians, the families with sons and husbands and fathers in uniform – knowing, or at least suspecting, but somehow not breathing a word. A million people keeping a secret. It was almost more astounding than the sheer force of arms, that force of will. He had wanted to ask someone about it, but around him the men in the stockade hadn't breathed a word about the invasion to each other, just stared

302

out through the wire as if they couldn't believe their eyes, as if it were all invisible. And yet there was nothing else to talk about. It was as if, he thinks now, we were keeping the secret ourselves.

He remembers, amid the long line of men moving past him, focusing on the small white cross on a chaplain's helmet as it bobbed along in the column, coming closer and closer, and then as it passed he saw the man's pale face, the fear on it, and something about a priest's fear moved him. He wished he could comfort him somehow. He wanted to offer tips – tell him about the baker in the next village who sold passable wine from the back of his shop. He wanted to tell him not to worry, Father, that he'd make it, that he'd live. *You're going to win,* Karsten wanted to cry, and recoiled at once from the thought.

So he'd known it then.

The war was lost. Not quite over, but lost. That was the secret. The deserted shore defences he'd slept in had only confirmed it. But no, that wasn't quite right either. Really, it had been the girl who'd convinced him, or helped him accept it, rather. He'd felt such astonishment slipping inside her, as if he'd never quite believed it possible. It had seemed, even to him, the amateur conjuror, like true magic. He thought of a shining coin palmed snugly in the fleshy fold beneath his thumb; a still-warm pocket watch ticking in his hand beneath a silk handkerchief. Gone, disappeared. Just like that.

For a moment, he had thought the whole war had been waged for that purpose only; he had felt such peace, he was sure it must be over, that they'd separate and rise to the bright news of armistice. An end to the war that was neither victory nor defeat, just peace.

'What do you want to know?' he'd asked the camp leaders.

'Anything. Everything!'

'We're going to go home,' Karsten said. 'The war's almost over.'

'How do you know?' Schiller asked hopefully, and then another voice, sterner, daring him, 'Who's winning?'

303

He looked into Sulzer's face. 'They are.'

'What?' Schiller had wailed, but Sulzer had just turned away, and Karsten had marvelled, *He knows*.

They'd called him all the old names then – turncoat, coward – and he'd spat at them.

'You think it would have made a difference to fight to the death. What would it have meant? A minute's delay for the British, two maybe.' He stared at Schiller. 'Our deaths might have prolonged the Thousand-Year Reich by five minutes.'

'Traitor!' they howled. Karsten had known what was coming, but he leaned over the table and said it anyway: 'Before long they'll all have surrendered, all our countrymen. Will they all be traitors? Or just Germans?'

'Why, you,' Schiller began, and Karsten struck him in the face. It felt so good. He'd been dying to hit Schiller for weeks, he thought. And then he hit him again in the middle of his bloodied, surprised face, and this time Schiller went down. *It's a favour*, Karsten had thought viciously. *Now they won't think we're friends*. But then the others were on him, as he knew they would be. He tried to stay upright as long as he could under the flurry of blows, tried to remain conscious until he heard the whistles of the guards.

In the infirmary, he has begged, through his split and swollen lips, for a window bed, and the orderlies have taken pity on him, laid him down where he has a view of the fence and the trees and the hillside, where he can keep watch for her. The Welsh girl. The pregnant girl. It's growing dark now, though – the flame of his candle reflecting in the dark pane – and he knows she's not coming tonight.

He wonders about her baby, wonders if he should have said what he did. What business is it of his? And yet when she told him about it, he'd had a sudden impulse, *I can save it*, that same impulse, he thinks, that he felt towards Heino and even Schiller just before he surrendered. And he'd welcomed it.

Rotheram has been to see him that afternoon, but he seemed taken aback by Karsten's injuries, asking his questions gently and not pursuing them. *He thinks they did this to me because I talked to him,* Karsten realised. 'You'll get no more out of me than they did,' he said, and Rotheram replied, 'I see that now.' When he was done and packing his bag, Karsten told him, 'I never knew you,' and Rotheram barely glanced at his ruined face, then nodded.

Before he left, Karsten asked him for paper and pencil. Rotheram had slipped a pack of cigarettes under the lined sheets, which Karsten appreciated but hadn't meant to ask for. It's time to write to his mother again, he thinks. There are questions he wants to ask her about his father – how he was after the last war, how he was before. But first he must tell her the truth, tell her of his surrender. He thinks of passing down that long, dark tunnel out of the bunker, the blood pulsing hot in his ears, pushing himself on into the blinding light. And he pictures himself, at last, holding up his hands, though now as if he were waiting for someone to grasp them and pull him out. Like a second birth, he thinks.

He starts to write. In the swaying candlelight the lines on the paper look like strips of bandages, and he has the strangest impression of his writing hand, unwinding them as it moves across the page, revealing the words beneath.

Twenty-Four

M rs Roberts opens her door at the first knock, almost as if she's been waiting behind it. She seems old and frail in the evening light. Esther remembers her as a tough, bosomy woman in school. They were all a little afraid of her bustling energy. Now her previously round face is drawn, and her eyes bulge. She brings Esther through to the parlour, the best room, and insists on making tea. Esther's never been here before, and she feels self-conscious, left alone with Mrs Roberts's fine things: the gleaming brass carriage clock on the mantel, the etched mirror above. Beside the clock is a framed photograph, and it takes her a long moment to recognise Mr Roberts, stern beneath the bowler cocked low over his brow. And then she spots the familiar gap between his teeth. The walls, she sees, are covered with family pictures, rank after rank of faces peering down at her. Rhys is everywhere. He's rarely smiling – shy, for once, of his gap teeth, or perhaps advised not to by photographers, conscious of customer satisfaction – and his stiff features make him seem from another time, a contemporary of his ancestors. She hunches on the stiff horsehair sofa where she's perched, listening to her old teacher in the kitchen, trying to avoid their eyes. Instead, she meets the glassy glare of the stuffed and mounted robin on the sideboard, its beak gaping, breast puffed, but silent under its bell jar. She wonders if she can go through with this. 'Mrs R,' she calls, 'Mrs R!' But the shrill cry of the kettle interrupts her, and when Mrs Roberts calls back, 'Did you want something, dear?' her nerve fails her. 'No. Nothing.'

The whispered thought comes to her that there might be a baby picture of Rhys on the wall, and she steels herself to look up, glancing around wildly, filled with a sharp desire to see it, as if it were the future somehow, her fate. But there's nothing, and then Mrs R bustles back in, steam puffing from the spout of the teapot on the tray before her.

There's a lull while they stare at the tray between them, at the silver pot and solitary Eccles cake beside it, as the tea steeps. 'Oh, I couldn't,' Esther says at last, as if the cake has just materialised before her, but Mrs Roberts waves dismissively. ' "The funeral baked meats," ' she says almost gaily. 'I've been getting more food than I can eat. You'd hardly know there was rationing.' And after another pause Esther cuts the cake in half and says they'll share. She stares at the little speckled pastry on the Willow Pattern plate before her, the knife pressed to it, and tells *it*, as much as Mrs Roberts, that she's carrying Rhys's child. Spoken in English the lie seems more abstract, easier, as if someone else is telling it.

There's a moment when she thinks Mrs R doesn't believe it, a second of calculation when her features seem smudged in the lamplight, her expression indeterminate. She examines Esther with wary appraisal, as if they've never met, and the girl braces herself for judgement. But all she says at last is 'You're long-waisted. I see it now, of course. Don't know how I missed it.' She shakes her head. 'But that's always the way, isn't it? Never see what's right under our noses.' Her face tenses and then relaxes.

'*Duw*,' the old woman breathes. 'Thank God.' She is up, with her arms around Esther where she sits on the sofa, knife still in hand, shaking against the plate, and Esther finds herself weeping.

'There, child, there. You thought I'd be angry, didn't you? Disappointed, even.' She shakes her head, pulls a clean little hanky from her sleeve, touches it to Esther's cheeks. 'Truth is, I never thought you'd have him. He was so . . . well, a good boy, but not quick. Still, one never reckons with love, does one? Anyhow, don't cry. There's nothing to be ashamed of, not much. I know the fault isn't only on your side.'

Esther tries to pull away from her, but the old woman holds her tighter, puts her lips to the girl's ear.

'It's not the end of the world. Oh, there'll be talk and some jokes at your expense, it'll be hard for a bit, but it's not as if you're the first as ever fell.' She leans back, nodding. 'You might as well say it's a tradition in these parts. "The Welsh way," the English used to call it. "Welsh courtship," if you read your Mrs Gaskell. This is a hundred years ago now, but back then it was a winked-at practice, a betrothed couple who couldn't yet afford to marry sharing a bed before the wedding day. I dare say the practice isn't entirely dead, although there's some what abused it, reneged on the deal, which gave it a bad name. That's why they call it "welshing", you know. *That's* where it comes from.'

And now Esther does fight free, looks at her with frank astonishment.

'You didn't think I knew that, did you?' Her former teacher smiles. 'But I could hardly tell you in school. Some definitions you have to wait for until you're a grown woman.'

She means it all as a comfort, but when she looks at Esther's face, she seems to recoil, and Esther wonders what she sees there. Anger, perhaps. *It's your fault,* she wants to shout. *You taught me to speak the language.* And somehow the flash of hatred steels her in her lie.

'There, now,' Mrs Roberts says, groping for something more to offer. 'But my boy'll make an honest woman of you, mark my words.'

Esther hangs her head, almost gagging, puts a hand to her

mouth, presses her eyes closed. But even in the darkness the words appear before her – *honest woman* – scratched out on a schoolroom slate. It's as if the English words are mocking her now, flinging her lies back at her like a hollow echo, as if the very language is laughing at her. She dare not speak.

'Oh, I know,' the older woman cries, panicked by Esther's despair, and then, 'Here, here.' And when Esther looks up she finds Mrs Roberts wringing her hands – no, twisting at her finger, pulling at a ring. 'See!' she says, beaming triumphantly. 'This is the ring his old father gave me. Welsh gold, it is. It'd be yours soon enough, so why not now? Yes! That's the ticket. I'd have given it to Rhys for you if he'd only asked. We'll say he wrote to me. In his last letter. To give it to you. You won't have to feel a bit ashamed.' She nods rapidly and holds it up before Esther, a little golden O, and Esther feels her lips slowly forming the shape.

She should make fists of her hands, jam them in her pockets, sit on them, anything. But when Mrs Roberts takes her hand (*takes my hand,* Esther thinks, shying more from the phrase than the touch), it feels limp, numb, not her own at all, and she watches in horrified fascination as the older woman slips on the ring, pressing it gently over her knuckle.

'There!' She turns Esther's hand back and forth in admiration. 'You're a Mrs R yourself now, and it'll be a proper little Welsh babby, and no one can say any different.'

Esther is still staring at the ring when Mrs R says, 'May I?' And it takes her a slow moment to realise she wants to touch her. Esther nods minutely and submits, leaning back and watching Mrs R smooth her hands over her belly, like a Gypsy over a crystal ball. She wills herself not to flinch under the span of the dry fingers, looks away as they slide over her, imagining Mrs R's hands still dusty with blackboard chalk, stares at her rapt face instead. The swollen crescents beneath the old woman's eyes look like blisters in the half-light, and for a moment it seems to

Esther as if they've finally split. *She's crying,* she thinks, and yet there's a gleam of light in Mrs R's eyes. It's the light of inspiration, and something more, Esther sees.

'There, now. It's going to be all right. He'll come now,' Mrs Roberts says vehemently. It's her classroom voice. The voice that will brook no more dullness. For all her stoicism, Esther sees with astonishment, a current of hope has been coursing through Mrs R like an underground stream. 'He'll come back now, mark me. We just have to have hope, girl. Do you have hope?'

Esther looks at her through her tears and nods slowly. She does have hope, she realises. All this time she's thought Rhys dead, and now she hopes, prays, that he is.

And then she does gag, cupping her mouth, her eyes wide with panic as she looks around the parlour, at the polished wood, the lace antimacassars, the cut glass. But in the end it's only tea she spills, bumping the low table as she rushes out, down the tiled passage, and out of the door, to the yard and the privy. And by then she's swallowed it down again, the bile searing her throat, so she can only spit, over and over, in an effort to get the taste from her mouth.

After a few moments she hears the door to the yard open, and she's sure she's given herself away. She pictures Mrs R, ruler in hand, stalking between their desks during tests, ready to smack the knuckles of cheats. Once she'd actually broken her ruler across a boy's shoulders. Esther had been too afraid to cheat, she thinks now. That's why she'd always worked so hard. It wasn't so much the ruler, but the shame of being caught in front of the whole class. And it occurs to her that it wasn't just some boy whose back Mrs R snapped her ruler over. It was Rhys. Trapped in the tiny cell of the privy, amid the stink of bleach, Esther wishes she had cheated all those years ago, had been beaten for it.

There's a soft knock at the door. 'All right, dear? Never mind. It's only natural, morning sickness.'

And perhaps because it's dark out, just a powdery moonlight sifting through the high window of the privy, Esther misunderstands her, hears her say 'mourning sickness', before Mrs Roberts adds: 'Silly name for it, really. It can come over you any time.'

It's a long, dark walk up from the village, pushing the bike, the night wet and windy. Mrs R's ring is too big for her, rolling loose around her finger. She'd take it off, but she feels faint at the thought of losing it, so she makes a fist until the ring stands up like a new knuckle. What she'd give for a cigarette to take away the taste of sick on her tongue. She's calmer now, trying to decide how she feels about what she's done, probing the lie, testing it. How bad has she been? She feels a wave of tiredness, totters from it. It's been an endless day, but she takes her exhaustion for relief, though she can't quite shake the nagging sense that she's completed Colin's work, dishonoured herself finally and irrevocably. In the end, though, she's a farmer's daughter, and it's pragmatism that wins out.

Her mind turns to the last lambing season. It's her favourite time of year, she and Arthur working closely together, his fierceness tempered by tenderness for the lambs, but the previous spring had been a hard one. Too many stillbirths, and too many of those females. The male lambs, the wethers, meant money; they'd be sold off after a year for meat. But the females, the ewes, were what the future of the flock depended on, the carriers of the *cynefin*.

Towards the end of the lambing, they'd both been sitting up through the night, nursing two of the last ewes to deliver. Around three, Arthur's lamb had been stillborn, the mother circling it for a few minutes, sniffing at it lugubriously and then withdrawing to a corner of the makeshift pen of hay bales, crumpling with exhaustion. A half-hour later, Esther's ewe gave birth to a healthy lamb, but the mother haemorrhaged within moments of the delivery and swiftly bled to death, despite their best efforts. They'd tried setting the orphaned lamb in the pen with the bereaved mother, but she wanted nothing to do with the newborn, turning away when the lamb tried to press its head against her flank, kicking out when it followed shakily behind. Esther had to lift the lamb out of the pen to save it from being trampled. She'd gone in search of a bottle, thinking to hand-rear it, though she'd never managed to with one so young.

When she came back into the circle of yellow lamplight, Arthur was cradling the dead lamb in his big hands, its head flopping over his wrist. He watched as she touched the snout of the bottle to her lamb's mouth. It licked the teat once, twice, then twisted away, struggling feebly in her arms, and Arthur shook his head. He'd pulled a knife from the hay bale beside him and set about the lamb in his hands, skinning it swiftly and neatly, and she watched, horrified as he tugged the fleece from the filmy blue flesh of the body with a soft tearing sound, the bloody carcass emerging, almost as if it were being born a second time. He set it gently beside him when he was done, came towards her with the wet fleece, and numbly she held the tiny kicking beast while he plastered the dead lamb's skin over it, tying the strips that had been its legs beneath the warm, trembling belly. By the end of it their hands were slathered with blood. They'd set the lamb on the floor of the pen and stood back as it tottered under the new weight. It had looked piteous, grotesque, the butt of a cruel joke, but the ewe had roused herself, recognising the scent of her own lamb, and approached, and this time when the lamb nosed against her, she stood fast.

Esther's tired mind can barely make sense of the parallels. Has she deceived, or been deceived? Is she the lamb, the ewe, the shepherd? Perhaps all three. All she knows is that having lied about who the father is, the baby feels finally, firmly hers now, hers alone.

Thoughts of the flock make her think again of *cynefin*. That knowledge, the sense of place, passed from mothers to daughters, without which their very lives on the farm would be impossible. It's what keeps the sheep on the land, and the sheep, she thinks, are what keep the people here, so perhaps they all have it. There are those who'd call her a traitor for carrying an Englishman's child, a betrayer of her father, of Mrs R, of Rhys. But it comes to her now that *cynefin* is the essential nationalism, not her father's windy brand, but this secret bond between mothers and daughters, described by a word the English have no equivalent for.

She leans the bike against the wall to open the gate, pushes it through.

A boy? she wonders. When she recalls Jim's question, she realises it had caught her off guard because she'd never really considered the possibility of the baby's being anything other than a girl. Even now it seems simply outlandish to imagine a boy inside her, a boy coming from her body. All her old fears of having the baby, of dying in labour, come rushing back when she thinks of its being a boy. Clasping her hands to her stomach, she's somehow sure it won't be, can't be. And if it is a girl, she knows the name already. Eunice. After her mother.

She wheels the bike into the barn, lingers there a moment, thinking of the German. He'd asked her once about patriotism. Fatherland-love. Why fatherland and not motherland? she'd wondered. But now she thinks: Why should the love of fathers *or* mothers be equated with love of country? Couldn't you love your country by loving your children? Weren't they your nation, at the last? Your childland, then. Your child-country. It sounds about as awkward in Welsh, but then it occurs to her to wonder if there's a better word in German.

She'll look for him again tomorrow, or the next day, and ask. He'll know what she means, she's sure. It reminds her of the renewed talk of prisoners working on local farms, like the

Italians elsewhere. Harry's just done a skit on it: 'You've heard of "Lend a hand on the land". Now they're lending Huns!' She must remember to tell Arthur. They'll need some extra help about the place when she's laid up.

She props the bike next to the spindly question mark of Arthur's crook. *The Lord is my shepherd.* How many times has she heard that text in chapel? So often her mother used to joke that there were 'those hereabouts who'd like to think shepherding is next to godliness'. *The Lord is my shepherd, I shall not want.* The flock is sleeping, ghostly forms dotting the dark grass, and she finds herself creeping across the yard.

When she gets in, she sees it's still not quite eleven, and she twiddles with the radio knobs. She's forgotten all about Harry's tip to listen tonight, but she might just catch the end of the show. The wind must be buffeting the transmitter, because the reception flutters, but through the whoops and whistles of static she can just make him out, signing off, and she sits back disappointed, wondering what she missed. And then, as she arches her back against the settle, she hears it, faintly at first, the opening bars of 'Land of My Fathers'. Harry must have switched it for 'There'll Always Be an England'. It's a nod of respect, she supposes, though typically for Harry, not without its sly mockery. But for once she feels herself inside the joke, finds herself smiling wryly, even as she sits up, stiff backed, as if at attention, until the last notes fade out in the wind.

Epilogue

Rotheram will see Hess only once more. In mid-May of '45, the war in Europe over at last, Hess asks for him again. It's the eleventh hour. He's about to leave the Welsh safe house for London and a plane back to Germany. The powers that be – Colonel Hawkins, Rotheram suspects – grant the request in the hope of some last revelation. The orders catch up with Rotheram almost too late – he's been on the road between one camp and the next – and though he drives through the night, he arrives to find the house packed up, furniture shrouded in dust sheets, Hess sunning himself, perched on a tea chest in the drive like so much luggage. They nod to each other. Hurrying inside, stepping between two empty metal filing cabinets that flank the door like suits of armour, Rotheram reports to Major Redgrave, who tells him, studying his watch, that the only way to talk to Hess now is if he travels with him to London.

'Baker's around here someplace. He'll drive you.'

'You and Lieutenant Mills won't be travelling with us?'

'*Captain* Mills has gone ahead to brief the prosecutors, sit in on the interrogations. Hess isn't half as exciting as Göring now, you know.' Rotheram searches himself for a flicker of jealousy. 'And as for me,' the major adds, 'if he wanted to talk to me, he'd have done it by now, I think. No, he's asked for you. Seems you made an impression last time through. Honestly, I doubt he's

317

much to offer, but if you fancy a trip to town, I can authorise you to go up.'

Rotheram hesitates – he has reports to file, men to interview – and Redgrave tells him impatiently, 'Don't look a gift horse in the mouth. Most men would jump at the chance of forty-eight in town, especially this weekend.'

It takes Rotheram a slow moment. It's the weekend after V-E Day; he's seen the pictures of celebrating crowds in the paper. Though he can't quite share the abandon of those open, shining faces, he's stared at them, fascinated. He's not been back to London for more than six months, has tried to persuade himself that he doesn't miss it, but now the thought of being there grips him.

'That's settled, then,' Redgrave tells him. 'Hand him over at London Cage by this evening and they'll debrief you there.'

Hawkins, Rotheram thinks. And for all the anger he's felt towards his former CO, he just nods. It feels fated somehow to see him again.

Rotheram finds Baker in the billiards room, peeling safety tape off the windows, hauling it down in long ribbons, which he leaves dangling like so much bunting, when Rotheram asks if he's ready to go.

Hess is silent for the first few miles, cradling his sides. 'Stomach cramps,' he explains. But when they reach the main road, he leans over to Rotheram.

'I thought of you,' he says. 'When I saw those new films. You know the ones I mean?'

Rotheram nods. Hess is referring to the newsreels of the liberation of Belsen. Rotheram, as part of the denazification effort, has spent the last fortnight overseeing their screening at several POW camps. Eventually, all the prisoners will be made to watch them.

'I wanted to ask you,' Hess said softly, 'if they were true.'

Rotheram is silent at first, almost chagrined that Hess's question is no different from that of the humblest German private.

'You think they're propaganda,' he says.

'I hope so.' Hess smiles ruefully. 'At least ours was beautiful.'

'Why ask me?' Rotheram wonders, but Hess just looks at him, as if the answer is obvious, and after a moment Rotheram says simply, 'Yes.'

'You wouldn't lie to me?'

'Don't you *know*?' Rotheram asks a little roughly. 'You, of all people?'

Hess draws back. 'I know nothing about all that,' he says hurriedly. 'I had nothing to do with it.'

'Surely you don't remember what you had to do with or not.'

'I remember some things.'

'But not this? So how can you say for sure you weren't a party to it?'

'That,' Hess says quietly, 'I think I'd recall.' He blinks. 'To have done such things and not remember them . . .'

'You believe me, then? That they're true?' Rotheram asks, and Hess turns away, stares out of the side window at the scenery gliding past. Rotheram feels sure he's going to deny it, and then Hess nods, almost imperceptibly, and Rotheram shudders, oddly disappointed, as if he'd been the one asking Hess if the films were true, praying they weren't.

Most of the POWs he's shown the films to vehemently refuse to believe them. They claim they were made in Hollywood. One actually swore that he recognised Henry Fonda playing an officer. Even those who acknowledge the footage is real claim the voice-over is a lie, that the dead aren't Jews but cholera victims in India, or German POWs in Belgium, where the camps are reputed to be disease ridden. He'd seen men weep at that last thought. Despicable as their denials are, they seem almost desperately innocent to Rotheram, and he's come to doubt

319

the War Office's policy of showing the newsreels to the men, obliging them to watch them.

They're never told what's coming; just another newsreel, another feature, they think. Rotheram stands at the back of the mess hall as the lights go down and the projector begins to whirr. There's the usual murmur of conversation at first – once the Pathé News cockerel has been greeted with clucking – and then a slow stifling of the noise. The first thing to get the men's attention are the fences, the barbed wire, and the low barrack huts. For a second, Rotheram is convinced, the men must wonder if they're about to see themselves up there onscreen, larger than life.

It's his job, thankfully, to watch them, the prisoners, rather than the film. He stares at the way their cigarette smoke swims up through the rays of the projector like watery ghosts, or how the reflected light silvers their shoulders, yet still he finds his eye drawn back to the screen, catching fragments of footage. A hut being burned to the ground with a flamethrower. The blank, masked faces of onlookers, local people, soldiers. An arm slipping off the side of a cart, swinging there lazily, almost gaily, like a hand trailed in water. A wave of corpses breaking before a tractor blade.

Afterwards, when the reel runs out, the film fluttering in the gate like a caught thing, the screen goes white, bathing them in its searing light as if for a flash photograph. Rotheram snaps the projector off and in the darkness there's silence. None of the men know what to do, how to react. It's as if they're waiting, waiting for the reel to be changed, waiting for the film, the main feature, wondering what could follow that, what could make them forget. But of course, the show's over.

Rotheram knows of only one prisoner who's accepted the films completely – a fellow who claimed to have seen his own mother among the local German women brought to Belsen to bear witness – and he'd been beaten black and blue by the others.

Rotheram knows the films are true, yet they're being *used* as propaganda. At heart, he's simply not sure how or even if men can be forced to believe such things.

He can hardly bear to believe them himself.

He recalls becoming furious with his own mother once when she made him read a report about concentration camps in the newspaper. This would have been in 1937, less than a year after they'd arrived in Britain. She had him read aloud to her to improve his rusty English, but he hated it when she corrected his accent. He kept at it only because it was better than being goaded by the local children, calling him Adolf whenever he opened his mouth. She insisted he learn the language as a boy – 'it's your mother tongue, after all' – but he always chafed at it. For once she'd fallen silent as he read, and he thought he must be doing well, until he looked at her and saw she was crying. 'Such terrible things,' she told him when she had recovered herself, and he looked at the paper in his hands in surprise. He'd been concentrating so hard on his pronunciation, he could barely recall a word of what he'd read. He set it down, shook his head when she asked him to go on.

'Not if it's going to torture you. Besides,' he said, 'it may not even be true.'

He meant it to comfort her, but she looked at him fiercely, and he'd become defensive. She insisted they speak English to each other, but it frustrated him, made him strident. Even now, after they'd escaped, he felt their old fight about fleeing Germany still smouldering between them. He had tried to tell himself he'd done it for her, but in his heart he knew she'd made them leave for his sake. *You want me to be afraid,* he'd told her once, and she'd said, *I'm your mother. I'm afraid for you.*

'Weren't you the one,' he said, 'who told me about the British during the last war, their propaganda about German soldiers eating babies, raping nuns. They said that about men like my father.' He folded the paper. 'So how can you know that these things are true?'

'Even if they're half true, they're terrible enough,' she admonished him. 'I hope they're not true, but I fear they are.'

'Fear,' he sneered. 'Fear will make you believe anything.' Yet sometimes, he thought bleakly, he wanted the stories to be true, desperately, cravenly desired them to be the very worst things, the most terrible atrocities, however unbelievable, if only because it would mean he had run for a reason.

He looks across at Hess now, huddled in the corner of the car.

'But how can you believe me?' Rotheram explodes. 'How can you believe . . . that? Those pictures. How can you just take my word for it?' He stares at him aghast, as though if the films are true, Hess can't exist; if Hess exists, a man sitting in a car having a conversation, the films can't be true.

And without turning, as if thinking aloud, Hess tells him.

'You have to remember how successful we were, how much we'd achieved. Seizing power, reclaiming the Rhineland. Austria! We would look at each other and shake our heads in wonder. How could such things happen? You might think we were driven mad by power, but we – I don't speak for *him,* but the rest of us – we were the opposite of arrogant, we were humbled by these successes, we couldn't believe we'd achieved such things. Perhaps it was luck, but once you have enough luck, it starts to feel like fate. Like tossing a coin, having it come down heads again and again. Once or twice is nothing, but five times, ten? It's shocking. But how can you stop? So we set our sights higher. Poland, Holland, France. What next? What could top what had come before? The Soviet Union! We knew it was impossible, but everything else before it had been impossible.' He shook his head. 'And if you ask me, this . . . this thing was another impossibility. What if we eradicate a whole people? What if there were a world without Jews?'

'That's enough!' It's the most Hess has ever recalled, but all

Rotheram wants is for him to shut up. Some questions, it occurs to him, should never be asked, let alone answered. But Hess seems not to hear him.

'It's a hypothesis, you see, but the problem with a hypothesis is you don't know it's true until you test it. You can't believe a thing is possible until you do it. Yet until you do it, why even ask if you should? There's no morality about the impossible, Captain. To us, you must understand, this was like climbing Everest, like going to the moon. We couldn't believe such a thing was possible, and that's how we could do it.'

Hess looks over, almost beseeching, but Rotheram leans back against the upholstery, as if exhausted. It's madness, he knows now, and it comes to him forcefully how truly vain this mission has been from the start. Hess *is* mad, but not just now, not temporarily, not simply since his flight to Britain. He's always been mad, all of them have been, all the monsters and butchers. Lucidly mad, rationally mad, functionally mad. Under any other circumstances he'd say Hess was unfit for trial, and yet it's his very madness that demands to be tried.

'Maybe that was the mistake,' Hess is saying, as if to himself. 'Killing the Jews *after* our conquests. If we'd just got rid of them, driven them out of Germany, not invaded Poland, the rest, would the world have cared? Britain, America? About some Jews?' He shakes his head. 'Yet those victories, that glory, the binding loyalty of war, perhaps they were all essential to carry the people with us.'

'*Enough!*' Rotheram cries, lunging across the broad back seat, and having the satisfaction of seeing Hess jerk back, his head bouncing off the window. 'So help me! Say another word and I'll wring your neck myself.'

It takes them almost an hour from the outskirts of the city to the Cage, Baker working his way laboriously through streets blocked by joyous crowds spilling from pubs and cafés. Hess leans back in the staff car and hides his face, but the few times anyone pays them any attention, it's to offer a cheer or applause.

At the London Cage, they part in silence. Hess is led away to another car, never looking back, and Rotheram is told to report to Hawkins.

'Sorry about that,' Rotheram tells Baker as he goes.

'Not at all, sir. Always fancied stringing him up with piano wire meself.'

Rotheram finds himself sitting across the familiar desk. Hawkins offers him a cigarette and a tumbler of Scotch while Rotheram tells him, a little stiffly and before he is asked, that Hess had nothing new to offer.

'Didn't really expect it,' Hawkins admits.

'Where are you taking him?'

'The Tower.'

Rotheram nods.

'How've you been?' Hawkins asks. 'Missed you around here, you know. Could have used you, preparing for all this.' He gestures around the room, and for the first time Rotheram sees the boxes piled against the walls.

'You're moving?'

'Lock, stock and barrel. Nuremberg, they reckon. Though they haven't found decent digs for us yet, far as I know. Not that there's much to be had over there right now.'

Nuremberg, Rotheram thinks. Of course.

'Look,' Hawkins says, leaning forward. 'It was rotten the way things went for you. I tried, but you know how it is with orders. Still, I should have tried harder. Anyhow, the truth is I'd like you to come with us. You should be there. I mean, Lord, I saw those films. Sickening.' He reddens before Rotheram's eyes. 'What I mean to say is, you deserve to be there, if you ask me, and I'll move heaven and earth to make it happen.'

The desk suddenly seems very wide, a vast veneered plain.

Rotheram reaches for the edge of it, puts his palms on it to push himself up.

'It's not necessary,' he says. He sees a flash of hatred in Hawkins's eyes, but doesn't regret it. Better, he thinks, that you should hate me than feel forgiven.

Outside, he presses his way through the choked evening streets, hurrying at first, then slowing as he becomes caught up in the throng of bodies. Before a pub in the Tottenham Court Road, he pauses to watch a man in a trilby, staggering with drink, falling to one knee and being helped up by two others, who clap him on the back as if he's just run a marathon. Behind him a crowd pours out of one of the theatres in Leicester Square and sweeps him along towards Covent Garden. Someone starts to sing, and soon they're all at it – 'Lambeth Walk', 'We'll Meet Again', 'Pack Up Your Troubles', 'Bless 'Em All'.

Rotheram would break away, but he's hemmed in on all sides. He tries to join in, but he feels self-conscious. And then his arm is hooked, and he looks around to see a red-faced girl beaming at him. 'Can't sing for toffee myself.' And no sooner has he leaned in to catch what she's saying than she's spinning him in a jig or a reel, and soon the whole crowd is twirling. 'What do they call you?' she shouts, and he tells her, 'Joseph.' She points to her chest and yells, 'Lucy! Pleased to meet you, Joe.' Her bare arm is warm in the crook of his elbow, and Rotheram finds himself entranced by it, this point of contact about which they spin, and then he bounces off someone else's shoulder and catches her heel and she stumbles, sprawls. Seeing her open her wide mouth, he almost bolts, and then she starts to laugh, a raucous peal. 'Your face!' she cries. 'I'm not made of china, you know!' She holds up a hand and after a second he grasps it and hoists her back on to her feet. She gives him a sloppy theatrical kiss and swings off from arm to arm through the whirling crowd.

He works his way to the edge of the group, pulls up in a

doorway, watches them go, marching now to 'Lili Marlene'. It's too late for Rotheram to join in, but the lilt of the tune stays with him as he heads north through Russell Square, Islington, along streets of celebration and streets of rubble. Finally, sometime towards nine, he finds a little hotel. Out there in the night, he knows, couples are coming together and making victory babies. Nine months from now they'll be repopulating the Continent. As for Rotheram, he's been awake for two days straight, and he falls swiftly into a deep and dreamless sleep, drifting off to the bursts of laughter and snatches of song from the street below, his last thought that tomorrow he should visit his mother's grave.

It's the last time he'll see Hess in person, though two months later, in a darkened cinema, he'll see him in a newsreel, sitting in the dock at Nuremberg. Hess will look shabbier, like a prisoner at last, and haunted, his deep-set eyes sunken, cowled in shadow. He's expected to plead insanity. His lawyer has already made the case. Hess will be asked by the French judge to confirm his plea. He will rise and blink in the bright lights of the newsreel cameras and grip the rail before him. He'll waver for a second, then stiffen, straightening his back. The amnesia he has claimed all these years, he will announce to the hushed court, was simulated, for tactical reasons. He renounces it. He will sit back down in the long, long dock, which looks so disconcertingly like a jury box, and Göring will lean into him, smiling, and pat him on the shoulder.

The prosecutors won't challenge the claim – it's a gift for them, justifying their decision to try him. And after all, Rotheram will think, watching the camera pan across the row of stark faces, how is one to know one's mad amid the ranks of the insane? But then something about Hess will strike him. He's the only one of the accused not to don the simultaneous-translation headsets that International Business Machines has invented and donated to the proceedings. Rotheram will have read this in the papers. The headphones pinch his head, Hess has told the court, utterly unimpressed by the incredible technology, simply pointing out the poor fit. So he sits there oblivious, dipping into a copy of *Grimm's Fairy Tales,* which he rests on his knees, smiling and occasionally nodding in response to what, no one knows. And it will dawn on Rotheram that this is just another suicide attempt. These men will hang, and Hess, by asserting his sanity, is volunteering to hang with them.

He's getting away! Rotheram will want to shout at the screen. *Can't you see?*

And yet, for all this, Hess will not swing for his crimes. He'll be convicted on counts 1 and 2 of the indictment, Crimes Against Peace, Planning Wars of Aggression in Violation of Treaties, but not on counts 3 and 4, War Crimes and Crimes Against Humanity – the timing of his flight, before the full implementation of the Final Solution, sparing him. He'll be sentenced to life, instead of death. He'll grow old in Spandau jail. He'll be a prisoner for the rest of his days. He'll never escape. He'll never be freed. There will be pleas for his parole, but the Russians will block them every time, perhaps out of vindictiveness, a lingering suspicion, or perhaps – it is rumoured – because even in the frozen depths of the Cold War, the meetings between the old Allies go on at Spandau. Ostensibly to discuss Hess, they will provide a thin but unbreakable thread of diplomacy so that the human relic of one conflict will, in a stony irony, help in a modest way to avoid another. Hess will lose his hair. Hess will lose his teeth. Hess will lose his mind, again or for the first time, to senility. He will live to hear that man has conquered Everest, walked on the moon; that Germany has hosted another Olympics; that the American actor turned president, who likes to say he was in the war though he was only ever in movies of it, has visited Belsen on the fortieth anniversary of its liberation and even claimed (to the Israeli prime minister, no less) that he filmed the newsreels of its liberation. And Hess will shake his head in disbelief at it all. He will be ninety-three at the end. And then he will die, finally succeeding after all these years in taking his own life, hanging himself, his limp body as light and lifeless as the faded flying suit he wore to Scotland, which he will have kept hanging on a hook on his cell wall, like a shed skin, ever since.

At the last, though, it isn't Hess that Rotheram thinks of when in years to come he looks back on the end of the war. It's a lonely Welsh pub – the name forgotten, if he ever knew it. He'd stopped there one night while investigating an escape, the only one he'd ever work on, though one he thinks he'd recall among hundreds, if only for the prisoner in question.

He'd got a frosty reception from the camp commandant, who seemed to think Rotheram had been sent to investigate *him* as much as the escape – the man had lost an arm somewhere along the way, sheared clean off, Rotheram couldn't help thinking, by the chip on his shoulder. The commandant's self-serving theory was that the fellow had had help. 'Quite possibly,' Rotheram told him; he had begun interviewing other prisoners already. 'No,' the commandant insisted. 'Not them. I run a tight ship here.' 'Tight' being the operative word, Rotheram thought, judging from the man's red-webbed complexion. 'No. I mean he had help from the locals, the Welshies. They're as bad as the Micks.' It had seemed preposterous, but Rotheram saw that he was going to have to humour the man to get any cooperation. Besides, the theory had the virtue of suggesting the prisoner might still be close by, not miles away, and Rotheram persisted in the faint hope that if he could only recapture the fellow, Hawkins might yet reconsider his assignment.

At any rate, he drove to the village pub late one night by way of introducing himself to the locals and in case any of them had seen something that hadn't already been reported. It'd been a long day of interviews – first the prisoners, then the equally sullen guards – and when a violent rainstorm overtook him, the water rushing down the narrow lane as if it were a streambed, Rotheram began cursing the commandant for sending him on a wild goose chase. He'd have turned back if he hadn't been desperate for a drink. He pulled up under the swaying sign, plucked his cap off the seat beside him and jammed it low over his eyes against the rain.

He'd been so weary, he was relieved at first to be ignored in the pub. The place was almost deserted in any event; there'd be precious little to learn here. He took a seat at the end of the bar, glanced at the menu chalked up behind it, lost himself in thought, staring out of the window at the rain, feeling the fire behind him warm his wet woollen uniform jacket. Only slowly did he realise that he hadn't been served, that the conversation among the few locals had stilled. He looked up and smiled and called, 'Pint of your best bitter, please,' and the barman, a burly old fellow, had limped down the bar towards him, a damp rag in his hand, pushing crumbs and shreds of tobacco over the polished wood. He'd brushed them right past, making Rotheram sit back and almost lose his balance. Someone laughed behind him. 'Excuse me?' Rotheram called, and when the fellow ignored him, he might have knocked on the bar. 'My good man!'

There was a murmur from the other patrons, and beside him a florid bloke said, 'That's torn it.'

The barman stopped at the end of the bar and dried his big hands on a green apron.

'We don't have to serve your kind in here, you know.'

Even here, Rotheram thought with dull rage, even in this uniform. There was a policeman in the corner, and Rotheram looked to him for a moment, but the other just raised his glass as if to his own reflection in the mirror behind the bar, and Rotheram realised he was alone. He looked the bartender up and down and felt a bitter satisfaction that he was so solid. He slid off his stool and took the first step towards him. It seemed so simple suddenly, and he almost rushed towards the fight, but as he closed the distance he thought something else was required, some final insult, and then his line came to him, as if in a film.

'What kind is that?'

And the man spat, 'English.'

Rotheram stopped.

'English?'

'That's right. We don't serve no English here.'

There was a little ripple of pleasure through the crowd.

The barman crossed his arms on his broad chest, threw back his shoulders, and Rotheram began to laugh. It wasn't so much the ridiculous pettiness of Welsh–English antipathy compared to his own experience, but the combination of the man's certainty – his bullish, pugnacious conviction – and his utter inaccuracy.

'What's so funny?' he demanded.

And Rotheram bent over now, one hand on the bar for support, held up the other, and after a second said, 'You don't know who I am, do you? You've no idea.' The man stared at him, wanting to strike him, Rotheram could see, but somehow unsure, as if the idea of striking a laughing man was unfair. 'I'm not English,' Rotheram managed to cry at last, through his laughter.

He could see the man didn't believe him, didn't know what to believe. Beside him, the florid fellow was shaking his head, wide eyed.

'What are you, then?'

Rotheram shook his head, coughing out, 'Would you believe German!'

'Well, I think you'd better go, whoever you are,' the barman told him with icy propriety. And Rotheram was too delighted with him, too choked with laughter, to object. He just waved, unable to get out another word, and stumbled outside to the car.

The rain had stopped, the air smelling fresh, as if washed, and he sat for several minutes, bent over the wheel, wiping the tears from his eyes while the stern locals watched him from the windows of the pub.

Of course, it occurred to him, catching his breath, that it was only funny because he *wasn't* German – or English or Welsh, for that matter. And for the first time since he'd run, he felt free, as if he'd finally arrived somewhere, and even after he started the engine, he couldn't imagine anywhere he'd rather be.

He'd felt a perverse fondness for the Welsh ever after, so when the commandant brought up his theory again, Rotheram asked blandly, if there was any reason to think the locals and the Germans had come into contact. He knew, of course, from the prisoners that the village boys had been in the habit of hanging around the wire, but if so, it was in contravention of standing orders, and the commandant knew well enough to keep his mouth shut. Besides, within a couple more days the escapee had been brought in, at the end of a farmer's shotgun. 'So much for the natives being friendly,' Rotheram observed.

Still, he had meant to press the prisoner about a local connection – if nothing else, he assumed the fellow guilty of petty larceny, just to keep body and soul together. Only he'd not had the chance before the man was beaten up by his own side, and afterwards, staring into his ruined face, Rotheram didn't have the heart. Besides, there was something about the fellow, something he recognised, even if the fellow swore they'd never met, something that had made it possible for Rotheram to tell him he was Jewish.

At first Rotheram had taken his question as a challenge, refused to run from it, as he had with Hess. But afterwards, looking back, it was the fellow's lack of shame at having surrendered that he remembered. It had never occurred to Rotheram that he could be unashamed of fleeing, of escaping, of living. Of being Jewish – if that was what he was. And suddenly it felt not only possible but *right* to not be German or British, to escape all those debts and duties, the shackles of nationalism. That's what he had glimpsed at the pub, what had sent him into that fit of laughter. The Jews, he knew, had no homeland, yearned for one, and yet as much as he understood it to be a source of their victimisation, it seemed at once such pure freedom to be without a country.

He'd seen the escapee once more, too. He came through the same region in the summer of '45 – the war done, but the prisoners expected to be held for many more months, until the situation in Germany stabilised – screening men for a labour programme. A prisoner who'd attempted escape wouldn't normally be approved, but Rotheram had never forgotten the fellow, sought him out and graded him 'white', fit for work, over the commandant's objections. The major was a short-timer by then, a month from being demobbed, and besides, as Rotheram pointed out, the man had been beaten by his fellow prisoners, and if that didn't qualify him as an anti-Nazi, he didn't know what did.

In fact, though, it was Karsten's despair that had persuaded him. He'd seen the newsreels recently, like the rest. 'To be fighting for that,' he shuddered. 'And I was ashamed of *surrendering*.' Rotheram had been moved to see him imprisoned again by shame. He'd hoped that the work on the open hillsides might be good for him. His own transfer came through shortly thereafter – he'd finally taken a posting to Nuremberg when offered by someone other than Hawkins – but he made a point of requesting at least one report from the new commandant, and heard that Karsten had been a great help on a local farm in the bitter winter of '46, digging sheep out of the snow.

He'd not given him much thought beyond that, but in late '47 he'd been back in Wales a final time. Rotheram hadn't lasted long in Nuremberg: he couldn't stand the stink of damp, charred wood which seemed to cling to everything still. But he had been lucky enough to make some contacts among the French delegation and get seconded to a unit in Paris assigned to sift through captured documents in order to build more war crimes cases. It was grim work, but at least the city was whole, and he stuck with it for almost a year until he found a pair of names he knew. All this time he thought he'd been hunting for evidence against the Nazis, and really he'd been looking for his grandparents. He'd submitted his last transfer request that day, and since Paris was an attractive posting, he'd been replaced and on the ferry back to Britain within a week. His own demobilisation wouldn't be far off, he knew – he'd already outlasted Hawkins, who'd retired to the south coast for the bird watching – but he had no idea what to do with himself after the army. In the meantime, he toured the remaining work camps and wrote reports that he was convinced no one but historians would read. There were no interrogations, of course, no investigations, but from time to time he was called in to assess the cases of men who had petitioned to stay in Britain permanently. Several he interviewed had met women, and wanted to marry.

One such case brought him back to Snowdonia that autumn. The Welsh village's name, that jumble of consonants, hadn't rung any bells, but he recalled the pub as he drove past it, and recognised the constable in whose 'station' – the parlour of his little house – he conducted the interview.

The constable offered him tea, and they reminisced about the escape. 'Always wished I'd caught the blighter myself,' the policeman said. 'You know, done my bit, so to speak. Too young for the first war, too old for the last one. Story of my life.'

Rotheram thought doing one's bit was overrated, but he nodded, asked about the couple. 'Girl know what she's doing?'

'Reckon so,' the constable said mournfully. 'Won't be talked out of it at any rate.'

'And the fellow—?' But they were interrupted by a bustling in the hallway, and the constable jumped to his feet with a whispered, 'You tell me.'

Rotheram had half expected to recognise the prisoner when he met the applicants, but the man was a stranger to him: a brawny, thick-necked Thuringian, marrying a roly-poly called Blodwyn. Rotheram had no illusions about the role of love in these unions – they owed more to desperation and loneliness – but he was inclined to approve them anyway – he couldn't quite say 'bless' them – provided they seemed founded in equal need. Why not after all? Who was he to judge? If he couldn't be sure who was lying, how was he to know who was in love?

The Thuringian and his Blod weren't much different from the rest he'd vetted. He saw them separately and then together, and they sat on the polished wooden bench in the policeman's hall and clutched each other's fat little hands. 'Oh, thank you, sir,' they'd chorused when he'd signed the paperwork. He asked the Thuringian if he didn't miss home, and the other frowned and told him, 'Yes, sir. Only it's not there anymore, is it?' And Rotheram nodded. 'If I'm going to start all over, might as well begin here as there,' the big man added, warming to his theme. 'You love him?' Rotheram had asked the girl, and she'd blushed deeply, which he took for a yes. Afterwards he heard the pair of them chattering away in a language he didn't understand – Welsh, it dawned on him at last.

Only when he handed over the paperwork did he realise that the constable and the girl shared the same name.

'Your daughter?'

The other gave a slight nod. 'When they started working, I wanted to keep an eye on them, stand guard, in a manner of speaking, and she used to bring me my lunches.' He shook his head. 'Looks like we caught a Jerry after all.'

Rotheram offered a cigarette, and they smoked in silence for a while.

'He's all right.'

'Better bloody be, if he knows what's good for him.'

Rotheram left him then. He'd parked outside the pub, and he walked that way now with a thought of getting a drink, but when he reached the door, he found it was closed. Not yet opening time. He asked around instead for the farm he'd heard Karsten had been assigned to, the same one he'd been captured on. Cilgwyn. The name had stayed with him. It meant 'white hill', apparently, though to Rotheram's eye it seemed as green as the rest. Still, it had struck him as an appropriate spot for surrender.

There'd been a girl there too, Rotheram thought, but when he knocked on the door, an old woman answered and told him the German was 'gone home'. Not surprising, really, he told himself. Most of the prisoners had been repatriated by then, but still, it disappointed him somehow.

There was a small child staring at him from the barn when he turned around, and he smiled and gave her a little wave. She took an uncertain step forward and he called, 'Hello there!' which only made her run back into the shadows. He was deciding whether he should follow when a woman – it was immediately apparent she was the mother – emerged from the barn, one hand raised against the light, to squint at him.

Rotheram began to apologise for startling the child, but she told him it wasn't his fault.

'She thought you were someone else at first.'

The woman was wearing an embroidered blouse, tucked into men's trousers, cinched at the waist with a broad belt, a combination that seemed to accentuate her figure.

'Can I help you?'

'You had a German prisoner here,' he said. 'I wonder if you have an address for him?'

'You knew him?'

'In a manner of speaking.' She searched his face, took in the uniform. 'Do you have an address?'

'Why do you want it?'

'I'm going over there,' Rotheram told her, and as he said it, he thought, *Why yes*. That's what he must do next. 'To help with the reconstruction. I thought I might have a job for him. Heard he was a good worker.'

'Oh, he is!' And she recited the address there and then, her accent flawless. 'His mother's place. I'm not sure it'll do you any good, though,' she said sadly. 'He's not replied to anything we've sent.'

It was the East, he knew. Soviet control.

'I'll make some enquiries.'

She nodded.

'Well . . .' He shifted his weight.

'If you do contact him . . .'

'Yes.'

'Could you tell him, Esther said . . . that the flock's well.'

'The flock?'

'Only, he put his heart into saving them. After that winter we had. We lost a lot, too many, really, to keep going. But he told us to beg and borrow stock from other farms – pastured them in return for the lambs – and then he stayed with them on the mountain. They'd have strayed, new sheep, if someone didn't go up' – she jerked a finger over her shoulder to the jagged hilltop – 'and shepherd them. And he did that, almost eighteen months, in all weathers, until the new ones knew their place.' Her voice wavered slightly, and Rotheram didn't know what to say.

The child had crept out of the barn and now ran to her mother, rubbing her face against her leg, but then looking up at Rotheram with a boldness that seemed beautiful to him.

'It's all right, *cariad*. Mam's fine.' She smoothed a hand over the child's silky head. 'My guardian,' she told Rotheram.

He smiled, and she swiped her eyes.

'Sorry. Only, there've been sheep here for hundreds of years, and it'd have been a shame to let them die out.'

Rotheram nodded slowly. 'I'll tell him.'

'In truth, I think he rather liked it up there,' she said, turning to stare up at the hillside, and Rotheram looked with her to where the sheep were drifting across it like a white cloud.

'*My* sheep,' the child whispered, and her mother laughed and pulled her close.

Later, in the pub, he heard her story: the father fallen to his death in the quarry, and the lover who never came home from the war. 'Local hero,' the chatty barmaid told him. 'Tragic, really, though the boy's mother's been a great help to Esther. Don't know what they'd have done without their German, mind.'

The barmaid was a big, blowsy girl, friendly in an oblivious way, and he was happy to listen to her. Down the passage, in the public bar, he could see a man's back moving to and fro, the same man, he guessed, who'd refused him service three years earlier. But when the old fellow limped past him to ring up an order, he looked at Rotheram without a flicker of recognition.

The couple from earlier in the day were at a corner table, and as Rotheram finished his pint, the barmaid asked, 'Another? It's on them.' Rotheram nodded to them.

'Young love,' the barman, who'd lingered, sighed, and Rotheram wondered what he disapproved of – the generosity, perhaps, or something more?

On the ceiling, Rotheram noticed a line of hooks screwed into the wood.

'Must have lost a lot of men hereabouts.'

'Just that one to the war,' the fellow said. 'Other lads never came back from the factories or the coalfields. Lost 'em to work, you might say. Been losing them that way for fifty years. Got so bad that now the girls are running after them.'

'Jack!'

'Well, it's true, Hattie.'

'You make it sound like it's not decent,' she cried. 'I'm

engaged,' she said to Rotheram. 'Met him when he was an evacuee during the war. Now he's working in Liverpool.' She gave the barman, Jack, a stern look and busied herself at the other end of the counter.

'Looks like you've one fellow who's staying here,' Rotheram said.

'Who? Jerry? He ain't so bad.' The barman dropped into a whisper. 'Told me he never even got a shot off. Said he was on the shitter when he got captured. Didn't know whether to put up his hands or pull up his drawers.'

Rotheram grinned with him.

'What are you two whispering about?'

'Nothing, nothing,' Jack cried, retreating down the passage.

'Congratulations,' Rotheram told her, raising his glass.

'Thanks!'

'You think she'll marry?' He bobbed his head towards the hills.

'Esther?'

The other shook her head. 'That's another story. Dead man's a hard act to follow, I reckon. None of the boys around here have the gumption to marry a hero's widow.'

She wiped the bar down, working in decreasing circles.

'Ashamed, isn't it? What did they do during the war, after all?'

'What about her German?'

The barmaid gave him a narrow look. 'Not that there wasn't talk, mind. Even went to the pictures together once before he left. But how would it have looked? And her with the dead man's daughter on her apron strings. Dead man's mam in her home. Besides, he was a right respectful bloke, that Karsten. Handsome and all.' She giggled, then went on more soberly as Jack approached. 'Hard worker, too, by all accounts. Lads used to call him "the German shepherd"! Said he took to it because it was just like guard duty. But he never liked that, said he'd rather be a bad shepherd than a good guard any day.'

'You don't mind serving them, then?'

'Not if they're good looking!' Hattie cried, but Jack gave her a look and she drew back, miffed.

'Frankly,' Jack confided, 'I need the business. Besides, they can drink, you know!' He waggled his eyebrows. 'And they keep the English away, to boot.'

He stared at Rotheram for a moment.

'No offence.'

'And none taken,' Rotheram told him, holding the barman's eye over the rim of his glass as he drained it.

'Another?'

Rotheram shook his head. He set his glass down in the wet circle it had made on the bar, and made sure to wish the young couple luck on his way out.

Acknowledgements

I'd like to thank the National Endowment for the Arts, the Guggenheim Foundation and the Department of English at the University of Michigan for their generous support during the writing of this book. I'm lucky to have wonderful colleagues at Michigan, in particular Eileen Pollack and Nicholas Delbanco, who read drafts of this book, as did Marshall Klimasewiski, who's been my sure sounding board for many years now.

I'm also indebted to the various editors who published portions of this work in journals and annuals: Ian Jack at *Granta*, Don Lee and guest editor Gish Jen at *Ploughshares*, Katrina Kenison and guest editor Barbara Kingsolver at *The Best American Short Stories*, and Ted Genoways at *Virginia Quarterly Review*.

My editors, Janet Silver at Houghton Mifflin and Carole Welch at Sceptre, have been great champions of this work, and their colleagues at the respective companies have made those publishing houses real homes for the book. Janet's patience and faith over the years, in particular, have sustained me more than I can possibly say.

I owe, too, an enormous debt to my wonderful agents, Maria Massie and Arabella Stein. Over the years of writing, Maria especially has performed that vital service so essential in an agent–author relationship: unwavering belief in the book and its author, even when I doubted both. This would be a lesser book without her.

Various sources for this work are listed in the Author's Note, but I want to single out my debt to my father, Thomas Enion Davies, for his vivid memories of Wales in wartime, and to my mother, Sook Ying Davies, for helping to draw those memories out and faithfully recording them.

Finally, I couldn't have written this book, or any other, without the surpassing support of my wife, Lynne Raughley, my first, ideal and essential reader.

Author's Note

Many books were consulted in the course of writing this book. What follows is only a partial listing.

On sheep farming in North Wales, I owe a great deal to Thomas Firbank's *I Bought a Mountain*, where I first encountered the concept of *cynefin*. *Small Scale Sheep Keeping* by Jeremy Hunt, *Snowdon Shepherd: Four Seasons on the Hill Farms of North Wales* by Keith Bowen, and *Welsh Sheep and Their Wool* by John Williams-Davies, were also valuable sources.

On German prisoners of war, their attitudes, conditions, and treatment, I'm indebted to the following: *The London Cage* by A. P. Scotland, *Group Captives: The Re-education of German Prisoners of War in Britain, 1945–1948* by Henry Faulk, *The War for the German Mind: Re-educating Hitler's Soldiers* by Arthur L. Smith, Jr., *The Barbed-wire College: Reeducating German POWs in the United States During World War II* by Ron Robin, *Thresholds of Peace: Defiance and Change Among German Prisoners of War in Britain Between 1944 and 1948* by Matthew Barry Sullivan, *Paper Hero: 'At His Majesty's Pleasure': An Account of Life as a Manx Internee During World War II* by L. N. Giovannelli, *They Will Rise Again* by R. M. Zammit, *Enemies Become Friends* by Pamela Howe Taylor, *For Führer and Fatherland* by Roderick de Normann, *Prisoners of England* by Miriam Kochan, and *Nazi Prisoners of War in America* by Arnold Kramer.

The circumstances surrounding Rudolf Hess's flight to Britain and his subsequent mental state remain uncertain – an uncertainty, of course, that invites fictional exploration – and have given rise to a variety of texts by his contemporaries and subsequent historians, ranging from the sober to the sensational and slanted. In the absence of a consensual historical understanding of his behaviour, I sampled an array of this work, including *The Nuremberg Trial* by Ann and John Tusa, *The Infamous of Nuremberg* by Burton C. Andrus, *22 Cells at Nuremberg* by Douglas M. Kelley, *Hess: A Biography* by Roger Manvell, *The Case of Rudolf Hess* by J. R. Rees, *The Murder of Rudolf Hess* by Hugh Thomas, *Hess: The Missing Years* by David Irving, *The Loneliest Man in the World* by Eugene Bird, *Interrogations: The Nazi Elite in Allied Hands, 1945* by Richard Overy, *Nuremberg Interviews* by Leon Goldensohn, and *A Train of Powder* by Rebecca West. My subsequent portrait of Hess draws on (and in some cases responds to) these works, but is also informed by the imagination and certain exigencies of plot (concerning the timing of events, for example). Rotheram and all the officers and men guarding Hess are fictional.

I'm also grateful to Ben Wicks's *No Time to Wave Goodbye* for information on evacuee children, and to Jan Morris's *The Matter of Wales* for details of Welsh history. In addition, exhibits at the Imperial War Museum in London and Duxford, and the United States Holocaust Memorial Museum in Washington, D.C., were invaluable resources, as were the holdings of the libraries at Cambridge University, the University of Oregon and the University of Michigan.

Lose yourself
in a good
book with Galaxy

Curled up on the sofa,
Sunday morning in pyjamas,
just before bed,
in the bath or
on the way to work?

Wherever, whenever,
you can escape
with a good book!

So go on...
indulge yourself with
a good read and the
smooth taste of
Galaxy chocolate